# in·ten·tion

*a novel*

# AVA HARRISON

*in·ten·tion: a novel*
Cover Design: Hang Le
Cover Photographer: Specular Photography
Cover Model: Olly Hines

Line Edit: Lawrence Editing, www.lawrenceediting.com, My Brother's Editor
Content: Jennifer Roberts-Hall, Becca Mysoor
Proofreader: Marla Selkow Esposito, Editing4Indies
Formatting: Champagne Book Design

Dedicated to Livia.
Thank you for always believing in me.

in·ten·tion
**NOUN**
a thing intended; an aim or plan.

*I've made a lot of mistakes in my life,*
*but if*
*every single one*
*had to happen to make sure I was*
*right here,*
*right now,*
*to meet you,*
*then I forgive myself*
*for them all.*
—K. Towne Jr.

# chapter one

## NATHANIEL

*Saint-Tropez*

B LOODY HELL, THAT'S SMOOTH.
*Nothing beats the first shot of the night.*

The way it pours down your throat, searing a path in its wake. It's a symbol of the possibilities, and right now, those possibilities are endless.

Here I am, at the most posh club in Saint-Tropez with my best mate, Oliver. Drinks are flowing. Women are plentiful. Life doesn't get much better than this. Well, I guess if I were getting a blow job right now it would be better.

My lip turns up into a wicked smirk as I take in the blonde beside me. She's just my type—long, lean, and straight off the cover of a magazine. And that's not just a figure of speech. She's literally straight off the cover of *Sports Illustrated*. I'm pretty sure she's last month's cover girl for *Maxim* as well. She's stunning, but one thing is for sure. Her looks are the only thing she has to offer me.

I tried to have a chat with her, but alas, that's not going to happen, so I'll settle for a good shag.

She moves to stand on the leather banquet at the VIP table

Olly and I are occupying, and now I have a perfect view of her tight arse. As if that isn't enough for a visual, she starts to seductively dance with another leggy blonde. Grinding and putting on quite the show, actually. The thumping bass is a nice backdrop to the way they sway against each other.

Smoke swirls through the distance, stretching across the space around us, making the room look gray and hazy. Between that and the low lights, I can barely see in front of me, let alone the dance floor only a few steps away. It makes no difference though. Despite the dancing bodies, they don't interfere with us. We're secluded in our private nook behind a translucent veil so the masses can't see us.

I glance over at Olly, who's also enjoying the show. Lifting the bottle of Grey Goose off the table, I decide to bypass the glass altogether and take a swig. When I motion to the girls, Oliver lifts a brow with a smirk.

With a lift of my arm, my body begins to move as the music thumps. That combined with the booze coursing in my blood has me shutting my eyes and pushing down all thoughts but the here and now. The feeling is sublime. Nothing matters but the bass, the vodka, and the *company*. As if reading my mind, hands touch me, and I open my eyes again to find the blonde pressed against me. I pull her closer and begin to sway my body with hers. My hands touch and trail, the warmth of her body is electrifying, fueling a need to leave and have my way with her.

But first, a drink.

It's not often Olly is free, so as much as I want to sink into her, it can wait. I grab the bottle, swallow, then give it to her. Once she takes a swig, the bottle is passed to Olly and the blonde beside him. Before long, the bottle is polished off, and I know it's time to go.

A grin from across the table tells me I'm not the only one ready.

"Who wants to get out of here?" Olly asks. The girls jump up at his words. Olly's hand touches my arm. "I'm out the back exit. Meet you at the hotel?"

I nod. This is Oliver's typical MO. He can't be seen, so when we party, we arrive separately and leave separately. I don't care what the paparazzi say about me, but Oliver has to be more careful. His name is more than a name . . . it's a title. An earl, to be exact. He's even in line for the throne.

Within a moment, Oliver is walking away from us, slipping out the back door of the VIP member's only club, and I walk toward the front door arm in arm with two of the hottest and most desired models in America.

The door swings open, and the brisk autumn air smacks me in the face.

Cameras fire off in rapid succession as we emerge from the club and out onto the street.

*Snap.*

*Snap.*

*Snap.*

Just as I suspected.

*Paps.*

"Let's go, ladies," I say, pulling them closer to me. My arm wraps around both their waists, eliciting giggles from the girls and cheers from the crowd.

"Where you off to, Harrington?" one yells. The flash of cameras has my lids blinking rapidly and my vision stolen from me momentarily. Another screams our way, all while still snapping pics. Blind to the world around me, I shift my shoulders back and walk without a care in the world. As if I own it. My superiority is my armor right now.

*Snap.*

*Snap.*

"Another after hours?"

I shake my head and answer the question with a gesture.

"Two girls tonight?"

This time, I smirk.

Another one hollers, "I want your life." I allow myself to laugh, playing up the role.

**British Playboy.**

**Billionaire Party Boy.**

I'm not sure what the headline will be this time, but I immerse myself in the part with a smile and a wave.

"Look at the camera."

With a turn of my head to the left, I do as they ask. The left side of my lip lifts up with a cool detachment from what I'm doing. I wish they would stop already. I'm ready for the next stage of my night to proceed.

"She looks like Cecile," a man's voice rings through the blaring noise. That makes me hold my steps. The comment sobers me up for a minute as I realize it's true. She does. "You certainly have a type, Harrington," the same man responds, trying to goad me. It hits its mark as Cecile pops into my head.

My ex.

The only girl I've ever cared about. The one who got away. Will I ever be rid of the feeling I have when hearing her name? God, I hope so.

I shake the thought out of my head. *She's happy, married, and you're over her. Plus, you have two women on your arms. Losing yourself in one of these women will certainly help.*

I turn my head and look at the woman on my right arm.

Then I look over at the one on my left—the one who doesn't look so much like my ex—and decide she'll be the one I sink into tonight.

"What party are you going to?" another pap says.

"No party." I turn to my girls, a Cheshire cat grin spreading across my face. "Well, at least not that kind of party." I wink as the girls giggle.

"Lucky man."

Isn't that the truth?

---

A text . . .

**Diane: The plane is being sent for you.**

More like a summons.

This is not good.

As I read the message, I see there is also a voice message. This time, it's not Diane, my grandfather's assistant. My muscles go rigid. The tone of the message is cold. Sterile. Not like the usual banter I have with the man who raised me.

**I expect you at the house as soon as you land. I have some important business to discuss with you.**

Important business? What could possibly be so important that I need to show up to dinner? As much as a family dinner usually does happen when everyone is in the same city, either London or New York, I have been excused for years.

One of the perks of being the favorite.

If I'm in town, I always go, but seeing as ninety percent of the time I'm not, I can't even remember the last time I've been to one.

Maybe two months?

Maybe longer?

The scratch of the tires brings me out of my thoughts. When the plane comes to a full stop, I unbuckle my seat belt and stand. Once fully up, I place my phone back into my pocket and make my way out the door of the Harrington private plane.

Another family perk.

We've landed at Teterboro Airport. A small metal stairway that leads down to the runway is waiting for me. The frigid air of late autumn hits me in the face as I step down. My car waits on the tarmac next to the hangar of one of the many fleets of private planes the Harrington family owns.

Perk number three. There are many perks for my position in life, but being the only namesake to the world-renowned Nathaniel Harrington is the biggest. *Nathaniel Harrington III*

Women, money, and prestige are the others that come to mind.

The car is already running, the driver standing beside it. The sounds of planes taking off in the background mute the engine's hum, but I know it's running from the puff of exhaust billowing from the parked vehicle.

"Roger," I say as I walk over to the familiar face. Whenever I am in town, Roger is my driver.

"Sir." He opens the door and then shuts it behind me.

As the car is already warm, I slip my coat off and recline back into the leather chairs of the Mercedes Maybach. Pulling out my phone, I furrow my brow.

My grandfather's message has me perplexed. It's not like him, and that fact has me on edge.

What could be so important that it couldn't wait until tomorrow? Why summon me to dinner the day I return to New York after a lengthy and exuberant trip to the South of France?

Surely, he must know I'd be tired? Luckily for me, I'm not,

but he doesn't know this.

I don't relax for any of the forty-five-minute drive to his home. Instead, I stare out the window and wonder what is going through his head.

By the time we reach the sprawling Harrington Estate, I have decided by the images I pulled up on my phone that Grandfather is probably not at all thrilled by the latest article of me on Page Six. That or the rumors I impregnated some supermodel in Italy.

That's got to be it.

I laugh to myself at the prospect of this conversation. He'll tell me to be more careful, and I'll agree. We'll both know that it's bollocks, and then we'll have a good laugh about it over hundred-year-old scotch.

A smile spreads across my face as I think of the old man who raised me.

When the car comes to a complete stop, the door to the back seat opens. Stepping out, I head to the large entrance of the house, but those doors swing open before I even have to knock. With a nod to his butler, I move briskly down the hall.

As my feet hit the marble, I can hear the clicking sound against the quiet of the house. I wonder where everyone is. I'm not that late that they would be eating dinner, am I? I lift my wrist and glance down at my watch. Shit. I am. Picking up my pace, I walk into the formal dining room. Just as I thought, everyone is already seated around the table. My gaze skates across the view in front of me until I meet the eyes of my grandfather.

"Sit," he says. His one-word command gives me pause. Maybe I was wrong about my assumption for the night.

I make my way down the table to my usual spot, but it's already taken. My second cousin, Edward, occupies my seat, and beside him is his very pregnant wife. I narrow my gaze at him, and his lip turns up into a smirk. I can tell from the gleam in his dark eyes that he loves the fact he is beside my grandfather.

"We didn't think you were coming," he taunts, his voice dripping with contempt. There is no love lost between us because we have never gotten along. He has always resented me. Resented my place within the family and, in turn, his lack thereof. But by the smug look in his eyes, he's pleased with the fact he's now sitting where I should be.

"No problem, Eddie," I deadpan, and his jaw tightens at the nickname. *He hates when I call him that.*

Once I know he's positively chaffed, I look around the room. The seat across the table is open. The seat reserved for a guest. I know everyone is looking at me, wondering what I'll do. So, with a large inhale of oxygen, I make my way over to it and pull out the chair. The scratch of the wood against the floor echoes in the now quiet room as I take a seat.

All the stares leave me and return to their plates in front of them. One of my grandfather's staff approaches me with my dinner before scurrying away.

Conversation is tight as we eat. It is obvious to all that my grandfather is in a mood, and by the way he keeps glaring at me, I'm clearly the source. I'm not used to this reception. So what if I'm a little late? At least I'm here. At least I'm back in America and made it to dinner. Shouldn't he be happy?

When the meal is over, my grandfather stands abruptly, his chair making a scratching sound as he pushes it back and then locks eyes with me.

"My study. Now!"

Before I can even stand from the chair, he's gone, stalking out of the room. Hushed words from across the table draw my attention to Edward. I don't have to hear what he's saying to know he loves every moment of my current fall from grace.

With brisk steps, I make my way into my grandfather's office where I find him sitting behind his desk with his arms folded across his chest. I take a seat across from him, crossing my right leg over my left, and recline back. On the outside, it looks like I don't care, but on the inside, he has me on edge.

"What's on your mind, Grandfather?" I say, cutting right to the chase.

"This." He flings a magazine in front of me. Not just any magazine, either. This one has my bloody face on the cover.

*Just as I suspected.*

"I have better angles, I suppose," I joke, trying to lessen the tension in the air.

"Quite. I'm especially fond of the one where you do not embarrass your family. Is that all you have to say?" He glares at me, the familiar bluish vein on the side of his forehead pulsating with anger.

"What do you want me to say? Paps are the nature of the beast." I shrug. It's true, and he knows it. "I'll try to not get photographed next time."

"Next time? There will be no next time, Nathaniel. This is unacceptable. This article talks about your endless string of conquests, ranging from London to America, with pit stops in France."

"So I like women. When did that become a crime?" I ask, not quite seeing the problem. This is hardly a new thing because I have always been like this.

"It became a crime when you became the heir to my fortune." He lifts an eyebrow.

He does have a point. I am the heir to the Harrington

fortune, but I'm still not making the connection. "The women I bed have no impact on my ability to do my job—when the time comes."

"See, and here is where we have a difference of opinion, and so does the board."

His words wash over me, making me lean forward in my chair. "What does the board have to do with my love life? I don't even work for you yet."

"Everything. And right now—"

"Grandfather, when the time comes, I promise—"

"The time has come," he huffs, and my eyes widen as I shake my head.

"Nonsense," I fire back. There is no way that can be true.

He lets out a long-drawn-out sigh and then runs his weathered hand across his face, covering his eyes for a beat before pulling it away and looking at me. He looks tired. Old. My grandfather has always had life and fire, but right now he looks deflated.

"They are like vultures circling a dead carcass," he breathes out. "They're demanding change. They are demanding you take a hands-on role. They are demanding you prove to them that, when the time does come, you can lead them."

I cock my head at him. "I can do that, Grandfather." My lip tips up. "I was born to lead."

He shakes his head as he picks up the magazine. "This is all they see, Nathaniel. And all this proves is you can be led along by your dick," he hisses, making my mouth gape open at the profanity that fell from his mouth.

"Don't be scandalized. I was young once. But when the moment came, I took over, and if I have anything to say about it, so will you. Because right now"—he gestures to the door—"your cousin is making a play for your spot, and I can only do so much to keep that from happening."

"That's nonsense."

"It is. But it doesn't make it any less true. Unfortunately, the board's power has grown significantly over the years. I own the majority, but they have the power to make change. Right now, your cousin is pushing for your incompetence."

"What in the bloody hell are you talking about?"

"Quietly, he's making alliances and building doubt, all while building himself up as the next successor. And you? You are playing into his hands. This article and the three before are the perfect ammunition for him to strike."

I sit back in my chair, running my fingers through my hair, pulling it almost violently as I will myself to think of a plan. I have no choice. What could I possibly do to prove that not only am I ready to work, but I'm also ready to take over? I need a job, but not one working under my grandfather. No. I need to show I can do it on my own and do it well.

Now to find a company to buy. One that is running smoothly and requires minimal work.

One that will solve all my problems.

# chapter two

## MADELINE

*New York*
*Three Months Later . . .*

"I'M SORRY I'M LATE," I SAY TO VALENTINA AS I QUICKLY stride into the showroom of Valentina Fisher, the fashion brand I work for.

Valentina and I have worked together for a long time. She's the lead designer, and I'm the CEO. Working with your best friend is the ideal situation, but there is one thorn in our side. Her uncle Gary, *the actual owner of the company.*

He's been a problem from the beginning. He's tight-fisted with his money and never comes to the office. He's hard to speak to when problems arise within the company, and the worst part is he threatens to sell us every day via email.

Working here, under his rule, is like a ticking time bomb. He hasn't shut us down because he must really care for Valentina deep down inside his cold exterior. Either that or he hasn't gotten a big enough offer to make him sell out his niece.

Today is going to be a busy day. I've started to compile a plan for launching a social media campaign and need to discuss the logistics with the team, so I place my bag down in my office and then head back to where everyone is congregating. In the middle of the large vacant space of the showroom is Gary. What's he doing here?

He spots me and waves me over. Valentina's face looks tight. Her lips pulled into a thin-lipped smile, but it's the line between her brows that gives her away. Whatever he just told her is weighing heavily on her, and it makes me nervous.

"Sorry," I say again when I'm finally standing in front of them. As much as Gary technically owns the company, this is actually Valentina's company, and I'll apologize to her, not him.

"Don't worry about it, but if you have a minute, we need to talk."

"Okay. Do I have time to grab a cup of coffee? I had an early appointment this morning."

"Is everything okay?" she asks.

I give her a tight smile. "It will be." My voice isn't convincing, and I can tell by the way she bites her lip that she is trying her best not to question me further. Not that I would tell her if she asked. The doctor's words are still too fresh in my mind, and I'm still too raw from hearing them. The appointment didn't go as planned, and I have some big decisions to make, but such is life. This is not the time or place to dwell on things that can't be changed. Instead, I push the feeling that wants to take root inside me, square my shoulders, and nod to Valentina.

"I'll grab that coffee and meet you where?"

"The conference room." Gary steps forward.

I glance over at him, surprised he's still here. I head over to the Nespresso machine set up in the corner. As the machine comes to life in a series of loud pitching, churning, and steaming, a robust aroma fills the air. I take a sip and let the taste explode in my mouth, my fingers wrapping tighter around the mug. My fingertips absorb the heat from the mug, instantly giving me the jolt of energy I need to sit through a meeting with my bosses. After two more long and satisfying sips, I head over to the conference room.

The heads of each department sit around the long metal table. The room, like the whole space of the showroom, is cold, cutting edge, and very industrial. I take the empty seat; the chair scratching on the concrete floors. All eyes are on me now, and I do my best not to let my cheeks warm. I have made it my life's mission never to show fear. I wouldn't have gotten to where I am in life if I'd showed my true feelings. I know that my attitude isn't conducive to friendships, and my only friend here is Val. I also know they call me the Ice Queen behind my back, but that's okay, because I get shit done. I have no life outside of work and I don't need one.

No time for a social life.

No time for a boyfriend.

No nothing.

As the thirty-two-year-old CEO of a startup company, I live, breathe, and sleep my job. I'm okay with the title. At least this way, no one will try to get me to go out, or even better, no one will try to introduce me to someone. I'm basically unapproachable.

This is my life.

"So let's get started," Valentina says with authority. More authority than I have ever seen before.

*This is going to be bad.*

Valentina is holding on by a thread, and her defense mechanism is to show no emotions. I'm the same way, so I recognize it from a mile away.

"Do you want the good news or the bad news?" Gary's voice

cuts through the room, heavy and full of dread. When no one answers, he takes it upon himself to continue. "Okay, let's cut to the chase. The good news is I'm retiring. I'm sure you have all noticed I'm not here as often. That's partially because I know nothing about fashion, but I'd also like to have more free time."

It's eerily quiet as we wait for our fate.

"So what does this mean for us?" I finally blurt out.

"Well, that's the good or, well, bad news, depending on how you look at it. Valentina Fisher isn't profitable yet. Although the meeting we had last quarter was a success, it didn't yield enough orders or profit for Valentina to buy me out . . ."

My stomach tightens. The other shoe is about to drop.

"About a month ago, a very successful company approached me. They are currently in textiles but are looking to branch out into small brands. At first, I gave Valentina the benefit of the doubt and gave her time to see if she could find the funds herself. When she couldn't, the offer was sweetened, and I couldn't say no. I got bought out."

From across the table, I can see Valentina's lip tremble. She doesn't want this. A new investor changes everything, and the direction of Valentina Fisher is uncertain now. Her dream. Her baby. And, to be honest, I feel sick too. I came here, left my job to be a part of something special, to help grow a brand I believed in.

"When does the change happen?" Placing my arms on the table in front of me, I lean in and narrow my eyes.

"Now," he responds with no emotion at all in his voice. As if he doesn't care that he just pulled the rug out from under us.

"What?" There is no holding back the surprise and disgust I have for this man.

"Today. Your new investor should be here any minute."

Chatter breaks out amongst everyone. I know what they are whispering about. It's mass chaos. *Will we have jobs tomorrow? Hell, will we have jobs in five minutes?*

"I hope you see this as a good thing. The vast capital they have can change everything."

"Or ruin everything," I mutter.

"Is this going to be a problem, Madeline? Because until the papers are dry, I still have the potential to let you go."

"It won't be a problem," I say through gritted teeth. Valentina needs me, and I won't be abandoning her. No jumping ship for me. I turn to Valentina. "No problem here."

She bites her lip and nods her appreciation.

"Well, if that's it, I'm going to head out and get to work," I say, not wanting to hear anything more from his lips.

"That's all—" He starts to say more, but I'm already out the door.

I don't like change. I like control. Order.

Meticulous order.

Not everything is in my control in my life, but this is. Work is. And no matter what obstacles get thrown my way, I will rise above.

# chapter three

## NATHANIEL

TODAY IS MY DAY.

The day I start my plan to prove myself.

I hate that I have to do this, but my grandfather—or really the board—has left me no choice.

It's an obligation, one that hangs over my head, but no way is that bloody wanker of a cousin going to take over my legacy. I don't care if Harrington blood runs through his veins. At the end of the day, his flow is tainted. His family was our ruin, but my grandfather saved us, and I'm not going to let this little shit take what's rightfully mine.

The truth is, at thirty years old, I don't feel like I'm ready for this. I don't *want* to be ready. But I haven't been left with much choice. I enjoy my life, enjoy my women, and I'm right pissed off that I have to fulfill this objective now, rather than later.

The worst part is not the how but the when. It's too soon. I didn't expect it. It came as a massive shock when my grandfather sat me down and gave me a piece of his mind, but it wasn't really the topic that made me take pause. I have always known the board hates my antics, but my grandfather has always allowed me to "sow my oats" so to speak. He's never harped on what I should be or not. He knew I'd take over because I was groomed to be this man. The best boarding school his money could buy, then Oxford, but when he confronted me, it was like something more was at play. I was given an ultimatum.

I spent the first month drunk. Sitting in a member's only club nursing a tumbler of scotch every day. As I was drowning my sorrows in three fingers of scotch at Soho House, I happened to be sitting right next to Gary Fisher, who was also drowning his sorrows. Apparently, he wanted to retire, but he had too much money sitting in his niece's startup company. I instantly knew the solution was simple.

It felt right.

Lucky for me, Gary wanted out. And out he got.

I chose to buy Valentina Fisher over my fifth glass of scotch. The numbers weren't great, and without an influx of money, they'd be dead in the water, but what they did have, according to Gary, was drive and an expert team. People loved their brand. The team was hard working; they just needed more capital, and he didn't have it. The best part, he didn't need to do anything other than give them money. It was perfect for me. I had plenty of money and no desire to actually do anything.

I always get what I want.

So here I am now, two months later, about to kick start my plan and turn this promising brand into the next Alexander McQueen. It will take six months, one year tops to prove to everyone that I have what it takes to take over Harrington Textiles when the time comes.

When I pull my motorbike up to an old dilapidated warehouse, I'm shocked by what I find. How can this be the headquarters of the company I've just purchased? The building appears to be abandoned with brick that is cracked, weathered, and faded with age. It isn't until I see a door and the words etched into the frosted surface that I know I'm in the right spot.

I park in front, then throw my helmet off and head through the glass doors. We are experiencing a rare winter day; it's warm, there's no snow on the ground, and the sun is shining bright. Taking full advantage of the situation, I donned a leather jacket instead of an overcoat. I don't look like a boss, and I certainly don't look like the heir to a billion-dollar fortune, but I never did play by the rules. Until the dotted line is signed and the weather turns back to the winter shitshow it's been, I don't see the need to turn in my Harley for a chauffeur-driven Mercedes Maybach like my grandfather travels in. Though once I sign these papers, I probably won't have a choice. Once my grand-father finds out I'm in New York City and working, he'll insist I act the part.

Pushing open the glass doors, my lip turns up. The inside is nothing like the front facade of the building, and I like the place already. White walls, white concrete floors, and white furniture greet me. It's cutting edge. Not trying to conform. Not exactly what Grandfather had in mind when he told me to prove my-self, but it will do.

Plus, to be honest, the designs and team seemed decent. That was one thing I'd insisted on before signing the papers, and although I might not follow fashion, I do know a lot about women, and the designs were exactly what women all over the world would want. Sexy and sophisticated all rolled up into one pretty package. They obviously know what they are doing, so I won't have to work hard. Which is good, because right now, I don't want to. All in due time and whatnot. I'm still young. Fuck, I'm only thirty and still in my prime. I shouldn't even need to prove myself right now. But here I am, apparently doing just that.

When I flew home from the South of France, I thought I would party it up in Manhattan for a few weeks, maybe a month, before returning home to my grandfather's estate in England. No need to kill myself was basically my motto until that fateful day in his study. Now I'm here, but as long as the team keeps up with what I'm doing, I can leverage this. I have plenty of time before my grandfather gives me the reins.

Movement, sounds, and a commotion greet me at the door. Creation is in the air. It pours into the communal space, vibrant and exciting. I instantly bask in the energy, and I'm happy I decided to buy this company.

A woman behind a Lucite desk smiles up at me. She's pretty if you like the wide-eyed, innocent look. I prefer my women with a little more bite. "Can I help you, sir?"

"Nathaniel Harrington," I say for introduction. "I have an appointment with Gary."

"He's in the conference room. It's all the way in the corner. He's expecting you."

I stride over the concrete floor. The sound my boots should make is lost in the sounds of people talking—gossiping by the looks of it. They are talking animatedly, hands waving around for emphasis. Voices loud, they sound like birds chirping. As I pass, they look up and their voices silence.

One, in particular, captures my attention. She's tall and resembles my typical type. She's got to be around six feet tall, and I wonder if she's a model. I let my eyes appraise her, and her cheeks flush in return. I'd stop to introduce myself, but I've already been announced, and I don't need anything derailing this transaction. No matter how pretty this blonde is. So instead, I pull my gaze away and walk right past the group until I'm standing in front of the glass window and door of the conference room. Taking a deep breath, I enter, ready to get this over with.

"Nathaniel." Gary stands and raises his hand to me. He looks more relaxed today than in the past, the lines that once circled his eyes have faded. *Maybe it's because this is finally over for him.* I'm not sure if this revelation scares me or excites me. Either way, I lift my own hand in greeting.

"Gary." I shake his extended hand before turning my attention to Valentina, the head designer. "Valentina." I've never met her in person, but I recognize her from my research. Valentina looks nothing like Gary. Where he's short and aging, she is tall and flawless with a willowy frame. With long brown hair and deep brown eyes, she has an exotic look to her.

She glares at me. It's obvious the news hasn't gone over well with her. "Let's get this over with. I have designs I need to work on," she hisses, more to her uncle than to me.

"Very well." I shrug. "All the papers of importance have been signed. Valentina, we just need for you to initial where my solicitor has indicated."

"Shouldn't I have my lawyer look this over?" she asks.

Her uncle steps forward. "My lawyers already have. Nothing will change whether you sign this or not, dear. It's a done deal."

*God, this man is an arse.*

Tears begin to form in her eyes, but she still signs.

"Now you officially own Valentina Fisher," the tosser says to me, and I have the urge to tell him to shut the fuck up. Can't he see how upset his niece is? But instead, I bite back my retort and give him a tight smile.

"Thanks, Gary." I cross my arms over my chest, showing him I'm not his friend. Now that this is done, I don't need to hear him speak.

"Should we make an announcement?"

"All in good time. Where is your office, Gary?"

"He doesn't have one," Valentina says, and I cock my head at her. "I mean, he does, but since he's never here, we keep our overflow material in there."

"I need a place." I smile tightly.

"I'll find one ASAP."

"Make sure you do. In the meantime, I'll make myself comfortable."

I find an office and open it. Through the glass windows, I see it's vacant. I'm not sure if it's anyone's office as everything in this place is so minimalist, but I walk in and make myself right at home at whoever's desk it is. It's mine, actually, since I do own the place now.

The first thing I do is kick my feet up on the desk. Might as well make myself at home. I fire up the computer in front of me and find it's not password protected. With a shrug, I open it up, interested to know whose desk I'm stealing. Looking through the files, I don't find anything of interest. Whoever uses this computer is very organized. There are files for everything. I open the email next. Each of the emails are addressed to a "Madeline." I wonder if she's one of the women I saw earlier. *Maybe this desk belongs to the blonde?*

Having nothing better to do with my time, I continue to scroll through her inbox. When the phone on her desk rings, I decide to answer it.

"Valentina Fisher," I answer.

"Is Madeline Montgomery there?" a woman asks through the phone.

"She's stepped out of her office. Can I take a message?"

"Will you please have her call back Dr. Martin's office."

"Most certainly. Is there a message I can relay to her?"

The woman speaks, and I respond before I hang the phone up and then lower my gaze back down to the computer. A few emails haven't been read yet, so with a smile on my face, I get even more comfy and start reading.

I'm deep into reading emails when I decide to rummage in her desk, looking for something to eat. Bingo, just what I was looking for. *Food.* Unwrapping the breakfast bar, I'm mid-bite when I hear the door open.

"What the hell do you think you're doing here?"

"Why, hello to you, too," I say, my words coming out mumbled around the food in my mouth.

"Are you eating my granola bar?" she hisses, and at that, I smirk at the fiery little thing standing in front of me. She's tiny. Maybe five foot two. Long brown wavy hair falls past her shoulders. For someone so small, she sure does pack a punch, though.

"She's sharp, too."

"That's my breakfast. Are you out of your damn mind?" She slams her hands on the desk. "I'm calling security."

"You do that." I shrug, lifting the bar up to my mouth to take another bite. Her blue eyes widen as she stares at me, and I swear if steam could pour out of ears, I would expect it now. She looks like she's about to lose her mind. I should probably stop taunting her, but I don't. Instead, I just smile as I continue to stare at her as I eat her breakfast. *I'm a wanker like that.*

She moves quickly for such a small thing, but just as I'm about to take a bite, she snatches the granola bar from my hand.

"Get out," she hisses.

"No."

"Forget security, I'm calling the police."

"Is that how you talk to the owner of your company, Madeline?"

"How do you know my name?"

"I'm Nathaniel Harrington, and I know everything."

Her eyes go wide and something I don't expect happens. She shuts up.

# chapter four

## MADELINE

THE NEW OWNER? WHAT THE FUCK DOES HE MEAN HE'S THE owner?

That's when the early meeting in the conference room slams back into me. Gary sold the company, which means someone bought it, and that someone is this man.

This prick.

This prick is my new boss. He's the man who bought the company. He's the man who holds this company's future in his grasp.

I stare him down, my eyes shooting daggers if I could. He looks like he would fit right in—if he were a model, not the owner. His hair is short but unruly. Like he can't be bothered to run a brush through it. Like he probably rolled out of bed after fucking some nameless girl. His face is magnificent; however, it looks like it hasn't been shaved in days. At least two days' worth of stubble line his perfectly chiseled jaw. And not only is he not wearing a suit, which is what I would have expected from someone in his position, but he's in a leather jacket with a white T-shirt underneath. His distressed jeans and boots are resting on my desk.

My desk.

Not his.

"Get your feet off my desk."

"Well, technically, it's my desk." He smirks, and if I didn't want to keep my job, I'd march up to him and smack the smug look off his face.

"You might own the company, but you are in *my* office. And that is *my* desk. And if you don't mind, I would ask you kindly—"

"Is that how you're asking?" he interrupts.

"If I could ask you kindly to vacate."

"You really are lovely when you're angry." His full upper lip tips up into a smirk that would make any girl go weak in the knees. Not me, but any other one with a pulse.

"Yes, so I'm not sure how you handle business over the pond, but referring to me as lovely here in the States is grounds for sexual harassment."

He lifts a brow. "Oh, is it?" The damn smirk deepens. I narrow my gaze and place my hands on my hips.

"It is," I say.

"Pardon my mistake." His voice is laced with humor, and there is no apology in his words. It's actually more of a challenge. Since he's not budging, I lower my hands and try a different approach. What's that saying? *You get more with honey than with vinegar.*

"Please, leave."

"No."

*Honey.*

"No?" I say softly, trying my hardest to keep my anger in check.

"You heard me. No."

*Honey.*

"You have your own office." I turn and point. "See right over there . . . that's your office."

He actually has the nerve to let out a throaty chuckle.

*Honey. Honey. Honey.*

"And seeing as right now it's a storage unit, I don't. So until that job is done, I'll reside here."

"And where do you see me working?" I fire back.

"To be honest, I don't bloody care. But while I have you here, your doctor's office called to confirm . . ." His gaze lowers until he's staring right at the lower part of my body.

"What?"

"I confirmed." He smiles.

"Let me get this straight. First, you have your feet on my desk. Then you eat my food. Then you took it upon yourself to answer my phone—"

"Don't forget to add I checked your email to the list."

"Y-you answered my email?" My voice rises as my nails dig into the fleshy part of my palm.

"Yes. Oh, and by the way, I responded yes to dinner with your mum for you. You're welcome."

I start to pace. Not knowing how to even respond, how to speak. My jaw is clenched so tight, I'm afraid it will break. "Why the fuck would you do that?"

"I was bored."

*Fuck honey.*

"That's it. I don't give a shit who you are. Boss or not, get out of my office!" I scream.

The sound of my door swinging open pulls me out of my heated haze. "Mad, can I speak to you," a voice says from behind me.

Without another word to my "boss," I turn on my heel and head straight back to Valentina's office and let myself in, her trailing me.

"He has to go!" I scream.

"Madeline . . ."

"He's a little boy. He can't run this company. There has to be someone—"

"There's not. It's this or shut down. You saw our profit margin last quarter. No one else will buy us, so our hands are tied. If we don't get an investor, we will shut down, and we don't even have the money to pay severance. Without him, we can't help Jean. And what about Lucy? She has college loans. I know this is hard, but there is more than you and me at stake. There are people who need this money. We can't fold."

I let out a long-drawn-out sigh. She's right. I know she's right. But that doesn't make this any easier.

"What are we going to do?" I groan.

"It's only temporary." Her voice is soft and reassuring, but I don't know who she's trying to convince: her or me?

"I know," I grumble under my breath, running my hands through my hair. "We need a plan. I mean, for crying out loud, he's in my damn office with his feet on my 'bloody' desk." My voice is way too loud. I'm sure everyone in the office can hear me now, but I refuse to look out the glass that faces the common room.

"We'll come up with a plan . . ." She starts, but her voice cracks with unsuppressed tears. "This is a nightmare. No. This is worse than a nightmare. At least with a nightmare, you eventually wake up."

"I promise we'll come up with a plan to get it fixed together. Everything happened so fast." She worries her lip at my words.

I blow out my cheeks and step closer, lifting a hand to touch her shoulder. "I know. I'm so sorry. I can't imagine how you must feel," I whisper. I might be the CEO of this company, but it's her company, her brand.

"It's okay. We'll get through this."

"Together." I nod. "We'll get through it."

"Thank you, Madeline." She gives me a tight smile, but I know it's fake. By her swollen and glassy eyes, I can tell she's been crying.

"So what do you want me to do? Where should I work?" I ask her.

"I don't know." She sighs.

"Maybe I should set up shop in my office and annoy him until he decides to be like Gary and just not come into the office." I laugh.

"That might not be such a bad idea." And for the first time today, she laughs too. "Should I have Eric bring up a desk?"

"Yes. Let's force this fucker out."

"He is kind of hot, though. At least the view won't be bad."

Shaking my head, I glare at her. "I don't fraternize with the enemy."

"He's not really the enemy, Mads."

"Until he's out of my office, he's my enemy."

"Whatever you say." She picks up her phone. "Eric." She smiles when he says something. "Can you please move a desk and chair into Madeline's office? Yeah, um, okay." She looks lighter as she hangs up the phone. Interesting.

"Everything okay?"

"Yep. He's right on it."

An hour later, I'm back in my office. Facing the enemy. But as I stare at him, I have to admit Valentina is not wrong. He's gorgeous and not normal gorgeous. No, this man is so much more. That word doesn't do him justice, and if his good looks weren't enough, he's dressed to blend as if he's a model, not the owner. He doesn't blend though. He's too good-looking to blend. Too striking. He's more handsome than any model I have ever seen before. I know I said I knew what I was doing, but there is no way working in this office, staring at this man is a good idea.

This is a bad idea.

A very bad one.

I can't stop staring. It's a major distraction. I haven't gotten anything done because as much as I hate him; he hypnotizes me. I need to get him out of here. But until I have another option, I'll have to suck it up.

The day drags on way too slowly, and the insistent tapping makes me want to bash my head on my desk. That or pray for peace and quiet. From where I'm perched at my makeshift desk, I can see his hands. His very masculine hands. I can't help but stare and watch as they play a beat on his desk. The way his knuckles move. The way the vein in his wrist flexes at the tap.

*Tap. Tap. Tap.*

Those hands can probably do wicked things . . .

My lids flutter closed for a second as the thought of his fingers strumming a beat somewhere else filters in through my brain.

Shit.

My face warms, and I need him to stop. Now. "Do you mind?" I groan louder than I want but enough to get my point across that I mean business.

"Mind what?" He feigns ignorance.

"The drumming on my desk. It's annoying."

"Don't you mean *my* desk?" He raises an eyebrow to challenge me.

Like the mature individual I am, I decide to accept his challenge and annoy him back. I start to hum to myself, each second letting my voice get louder. From the corner of my eye, I can see it has the desired result.

"You have an awful voice." He covers his ears as I continue to sing a full song in my office.

"If it's so annoying, you could always leave."

"I'm good right here. But thank you for your consideration." The drumming of his nails picks up.

I pick up the phone. From having two brothers, I know the one thing that is kryptonite to men: women on the phone and pestering.

Operation: Drive this man insane until he leaves is in full effect.

*Ring. Ring. Ring.*

"Madeline." I hear through the earpiece.

"Hey," I say in a voice that is so off pitch and not me that I know Eve will ask what the hell I'm doing.

"Um, Madeline, are you okay?"

"Yep. Just have a rodent problem I'm trying to get rid of." I glare at him.

"A rodent problem? Now, this sounds interesting. Work related?"

"Yep."

"He or she?"

I stare at the intruder. *All man.*

"The first . . ."

"Is he at least good-looking?"

"Not the issue at hand."

"So he is?" She laughs.

"You're not helping, Eve."

"What does he look like? I have been with your brother so long, I forget what it's like to be single. Let me live vicariously through you."

"Goodbye, Eve." I slam my phone back on the desk.

"Wasn't helpful?" Nathaniel asks.

I turn to face the other direction, trying to think of a witty retort but come up empty-handed, so I stand, pull my chair to his desk, and lean forward, propping myself on my elbows. "So what are you working on? Have you always wanted to own a fashion brand?" He doesn't answer. "Do you live in New York full time?"

I fire question after question until he lets out a long groan, stands, threads his fingers through his hair, and walks out the door.

*Bingo.*

# chapter five

## NATHANIEL

THIS WEEK HAS CERTAINLY KEPT ME ENTERTAINED. I'VE taken up residence in my new office and watching Madeline has become my new favorite pastime.

I've learned many things over the past four days . . .

One: Madeline is the neatest person I have ever met. Even with her makeshift desk set up in the corner of the office. She has color-coded files, pencils, and pens in perfect order, and when she leaves, nothing remains on her desk.

Two: Madeline is a control freak. No matter who comes into the office, she steers the conversation in the direction she wants. The outcome always what she deems best.

This has been my favorite piece of information I have cataloged in my mental Madeline file because this information means I drive her crazy, and no matter how hard she tries, she knows she can never win with me.

Three: She's incredibly stubborn. I don't know anyone else who would put up with me in her office, feet on her desk, and drumming my nails on the desk but her. She refuses to admit defeat.

Four: She never stops working. She's apparently the first

person in the office in the morning and the last one to leave.

Five: She looks sexy as hell when she's mad . . . This, by far, is the most dangerous of all the things I've learned this week.

My mobile vibrating in my pocket pulls me out of my thoughts. Grabbing it, I look down to see my grandfather's name on the screen. I've been expecting this call, but knowing it's coming and actually being prepared are two different things. I'm surprised it took this long, to be honest.

"You bought a company?" His voice is curt and to the point.

"You said I needed to take initiative," I retort, not seeing the problem.

"I meant coming into the office." He pauses. "I meant working for me."

I let out a deep, drawn-out breath. I had thought about that, but in the end, it wasn't enough shock and awe for what I needed. This was. Buying my own company would prove once and for all that I could handle running Harrington Textiles.

"That wouldn't be enough, and you know it," I finally respond.

"Nathaniel, you can't go off half-cocked like this. Even this move proves to them you aren't ready."

"Grandfather, I don't need to be ready now. You aren't going anywhere. This is a good way to prove I'm serious." I leave out the part about not having to work nearly as hard as I would if I had the watchful eye of the board at Harrington glaring at me all the time. But that's what this is. I'm not ready to be at Harrington yet.

"I hope you know what you're doing." He sighs, clearly giving up on this conversation.

"As a matter of fact, I do."

"You better."

The line goes quiet. I look down and see he's hung up on me.

Great. Just great.

I shake my head and place my mobile back down, this time on my desk. From across the room, I hear the tapping of Madeline's fingers on her keyboard. Was she listening to my conversation? I had forgotten I had an audience. Probably not. It seems she's too immersed in whatever she's doing. *Like always*. Does she ever stop working?

"Is there something I can do for you?" she says, pulling me out of my haze.

"Nope," I answer truthfully. Neither she nor anyone else here can do anything to help me get out of the bind I've gotten myself into. The only thing she could do is take my mind off all my problems, and I highly doubt she'd entertain the notion of letting me fuck her on my desk right now.

*Fuck her on my desk.*

Now that idea has promise. She really is something. I wouldn't mind burying myself in her. Although she's not my typical type, with long brown hair and full lips, she's stunning, but that's not what makes her different. The women I find myself attracted too are easygoing and not a challenge, but somehow, it's her fire that actually turns me on the most. She's a hellion. Ever since Cecile, I've had my fair share of women, too many to count, and all these women were forgettable—nothing more than a great shag. But something tells me this one would be more. So much more.

"So you're just staring?" she says, and I shake away all thoughts of her lying naked before me.

"Yes," I deadpan.

She lifts her hands from the computer and places one on

her forehead as if this banter is giving her a headache. "Can you stop?" She's glaring at me now, and I can't help but chuckle.

"Nope."

"You are the most infuriating person in the world." There is a newfound edge to her voice. Like an onion, Madeline has different layers of pissed off. Something tells me I haven't even delved past the second layer.

"Whatever you say, Tink." The nickname slips out, and it makes my lips pull up. *It's perfect.* If I can't fuck her, I might as well fuck with her.

"Excuse me, what did you call me?"

"Tink."

"Tink?"

"Yes. Tink," I assert, smiling widely. It's genius. "As in Tinker Bell." Her eyes widen at my clarification, but she still doesn't speak. "As in Peter Pan."

"I know who Tinker Bell is," she hisses.

"So then you know to whom I'm referring?" I'm such a dick, but watching her face furrow with anger is worth it.

"Yes. But I'm not understanding . . ."

"Well, clearly I'm calling you Tinker Bell."

"Because I'm short?"

"Well." I lean back in my seat, shrugging. "Tinker Bell was a bit of a party pooper, let's admit it. Raining on Peter and Wendy's parade. Trying to sabotage Wendy's life. Plus, you both have the tendency not to buzz off even when the situation calls for it."

Her mouth drops open. She stands, shakes her head, and storms out of the room.

Good, maybe now she'll move out of *my* office.

No such luck. Instead, she comes back, not even ten minutes

later, this time holding her mobile in her hand she points it to me and presses the icon for the music app.

"What are you doing?"

"Well, if I'm annoying, I might as well live up to the nickname."

I'm not quite sure what she's going on about, but when atrocious heavy metal screeching music blares through the room from the tiny speaker on her phone, I get it.

"Well played, Tink." I grin.

The rest of the day drags long and tedious. I distract myself by playing solitaire online. I can't even imagine having to do this for the next six months, let alone a year.

Maybe I didn't think this through completely.

# chapter six

## MADELINE

I IGNORED HIM THE WHOLE DAY. HELL, I IGNORED HIM THE DAY after that, too. Then came the weekend, which was a much-needed reprieve from my new boss and officemate. Yesterday, Monday, I'd been in and out of meetings, and today I'm working from home.

*Sick.*

*Again.*

The phone rings. It's on the coffee table lying beside the heating pad and pain pills that have become my salvation today. I groan from where I'm lying on the couch as I grab it. Val's name flashes across the screen.

"How're you feeling?" she asks before I can even say hello.

"I'm officially dying," I mutter.

"Dramatic much?" The sound of her laughter makes me join her, but the movement causes a sharp pain to radiate through my body, making my breath hitch.

"No, seriously." My voice cracks as I hold back a tear. "I'm dying."

"Shit." She's serious now. She knows I'm not joking. "You don't sound good."

"I don't feel good."

"I'm coming over," she says forcefully.

"You really don't have to."

She lets out a sigh. "Mad, I know I don't have to, but I want to. Let me come over. We can talk shop. I'll grab a pizza. We'll gossip. All the things you love to do."

"You must have me confused with someone else because I'm sure I don't like any of those things." A laugh escapes, and again, the movement has me groaning while clutching my stomach.

"Don't laugh. You sound awful."

"Gee, thanks. But seriously, if you want that kind of night, you might be better off calling Lucy." As the resident party girl in the office, young and freshly out of college, Lucy always wants to go out, drink, and gossip.

"You're an ass. I'll be over in thirty." I hear her rummaging through papers and then her chair scraping against the floor.

"Are you coming from the office?"

"Yeah."

"Is he still in *my* office?"

"He is."

I groan again, but this time not from pain but from annoyance.

"See you in thirty."

She hangs up, and reluctantly, I stand. No matter how much pain I'm in, I can't let Val see me like this. I look like a car—make that a truck—ran over me. Each step hurts as I walk to the bathroom. I wonder how long it will take for these pills to work. I'm on a new prescription from my doctor. This one is stronger, and it helps more, but when I take it, I feel sick. Not that I don't normally feel sick, but these pills I only take when

I desperately need it. Usually, it coincides with that time of the month . . . *lucky me.*

I look in the mirror and grimace. My eyes are hollow. The blue of my irises dull, and mainly only my pupils showing. My skin appears drab and a bit gray. It's not a good look for me. I try to lift my arm to open the medicine cabinet to get some makeup, but even that hurts. According to my doctor, this is the nature of the beast.

Endometriosis.

I was formally diagnosed a few years ago. It's been a steady, painful battle ever since. The pain I feel during my period, though, is something completely different. It's like shards of glass are ripping me apart.

Knowing I can't do anything to make myself more presentable, I let out a long-drawn-out sigh and waddle back to the couch. Val and I have worked together for years. When we first met, she was one of the designers at the first brand I worked at. She was just an intern then, and I was fresh out of college. Together, we rose up the ranks. Then when she decided to branch out and start her own brand, she brought me with her. Sure, it was a gamble, but she's one of my closest friends, the only one who knows why I am solid ice and loves me anyway.

In the distance, I hear a jingle of the key and then the door opens. "Hey, girl," she says as she walks into the apartment.

"In here," I respond. The sound of her clicking echoes through the air.

"Holy shit." She gasps.

"That bad, huh?"

"I love you, but yes." She sits next to me and places her hand on my head like a mother. If it didn't hurt to laugh, I would, but it does, so I refrain. "Should I . . ." She pauses and worries her lip. "Should we call your doctor? You don't look good." She looks pale now as if my symptoms have traveled into her body.

I lift my hand and touch her. "I'm okay. Nothing I haven't lived through before. The pain pills will kick in soon."

"Okay," she mutters, unsure, but I give her a reassuring smile and watch her take a deep breath. Her shoulders rise and then fall. "Let's eat this pizza before it gets cold."

When she says the word pizza, I look over at the coffee table. How did I not notice it before? My stomach lets out a painful growl. I can't remember the last time I ate? Maybe yesterday?

Pulling my body up to sit, I take a slice and set off to eat. Once I'm done with my slice, I finally start to feel better. "So you said you wanted to gossip?" I ask.

"I do . . ." She perks up.

"About?"

"The big giant elephant in the room . . . or rather, your office."

I let out a puff of air. "Do we have to?"

"Yes."

"Fine. What do you want me to say? We are fucked," I deadpan.

"Maybe it won't be so bad." She's staring at me intently, probably hoping I'll agree with her new assessment. I won't. We *are* fucked.

"I found him a few days ago playing poker online."

"Shit."

Shit doesn't even begin to cover it, but the situation basically holds the same aroma.

"Well, there is only one thing we can do."

"And what is that?" I ask.

"Google stalk him, obviously."

I shake my head at her. Of course, she would suggest that.

"Where's your laptop?"

"No clue."

She pulls out her phone. "Damn, for some reason, mine's not connecting to the internet. Give me yours." I let out a groan and point at the table. She grabs my phone and types frantically in it. "Oh Lord, we are so fucked."

"Why? What did you find?"

"Well, not only does he like poker, but apparently, he likes women, too, and clubbing."

"So he's basically the playboy trifecta?" I huff.

"Yep."

"We'll be lucky if we are still in business in a year."

Her eyes go wide, and I instantly feel bad.

"I didn't mean it. Of course, we will. We are a team. And a damn good one at that," I affirm.

"We are, right?"

"The best." My voice is confident, leaving no room for doubt. "So first things first, we come up with a plan, and then we implement it."

"Okay, where should we start?" she asks.

"Tomorrow, we call an emergency meeting in my office. We tell him to either help or get out. If he gives us shit, well, I'm not sure. But I'll figure out a threat that will work. If I can't think of one, we'll annoy him enough to leave."

"It's too bad he's such an ass."

"Why?" I ask.

"'Cause he's gorgeous. Seriously one of the best-looking men I have ever seen."

I stare at her blankly. "I mean, sure, he's hot, but one, he's a dick, and two, I hate to be Prudish Paela, but dating in the office isn't cool. Who shits where they eat? It's tacky." I shrug.

Val doesn't say anything, so I turn to her. Her brow furrows, and she looks upset.

"What? Are you okay?" I ask.

"Yeah. I just have to go." She gets up and walks toward the door stiffly. "If you need me, call me."

"Okay."

I'm not sure what I said, but that was awkward.

---

Today, I feel much better. My medicine's working now. I'm on my way back to the office. No subway today. No walking either, so today I uber it. I'm still drained from yesterday, but I have things to do, so a meeting today is imperative.

With determination pounding in my blood, I walk into the showroom common space and turn to Val. "Meeting. My office." I smirk at her. Now we find him.

It doesn't take us long. He's exactly where we were expecting. In my office, feet on the desk. He looks up and doesn't even bother trying to pretend he's working. Making my way inside the office, I stand by my desk. Val trails me, but she stops in the doorframe.

"You're still here?" I mutter. I knew he would be—he enjoys bothering me too much—but a small part still prayed I'd be wrong and he'd have gotten sick of coming into the office.

"Yep."

"God, I thought for sure you'd grow bored of being an adult and go fly off somewhere," I groan. I look at him, reclined back as though he doesn't have a care in the world. "Can you at least make yourself useful?" If I'm going to be stuck with him, he might as well do work. Do something. Not just sit there looking so damn hot. It's infuriating.

"What would you like me to do?"

"Do you have any talents?" The moment his lip quirks up into a wicked smile, I realize my mistake.

"I do have quite a bit. Interested in having me list them?"

My face begins to warm, and I shake my head. "Not those kinds of talents. Actual work talents."

"Such as?" The mischievous look in his eyes as he speaks should be illegal. I puff my cheeks to distract myself from the thoughts that are starting to spiral out of control.

"Seriously. Why are you even here? You obviously have no interest in working. You want to be a pretty face in the office, fine, but can you at least do it someplace else?"

"So you think I have a pretty face?"

"Really?"

"Really."

"You are infuriating." I place my hand on my hips. "This is such a joke. Maybe if you knew the company you were buying, you'd know what needs to be done. Maybe you should have done your due diligence—looked at financial statements."

He cocks his head at me and nods. "Okay."

I'm taken aback. "Okay?"

"Yes. Okay. You're right. Get me the files."

I swear my mouth drops open and I'm at a loss for words. "Umm . . ."

"Cat got your tongue?" he jests.

My mouth snaps shut, and I'm pulled from my haze. If he wants information, then information he'll get. I'm about to head out and get it when I take in his computer screen. A groan escapes my mouth. "Apparently, today is no different from yesterday." I move his screen so Val can see what I'm looking yet.

"Poker." I lift a brow.

"Is there something else I can help you with, or can I get back to my game?" He crosses his arms across his chest in challenge. "I don't get you. You storm in and are practically sitting on my lap. Is there something else I can do for you, Tink?" He smirks as he runs his gaze down the length of my body. "Because if you want that, that's fine." He licks his lower lip as if he wants to devour me. Warmth spreads through my stomach, and I hate my treacherous body at this moment. "But if you want that from me, if you want me, a heads-up would be nice. Unless"—his brow pulls up—"was this my heads-up, Tink?"

"Would you just shut up?" I hiss, stepping back before I throttle him. "This is your heads-up . . . just not for what you think."

"What do you mean?"

"If you're going to do this"—I gesture around my office—"if you're going to own us, be silent, but if you are going to take over my office, you need to work."

"I am working. I'm counting my money and playing poker." He winks.

"I'm being serious."

"So am I."

"Here are your choices . . . One: you're a silent partner, and you get the fuck out of my office or two: you come up with something to do here and . . . get the fuck out of my office."

His eyes widen, but at the same time, I see his lip tip up. Fuck. He's enjoying this. Great. Just great. He continues to stare at me amused, and I shoot daggers at him with my eyes. We are at a standstill. Neither of us speaking for way too long.

Finally, I step forward, blowing out a breath. "Nathaniel." I stop and think of how to get my point across and not kill him

45

at the same time. "There must be a reason you bought our company. There must be a reason you're here. I have to assume that's because you either want or need us to be successful. But whatever the reason you have"—I pause, and I'm shocked by the words that come out of my mouth—"help us."

Nathaniel doesn't blink for a second. He just stares at me and then pulls his gaze away to look past my shoulder at Val. Then he does something I don't expect. He removes his feet from my desk. Leans back. "What can I do?"

The words shock me. My mouth hangs open, and I'm not sure what to say.

"I like seeing you like this, Tink."

"Like what?"

"Shocked. Speechless."

"You're a dick."

"Don't I know it?" He laughs and shakes his head in exasperation. I step away.

So much for him being serious. The worst part of all this, though, is I don't like the feeling in my stomach at the sound of him laughing. I hate him. Just because he's gorgeous when he laughs doesn't change anything. Needing space, I storm out of the room and make my way to what should be "his" office even though it's still a catchall. No one has cleaned it out yet, and if I had to harbor a guess, they won't. Because knowing Nathaniel Harrington for only a short time, I know he probably told them not to. He enjoys annoying me too much.

Moving to the back of the room, I find the file cabinet I'm looking for and bend over to grab the files on the bottom shelf. We really should transfer all these files to one secure file on the computer, but we've been so busy with everything else that we haven't. With five huge files in hand, I have everything he needs. Last quarter's numbers. This quarter's buy sheets, and the projections from the show. I have the Excel spreadsheets on the samples being sent out. I even grab all the files from last quarter. If he's going to start, he should know what he's dealing with. So I pile it on. All the files from before his purchase. I'm sure he had the sales figures, or why else would he buy, but now he has all material costs, all the vendors. Everything.

And I can't wait to see his face when I give him enough work to last a year.

Trudging back to my office, I find him on a phone call. He doesn't look happy at all. A line forms between his brows. "I don't understand the rush," he mutters into the phone. Then he waits and listens to whoever is talking to him. "Very well. Yes. I understand. I'm working on it now." He worries his lip as the conversation becomes one-sided again. "Yes, Grandfather." When he finally hangs up, he notices me standing in the doorway.

"Trouble in paradise?"

"Bugger off," he hisses before turning away from me in dismissal.

Whatever was said to him has him on edge, and although I don't like the man, I can't help but feel sorry for him. Stupid, I know. But I can't help it. I know what pressure Jace, my brother, always put on himself to succeed, and by the sound of the conversation I heard, it seems he might be under the same pressure my brother was under.

"Where did Val go?"

"She gave me privacy, unlike some people. It's bad form to eavesdrop on a conversation."

*So much for feeling sad for him.*

"Here are the files you wanted to see."

He raises his gaze and meets mine. His green eyes are piercing. They are a darker shade of emerald than before. As if his emotions amplified the color. Like a fresh morning sun on moss. Vibrant and alive with emotion I can't even begin to understand.

I pull my gaze away, not wanting to get lost in his eyes. Instead, I watch as he takes a breath, the muscle in his jaw tightening and then loosening on the exhale.

"Thank you."

"No problem." I place them down and leave. Needing space. Needing to not see him as anything more than the asshole who bought this company. I can't allow myself to humanize him.

I walk out the door and straight into Lucy. "Whoa, there," she says as she straightens her dress.

"Sorry about that." I lift my hand to steady myself so I don't fall.

"Not paying attention? Got something on your mind?" Her questions take me off guard.

"Something like that," I mutter.

"Is it the hot man candy in your office?" She widens her eyes as she speaks and starts fanning herself. Normally, I might chuckle at her dramatic flair, but right now, I'm just not in the mood.

"He's not hot," I lie through gritted teeth, not wanting to admit to Lucy that I think he is.

"Fine, you're right. He is so much more than hot. And I also heard from Jean he's British."

I roll my eyes at her. "He is."

"Shit. It's true. I need to hit that."

"Lucy," I scold.

"What?"

"Don't what me. You know you can't hit that."

"Why the hell not? There's no rule against sex in the workplace." She smirks.

"Even though there is technically no rule, it's frowned upon. He's our boss."

"One, he's not really our boss. Valentina is. And two . . ." She drawls out before smirking. "Hello, Valentina is banging Eric."

Oh my God.

It all makes sense now. Valentina's reaction last night. What I said to her. I feel like a complete asshole. "One, as you so aptly put it, he's our boss. He bought the company, and just because he isn't technically our boss, he is still our boss. And two, Valentina doesn't count."

"You really are no fun." She rolls her eyes at me. I wish I could be like her sometimes, light and carefree, but I'm not. I never will be.

"This is a place of work. It shouldn't be fun." *And I really don't want anyone else to have fun if I can't.*

"So I guess that means you won't be going to happy hour today?"

She asks me this question every week, hell, probably closer to every day. "Nope. I have work to do." I give her the same answer I always do.

"You work too damn much."

She's right. I do, but the thing is, it's all I have right now. And it keeps me distracted, so I'll take it.

"Can you at least do lunch?"

"I don't know if I should laugh or be horrified by you." I shake my head in disbelief.

She shrugs. "Why?"

"Because I'm also technically your boss."

"I know, but you love me. What would you do here without me?"

"Maybe hire someone who does more work." I let my lips twist up into a smile. Lucy laughs at that and heads back to her desk.

The truth is, she's right. She's always exactly what I need to lighten my mood, and as much as she fucks around, she always gets her work done, and when needed, she is of the utmost professionalism. I grin to myself and head for Valentina's office.

It's time to say I'm sorry and grovel.

---

A few days have passed. Surprisingly, it appears as though Nathaniel is going over all the files I gave him.

From across the common room, I hear a loud crash against the floor. Looking in the direction of the disturbance, I see Jean kneeling over, trying desperately to clean a mess she's made. Jean is the resident grandma in the place. As the mother hen, she is also around eighty years old and very klutzy. I watch as she cleans her mess and scampers off. A few minutes later, I hear a large groan in my office.

"She needs to go."

"Who?" I have no idea who he is even talking about, but then I follow his gaze. Jean is now fetching coffee for Valentina. Her movements are slow, and she's spilling liquid on the floor as she walks. The hot beverage sloshes against the rim of the mug, hitting the floor beneath. The sound as each drop crashes to the floor echoes in my ear.

"Jean can't go."

"Of course, she can. She should be retired at home, not trudging along bringing coffee, slowly."

"She can't. She's been with us since the beginning."

"The beginning of time."

I turn away from Jean and glare at him. *What an ass.* "No, not the beginning of time. She's been with us since Val started the brand."

"She needs to be let go. It's unseemly to have her here. I will speak to Valentina." He stands and goes to walk toward the door. I stand and block his way, placing my hands on my hips and staring him down.

"You cannot fire her."

"Try me." He sidesteps me.

"You are a horrible man," I call from behind him, making him stop in the doorway of the office and turn around.

"That might be so. But I own this company, and this is a work hazard. A model could slip. Fall. Sue me."

"God forbid you get sued." I roll my eyes. "You don't understand. She was her nanny. They kept in touch, and eventually, she fell on hard times. She . . ." My voice cracks at the thought of Jean's life. "Her daughter died. She and her husband . . . she took in her grandchild. She needs this job. She's raising him. Supporting him."

He goes still at my comment. Painfully still. It's almost as if he's not breathing. But the rise and fall of his broad chest tell me he is. He blinks once. His eyes are lost and unfocused.

I've never seen him look like this.

"My decision is already made. She needs to retire." Without another word, he turns on his heel and leaves me standing alone as he stalks toward Jean. I want to say something, to demand he stop, but I can't. I'm stuck. My feet glued to the floor with what just happened.

Together, they walk off into the office—Valentina, Nathaniel, and Jean. When the door closes, the sound of it wakes me from my haze. "Bastard," I hiss to myself and then head back to my desk. "Fucking bastard." Thirty minutes must pass, and from my office, I see when the door opens. Jean hugs Valentina and walks out the door. Tears fill my eyes. Nathaniel is nowhere in sight, so I prowl across the space until I'm standing right in front of Valentina.

"How could you let him do that?"

"Do what?" She tilts her head at me. The confusion evident on her face.

"What do you mean do what? You saw what he just did. Valentina, did you see what he did to Jean?"

She looks at me like I have two heads now. "What are you so mad about?" she finally asks as she scrunches her nose.

"I'm not mad at you. I'm mad at him."

Lifting her hands up, she shakes them as if to stop me. "What do you think he did?"

My mouth drops. Is she kidding me right now? "He fired her," I grit between my teeth, not wanting to scream. Instead, I bite my cheek until a copper taste fills my mouth.

"No. He didn't fire her." Her words make no sense. I saw him.

"He did. She's gone."

"She retired."

"He forced her retirement. She has her grandson. His school. His tuition. He's a monster."

Nathaniel chooses that moment to walk out. His gaze catches mine, and I narrow my eyes. I might not say it, but my intention is loud and clear. He's a monster.

Valentina pulls me into her office by my arm. "What are you doing?" I lift my brow.

"Saving you from doing something you will regret," she says.

"Such as?"

"Going off, losing your temper. Losing your job."

"If this is how it's going to be, I don't know if I can work here. Work for him."

"Madeline, I'm going to say this one time, and then you're going to shut up and go back to your office."

I don't speak.

"He didn't fire her, and he didn't leave her in the lurch. Quite the opposite. He paid her a severance."

"But her gran—"

"Stop." Her hand lifts, silencing me. "He paid that too."

"What?"

"He paid for her grandson's college. All of it."

The room goes quiet. My heart hammers in my chest. I don't blink as I let the information soak in. The silence around us is deafening.

"He paid?" I whisper in shock.

"Yes."

"Oh."

"Exactly. You owe him an apology. Now go back to your office. I have a phone call to make."

I turn and leave, barely able to swallow at the revelation just presented to me. How could I have been so wrong?

And if I was this wrong, what else am I wrong about?

# chapter seven

## NATHANIEL

THIS IS MORE WORK THAN IT'S WORTH.

All the paperwork and looking at a rundown on the logistics is monotonous, boring, and tedious.

Meeting after meeting.

Spreadsheets.

PowerPoints.

By five p.m. yesterday, I had been told about all the plans. The shows. The parties. I also have a full rundown on pending orders. And plans to get more. The last investor was silent, and seeing as I don't really understand this business, I'm considering going home and being silent as well. Maybe my grandfather was right and instead of buying a freaking company, I should have worked for his. But I know I can't.

One: I'm supposed to be proving myself.

Two: It's kind of fun pissing off Madeline.

When I'm finally done for the day, I head home, and the first thing I do is pour myself a big helping of scotch. That should make everything better. I'm not even done with my first glass before my mobile rings. Looking down at the screen, I swipe it and answer.

"I'm in New York," he states.

"I'm starting to think you're following me, mate." I laugh.

"Nothing to think about . . . I am." He chuckles back.

"Seriously, what are you doing in New York so much?" I ask.

"Visiting a friend." He doesn't give anything else away, so I place my glass down on the table, interested to know more.

"Does this friend have a name?"

"Don Julio . . ."

"You're such an arse."

He lets out a throaty chuckle. "But seriously, are you going to meet me?"

After the day I've had, there is only one answer. "Yes."

"That took a lot of convincing."

"I'm working with all women. I need a night out with my best mate." As the words pass through my lips, I know how true they are. I need to go out. I need to get laid.

"See, aren't you happy I stopped in New York now?"

"I am, but don't you have work to do? Or is it all just fun and games to be the sixteenth earl to whatever your damn title is?"

"See you soon." He laughs through the phone, and I can't help but shake my head at him.

*Olly.*

At eleven, I roll up to the private lounge where I always meet Olly. This is his MO. Private clubs. Places he can come and go under the radar. It's not that he's an elitist arse, but his family is. He can't be seen in a bad light. And heaven forbid he be photographed. So a private club it is.

A few minutes later, I find him, and the table he always

occupies. On the table, a bottle of Don Julio 1942 waits for me. "It's a tequila night, I see?" I lift my brow.

"It is." He looks pissed off. Or upset. Not a typical look for him. Sure, he's an arsehole half the time, but upset . . . not like this.

"Want to talk about it?" I ask. He won't. One thing about Olly is that he's private about his life. He's always got his nose in my business, but his is private. But I respect him enough not to press when he shakes his head.

A waitress comes over and smiles. "Can I get you something, sir? Shots perhaps?"

"Sure. I'll have a shot but also get me a bottle of Grey Goose."

"Mixing." He shakes his head in mock disapproval.

"I'll be fine."

A minute later, the waitress brings my vodka and a shaker. Once I have my drink, she goes about shaking the tequila, making it extra chilled like Olly likes. After the shots, Olly stands and signals a girl over to him, who proceeds to sit on his lap. She's whispering in his ear. Leaning back, I watch as my friend works his magic. No question he'll be getting laid tonight. Me, on the other hand, I'm not finding anyone in this room I want to fuck.

My gaze runs the full length of the wall, taking a moment at each table to scope out the ladies occupying the space. Although the girls are all beautiful, not one piques my interest.

"Searching for someone? Maybe me?"

My back goes ramrod straight at the all too familiar voice of my ex. *Cecile.* "What are you doing here?" I grate out, not at all happy to see her here.

"Nathaniel." She smiles. "You know I'm a member."

"No, Cecile. What are you doing in America? Shouldn't you

be in England with your husband?" I spit out.

Her eyes grow wide at my tone. "I'm here for the cocktail party."

"You're a bit early for that." Her answer is bullshit. I know it, and by the way she furrows her brow, she knows it too.

"I'm here for another party as well."

I look over her features. Her eyes are blue, strikingly so, but not the same shade of blue as Madeline's. Madeline's eyes are otherworldly. Like sapphires plucked from the ground, raw and magnificent.

*Madeline.* Why am I thinking of her? *Because anything is better than thinking of Cecile.*

"I guess I should get back to my group."

"You should," I say as I reach for the bottle of Grey Goose and pour more into my now empty glass. "Lovely seeing you, Cecile," I lie. It's never lovely to see her.


The night goes by in a haze of booze and more booze. Glasses of vodka chase shots of tequila. Before I know it, the alarm on my mobile blares through the space.

"God," I groan as I fling my arm over my head. As it keeps singing to me to wake up, I finally do, throwing my hand and swiping the screen to silence it. There is a jackhammer in my brain as my head becomes cloudy with bits of memories hovering above me.

The club.

The booze.

The Cecile.

I shouldn't have drunk as much as I did, but when I see her, I can't help it. As much as I try to convince myself I don't care, it's obvious I'm still not ready. Although the wounds are a few years old, they are still as deep and gaping as ever. And today, I pay the price for my weakness.

Reaching across the nightstand, I grab my water and then take a few pills to help with the pain. I need to get to work. The stink of booze on me makes my nose scrunch in disgust and my stomach roils.

*Or maybe I shouldn't.*

An image of the small petite brunette I share a space with filters in through my eyes. No, I'm going in. The only thing that will make me feel better today is messing with Tink. Teasing her, toying with her, and watching her rage for some reason makes me happy. It's sick, I know. But true nonetheless. I get joy from watching her squirm.

Squirm . . .

Shit.

Now another thought invades my mind. Her. Naked beneath me. Me. Thrusting in and out of her tiny little body. I imagine she'd be tight. Perfect. Fiery. The vision of laying her out across my desk is so promising, I swear my hangover subsides for a moment.

Not long, but long enough for the idea to take root.

---

Yesterday was awful. My headache persisted the entire day and night and I swore I would never do that again. So today I'm here early with a new resolve in place. I like the quiet and peace it brings. It also allows me to spend time sans Madeline formulating the best plan to make this investment pay out as fast as possible.

As shocking as it is, I don't mind working. Or at least, I

don't mind working here. I'm reading through my correspondence when a throat clears, making me look away from my computer. "And here I thought you wouldn't be in today. After your hangover yesterday . . ."

"I am happy to disappoint," I say as I flash her my pearly whites. "But I am here today, and I did my homework." I speak really slowly, painfully slow. "The files were interesting. Fascinating really." I lift my coffee in hand and take a sip, wetting my throat, making her wait for what I'm about to say. Her large blue eyes widen considerably as she watches me.

"Why are you still here? I really don't get it. Aren't people as big as you actually too busy to work? Don't you have a bigger enterprise to run? A private plane to ride or something?"

"Not particularly."

"There really is no need for you to be here every day. Gary never came in."

"I'm not Gary," I fire back, not liking being compared to that prick. I might not have a huge sense of morality but selling your niece's company goes against even the little bit I have.

"How about you go home, or to wherever else you can be more useful? I promise if there is a crisis, I'll call you."

"Madeline," I say, and she halts her movements. "Sit." She moves to sit at her small desk set up in the corner of the room. "Not that one. Please sit with me."

"I-I . . ." she stutters.

"I won't bite, Madeline." Her face flushes, and I want to smile. I don't, but I want to. It seems she isn't unaffected by me after all.

Good.

I like that.

When she sits in front of me, she pulls at her skirt, trying to lower the hem. Only, it does the opposite of what she intended. Now it's actually rising up her leg inside. Her creamy white tights are in perfect view from where I'm perched on my own desk.

"I want to talk about these numbers."

Shock mars her features, but she rights them quickly. "Valentina isn't here yet."

"We don't need Valentina yet."

"She's the designer."

"And these are the numbers. This might be her company, but really, you're the brains behind the operation."

Her mouth drops open at that.

"Yes. I have done my homework. I saw your work and your experience. You have done a great job—"

"But . . . why do I feel like there is a but here?"

"There is."

"And what is the but?" she asks as her upper teeth bite down on her lower lip.

"It's not enough," I respond, unfazed.

"Not enough?" She stands abruptly and starts to pace around the office. Keeping her focus on the floor, she grits her teeth as she clenches her jaw.

"Please, sit," I say softly as if she's a wild animal that I don't want to spook.

She glances up and narrows her eyes.

"I don't think I will. You don't get to come into my office and tell me I haven't worked my ass off."

"I never said that. Actually, I do believe I said it's apparent that you have, but what it also shows is that it's not enough. We need more. We need to expand."

"And you have experience in expansion?"

I don't answer. I don't, but just because I don't doesn't mean I can't see the numbers plain as day.

"Just what I thought. You come in here all high and mighty, acting like you know everything, yet you probably haven't worked a day in your life."

"That may be true, but you need me."

"I don't need anyone." Her words come out strong, and by the tone, I know it's not just about work.

"Again, that may be the case, but my money is holding this place together until the orders come in, and seeing as I just looked at the books, it's also obvious that even I won't be able to hold you afloat if we don't do more."

"Does Valentina know this?"

"I haven't spoken to her about this, but she's in a bad place right now."

"That doesn't make any sense. The feedback for the line has been amazing."

I lift my hand and run it through my hair, trying to think of the best way to explain this to her. But there only really is one way—honesty. "It was. But there just isn't enough money."

"So what do we do?"

"Expand. We need department stores to pick us up. But to fix the immediate fund problems, we need to cut back on material costs."

"And you think you have an idea for that?"

"For the materials, yes. I can have Harrington Textiles supply them. That will help tremendously. For expansion, I don't have an idea yet."

"Well, thank you for your time. This has been enlightening, but now I need to figure out what you failed to do."

"What do you have against me, Madeline?"

"Everything."

"Such as?"

"For one, you are still in my office. Two, I have worked my ass off. Three . . ." She trails off, trying to think of something else to throw at me.

"Yes?"

"Nothing," she hisses through clenched teeth.

"Very well."

My phone rings and after I glance at who's calling, I have to cut our conversation short. "Do you mind? I have to take this."

She groans loudly.

"Hello, Grandfather."

"I'm in town."

Every muscle in my back tightens at the information. *Shit.* "Excuse me?"

"I need to see for myself that you are taking your life seriously. The board is asking for numbers."

"You cannot be serious right now."

"I am."

"Isn't it enough I'm here? Working."

"Harrington Textiles is a billion-dollar company. You have acquired a new acquisition, and it is in our right—*my* right—to see what you are doing with this investment. Nathaniel, I know this isn't ideal, and I don't want to force your hand, but you have left me no choice."

"Fine."

"I'll be in the New York City office at the end of the week. Be prepared."

Hanging up the phone, I blow out the air in my lungs. I knew I was going to be micromanaged, but this is a bitter pill to swallow. I never expected my grandfather to be this on top of me, and it has me on edge. I'll need to schedule a meeting to come up with a game plan for expansion. By the end of the next quarter, the board will expect growth.

I can't lose the board's approval. My grandfather might run the company, but he set it up in a way that, after what his brother did, no one would have too much power. I understand why he did it after all he lost, but now that I'm in the line of fire, I don't like it. Harrington Textiles is my legacy. I'm Nathaniel Harrington, son of Nathaniel II and grandson to Nathaniel I.

I won't let him down.

———————◆———————

The time has come for my grandfather to summon me yet again, this time to the Harrington Textiles office in New York. I'm on edge even though I shouldn't be. After working the past several days and into the late night with Valentina and Madeline on the expansion plan, I know we have a solid pitch. But even knowing that doesn't stop the impending doom I feel hanging over me. This isn't something I should be worried about. This man raised me, making me the man I am today, yet it still doesn't matter. The mere thought of him being here still feels like a hot poker being shoved into my stomach.

This was one of my many rash decisions. Buying Valentina Fisher. I hadn't really considered the ramifications of my actions. For some reason, I assumed buying it would be enough to foster goodwill amongst the board and they wouldn't try to bypass me in the line of succession. I was wrong, of course. They are asking for proof. And my grandfather is here to gather it.

I stand from the desk I have decided is my own. Madeline looks over her shoulder.

"It's time?" She's lost and distracted by whatever she's

looking at on her phone. Not like her to be distracted, but I have enough going on in my life than to worry about her.

"It is, Tink."

Her glare burns through me at the use of the nickname.

"Can you please stop calling me that?" Pissing her off shouldn't make me smile, but I can't help it. It does. For some reason, riling her up is the highlight of my day.

"Nope."

"Does it make you feel better to treat me like shit?"

I shrug. "I hardly think I am treating you like shit."

"Oh no?"

"No."

"So nicknaming me after a fairy is nice?" Her left eyebrow lifts in confrontation. This time, I let my lips part into a huge wicked smile.

I step closer to her until the toe of my shoe touches hers. "I never said I was nice, Tink, but I don't treat you like shit."

"Intolerable. If I'm Tink, that must make you Peter." She raises her chin and then it's her turn to smirk. "Pretty fitting, actually."

"How so?"

"The boy who wouldn't grow up . . ."

Her words hang in the air, the weight of the words so relevant right now. But isn't that what I'm trying to do, grow up?

*Hardly.*

*You are trying to appease a board. You still haven't actually worked. Nor will you.*

I move past her, turning over my shoulder. "Go get Valentina, so we can head out."

"She's actually meeting us there."

"Then let's go."

It takes us thirty minutes to make it to the oppressing office. The magnificent structure stands tall in the middle of the city. One that clearly states how much money it brings in.

Once inside, I lead us to the private lift that will take us to the conference room on the top floor of the building. Tink is silent, looking around in complete awe of the space. It is quite a lot. Even though I have grown up coming here, I am still in awe.

We move toward the large glass window that surrounds the conference room. Coffee and tea are set up. Everyone is sitting around the table sans my grandfather and us. We don't have to wait long for him to appear, though. It's only mere minutes before his larger-than-life stature enters the room. For as old as he is, he's intimidating. Not to me, but I can see it in Madeline's eyes. She knows what his presence means. He can make or break this company. By proxy, so can I, but where she doesn't take me seriously, she takes him very seriously.

"Hello, Grandfather."

Valentina is the first to introduce herself, followed by Madeline. The whole board does introductions before slides are shown, numbers recited, and a game plan to create our own version of fashion week is pitched. We might not have taken part in Fashion Week this year, but we will hit up every city with the hopes of landing Valentina Fisher in all the major boutiques and department stores. The proposed trip is laid out, the calls to Harrods and Selfridges. The private parties and social media influencers we'll use.

My grandfather fires off the obligatory questions. He nods and smiles, and all in all, it seems to be going well.

"Nathaniel. A minute."

"Yes, of course, Grandfather."

When the door closes behind everyone, we are left alone in

the quiet of the room.

"My lad," he starts. "This is a big undertaking. Are you sure you are up for it?"

His words hit me in the gut. The man who always believed in me doesn't think I have it under control.

"This isn't anything against you, son. Your cousin is out to get you. He wants to prove you unworthy. I never meant for this to happen. I was just trying to protect our legacy."

"I know."

"You will have to travel with the team from Valentina Fisher and help them execute the plan for expansion."

I never thought that far ahead, but now that he says it out loud, I know he is right. "I will."

"You need to ensure success. It's imperative."

"I understand."

"There is another thing."

"And that is?"

"A wife."

*He didn't just say what I think he did.* But when he doesn't smile, just keeps a straight face, I know he did. I shake my head. "I'm not getting married."

"I know, but you also can't be photographed with every woman."

"Who I'm shagging is none of the board's business."

"And that's where you are wrong once again. Who you *shag* is every member of the board's business, because you make it their business when it is splashed all over the news." He stops and sighs. "You need to be above reproach. Your cousin—"

"I don't give a shit about my cousin."

"He has a wife. He has a child on the way. He works for the company. You should care about your cousin because he cares about you. He will do everything to steal back the legacy he thinks is his. Do you understand?"

"Yes."

"Do I need to find you a—"

"I'm seeing someone," I say before I can stop myself, digging myself into a hole I'm not sure I can pull myself out of.

"Bring her to dinner next week."

And just like that, he calls my bluff.

# chapter eight

## MADELINE

THE MEETING WENT WELL. ALTHOUGH INTIMIDATING, Nathaniel's grandfather kept relatively quiet and seemed quite nice.

Nathaniel steps out of the conference room, and his eyes go wide when he sees me. "You waited?"

"I did."

His gaze softens. I'm not sure why I waited, but when Valentina was leaving, something told me to stay. *Stay for him and make sure he's okay.* Seeing the way he looks at me now, a feeling spreads through me. It rests in my belly, making it grow warm. Heat creeps up my neck. I'm not sure what this feeling is, but I need to pull away from it.

I take a step forward, heading to the elevator we used earlier. Nathaniel presses the call button, and he's still giving me this strange look. When the doors open, I'm quick to enter. Neither of us talks as we start our descent, but all of a sudden, the elevator is sputtering down, and I'm starting to regret my decision not to go with Valentina. The light between floors illuminates as we slowly drop. Just as the little arrow moves to hit the second floor, the small space vibrates, sputters, and stops.

"What the—"

The lights around us shut off, and my heart pounds in my chest. It's dark, so dark that it feels like I'm in a coffin. The air feels heavy, and my heart rattles in my chest. I frantically jam the call button.

Nothing.

No sound. No alarm.

I keep hitting my hand against the button, but when nothing happens, I notice another button beside it. This time, I hit that button, the red emergency button. "I don't understand what's happening?" I grab my phone out of my bag and start to wave it frantically around. The little flashlight is now on, illuminating the space with a tiny stream of light.

"I don't have service. Do you have service?" I ask. My voice cracking as I feel a sweat break across my brow.

He looks down at his phone and shakes his head. "No. Are you okay?"

"Is it hot?" I start to push up the sleeves of my blazer. "Do you feel hot? Do you think the building is on fire?" I start to pull at the collar of my shirt. It feels like I'm suffocating, like the material around my throat is grasping at my lungs and making it hard to breathe. The room feels too small. Too tight. His body is so close, and I know he can feel the inhales of my body as my breaths come out tight and shallow.

"It's going to be okay," he coos. His hand touches my spine as he lets me step around him, and my heart pounds harder, but this time I'm not sure if it's from the elevator but rather from the proximity to his body. "I got you. Slow, deep breaths," he commands.

But I can't see through my own need for control. Everything in my life is controlled. I hate to lose control. I need it to function, and without it, I feel like I'm suffocating.

I have never been good at handling things I can't control, which is why I am such a workaholic. I need to make sure everything is right and can't leave it to chance or luck. And that's why right now, in the small confines of this elevator, that will most certainly fall, killing us both, I'm having a meltdown.

I shake my head. *No. I can't think like that.* But as much as I can't, I hear the words leaving my mouth. I can't stop them.

*"We're going to fall."*

*"No one will find us."*

*"We are never getting out of here."*

Time stretches. Minutes. Seconds. Or maybe an hour. I know it hasn't been that long, but it doesn't matter what my rational sense says. A minute might as well be an hour because I can't change anything. I'm stuck. Actually, we are stuck, and I can't find any oxygen in the room.

"Look at me." Nathaniel's voice cracks through my panic.

"I can't see you."

"That's not true. Open your eyes," he asserts.

I do as I'm told.

"Good girl. Now let them adjust. Don't close them again."

His authoritative voice is raspy and sexy, and I can't help but fall into his voice, to allow myself to be swept away by it, by the tone. By the cadence that baritone commands.

Just as he said, I keep my eyes open and allow them to settle. A faint light peeks in through the crack in the elevator door, and I see him. He's at eye level with me. I can't see the color of his eyes. It's so dark, they appear black, the pupils merging with his irises. They look at me intently. Gauging me.

"Are you okay?" His fingers lift and start to trail across my skin. My breath hitches at the contact as he tips my jaw up for a better view of my eyes. "I have you," he assures again. "Take a deep breath."

I do. My heart rate slows in time with his demands. His finger strokes me, trying desperately to calm me. When I don't calm, I feel him step in until his chest touches mine. Until his heart beats with mine. I'm dizzy now, but it's not from the frantic burst of oxygen I'm inhaling. It's from him, for him.

I'm no longer in the elevator. I'm no longer stuck in my mind. No. No, now all I am is a girl, a girl who needs to be kissed by this man I hate. I do hate him, right? It's so unlike me to feel this way, to want anyone, but still, I find myself lifting onto my toes. Our faces are so close that every time he lets out a soft exhale, the air leaving his mouth tickles my lips.

Any lingering doubt vanishes with my need to see how soft his lips will be. I move closer, and this time, I'm not sure if they touched, or if it's a phantom touch. My eyelids flutter shut of their own accord, and I lean in . . .

*Sputter.*

*Sputter.*

*Sputter.*

I'm pushed back. More like jerked back. What the hell was that? Then the reality settles in. The elevator has moved. My lids open, and before I can even turn to look back at Nathaniel, the doors to the elevator open. The bright light floods the elevator and blinds me, causing me to blink rapidly to acclimate.

"I—" I start to say. I have no clue what, but I need to say something. He saw me at my worst and comforted me. I want to ask him why he didn't kiss me? I want to throw caution to the wind and go against everything I am and continue our moment. The perfect moment, when I thought he might kiss me, and I thought I might want it.

But just as I go to speak again, his gaze pulls away from me, and it locks on something within the room of the lobby. I try to see what he's looking at, to see who has captured this man's attention.

"I—"

"I have to go," he says while he's stepping out of our enclosed space.

No goodbye.

No farewell.

It takes a while for me to right myself from what just happened, and then I realize he left me alone in the elevator after I waited for him.

---

After a long week, Friday finally arrives, and when I glance at my computer, I see it's already four p.m. With Nathaniel God knows where, I was able to immerse myself in my work. I'm not sure how long I've been alone, but my body's stiff from slouching over the computer. I'm lifting my arms into a stretch when the door to my shared office opens.

"Hey, girl, we're ducking out early. Want to go to happy hour with us?"

"I'm probably going to stay a bit longer. In order to make our goals . . ." I trail off all while giving Lucy a very dry, sarcastic look.

"Blah, blah, blah, all I hear is nothing. Come. You've been working your ass off ever since you started here. Isn't it time to unwind?"

"I'm not sure if I can."

"Come on."

I let out a puff of oxygen and run my fingers through my

hair. "Fine." I sigh. "I'll come."

"Woohoo."

"Did you really just say woohoo?"

"I did. Do you have a problem with that?"

"I actually don't." I laugh.

"Are you coming too?" she asks, and I turn to where her gaze is. Nathaniel is back and striding into the office. He's looking at us with his head cocked and his brow furrowed.

*Please say no.* I'm still ignoring him for being a dick after the elevator incident. I'm more mad at myself, though, for wanting him to kiss me.

"That would be lovely."

I grit my teeth. Great. Just great. I finally decide to go out with the team, and he's coming with.

"Okay. Great. We leave in twenty." The door shuts before I can object.

I turn back to him and narrow my eyes. "Why are you coming?" I say, the tone of my voice making it very clear how I feel on the matter.

"Because I was asked."

Without a rebuttal, I continue to type furiously at my computer.

"What's your problem with me, Tink?"

I turn and glare at him. "Well, you call me Tink. And if that isn't enough, you have forced yourself into my life, my office, and now my happy hour. Actually, this is where I draw the line. They call it happy for a reason. Let me be happy!"

"You do realize I'm your boss, right?"

"You do realize you are supposed to be a silent investor?" I snap back.

"I never said anything about being silent." The way his eyes beam makes me even angrier than before because he's right. He does technically own the company now, and if he doesn't want to be silent, who am I to tell him he needs to be. And worse than that, if I keep up this attitude, I'll probably get fired. But I have no intention of being nice to him. However, maybe I should stop the verbal sparring.

"Fine. Come." That's the best I can do right now. Closing down my computer, I stand, straighten the skirt on my black A-line dress, and make my way out the door.

"Let's go," I say to Lucy, who isn't moving.

"We need to wait for Nathaniel."

"Mr. Harrington," I correct.

"I can call him Mr. Harrington." She smirks. "That's kind of hot."

Women burned bras so this person could work next to me. Unbelievable.

He saunters toward us, and sauntering is the perfect word to describe how he walks. Without a care in the world, it's as if he owns the place, which he technically does. But it's more than that. His short brown hair is unruly as though he just ran his fingers through it. His tailored suit fits him to perfection. He wore it for another meeting with his grandfather, one I didn't attend, but now that his grandfather isn't here, his jacket is open. He's also removed his tie and popped one button on his shirt, allowing a hint of his olive skin to peek out. He's tan for this time of year, and I imagine, before he decided to grace us with his presence, he was off jet-setting around the world, island hopping or whatnot.

He walks up to us and doesn't speak, just owning us with a look. I hate myself for the way it makes me melt. Hate myself that when his gaze hits mine, I lose my breath at his mere beauty.

I turn without a word, needing to break the trance he puts me under. Needing to sever the connection. Behind me, I hear his crisp British accent and the faint sound of giggles from Lucy. I don't pay attention to her, though, or the yammering going on behind me. I just focus on making my way out of the building. The clacking of my heels on the concrete and the scratch of the glass door as I swing it open.

Once outside, the air hits me, and I pull my blazer tighter around me. Even though it's not freezing today, I should have worn a coat. The air temp is rising, and winter is hovering around us. Before long, the launch of our new line will get here. Only a few months of planning. I'm excited.

Truth be told, I love to work. I love my job, and I love throwing myself into work. I have no life outside of this. Nothing at all. Other than occasionally seeing my niece and nephew, I'm either working or reading, which explains why Lucy basically threw me a party when I said yes.

After about a block of walking, I see the awning for the bar. I've never been here before, but I know this is a regular Friday spot for the team. Once inside, I head over to where Valentina is, and to prove this isn't a normal company, she's draped on Eric. No fraternizing rules in this place. I'm sure the thought makes Lucy as happy as a clam.

The thought of Lucy and Nathaniel Harrington makes my jaw clench. I'm not sure why the thought makes me angry, but it does. *It's probably because I view him as the enemy*, I tell myself, but as I watch him lean across the bar, I know that's not it. My treacherous body has a mind of its own, and I want to yell at myself for allowing me to want someone like him.

"Shots all around," Valentina shouts. It's completely unlike her. And I'm not even sure what we are celebrating or maybe we are drowning our sorrows, but by the way her lips pull up into a huge smile, it's the former and not the latter.

"What are we celebrating?" I ask.

"The meeting Nathaniel had today. Travel has been approved. First stop, London and then Paris."

"So it's official? The meetings have been lined up?"

"Not officially, but they will be."

"Wow. Congrats, Valentina."

"Congrats to you, Madeline."

"Cheers," I hear from beside me. Nathaniel is there now, holding up a shot of tequila. "To your success."

"Our success," Valentina cheers back.

I clink glasses before turning back to the bar.

"You can't avoid me forever, Tink," he whispers close to me, the warm air from his mouth caressing the shell of my ear. A chill runs down my body, causing goose bumps to form on my exposed skin. When I hear a faint chuckle, I know he can see them. He can see how affected I am by him. I might despise him, but my body hasn't received the memo.

"I can. And it won't be forever. Just until you get bored." I shrug.

"That may be so, but I'm here right now."

"And for right now, I'll avoid you."

"You're going to find that hard to do." He chuckles, and the sound tightens the muscles in my back and causes flutters in my stomach at the same time.

"And why is that?" I ask tentatively. A part of me fears what his answer will be and how I'll feel about it.

"Because you'll be working with me to prepare."

On those words, I turn around and am met with his large green eyes. I search them for anything but the truth, and I find nothing. "Why would I work with you?"

"Because I know everyone. And if you want this to be a success, you'll use me. Use my knowledge."

"Use your knowledge?"

He nods.

"I don't think so." With no more to say, I turn and grab another drink.

Drink after drink, I start to loosen up. The party has moved from the bar to a private alcove in the corner of the room. Everyone is letting loose, excited about what the potential of a European expansion will mean for us.

The last drink has gone to my head, and I need air, so I move to walk outside. Once there, the air hits me. It refreshes me but at the same time brings a chill. I'm standing against the cold wall when I see him.

So much for peace.

With a shake of my head, I duck back inside, bypassing him. I'm not even halfway inside when his hand touches my arm. I stop in the dark hallway and turn to him.

"Do you mind?"

"Why do you hate me so much?" He takes a step toward me. I take a step back, but my back hits the wall. He moves closer until he's caged me in.

"I am indifferent to you."

"It doesn't appear that way." He pulls his gaze away from mine and trails his eyes across my skin. Again, the damn goose bumps. "It doesn't appear you are indifferent at all. What is it about you, Madeline?" His head peers down, his gaze alarming. Predatory. "I like getting under your skin."

"Maybe you need a new hobby. Or better yet, maybe you should become useful."

"I can be useful." He lowers his head until his mouth is so close to my skin, I fear if he touches me, I'll be engulfed in a flame so hot I'll never be able to put it out. "Can't we get along?" His accent . . . his breath, it caresses the soft skin on my lips, and my eyes close of their own accord.

I snap my eyes back open, remembering where I am. Remembering who's standing in front of me. Remembering his lips hovering over mine.

I sidestep him, getting the distance I need. "Not happening, Peter."

"That's what you think, Tink."

Frazzled about not being able to be in the tight space with him, I head back to the alcove. When I sit down, I pick up the glass of vodka I left behind and take a long swig.

"Damn. What has you so riled up?"

"Nothing," I respond to Lucy.

"Oh, come on. I can tell something is up. You are all red and flustered. That and also the way you just downed that drink. It's obvious something has gotten to you. So what is it? Talk to me."

"Him," I say as I point at the culprit.

"Nathaniel?" She looks perplexed. "What did he do?"

"He's just such an ass."

"Yeah, I know. Isn't he great?" A giggle escapes her mouth, like a schoolgirl with her first crush. I roll my eyes.

"No. He's not." I slam my drink down and move toward the bar. "Another shot of Don Julio, please," I shout to the bartender.

"I'll have one too." I feel his presence before I see him. How long has he been there? Did he hear? My face burns with the knowledge he might have heard us talking about him. His ego doesn't need any more inflating.

"Then you're buying," I mutter back.

"My pleasure." His voice is husky, and I know the innuendo is there.

"You're playing with fire."

"But isn't it fun to get burned?"

When the shot is placed in front of me, I lift the glass to my mouth and take it fast. It scorches my throat, burns my lungs. Makes me dizzy.

Like him.

# chapter nine

## NATHANIEL

A WEEK HAS PASSED, AND THE FAMILY DINNER WAS CANCELED due to something coming up for my grandfather. I'm not sure what that is all about, but I welcomed it. It gave me an opportunity to breathe for a few days and to concentrate on work. Which is pretty much the same old, same old.

I'm back home and exhausted. Working full time is not easy. I'm reclining on my sofa in the flat I keep in New York City when I hear footsteps in the room. Opening my eyes, I'm shocked by who I see.

"Grandfather."

He steps forward, walking farther into my space.

"To what do I owe the honor? I thought you would be back in London by now."

"Hoped?" He raises his eyebrow, and it makes his well-weathered forehead scrunch and wrinkle more than usual.

"Of course not."

I knew giving him a set of keys was a bad idea. Because here he is now, and I don't want to admit out loud that as much as I love my grandfather, I don't want him here right now. It feels like he is checking up on me or better yet spying. I'm not used to living my life under the watchful eye of anyone, let alone him. He has always raised me to be independent. He's allowed me to sow my wild oats and never demanded anything of me. And I always just assumed that when the time came, I'd lay down my hat and focus my enthusiasm elsewhere.

Instead, that dream was ripped away from me by one phone call, one meeting, and one company.

"How are you?"

"Good, I suppose. Better, if things were more stable."

"You look annoyed, Grandfather, although I'm not sure why. The company is doing well. We're almost ready to launch the new line. Meetings are lined up. I'm working hard. Isn't that what you wanted from me? I sent you all the perspectives."

"It is."

"But . . . ?"

"I need more from you."

"More? How much more? I don't know how else I can prove myself."

"A relationship."

I shake my head, confused. Is he going senile? "We spoke about this already, and I still don't see what that has to do with my ability to run Harrington."

"Your cousin," he responds.

"Again, we spoke about this. Fuck that wanker."

"Mind your tongue," my grandfather barks back, and my eyes widen.

"Sorry, but he needs to sod off."

"That may be the case, but he's causing trouble. Going on about your personal life. Your need to be constantly in the papers."

"It's been months since I've been photographed." I huff.

"Doesn't matter. He's still going on about it." My grandfather shakes his head, and I know he isn't happy about my cousin's quest to discredit me as much as I'm not.

"Why does that even matter? I have plenty of time to settle down. Shouldn't my involvement with Valentina Fisher be enough to keep the vultures at bay?"

"It matters. More than you know." He looks so serious, as if he's holding back a myriad of things. What is really going on here?

"What aren't you telling me?"

"Never you mind. I just need you to prove that you are ready for this. That you are ready to lead, start a family . . ."

"Start a family? Can't we take one step at a time?"

"Maybe if you were serious—"

"I am. I told you this before." The lie slips through my mouth before I can stop myself. By the way he watches me, I know he doesn't believe me one bit.

He narrows his eyes. "Very well."

"Is that all?" I question, annoyed by where this conversation has gone.

"Yes."

"In that case, I do have some *work* to do." I stress the word work. What I really need is to be alone so I can come up with a plan.

"I shall get out of your way."

Together, we walk toward the door. I open it, and he takes a step out. When I move to close it, he halts my progress. "You said you'd bring her to dinner."

"What?"

"The girl you are dating. Last time I saw you, I asked you to bring her with you."

"I-I," I start and stutter, not even knowing how to get myself out of this mess. "You canceled dinner," I say too quickly.

"Next time, then."

"But won't you be heading back home?"

"Next week." He gives me a knowing look, calling me on my bluff.

"Very well, I will."

"Good. I will be in touch."

After I close the door, I make my way to the bar in my living room. Pouring myself a glass of scotch, I sit down to devise a plan, but halfway through the glass, I have nothing. Adding another finger, I drink that too.

Still, nothing.

I'm midway through my third glass and I have dismissed every woman I have slept with in the past year. Any women I have previously been with were after one thing and one thing only, to be Mrs. Nathaniel Harrington. If it were just for a night, it would be one thing, but one night on my arm won't fix my problem. I need a girlfriend. And I need one now.

One who doesn't want a relationship.

One who will understand this is simply a business transaction.

One who will be pliable to my needs.

One I won't fuck because that will complicate shit.

Needing inspiration, I pick up my phone starting at the A's looking for anyone who might fit the bill.

No A's.

No one in the B's.

I make it all the way to the E's before I stop. Narrowing my eyes, I look at the name Elena . . . She's a possibility. I haven't spoken to her in years. Why did we stop fucking?

Oh yeah, because she's clingy.

Next.

I keep moving my finger, past the F's, G's, H's. Stopping again, I look at Harlow's name on my phone. She'd be perfect. Not clingy, beautiful, right good shag, but she's in London and I'm here, and I really can't do a fake long-distance relationship. *No, that wouldn't work at all.*

Who do I know in New York? Juliette. Juliette would be perfect. Without second-guessing myself, I dial.

"Hello?" a man's voice answers.

"Is Juliette there?"

"No. Who is this?"

"Who's this?" I fire back.

"Her husband," he growls.

I hang up and pour myself another drink. The only women I see on a regular basis these days are the women who work at Valentina Fisher. Lucy would be game, but she'd most certainly confuse shit. Valentina is in a relationship with Eric, and that only leaves Tink.

*Tink.*

She would never agree, but Lord, she would be perfect. She hates me, so I'll never have to worry that she'll fall for me. I don't have to worry about lines being crossed. She's perfect. Bloody fucking perfect. She'll do anything for her job. I just need to approach this right. Get the ammunition I need to lead her into my trap and convince her to help me.

Across the table, I see the sales pitches and the department stores in front of me, and an idea forms in my brain. Maybe I'm drunk and maybe I'm not thinking, but right now this is a bloody good idea. And what other option do I have? I need a girlfriend, and I need a girlfriend yesterday.

Pouring one more glass, I nod to myself. This will work. It better work because letting my grandfather down isn't an option. Failing isn't an option. I will do what I need to do to win, even if that means I need to be a prick.

I will.

# chapter ten

## MADELINE

ARRIVE AT WORK EARLY MONDAY MORNING. WELL, AT LEAST I arrive earlier than most, but that is normal for me. Normally, I open the place up. However, today, when I open the door, I'm taken aback that the lights are already on.

*Odd.*

I walk farther into the space, and in the silence of the showroom, my heels click on the floor like a stampede or a freight train.

I look in every direction, but no one is here. Did someone leave the lights on?

Then I see my office light is on, the light a stark contrast to the offices next to mine. Did I leave it on overnight? I shake my head. That's not possible, but then I see him, and I know exactly what has happened.

He's in my office.

He's seated at my desk.

His head is down looking at something on *my desk*. Picking up my pace, I make my way over and swing the door open.

"What are you doing here?"

"Same old song, I see." He lifts his gaze. "I thought you'd be used to me being here already," he states in a mocking tone that sets my blood boiling way too early in the morning.

"I mean, what are you doing here so early?"

"Well, isn't it obvious?"

"No."

"I'm working, Tink." My mouth drops open at his words, and he chuckles. "Positively shocking, I know. But I am."

"What are you working on?" I move into the room tentatively, not knowing how to handle this side of him.

"Email correspondence."

"With?"

"My mate who works for Harvey Nichols."

That piece of information leaves me even more confused about everything. Maybe I was wrong. I take off my coat and hang it on the chair before turning it to face him.

"Were you able to secure us a meeting?"

"I was," he says, barely acknowledging how huge this moment is.

I cock my head at him, not really understanding why he isn't more excited. "What is it?"

"We have something to discuss, Tink." His tone has me instantly on edge.

Every muscle in my back tightens as I swallow before finding my words.

"How come I have a feeling I'm not going to like this?"

"Because you're not." His voice is level, and it doesn't help to calm the raging storm of anxiety that has taken form in my body.

"Jeez, that's some way to start a conversation," I deadpan. I try to sound sarcastic. I try to hide the tremble I feel in my stomach, but something tells me that I'm not going to be happy with whatever he tells me.

"I'm not one to beat around the bush."

"Encouraging." Or dreading. Why am I scared?

He shrugs. "So do you want the good news or the bad news?"

"Bad."

I'd rather have no false illusions.

He's about to open his mouth and drop the bad news on me when Valentina pops in. "Hey, guys. You're here early."

I turn in her direction. "You're one to speak. You're never here at eight."

"True, but we have so much work to do."

"Speaking of work, Harrington over here landed us a meeting with Harvey Nichols."

Valentina's eyes widen considerably, and she turns toward him. "Is that true?"

His lips part and he gives her an earth-shattering smile. "It is."

"Oh my God." She jumps while letting out a high-pitched scream. I don't think I have ever seen her this excited. "This is really happening. Between the meeting with Bergdorf and now this . . ." She screams, her shoes clanking on the floors as she jumps. "I have so much work to do. Thank you so much. You just made my day." She skips out of the room like a kid in a candy store.

Once she's gone, I see that Nathaniel is still looking at me. "What?"

"There are always strings."

"Excuse me?"

"You heard me. Nothing comes without a price."

My back stiffens at his words. "What do you mean?"

"Your boss is happy. What would you do to ensure that happiness?"

"What the fuck do you mean?"

"Exactly what I just said. What is your price? Everyone has a price."

"I don't have a price. I can't be bought."

"Not even for Bergdorf? Not even for Harrods? Or Selfridges?"

"I'm really not following you."

"Here's how I see it. I have something you want. And you"—his eyes linger over me—"have something I want."

My stomach bottoms out. Is he saying what I think he is? "I am not a whore. I am not fucking you, you piece of shit."

"Who said anything about fucking, Tink? Take your head out of the gutter. Although I find you quite lovely, I'm not after that."

"So what then? What are you after?"

"You."

"But you just said—"

He holds his hand up. "I know what I said, and I mean it. I don't want you. I want what you can give to me. I need you to help me with a situation I have gotten into."

"Absolutely not."

"But you haven't even heard what I have to say." He smirks. And I want to slap the smirk right off his face.

"Nor will I."

"If that's how it will be, I'll make the call," he responds off-handedly as if I know what he's talking about.

"What call?"

"To Walmart, of course."

"Walmart?"

"Well, yes. Seeing as I own this company and want to make a profit, I have decided on a new course of action. I see Valentina Fisher as mass market. Every Walmart across the country. Think of those twins in the nineties . . . Mary something? And her sister? Didn't they make a fortune making clothes?"

"I-I," I stutter, trying to form words. "We aren't selling to—"

"How about Kmart then?"

"You're insane. You come in here on your high horse demanding you take over my office. I'm sick of you and your Peter Pan ways. Grow the hell up. People don't do business like this," I fire back. "You know what? I'm done. You want to piss away millions of dollars? Have at it. I have a great résumé."

"You might bounce back, but will Valentina? Will Lucy?" He has a sly grin on his face.

His words knock me in the gut. I have to stop being selfish. I need to hear him out. "What do you want?" I hiss.

"Your company." I open my mouth to object, but he lifts his hand. "Before you say something you will regret, let me lay it out for you. You pretend to be involved with me, come to a few key events, and I will do everything I can to ensure your success. You don't, and I . . ." He trails off for impact.

It works.

"So let me get this straight . . . if I don't pretend to be your girlfriend, you'll ruin us?"

"Now we understand each other."

"No way."

"Before you do anything rash, Tink, I want you to think long and hard. I want you to spend your whole day listening to Valentina celebrate and then give me your answer."

"Why me?"

"Why not?" He shrugs.

"I want a reason."

"Because you won't fall for me."

"Wow. You. Are. A. Dick."

"I'll give you until five to decide." He then steps up and grabs his laptop.

"What are you doing?" I say, motioning to his computer.

"I had my office cleaned out. Good faith gesture. Think about what you want to do."

Shit.

# chapter eleven

## NATHANIEL

SHE NEEDS MORE TIME.

Not the answer I wanted. Not the answer I needed. I was hoping I would be able to take her with me tonight. To make my first official appearance with her by my side.

No such luck.

Instead, I'm dressed and heading to the cocktail party alone. I feel like I'm suffocating. My tuxedo is cut to perfection, measured to my every inch, but it feels like the tie around my neck is strangling me. Even though I know all the people I will see tonight. Normally, I wouldn't give a fuck, but tonight I do.

Firstly, I'll see my grandfather. He's in America to go to this party. Secondly, my cousin Edward will also be in attendance, and last but certainly not least, Cecile. She's always there. The one woman to steal my heart. The one woman I let in.

*The one who got away, married your best friend, and most importantly, the woman I hate.*

Tonight would have been so much better if Madeline had just said yes. Then I could have killed two birds with one stone. Flaunt her beauty not only in front of my prick of a cousin but also in front of my ex. Not that I still want her, but I hate the way she looks at me whenever she sees me. Pity maybe? Lord knows.

Stepping out of the car, I make my way up the stairs that lead to the converted loft space. A New York City landmark has been transformed into the perfect location for a gala. The door swings open as I make my approach. Two men dressed in elegantly appointed tuxedos hold the door open and take my overcoat. Stepping into the large space, I find the air in the lobby still brisk. I move farther into the room, and it warms considerably. In the corner, a crowd has formed to talk, socialize, and people watch. All things I hate about these events. Instead, I move toward the bar. I've only been here a moment, and I'm already itching to leave.

"Cousin," I hear from beside me.

"Eddie. Apparently, it was too much to ask that I have a libation before you approach," I call over my shoulder.

"Don't be daft. I planned it this way," my smug as shit cousin chides. "I want you to be sober. That way you won't miss how I take apart your life in front of your face." Those words make me turn around and look at the pompous arse.

"What are you going on about?" The bartender brings me my drink, and I lift the now filled glass to my mouth.

"Taking your legacy, of course."

I don't even bat a lash at his suggestion. "Hardly."

"That's what you think, but as you sit here nursing your drink, I have already spoken with everyone of importance. You might think you have this settled, but I'm the one holding the cards. It's only a matter of time before you lose."

"Sod off." I take another swig and move to leave, but his hand stops me, mid-step. I glare down at where he is touching me and narrow my gaze.

"Not before I let you in on a secret. No one is fooled by your little purchase. At least no one on the board. And when they vote you incompetent, I will bide my time, and when the times does come, I'll dismantle your grandfather's legacy."

I'm too stunned by his retort to speak. I don't like it.

This won't do.

Won't do at all.

I push away from the bar, away from his grasp, and with my drink still in hand, I walk away all while taking another swig. It burns. Scorches really. But it does the trick, relaxing my shoulders. When I turn the corner, I see Cecile in front of me. She has a large smile brimming on her face. Plastered more like it, pained on with perfection.

Just like the last time I saw her, I feel nothing when I see her. There are no feelings of want or need anymore. She took that from me years before, leaving a hollow hole in my heart from where she used to be.

"Hello, Nathaniel," she speaks as she moves closer to me. Her familiar scent wafts in through my nose.

The scent of early mornings in the country, of youth, but that's all it is. A distant memory, one I need to push down. One I can't let back in, and luckily, right now the scent does nothing for me. Other than annoy me.

"Hello, Cecile. Don't you look lovely tonight."

"Thank you, Nate."

I cringe at the nickname. She's the only one who calls me that, and it feels too intimate right now.

"How are you? It's been too long." She gives me a strange look. As if she is trying to read me, to see my emotions. What she doesn't know is those emotions have been turned off.

"It's been two weeks," I deadpan. "I'm well, thank you," I respond, looking around the room for an exit.

"Darling," I hear from beside me. My back stiffens. I know the sound. I know the voice. My former best mate from university. "Harrington, how long has it been?"

"Not long enough," I respond, and Cecile's face grows tense.

I feel no need to play nice. I'm here for one person and one person only, and neither of these two are him. "I must be going. The pleasure was all mine." By the grimace, my sarcastic quip isn't lost on Cecile.

I step away and head to the far corner of the room where I see him.

"Nathaniel, dear boy, you startled me."

"Sorry, Grandfather."

He looks around and then back at me.

"Are you here alone?"

"I am."

"Oh pity, I was sure you would bring your young lady friend." He quirks his gray eyebrow, and I know what he's saying without him having to say it.

"I would have, but she had to work late."

"And what is it she does?"

Before I can stop myself, I answer, the words leaving my tight mouth. "She's the CEO of Valentina Fisher. You met her last week." There, it's done. Now I just need to get her on board.

"Is that so? Darling young lady, but why didn't you mention it?" He's calling my bluff. I know it. He knows it.

"We didn't want anyone to know with work."

"Well, that won't do," he says as he glances around the room at where my cousin stands with his wife and a member of the board. "Won't do at all."

I nod. I know what he's saying, and I know what I have to do.

I need to convince Madeline to go along with this farce.

No matter what.

# chapter twelve

## MADELINE

'D LIKE TO SAY I WORKED ALL DAY. I'D LIKE TO SAY I accomplished something—anything. I'd like to say a lot of things, but I can't. Because the truth is, I did nothing. I am completely useless. Ever since Harrington's bombshell, I have sat in my office alone and thought. Now today, I'm doing the same thing.

I thought the idea of having my space back would ease my worry and give me comfort, but instead, it's had the opposite effect. Instead, it's too quiet. I swear I can actually hear myself thinking from the eeriness.

I have no idea what to do. The funny thing is, every single time I think about my decision, I scold myself.

There is no decision to be made. Say no.

Tell him to fuck off.

But you can't.

Every time I think of saying no, I see Valentina jumping up and down. Her squeals echoing in my mind amongst the quiet of the room. How can I say no? How can I crush her dreams? She has told me of her dream to be in Harrods. Of her dream of participating in New York Fashion Week someday. We are so close to her dreams.

My nails tap on the desk as I consider my options. How bad could it be? He made it quite clear he didn't expect it to be real. That it was for show only. A few small appearances, so what? He doesn't want me to fall for him. Well, that won't be hard. I hate him. How could I possibly fall for him?

*Because he's beautiful.*

I shove that thought out of my mind. I have done a lot of things to get where I am in my career. This would just be another hurdle.

I can handle this.

I can handle anything.

With my mind made up, I'm finally able to work. I open the browser on my computer and start to type furiously. So little time, so much to do. I get lost in my thoughts, and before I know it, I hear the door open, followed by the familiar sound of footsteps entering the room. Looking up, I see him standing there. Hands in his pockets, head cocked to the side, a smirk gracing his face. The five o'clock shadow on his face that wasn't present this morning.

"Have you made a decision?"

"I have."

"And what pray tell have you decided? Will it be Bergdorf or Walmart?"

I stand, my shoulders pulled back, and step up to where he is. I will not back down, and I will not show fear. I have not made it to where I am by being a timid mouse.

"Bergdorf."

"Good." He smiles, liking that he won, I'm sure.

"But before you have a celebratory party, I have rules. Conditions."

"Certainly."

"A long list." I quirk my brow. I really don't have a long list, but I want this on my terms, so I start to mentally tabulate everything I want.

"Go on."

"Not here."

"Very well. Dinner tonight. Our first public outing. We can go over any rules and regulations you have."

"No dinner. Just drinks." I need liquid courage.

"Fine. When will you be ready?"

"Six."

"I'll be back in an hour."

He walks out of the room, and I let out the breath I didn't realize I was holding. The room is sweltering. Even though the air is on full blast, I'm heated to the core from a combination of anger and nerves. I push it all down, though. This will work well for me. If he needs this, then I also need things. I need his full cooperation, and I need a bigger budget. This will play out perfectly if I play my cards right. I'll be able to do everything in my power to make the spring launch a success.

The hour passes with a wave of ideas. I write everything in a small notebook and have secured it in my tote just in time to see him walk back through the door. "Harrington," I say.

"Nathaniel," he corrects. "If this is to work, you must use my given name."

"Nathaniel," I grit out.

"Are you ready?"

"Ready as I'll ever be." I step past him, and he places his hand on the small of my back to guide me. My head turns quickly at the gesture, and I stare at him wide-eyed.

"In order for this to work, I'll have to touch you, Tink."

"Shouldn't you call me by my given name?" I bite out.

"No. Tink is a term of endearment. It will work just fine."

I roll my eyes and continue the path through the office and out the door. No one is here at this hour, so I don't have to hear any office gossip about him touching me, but tomorrow I will. Mentally, I note this as another topic of conversation once we are alone. He steps forward and holds the door open. His chivalry just infuriates me more. But I must play along. Everything depends on it.

*Everything.*

Everything I have done over the past few years has led me to this moment, and I refuse to let this derail my course. Work is everything to me. My reputation is everything. No one will ruin this.

Not even my "boyfriend" Nathaniel Harrington.

# chapter thirteen

## NATHANIEL

"Very good. I will have my solicitor draw up the paperwork," I say once all the details are settled.

"Paperwork? But why would we need paperwork or better yet a paper trail?" she asks me, her nose scrunching in confusion.

"It's not that I don't trust you . . ."

"But you don't trust me," she quips, and I can't help but laugh, the sound lightening the mood.

"You're right. I don't trust you," I admit.

"And I don't trust you either."

"Which makes the need for paperwork even more important."

"Fine," she agrees, furrowing her brow.

"Tink." A small line forms between her brows at the nickname. "It's not you."

"Lord. We haven't even started 'dating'"—she air quotes—"and you're already breaking up with me."

I laugh again. "You're quite funny when you want to be."

"Thank you, I think."

"The thing is, Madeline . . ." I start, and she stops the drumming of her fingers to look up at me. "I'm a very wealthy man . . ."

"Say no more. We don't need to even talk about this. Have

your lawyers draw up the contract, but I also expect a clause to be written in about the money."

"Fair enough."

"And a clause about Walmart."

"Duly noted."

"And a clause that this is fake and that there will be no kissing."

I lean forward in my chair, squaring her with my gaze. "Denied."

"But—"

I hold my hand up to her objection. "No buts, Madeline. Once those documents are signed, you are my girlfriend . . . and whatever that entails."

She waves her hands in the air frantically. "No. No. No, not whatever that entails."

I flash her a wicked smile. "Trust me, Tink. If I set my sights on you, you wouldn't want to say no." Lifting my hand in the air, I order us another round.

"Now where to?" she asks.

"Home, darling."

"Darling?"

"Not sufficient?" I ask.

She lets out a sigh of agreement. "Better than Tink."

"Oh no, darling," I draw out. "You'll always be Tink."

"How can I be Tink and Darling at the same time?"

I give her a perplexed look, not understanding what she is saying at all. People often have numerous nicknames.

"You're calling me darling as in Wendy Darling as in Peter . . ."

Realization settles on me at what I said.

"How can I be Wendy if I'm Tink? You really do have a

thing for Neverland, don't you?" She winks.

"How could one not?" I shrug. "I grew up in London. Peter and Wendy are like our bible."

"You can't always live in the sky . . ."

"I know."

"Do you?" she asks before turning, walking out and leaving me speechless. Do I?

I'm not even sure what I know anymore. What I do know is for the first time since I have met Madeline Montgomery, I'm interested to find out more, and that thought alone scares me.

The moment I'm alone, I pick up my mobile and dial my solicitor.

"Nathaniel, looking to purchase another company?" He laughs.

"No."

My one-word answer makes him stop laughing. "Everything okay?"

"Yes and no," I answer truthfully as I lean forward, balancing my elbows on my knees.

"Jeez. Are you in jail?"

A chuckle escapes me, lightening the mood. "No. I am not in jail." Although technically, my world feels like a prison, but I'm not going to respond to him with that.

"I need your help on a small matter. But this is between us. No one can find out."

"I know we partied hard in university, mate, but I take my role very seriously."

"I need a contract drawn up."

"What kind of contract?"

"An agreement between me and a lady."

"What are you up to?"

Moving to a reclining position, I proceed to tell him all about the company he helped me buy, the need for a girlfriend, and Tink.

He lets out a long-drawn-out sigh. "I'm strongly advising you not to do this. This will end badly."

"No need to warn me. Although I do appreciate your concern, I have everything under control."

"Very well. I'll have the paper sent over by the end of the day."

"Thank you, Lawrence."

---

It took a week to have the contract drawn up. But now with it in my hands, it feels heavy. It's crazy how a little piece of paper can hold so many emotions and meaning. This paper is the key to my future. Tink doesn't know that, and I have to make sure she doesn't realize just how important she is to this whole mess and how much power she has until after she signs it. She never asked why I need a girlfriend and I don't need her to know. If she realizes, she might want to negotiate more, and I'm not sure how much more I have to give.

For your legacy . . . *everything.*

She could have me by the balls if she knew just how much was riding on this. Not just the money. The truth is, the money means nothing to me. It's the legacy that means everything. Making my grandfather happy is everything as well. Honoring my father . . .

I find myself at the nearest bar. A glass of Glenlivet in my hand as I wait for her. She requested a public place, and since signing this contract in front of the staff at Valentina Fisher isn't wise, I chose a place up the street. Having a drink is a bonus.

"Hello," I hear from beside me.

"Sit," I say, not even bothering to look up at her. I just proceed to lift my glass and take a sip. I'm on edge, the need for this to go smoothly weighing heavily on my chest.

Once she's sitting beside me, I slide over the paperwork. "What are you having to drink?"

"Glass of cab," she responds as she thumbs through the documents. I order as she reads, and when the glass is placed in front of her, she takes a sip. "Family meetings?" she asks, her eyebrow rising.

"Yes. Occasionally, you will need to come with me to them."

She nods, seeming okay with that, and I wonder what she will stop to question next. I watch her as she looks over each bullet point. Her brow furrows, her cheeks puckering in, but then she bites her lips and cocks her head toward me.

"If either party chooses to engage in sexual activities with a third party, they have to have written consent? I am not signing this."

"Why?"

"I will not be asking for your permission to sleep with someone."

"You can always sleep with me, then it won't be an issue?" I smirk.

"There is no way in hell I'm sleeping with you." She lifts the glass to her mouth, silencing herself and the rest of this conversation.

# chapter fourteen

## MADELINE

After my drink with Nathaniel and the damn contract, I head home. In the end, I took a marker and scratched out the clause about sex. As if I would ever sign that. Once the "sex" clause was off the table, I reluctantly signed it.

I'm about a block away when my phone rings. It's my mom.

"Hey, sweetie." Her voice instantly makes me smile.

"Hey, Mom."

"Are you in town?" she asks, and I know where this is heading. She wants me to come over soon.

"I am."

"Well, when can I see you?"

Looking toward my building and imagining what waits behind the doors, which is a whole lot of nothing, I know my answer. "I'm not busy now."

"Oh, wonderful. Your father will be so happy. I'll invite your brothers."

My lips turn into a smile. This is just what I need. Some time with my family. I haven't seen anyone since the show, and it feels like forever.

Bypassing my apartment, I head straight for the

underground garage in my building. Having a car at this moment is such a good thing. I often wonder with my travel schedule and cost if I should do away with this luxury. But at moments like this when I need to get away from the city and see my family, I'm happy I kept it. Sure, it costs a small fortune to have a car in New York, but it's well worth it. The idea of being stuck in the closed space of my one-bedroom apartment alone again tonight makes my stomach tighten.

Like being stuck in the elevator.

With him.

The fear that courses through me is strange. I have never expected to feel that way, but my control was taken away, and I need control in my life. There are so many things I can't control, so when I think I'm losing control, I tighten up. My stomach clenches.

Not only am I stuck with Nathaniel Harrington in my life, but now I need to pretend I'm his girlfriend. What that entails has my tension rising, my muscles tightening, and every nerve ending in my body coming awake. Truth be told, as much as I don't want to admit it, I'm attracted to him. I hate myself for it. I hate that I don't have the control over my body to stop the warmth that spreads through my chest when he's around.

Turning the music up, I allow myself to get lost in the beat that plays through the car. I weave in and out of traffic for forty-five minutes until I'm pulling up to the large Georgian colonial house that holds so many memories for me.

I park in the circular drive and step out of the car. I tighten my coat around me and walk to the large oak door. I knock on the large knocker and wait. The door swings open. and my mom's arms wrap around me. I inhale deeply, welcoming the comfort only a mom can give.

"It's so good to have you here." She holds me close until I hear loud footsteps. Pulling away, I see my dad. I walk up to him and launch myself in his arms next as if I haven't seen them in years, when, in truth, it's only been a few weeks.

"Is anyone here?"

"Not yet."

"Great, I have you to myself." I smile.

"Come, sweetie, let's open a bottle of wine while we wait."

"I have to drive."

My dad pulls away and looks down at me. "Stay the night, sweetheart. Your mom and I miss you. This way, you don't have to rush, and you can leave early before work."

The idea of spending the night in my parents' house is welcoming. I don't want to be alone in my mood.

"Fine. Twist my arm."

He lets out a chuckle, and we walk into the kitchen arm in arm. My parents are laid-back. As much wealth as they have, you would never know it by their demeanor. Sure, their house is beautiful, but it has an intimate quality despite its size.

They don't hire a staff; my mom preferring to cook for us herself. The only person who lives in the house beside them is the live-in cleaning lady, Linda, but she's practically family after residing with us since I was a child.

"Cab?"

"Of course." I wink.

"I just got a fantastic bottle of Screaming Eagle. Seems like a good time to open it." He smiles, and I laugh. Yes, a Tuesday night with your daughter is totally the right time to open a one-thousand-dollar bottle of wine, but that's my parents. They have acted like being with me is a celebration. A gift. I never appreciated it in my youth, but now, in my early thirties as the prospect of settling down and having a family of my own seems slim to none, I appreciate it. I love these moments. I would never trade them for anything.

"So tell me about work?" my mother asks as she brings the glass to her mouth.

I let out a large sigh.

"That bad?"

I'm about to open my mouth and tell them all about my company being sold and the man who drives me crazy, but I snap it shut. I can't. I can't tell them anything. As far as every person is concerned, starting now, my boss, Nathaniel Harrington, is my boyfriend. Shit. I didn't think this through. "Just a lot of work," I groan, hoping this is a plausible answer.

"But worth it?" my dad asks.

I nod. "Yes."

"Then I'm proud of you. Nothing worth doing is ever easy." If he only knew how accurate his words were. It's true. Case in point: my faux relationship.

My mother turns to me. "I hope you at least have time for a social life."

A warm feeling spreads across my cheeks at my mom's question, and her eyebrow rises. She reads my blush wrong, her eyes widening as she smirks. "Is there something you want to tell us? Are you seeing someone?"

This isn't the way I planned on them finding out, and I hate myself for having to lie, but I made my bed when I signed that contract, so I seize the opportunity and smile at her.

"You are," she exclaims. "Details."

"Oh dear, leave the poor girl alone," my dad utters, but in truth, it's not that he's trying to save me. He's trying to save himself from having to hear these details.

"Where is everyone?" I hear in the distance, and I can't help but smile. Preston is here, which means Eve is here as well. I haven't seen them since Jace and Sydney's wedding.

"In here," my dad calls out. The sound of their feet hitting the wood floors echoes in the silence of the living room as we wait.

I lift my glass to my mouth, allowing the room temperature liquid to wet my throat. The taste invigorates me, loosening the last of the corded muscles from work.

"Just in time," my mom greets them.

"For what?"

"To listen to Madeline tell us all about her new beau."

A large, dramatic groan escapes my mouth before I can silence it. "Mom . . . no one calls it that anymore."

My mother smiles, and Preston walks over to me. I place my glass down and stand, hugging him before stepping over to Eve.

"New boyfriend? You're holding out on me?" Eve laughs as she hugs me back.

"Holding out on what?" From the corner of my eye, I see Sydney, Jace, Logan, and Avery walk into the room.

"Apparently, Mad has a boyfriend," Eve tells the gang, and I cringe.

Preston is staring at me, and I realize how easy it will be for him to read my lies. I lift my glass again and down my drink.

"What do you mean you have a boyfriend? I just spoke to you last week." Sydney steps up to me and cocks her head to the side.

"I just . . ."

"You just . . . ?"

I try to think of a plausible reason and come up short. "I've been busy at work."

"Likely story," she jokes. Everyone laughs since it's obvious that all I do is work.

"Well, if that's the case, how did you meet this fella?" my dad counters, trying to join in the fun.

I groan. "We work together."

"You work together? How scandalous." Eve laughs.

"Hardly. Val is dating Eric."

"Oh, in that case. Details," Sydney says as she walks closer to me.

"Um. No."

"And why is that?" She smirks.

Without a rebuttal, I thrust the bottle in her face. "Shut up and have a glass."

She looks down at it, and her eyes dart toward Jace. "That's okay, I'm not in the mood to drink."

I tilt the bottle to Eve. "You?"

"Nah, I'm good," she says nonchalantly, but I don't miss the look there either. Both of my brothers' wives aren't drinking. My stomach clenches at the thought. I know without a measure of a doubt that they are both pregnant when Eve and Sydney look at each other for a moment. It becomes painfully obvious.

"But you only just got married." Eve laughs.

"Nice work, man." Preston taps Jace on the back. Jace smiles, and Sydney blushes.

In my peripheral view, my mom steps up, her hand covering her mouth. "Both of you?"

No one has said it, but the thundering in my heart knows the words. Both my brothers are having babies. Both are married. Both have started their own families.

My mom steps up behind me. "One day, you'll fall in love

too. And one day, you are going to have the most beautiful babies."

I turn my head to look at her and force myself to smile. Behind my lids are unshed tears. I want to be happy. This feeling of jealousy that weaves its way through me like poison isn't welcome.

All I've ever wanted is a daughter just like me. A son just like my husband. I want a little girl to have my face and my eyes. To see a part of me smiling back. I want a sassy daughter and a smart-ass son.

I want to be happy for them—truly, I do—but I can't help how I feel. So as everyone laughs and claps, I play the part. I smile and cheer. I toast and drink. I pretend I'm not envious of their life. I pretend for a moment that I don't want what they have. That I'm content with my life.

*Alone.*

It's late the next day. After my visit with my family, I came here early and haven't left my office. I'm numb from yesterday. It's like I have wounds all over my body, and if I let myself pay attention to the emotions coursing through me, they will gape and bleed. So instead, I work. I work and work and work until it's so late I have no choice but to leave. When I step into the common area, I'm shocked to see Nathaniel. I guess I shouldn't be shocked, though. Ever since his grandfather's impromptu meeting the other day, I've noticed he's been here earlier and working later. I also noticed that he's paying attention. Contributing. Interested.

I'm not used to it.

I'm not used to someone like him being here. In the past few years, I haven't really been around men like him. A gorgeous specimen of a man who oozes sexuality. Sure, I've been around very good-looking men, but none who look at me like he does. Even though he hasn't made a pass since the night at the bar, I can still see the way his eyes linger on me when I step into a room. Appraising me.

I'm not sure how I feel about it.

Obviously, I don't like him like that, but it isn't unwelcome to know he wants me either. It's been so long that anyone has looked at me, I don't actually mind the glances. The thought perplexes me.

"What are you working on so late?" I'm pulled out of my thoughts by his raspy British accent.

"I'm trying to figure out a way into some of the higher-end department stores. I'm picking my brain on who I know and how I can land a meeting with them. Of course, we'll send them invitations to the show, but I'd like to do something more. Have some one-on-one time."

"I think that's a brilliant idea. Making the buyer feel special will help us land them. Let me help you."

"You want to help?"

"Of course."

I stare at him blankly. Clearly, I misunderstood him. There's no way he wants to help.

My eyes narrow. "Why?"

"Other than the obvious reason?"

"Let's hear the obvious reason first?"

The left side of his lip tugs up, giving me the smirk I have grown accustomed to. A smirk that is so sinful it could melt a glacier and, if I'm not careful, melt the Ice Queen.

"I own the company," he responds, mocking me softly.

*Jeez, Madeline.* Get a hold of yourself. "Yeah, that makes

sense. Do you have any connections? Other than your *mate* at Harvey Nichols?"

He lifts a brow.

"Of course you do." My head shakes back and forth. "I don't know what's wrong with me tonight."

"Tired?"

"I'm just not feeling too well, I guess."

Understatement of the year. This always happens. Every month. I might as well be in bed with the flu with how useless I become. That and the painkillers I take when the cramps kick in . . .

*I swear I'm sick three weeks out of the month these days.*

Men have it way too easy. All I want is chocolate, wine, and a hydrocodone. But I don't respond with that. TMI for boss man.

"What's wrong?" he asks, his voice laced with concern.

"Nothing, I'm fine. Just stressed." Both of my hands lift, and I pull them through my hair, tugging at the roots as if tugging will take away the ache in my body. I'm so frustrated and angry for always feeling like this. With always feeling run down, and in pain, and needing a barrage of pills to make me feel better.

"Then it's settled. I'll handle London." His voice is authoritative. He's making a command, and he's leaving no room for objection.

It shouldn't make me feel warm inside, but it does, and I don't like the way it makes me feel.

"Why are you being so nice?" I'm not sure why he's offering to help me. There has to be a reason for his change in demeanor, and I want to know why.

"You mean why aren't I being an arse?"

"Pretty much."

"Everyone has to be nice sometimes."

"Maybe."

---

Bright and early the next morning, he walks into my office. I wasn't expecting him. He's pretty much given me space ever since I agreed to this crazy mess.

"Tink."

"Peter."

I gave up correcting him, and instead, I just counter with his own nickname. If I was a pesky fairy, then he was the boy who wouldn't grow up.

Case in point: this whole concocted plot. A fake girlfriend. Only a dreamer would think this plan would work, or worse, think it had any merit at all. Rather than grow up, take responsibility, and come down to earth, Nathaniel lives in a fantasy world where fake relationships are acceptable.

"To what do I owe the honor today? Going to make me plan a pretend wedding?"

"Maybe a child," he chides.

But at the mention of children, my back goes ramrod straight, and I tighten my jaw.

"Too much?"

"A bit." I let out the breath I'm holding and cock my head to the side. "What's going on? I'm pretty busy, and I don't have time right now."

"We need to discuss logistics."

"Okay. Does it have to be now?"

He shakes his head. "No, but soon."

"Why?"

"Our presence, or should I say *your* presence, has been requested."

That makes my body tense. "Requested where?" I ask through gritted teeth. This is really happening. I'm not ready.

"Dinner," he answers nonchalantly. As if this is no big deal when in truth it's a huge deal.

"How long do I have?"

"Four days."

"Four days . . ." I huff out, lifting my hand and rubbing my temples. "Shit. I thought I'd have more time?"

"Unfortunately not."

I can't possibly be ready in four days. I've just barely made peace with this arrangement, so pretending to be in a relationship will be impossible.

"I can't."

"You have to."

"No, I really don't think I can. I'm not that good of an actress."

"I think you're selling yourself short."

"I appreciate the vote of confidence, but I promise you, no, I am not."

"Then we shall have to remedy it."

"And how do you plan on doing that?"

"By spending time together." His voice is so calm. Too calm. As if this is the only solution. The truth is, it is. I don't like it, but he's right. We have no other choice.

"Fine."

"Fantastic. We'll have lunch together."

"I can't."

"Dinner then."

My eyes widen, and he laughs. "What?"

"I'm just shocked you don't have dinner plans. I wouldn't have pegged you for a man with no social life."

"Seeing as you're my girlfriend"—he smirks—"my nights are saved for you."

"Don't be getting ahead of yourself, champ."

He laughs, and the sound does something to my insides, liquefying some of the ice surrounding my heart. I can't let him in, though. I can't let myself thaw. So I glare at him as if that will stop this feeling spreading inside.

"Wouldn't dream of it."

"Good. Okay, dinner. I have a meeting outside the office. Where should we meet?" I square my shoulders and act as detached as I can.

"Do you fancy sushi?"

"I always fancy sushi."

"Very good. There is a fantastic spot by my flat."

He rattles off the directions and address, and I punch it in my phone. As much as I don't want to spend my free time with him, I know I must.

<hr />

"So you want to know my background?" he asks from across the table. He's lifting a chopstick to his mouth, and it makes me stare at his full lips.

"I do."

He eats the piece of sushi and swallows. When he's done, he places the chopsticks down and smiles.

"Very well. The Harringtons haven't always been in textiles. Originally, we hailed from Harrington, England . . ." He trails off. "Hence the surname."

"Got it."

"We weren't titled, but what we lacked in that department, we held in spades in wealth and land. My great-great-grandmother's family was titled, but she married a wealthy commoner. As far as they climbed in the world, there was always a disconnection, but then the world changed, and money ruled. Sons took over and passed down from generation to generation a coal business."

"Coal?"

"The one and only."

"That's quite a jump from coal to textiles, and from England to America." I lift an eyebrow.

He chuckles at my expression. "You don't know the half of it."

"So tell me," I say, curious. As soon as the words leave my mouth, I realize how much I want to know about him. How interested I am to hear about his family. It shocks me.

"My grandfather, Nathaniel—"

"Are you all Nathaniels?"

"There were three."

"So you're the third."

"Quite clever, aren't you?" he chides. "Do you mind not interrupting?"

I roll my eyes. "Sorry."

"So where was I? My grandfather, Nathaniel, worked beneath his brother. His brother was the oldest, thus it was his legacy to take over. Through a series of bad investments, and being an utter drunk, he lost everything."

*Holy crap.* "Everything?"

"Yes. Everything. The coal, the land, everything. Having nothing left to tie my grandfather to London, he traveled to America with hope and dreams and whatnot." He shakes his head at the notion. "He met an American and fell in love. There, he built Harrington Textiles."

"Your grandmother is American?"

"Was American. And that's the only part of the story you got?" Now it's his turn to roll his eyes at me.

"No, of course not. From coal to textiles, that's quite the jump."

"Not really. At the time, my grandmother's family was in textiles. So with his father-in-law's guidance, he started it. But it was his hard work and dedication that made it what it is today."

"A billion-dollar company."

"Yes."

"So how does that play into now?"

"As time passed and the company grew, he brought his brother in. Family means everything to my grandfather. And despite the mistake, he felt obligated to help him. The company grew, and Harringtons was born with my grandfather at the helm this time. Over the years, we've expanded offices in New York and London."

"That's so interesting," I mutter because, in truth, it is. There is so much about this man I don't know. It's fascinating.

"My father, Nathaniel the second, was born, and he was groomed to take over as well. Met my mother and had me." He looks off into the space above my head.

"What happened?"

His eyes look hollow now. "My parents died one night in London. Car accident."

My heart slams in my chest with this knowledge. It feels like I can't breathe.

"I-I'm so sorry." My voice cracks with emotion.

"It's okay." He smiles reassuringly. "It was a long time ago . . ."

"Who raised you?"

"My grandfather. He lived half the time in London, half the time in America, but like all good British boys, I was raised at boarding school."

"Hence the British accent."

"Hence the British accent," he agrees.

"So if you and your grandfather are so close, why the charade?"

"Well, that's where things get dicey. I haven't been the ideal heir. Partying. Drinking. Women." He smirks.

"Page Six."

"Page Six." He nods his agreement. "My cousin has been dropping seeds of doubt while I've been off seeing the world."

"Sowing your wild oats, you mean," I chide. He grimaces, and it makes me laugh. Once he stops chuckling, his jaw tightens.

"Yes, that too. He's been feeding a story that has put my future legacy at stake."

The easygoing Nathaniel is gone when he says this, replaced with a more somber version of himself. I incline my head and watch him for a minute. His shoulders are stiff, and his hands are fisted on the table.

I don't like to see him like this. I might not like Nathaniel, but no one should look the way he does when he speaks of family.

"But how can that be?"

His eyes shift to the side, but I can see he's lost in thought. Blinking a few times, he rights himself.

"The board has the final say. My grandfather never wanted what happened to the coal to happen to Harringtons again. He didn't want one leader. He wanted a board to oversee it, but his need to right a prior wrong has backfired on me."

I lean forward and place my elbows on the table.

"Why the bad blood between you and your cousin?"

"Because he's the direct heir of a lost empire, and I'm the heir to a new one. He wants what I have, and his jealousy clouds his judgment," he grits out harshly. There is so much hate and pain, and I'm shocked by all this information, yet I still don't fully understand what this has to do with me.

"So I understand all this. But why the ruse? Why the need for a relationship?"

"My cousin is married. I am not. While he has always worked—"

"You have not," I cut him off, and he nods.

"Exactly."

His one-word answer still has me perplexed. It still doesn't make sense why he bought Valentina Fisher.

"But why wouldn't you just go to work now for him?"

"I didn't want to. Since I haven't always been there, I thought it would be best to prove my worth in a different way. I wanted to overcome my indolence on a grand scale."

"And the relationship?"

"It was a white lie when he got on my case that I'm not sure how to get myself out of," he admits on a sigh. He looks so damn lost that I have the urge to reach out my hand and tell him it will be okay. But will it? It can't possibly because this is all a lie. Nothing good comes from a lie.

"But what is the endgame? We can't pretend forever. We can't."

"I know. I know, but while I prove myself, being in a relationship will take the spotlight off my extracurricular activities. By the time we end it, I will have proven to them I'm ready for the responsibility."

"And you really think you can pull this off?"

"Of course," he says matter-of-factly. His confidence in his abilities makes me laugh.

"Cocky much?"

"You don't know me, Tink. I get what I want."

Any emotion he had before is gone, replaced one hundred percent with the Nathaniel that has been present ever since the first time I saw him with his feet on my desk.

"And self-absorbed. A real winning combination."

"Don't forget arrogant."

I shake my head back and forth. "I don't know what I'm going to do with you," I finally respond as I roll my eyes.

"Pretend. You'll get good at pretending. Because when we are in public, I will touch you . . ." He pauses, and my heart thuds against my breastbone. "I will kiss you." *Thud.* "You'll be mine." *Thud.* "And no one can think otherwise. Do you understand me?"

"Crystal clear," I whisper breathlessly, and I hope he doesn't hear how much he affects me.

"Good. Well, now that that's settled, care to have a drink?"

Internally, I breathe out the tension that had collected that he might have realized what his words did to me.

"Why the hell not."

He waves the waitress over, and this time, we go straight for the champagne, a vintage Bollinger Cuvée.

"Fancy."

"Only the best," he replies.

"So what are we toasting?" I ask.

"To us."

I snort. "Cliché. To faking it," I retort.

"With me, you'll never have to fake it."

"Of course I will, because this isn't real."

The glasses clink, neither of us speaking after that comment. It might not be real, but at least we can enjoy the champagne.

———————•———————

It's only a day after our dinner, which actually felt like a turning point for us. Not that I like Nathaniel, but I understand him better after hearing his story. He's also been helping so much at work that we've called a ceasefire.

I got home from the office a few hours ago, and now I'm sitting in my apartment fresh out of the shower when I hear my cell phone ringing on the nightstand. An unknown number. I don't normally answer unknown calls, but it's early. Technically early enough to be working, and it could be one of the many people I have called over the last week and haven't heard back from.

"Hello," I answer.

"Tink."

His voice shouldn't make my body warm, but it does. My body never listens to me. "Nathaniel. To what do I owe this honor?"

"I need you."

Butterflies take flight in my body, but I shake my head. He can't see me, so I need to shove away the visual presenting itself to me. "What?" I choke out.

"I need your help tonight."

My stomach drops, and I realize what he's saying. He doesn't need *me*; he needs the charade. He needs the theatrics to begin.

"Now?"

"Yes."

"It's kind of short notice. I thought I had three more days," I say.

"I know, and I'm sorry. But I have no choice."

"Okay. Where are we going?"

"There is a fundraiser."

A fundraiser. Shit. There is no way I'll be able to get ready in time. "I-I—"

"Not like that. This isn't the fundraiser." He laughs. "But there is a Harrington Fundraiser my family throws every year. This is the dinner to discuss the logistics."

"How many fundraisers do you go to?" I ask in shock. Didn't he just go to one?

"A lot," he groans, and I can hear in his voice that he hates them.

"And you need me to come to this meeting? I don't understand."

"My grandfather called. With most of the board members in town, it seemed the most opportune moment."

"Oh. Um, okay," I mumble back.

"It will be fine." His voice sounds calm, but I'm not sure how. This is a big moment for us—for him.

"How long do I have?"

"I'll pick you up at eight."

I look over at the clock. It's only five p.m., so I have plenty of time. There's a blow dry bar down the block, and they also have a makeup bar. Maybe I'll get lucky and they can squeeze me in. As I hang up and dial, I send a silent prayer up in the air.

My prayers are answered as I find myself hauling ass to get to the salon in less than ten minutes. Once my hair and makeup are done, a smoky eye and a red lip, I pair it with a tight A-line black dress that hits me right above the knee. Sophisticated yet classic. And a hint of sexy.

I'm lost in my thoughts when the buzzer rings on my apartment. I hit the button. "Hello?"

"Hello, Ms. Montgomery, I have a Mr. Harrington here to see you."

"I'll be right down. Thank you."

Heading toward the closet, I grab my coat and clutch and head toward the elevator. The ride takes forever, and it reminds me of the last time we were in an elevator together. How long ago that seems. A lifetime truly. That day I wanted him. Wanted something I couldn't possibly have. Now I have him but not really.

This is my life. I have a faux boyfriend, yet a relationship is still out of my grasp. This is how it needs to be. Enjoy the free dinner and a night out, but don't allow yourself to hope for more.

You'll only get hurt.

The elevator doors open, and I see him instantly. How can I not? His presence is huge in the small space of the lobby. He's leaning against the wall, his legs crossed at the ankle, hands tucked into his pocket. He hasn't seen me yet. His eyes are downcast, brow furrowed.

My heels click on the floor, and he lifts his gaze. Our eyes lock, and my breath hitches. He shouldn't look at me the way he does. But I can't lie and say I don't love it. He peers at me through hooded lids. They trail up and down my face, stopping at the swell of my breasts. A smile tips his lips, a wicked smirk saying unseemly things, and I love it. Nothing will happen—it can't—but I can't help loving feeling wanted. Feeling like a woman when so often I don't. It's my own fault, but I won't think about it now. Instead, I smile.

His whole face lights up when I smile. "You look gorgeous," he says as he pushes off the wall and walks over to me.

"Thank you."

He reaches out his hand and takes mine in his. The touch of his skin sends a shiver down my spine. "This way."

Outside, I pull my jacket tighter around me as he leads me to a waiting car. A man walks around my side and opens the door, and we scoot in. We are so close that my bare skin on my leg touches his pants. His hand rests on my knee, his fingers burning me up.

"What are you doing?" I ask, looking down at his hand.

"Making sure you are comfortable with my touch." He says it so nonchalantly that I almost believe him, but when he traces slow, soft circles on my knee, I know this is more. This is for his own enjoyment. A part of me knows I should tell him to stop, but a bigger part says nothing and just enjoys the feel of a devastatingly handsome man touching me. Because for me, there isn't a happily ever after, no prince and no forever, so if this is all I'll have, I allow myself to immerse in the tale, even if for a moment.

I'm pulled out of my reverie by a cough reverberating in the closed space. "We're here," he rasps, and I look up at him. His hand is still on my leg, but somewhere during the drive, it had crept up. Now the tips of his fingers are playing a soft melody on the skin just beneath the hem of my skirt. I look into his eyes. It's dark in the car, so I can't see the shade of green that haunts my dreams. All I can see is the black of his pupils, large, dark, and ominous. His tongue juts out, and he licks his upper lip. A reflex? A promise? I have no idea, but the small move has me focused on his lips. His delectable lips.

I can't think this way.

I can't allow my lust-filled brain to think this way.

It's been way too long since I've had sex, and I'm starting to go crazy with the way he looks at me from across the seat. I pull my gaze away, but not before I see the side of his lip pulled up into a smirk.

Bastard.

I have to remember that we might be working together, but we are not on the same side. Sure, our agendas mesh, but it's for very different reasons. He might want Valentina Fisher to succeed, but not for the reasons I do. This is all a ploy for him to take over his supposed legacy, and although I don't fault him for it, I can't get wrapped up in this either.

"We're here," he repeats, and this time, I notice that the door to the car is now open. I step out, and he follows suit. His hand grazes my dress, the heat sending chills to caress my body.

So much for the pep talk I just gave myself.

I'm so screwed.

We enter through a back door. When we step inside, it's dark and dusty. Like we're in a storage unit. In front of me is an elevator, and I tense.

"No, this time there will be no elevator."

He chuckles, knowing full well my hesitation. "It's just down this hallway."

The building seems odd. It's not a restaurant and certainly not a place I can imagine having dinner at. It's an apartment building, I think. His hand still on my back, we walk down a narrow hall. We pass a door and then another. The hallway is dark, and when I see another set of doors, we step in, inside is his grandfather, his family, and the board.

I halt my steps, freezing in place. This is really happening. Am I really doing this? I already want this man too much. How will this not hurt me? How will I be able to keep my feelings concealed as we play this wicked concocted game?

As if he knows what I'm thinking, he steps toward me, and I step back until my back hits the wall. "Are you okay?" he asks. His voice is low, not wanting to alert anyone we're here, I'm sure.

"I'm not sure," I admit on a sigh. I never let myself fall so far astray, and that is what I am about to do. I'm walking toward a fire, a burning building, when I should be running in the opposite direction.

"What is going through that beautiful head of yours?" he asks as he lifts his hand, and his fingers touch the skin on my temple.

"I don't know if I can do this."

"Do you feel you can't pretend?" His finger trails from my temple, to my jaw, the pad of his thumb soothing me. "Are you not attracted to me?" He's so close now, his breath when he speaks tickling the top of my head. With his hand, he tilts my head up, bending his knees so we are eye to eye. Mouth to mouth. "For this to work, you have to want me."

I inhale a ragged breath as his words penetrate me; as his accent blankets me in a heat that shoots straight to my core.

"Do you want me?" He exhales, and I inhale his breath.

"Yes," I say.

"Enough to fool everyone?" he whispers against my lips as they touch for the first time.

"Yes."

His lips collide against mine, his tongue seeking entry.

I allow it.

Wrapped up in the feel of his strong body around me, I would allow this man everything. I know this is crazy, and I know the game hasn't begun, but I let him possess me. I let him own me in the hallway. This is real. The next minute, it won't be, so I indulge. I allow myself to get lost to him because as soon as we enter that room, it's over. Nothing will be real again.

"Good," he mutters between kisses.

*Good?*

His lips silence my thoughts again, and I know I should stop this. I shouldn't allow myself to dream, but I do. I hold on to the feeling of something real for as long as I can.

A cough and then a chuckle echoes into the space. My eyes are still closed, so I don't register the fact I'm pushed against a wall with a hard body pressed to mine until I hear the voice.

"Well played, cousin. But is a cheap girl in the hall the best you can do?"

A bucket of cold ice is dumped on top of me as I realize we have an audience, and then the next shoe drops.

This wasn't real.

The game had started. My back goes ramrod straight, and I move to push away. He holds me closer, tightening his grip.

"No," he says so low no one can hear. "No."

So I stay in place and will my muscles to uncoil.

Game on.

With a hand on my back again, he leads me past his cousin, who is appraising me in a way that makes me feel cold. I don't like the way he stares at me. It's as if I'm beneath him, a thing for him to squish, but at the same time, his eyes run up my body, and it feels like bugs crawling on my skin. He might want to squish me, but it's obvious he wants to fuck me too. Bile crawls up my throat. By the way Nathaniel tightens his grip on me, it's obvious he senses this too. As the door swings open and we step in, I feel like a lamb being led to the slaughter. All eyes are on me.

I imagine I'm still flushed from the kiss, and that thought makes me want to run and hide. But I am not that girl, and I will never be that girl. I don't back away even when I am uncomfortable. I face my problems head-on. And right now, this is my problem. Nathaniel has brought me into his world and his problem and made them my own. I square my shoulders, straighten my back, and walk toward the wolves.

We approach a group of men situated next to a long table. This seems to be a private party room within a restaurant. "Where are we?" I ask.

"The Lancaster."

"Why didn't we come in through the front?"

"This is the fast way in, and truth be told, as much as you think I like being photographed, I don't."

I cock my head at him. I would have surely thought he liked to garner attention, but this hasn't been the first time I have been wrong about him. I hate to admit it even to myself, but there is a lot I don't know about him.

One other thought that pops in my head and I try unsuccessfully to push it away is the desire to learn more. *You're on thin ice here, Madeline. Poke the beast and you're sure to get bit.*

"Grandfather," I hear him say as a man turns around. I remember him from the meeting a few weeks ago. He looks tired today. His skin dull, his eyes a tiny bit glassy. The last time I saw him was in the morning, and I wonder if this is just the aftereffect of a long day.

"Nathaniel." He turns to me and smiles. A kind smile. "Ms. Montgomery."

"Pleased to see you, Mr. Harrington." I find myself

bending my knees a little despite my best intentions. Without meaning to, I'm playing into this more naturally than I thought I would. Maybe I am pleased to see him? No. Not possible.

His lip tips up. "Please call me Nathaniel."

"Then you must call me Madeline."

"As you wish, my dear. I could never turn down a beautiful lady's request." My cheeks warm and the younger Nathaniel, my Nathaniel, chuckles. *Not my Nathaniel, jeez.* I need to get that thought out of my head.

The apple doesn't fall far from the tree with these two. His grandfather is handsome, weathered with age, and obviously a wicked flirt. Now that I know he raised his grandson, I can see the warmth in his eyes as he watches him, and the warmth he sends my way tells me he just wants his grandson to be happy. I hate the lie, and I hate that I'm contributing to it, but as I look around the room and see the tightened jaws and straight lips staring at us, I realize that maybe this really is necessary.

"Come sit, we have a lot to discuss."

Drinks are ordered, and the discussion of the fundraiser starts. Apparently, Harrington Textiles donates money to orphanages throughout the world. This does not surprise me. Knowing what I know now about Nathaniel and what I know of his grandfather, I understand completely.

I turn to Nathaniel, and he looks at me and whispers, "Ever since my parents died . . ." He starts and stops, and I nod with understanding. "It was my suggestion. My grandfather did so much for me, so we have a scholarship to send children with no parents to boarding school. To get the best education money can buy."

"How many children do you help a year?"

"Depends on the year. Some years it's more, some less. Last year, we gave scholarships to fifty students."

"And this year?" I smile.

"I hope to make it more."

"I know you can."

His lip tips up into the signature smile I have grown to wish for. This man is so different from the man I saw at the office that I'm almost dumbfounded by it.

"This is why you paid for Jean's grandson?"

"Yes and no. Yes, the foundation will pay, but typically, we handle primary school."

"And you made an exception because?"

"For you, of course."

"But why?"

He shrugs and turns back to the conversation at hand. Obviously, a sore topic. I'm sure losing his parents is the obvious answer.

"How are we on invitations? Are the key benefactors confirmed?" someone asks from the corner.

"Yes, we're in line to raise over a mil this year."

"And you're handling this?" an elderly gentleman asks, lips puckered as if he tasted something sour. He looks a little like Nathaniel, and I wonder if they are related.

"I am," Nathaniel responds.

I realize who he is. This must be Nathaniel's grandfather's brother. The one who lost all the money.

"You sure we should trust you with this?" he asks.

Nathaniel stiffens beside me.

From under his breath, I hear his cousin say, "Be careful. He's liable to blow all the money on coke"—and then he looks over at me and smirks—"and hookers."

My fists clench in my lap. Did he just call me a hooker? Any reservation I had before about this plan is gone. This asshole needs to go down. Lifting my hand off my lap, I place it on the table on top of Nathaniel's.

A united front.

# chapter fifteen

## NATHANIEL

TONIGHT WAS A SHITSHOW.

Hand in hand, we walk toward the exit. I can't get out of here soon enough. With each step, I feel the weight that has been sitting on my shoulders loosening. As we emerge from the building, I guide her to the waiting car. As my driver steps forward, I shake him off. No need.

I open the door for her.

She steps in and takes a seat, and I move in beside her. From where we sit in the back seat of my car, our bodies touch. I glance over and peruse her face, allowing my gaze to sweep down to her exposed neck. I always knew she was beautiful but tonight even more so.

Shit.

Is it getting warm in here?

I shake my head. I can't think about her skin or the way her lips felt when I kissed her.

Earlier tonight, I caught her off guard but took what I wanted. I played it off that I did it because of my cousin, but the truth is, I have wanted to do it ever since the elevator. I wanted to throw her up against the wall, lift her skirt, and sink into her heat. I feel my pants tighten at the thought. Again, I try to push the thought away, but she's so close, I can smell the soft scent of lilac in the air. It's intoxicating, and I do everything in my power not to devour her again.

I'm pulled out of my thoughts by the car stopping. We're at her apartment. Thank fuck. I would not be held responsible for what I would have done to her in the back seat of this car if we hadn't stopped. Truth be told, I wouldn't even give a fuck if we had an audience. That's how much I want to be inside her.

I get out of the car and hold the door open for her. As she steps out, I reach out my hand and take hers in mine, helping her out. Once we're standing on the street corner in front of her building, I look down at her.

She looks up. A strange tension hovers over us as if I'm supposed to kiss her. But this isn't a date, so I can't. No matter how much I want to taste her mouth again, right here, right now, I don't. Instead, I lean down and place a chaste kiss on her forehead. When I pull away, her eyes are dazed.

"Thank you for tonight."

She peers into my eyes but doesn't speak. Instead, she gives me a tight-lipped smile as she walks away from me, leaving me standing alone on the corner of the street.

I watch her as she enters her building and then climb back into my waiting car.

"Where to, sir?" Roger asks as he puts the car into drive.

"My place."

"Very good, sir."

It isn't even ten minutes later that I'm finally at my flat. Walking over to the wet bar in my living room, I pour myself three fingers of scotch. My favorite. Must be in the blood because as soon as I lift it to my mouth, I feel at home.

My mobile rings in my pocket.

"Hello."

"Hey," the familiar voice says on the line.

"Oliver. To what do I owe this honor?"

"Sod off."

"Still the same prick, I see." I laugh. "Tell me you are once again back in the States."

"Always. And yes, I'm in the States. Wanted to know what you're about?"

I think about what he's asking. A night out with Oliver offers a night of fun. As an earl with more money than God, all doors are open to him. The truth is, I could go. I could find a hot piece of arse to sink myself in, but for some reason, the thought holds no appeal. There is only one woman I can imagine thrusting into, and she's not a no-name girl you find at a bar.

"I'm good."

"Suit yourself."

I hang up the phone a moment later, but now what the fuck am I going to do? I'm rock-hard, and the options are limited. Maybe I was too hasty saying no to Oliver. Fuck. Because in the quiet of my flat, my cock is begging to come out. If only I could call her. If only my cock was out and her mouth was wrapped around me. Tongue and hands stroking. The throbbing inside my pants is painful.

I need a release, and I need it now.

Without preamble, I remove my shirt and then pull myself out of the tight confines of my pants. Leaning back, I stroke myself with my hand. Making long strokes with my palm, I drag my orgasm to the surface. I imagine it's her pumping her slender fingers on the base as her tongue swirls around the tip.

As the pressure builds, I grip harder, imagining the pressure of her tongue or her throat as I fuck her face. That's it. Just like that. I fall. Bursting into a million pieces. Breathing out a long exhale, I wait for my heartbeat to regulate. That was intense. And now I need to clean up this mess.

I stand from the sofa, kick off my pants, and head for the bathroom. With each step, I wonder what I'm doing and how I'm going to pretend with this woman when all I want to do is fuck her. I stop in front of the floor-to-ceiling windows in the living room. The city lights twinkle in the distance, casting a soft glow through the room.

Fuck. Why can't I control myself? This is going to be a problem. *She* is going to be a problem. But I have no choice but to follow this through, no matter the consequence.

Even if that means nightly reenactments of tonight.

---

Sunday night dinner never happened. *Canceled again.* The truth is, it was a good thing because I needed to process what happened the other night. After the kiss and the follow-up alone in my flat, I want to see her. I hate to admit it, but I miss Tink. Although she flitted around like a little fairy, barking orders and being a little pest, I miss having her in my space—well, I miss being in her space. Sitting here, looking over the notes from the early morning meeting and the timeline for presentations, I decide I can't work in here anymore.

I know I have an office. I know I have a private space within this converted warehouse to call my own, but I don't like it.

It's too quiet.

Too empty.

Grabbing my laptop, I head to the main room. There are

tables and chairs, but really, it's rubbish right now.

Valentina has fabric everywhere. Clothes are piled on top of what should be a table. I love the confusion, the congestion, and the energy here. It's not much unlike Harrington Textiles.

I'm used to materials of all sorts, trimmings and whatnot, but this is different. Seeing the fabrics my family created turned into more is eye-opening. And Valentina certainly has an eye. I look over at the model being fitted in the corner. Black lace covers her, and her dusky pink nipples peek out from the material. It starts at her neck, inspired by a Victorian fashion, but the see-through design gives it a modern edge. I turn to look at the materials lying beside her, at what else she is planning. The model smiles at me a seductive smile, and although she's gorgeous, I pay her no mind. I take a seat, pushing over the trimmings, and open up my laptop.

With the noise in the background a constant hum, I was able to lose myself in my work, but the room has gone relatively quiet, so I look up. The model from before approaches me. "Hi," she purrs. And now with her this close and me still in my seat, her nipples are in my direct line of sight. There is no question she's still wearing this on purpose. "I'm Lauren." She reaches her hand out, and I take it in mine.

"Nathaniel."

"Oh, I know." She licks her lips. I'm sure she knows who I am, and by the way she's eye fucking me, she'd be more than happy to be my plaything for a night or two. Like so many women before, she wants me for one thing. For my name. I'm not saying I'm not attractive. I know I am, but girls like her want me for what I can do for them.

After a second, I release her hand, but she's still standing there. "Is there something I can help you with, Lauren?"

"Yes . . ." she drawls out. I consider it for a minute. How easy it would be to take her to my office, close the door, and bend her over my desk. She's practically panting right now, waiting for me to say the word. The old me would do it. In a heartbeat.

I say that as if I'm a new man.

I'm not.

But I have changed. Enough to know if I am trying to put on a front that I am in a relationship with Madeline, I shouldn't be shagging some other girl in my office.

As if hearing my thoughts, I see Madeline step out from her office. She looks from me to the pair of nipples at eye level and frowns. A line forms between her brows, and I wonder how she'll handle this. I'm intrigued and can't wait to see how this will play out.

She steps toward us. I stand.

Before I know it, she's beside me. Staking her claim. It's obvious by the tightness of her jaw, but to confirm my thoughts, she places her hand on mine. Fuck that. My arms pull around her waist, and as unprofessional as it is to do this in the office, it's too fun not to, so I place my mouth on hers. Staking my claim right back.

I'm not sure why I do it. Some primal need, but either way, I hold her close and kiss her. Tongue slipping in, moans escaping from her lips. A round of claps is heard all around us, and she pulls away. Her face is flushed with heat or maybe embarrassment or both. I bite back my chuckle. She's cute when she's like this. I wonder what she would look like . . .

"Do you mind?" I hear her whisper.

"I do."

She rolls her eyes, feigning displeasure, but I felt her lips and tasted her tongue. I heard her little moans of pleasure. You can't fake that. She wants me.

And that fact alone changes everything.

Because this was just a plan, just a ruse, but that was before I wondered what she felt like, before I yearned for her taste on my tongue, and most of all, before I knew she wanted it too.

I'm having my cake and eating it too.

Every single delectable bite.

# chapter sixteen

## MADELINE

'M BOTH DIZZY AND DAZED.

I have no idea what I was thinking when I marched over to him and told the world, or at least the office, we were an item, but I did. By the sounds of the claps and cheers all around us, the message was read loud and clear. I shouldn't have done that, but I legit couldn't help it. When I saw that model hanging over him, her nipple practically in his mouth, I saw red.

Something that has never happened to me before, let alone to someone I'm not even dating.

God. I'm an idiot. The worst part is the cocky bastard loved it. Loved it. It was written all over every single perfect feature on his dashing face. He ate that shit up like it was the last meal on earth. Slowly and to the point, he kissed me. Playing right into the part I started but leaving me speechless and dumbfounded at the same time. How can a man I'm not with and don't even like make me lose all reason? *Because you do like him*, a pesky voice says in my head. I try to shoo it away, but instead now in his arms, being led back into my office, I can't silence it.

I do.

I hate myself for it.

But I do.

I don't like Nathaniel Harrington. I just want him. Not a good place to be, but things can certainly be worse. At least I rarely have to see him outside of work. I can't imagine his grandfather will be in town much longer or his cousin, for that matter. Nathaniel was quite clear that his cousin ran the business side of things in the London office and his grandfather has been spending more and more time in London as well. As long as I don't need to be alone with him, I should be okay. I have managed to succeed at not letting any man distract me from my goals. I won't let this one.

"A word," I hear from the doorway and look up to see Valentina looking at me. Her cheeks are sucked in, and her arms are crossed protectively against her chest.

"Okay," I mumble, knowing where this is going and not looking forward to it.

"I thought dating in the office isn't cool." Her head tilts to the right. "How did you say it? Oh yes . . . who shits where they eat? It's tacky."

"I didn't mean it," I whisper, feeling like the worst friend in the world again.

"Didn't you, though?"

I want to tell her everything. I want to confess all my secrets and beg her to forgive me, but part of the contract stated I couldn't tell anyone, so instead, I bite my lower lip and look down. The pressure of my teeth cutting my skin burns, but I deserve the pain right now.

"I'm sorry."

She doesn't respond to my apology, and I step up to move toward her, but she lifts her hand. "I'm not mad. I mean I am— but not for the reason you think."

"Why then?"

"You should have told me . . ."

"You never told me about you and Eric. Shouldn't the same have gone for you? We're supposed to be friends, but apparently, we are both leaving stuff out."

A fine line pops up between her brows, and she gives me a tight smile. "You're right." Her voice is low, weak. It doesn't feel good to be right, because the truth is, I still hurt my friend.

"Listen, we both made mistakes, but how about we put it behind us and try to do better?"

"Okay." She smiles. "I have a phone call. Talk later?"

I nod, choosing to keep silent. I don't know what confession will spew from my mouth if I don't.

When Val leaves, I turn back to my computer and throw myself back into my work. Not much time passes before I hear the door open again. Looking up, I see Nathaniel. He pushes open the door, and he steps in.

As soon as the door closes, I fire at him. "Why did you kiss me? You can't do that here."

"Why the hell not?"

"Because it's our place of business, and it's not professional." I place my hands on my hips, trying to convey how serious I am. I don't think I'm even buying it myself.

"And here I thought that was exactly what you wanted me to do." He smirks.

"I did not."

"See, that's where you have me confused. By the way you marched over, I thought you wanted to get the point across."

"By kissing me?"

"What better way?" He lifts his eyebrow.

"You can't keep doing that," I implore, but what I'm really

saying is please stop kissing me, or I don't know what I will do.

"And why is that, Tink?"

"Stop calling me that!"

"No."

I let out a deep breath. "Just don't kiss me at the office."

"Can I kiss you out of the office?" The way his eyes sparkle should be illegal.

"No."

"But we had a deal." Placing his hands on his narrow hips, I know he's challenging me again, and unfortunately, he wins this round.

"I-I mean obviously if someone from the board or your family is around . . ."

"What are you so afraid of?" he asks.

"I'm not afraid of anything." I straighten my spine, trying to appear taller than my five-foot-two frame.

He takes a step toward me.

I take a step back.

My body collides with the desk behind me. "Are you sure?" he breathes out, leaning toward me. There is a wicked gleam in his eyes. He trails his gaze over me, leaving me feeling naked and exposed.

"Yes," I pant, my voice betraying me. I sound desperate and needy. He knows it and chuckles.

"Keep telling yourself that, Tink."

"Is there something you need from me?" I ask as I sidestep him and put distance between us.

"There is a lot I need from you . . ." His words hang in the air like an invitation. "But for now, I need to go over your diary."

"My diary?"

"Yes, your schedule. We need to figure out our appearances

together." He makes it sound so clinical, the polar opposite of the searing kiss we just had.

I walk toward my desk and sit behind it. Then lift my brow for him to sit in the chair opposite me. "Okay," I say now that I have my calendar out. "When do you need me?" That comment elicits a smirk, and I roll my eyes at him.

"Right now, I'm thinking a very public dinner this week."

"How public?"

"Paparazzi public."

"Shit," I mumble. This is real. Pictures. Paparazzi. People knowing my business. What did I agree to?

"Yeah, I know. But if you do this, it will get them off my back for a while."

"One can hope. So what's the plan? We'll go to a club, drink, get photographed?"

"Yes." He nods.

"When?"

"Saturday . . ."

"And until then?"

He tilts his head in question. "What do you mean?"

I take a deep breath, not wanting to say it, but it weighs on me. "When we aren't together . . ." I trail off.

"Yes . . . ?" He's leading me, and I hate how smug he sounds. He knows what I'm asking but wants to mess with me. I really don't want to say anything, but then I think back to Miss Perfect with her perfect nipples hovering above him.

"Will you . . ."

"Will I what?" He smiles, and I can tell he likes how uncomfortable I am way too much. My face gets warm.

"Will you be . . ." God, why is this so hard?

"Fucking someone?"

"Jeez Louise. Can you be any more blunt?" I hiss under my breath.

"I could," he deadpans. "You'd be surprised."

I give him a groan in return. "But yes. While I'm pretending to be your love interest, will you be with other women?"

"Would that upset you, Tink?"

"No, of course not," I lie. For some reason, the idea of him touching anyone else has me clenching my fists under the desk. "But I don't want to look like a fool. If you have to—"

"If I have to?" he leads.

"Can you be discreet?" I want to say don't. I want to offer myself up on a silver platter to him, but my pride pushes the words down.

"If and when I decide to fuck someone, I promise to be discreet. Good?"

"Fine."

"Well, now that we have that settled, I'm starving. Have you had lunch?"

"I have." I haven't, but I can't have lunch with him right now. I'm too unsettled.

"Very well." He stands and makes his way to the door. "Until next time."

He closes me in my sanctuary, giving me peace from the crazy feelings rushing inside me. The confusing feelings. Feelings I don't want to think about.

So I won't.

# chapter seventeen

## MADELINE

AFTER AGREEING TO GO OUT WITH NATHANIEL, HE LEAVES me alone. It's quiet in my office, almost too quiet, and I can't help but laugh at the irony of the situation. All this time, I have wanted him out of my hair, and now I think I miss him. In the distance, I hear a commotion. Standing from my desk, I move toward the door to see what's going on. Nathaniel is chest to chest with his cousin Edward.

What's he doing here?

Without a second thought, I make my way over to them. I step up behind Nathaniel, and from where I am, I have the perfect view of his clenched fists. The situation is heated and needs to be cooled down, ASAP.

"Is everything okay?" I reach my hand out and touch Nathaniel's shoulder instinctively. His body startles, not expecting anyone to touch him. He looks over, and I can see that his pupils are enlarged. He's lost in his rage. I softly run my hands down his arm until I grasp his hand in mine. "What's going on?"

"My cousin took it upon himself to visit," he grits through clenched teeth.

"Needed to see what the old boy is up to," Edward says, and I take a step to the side so Nathaniel no longer blocks me. Edward is wearing a smug smile on his face. He knows his presence isn't wanted.

"How nice of you to join us. However, next time you should make an appointment. We're all quite busy here." He looks me up and down as we speak, his eyes narrowing at my hand entwined with Nathaniel's.

"Just wanted to make sure my cousin was working."

"Well, now that you see he is, I'm going to have to ask you to leave." I tilt my head in challenge.

He nods once before turning to look at his cousin. "I'll make sure to report back to the board that you were here." He winks.

"You do that," Nathaniel practically spits out as Edward turns on his heel and leaves. When he's finally out of the door, Nathaniel mouths to me, "Thank you," before he walks away across the common area and into the conference room. I'm left standing alone—well, except for the whole staff staring at me.

Should I follow him? Make sure he's okay. If he's anything like me, he'll want to be alone. I'll respect him enough to give him his space. With my decision made, I head to my office.

My phone chimes on my desk as I head back inside.

I don't recognize the number, so I allow it to be sent to voicemail. A minute later, the chime that rings through the air lets me know I have a message.

"Hello, this message is for Madeline Montgomery. This is Sara from Dr. Martin's office. We are calling to confirm your appointment tomorrow morning at eight forty-five."

My heart drums in my chest at the realization that my appointment is tomorrow. I've been putting off this appointment for weeks now. A feeling of impending doom always crashes upon me when I know a doctor's appointment was near. It's completely irrational, but the fear is real, nonetheless.

I try to put it out of my head by busying myself with work. A knock on the door pulls me from the list of events we have scheduled for the next month. I'm making sure all the vendors have been hired and deposits paid. This is not my job, but seeing as we are a small startup and I don't want to think about everything else going on in my life, I had offered to help. I'll still have to go over the figures with our CFO, but this keeps my mind busy.

I peer up from my computer, running my hand over my eyes to brush off the glaze making spots dance across my vision. Valentina steps inside.

"Can I come in?"

"Yes," I mutter, still rubbing at my eyes. When the spots are gone, I look at her. She isn't fully in my office, just peeking in, as if she's waiting for more. "What are you doing? Come in," I insist, and now with the forcefulness of my voice, she does. But she's hesitant. Her moves are slow and assessing. "What's going on?"

"Are you . . . are you okay?" she asks, her brow furrowed.

I tilt my head to the side and nod. "Yes. Why?"

"It's just . . ." She trails off, looking uncertain.

"It's just what?" I nearly snap.

"You seem stressed having Nathaniel's cousin here. The way you challenged him . . . I just wanted to make sure you weren't upset by him stopping by?"

Shit. I thought locking myself in my office would keep the inter-office gossip from spreading, but obviously, I was wrong.

"I'm okay. I just don't like him. And I don't like the way he treats Nathaniel."

She narrows her eyes. "He did seem pretty awful. Oh. Okay, I guess I'll get out of your hair." She looks at me again. "Is there anything else—"

I plaster on the biggest fake smile I can muster. "Nope. I'm great. And you are never in my way."

To that, she finally allows her shoulders to drop as a smile forms. I decide to share the news that I'll be late tomorrow. I didn't want to bring it up until later, but the truth is, I don't really want to talk to anyone right now. My mood is unstable, so it's best I stay away from anyone.

"Valentina," I start and then stop. I hate putting myself out there, and although she won't know it, taking time off to go to a doctor is just that.

"Yeah."

"There is one thing. I'm going to be late tomorrow."

"Oh?"

"Yeah. I just have a doctor's appointment," I say, a little bit too quickly, but I smile broadly, hoping to throw her off. "Nothing big, just the typical girl issues." I wink, and she laughs.

"Nothing serious, though, right?" She's silently asking if my symptoms have gotten worse. Gotten worse than me secretly popping my pain pills like they're candy . . . nope. I shake my head. "Being a girl sucks, right?"

"The worst," I agree, and right now, knowing I'll be poked and prodded tomorrow, I really do agree. Being a thirtysomething single woman sucks.

She steps out, and I let out the breath inside my lungs, dropping my gaze and losing myself in work once again.

The next day comes before I know it. Now back in the office, everything from my earlier appointment with my doctor plays in my head over and over.

"*Because of your age . . .*"

My age.

"*You need to consider your options . . .*"

My options.

"*What do you want?*"

I have no idea what I want, but right now, everything aches.

My body.

My mind.

My heart.

"*Do you want children?*"

Anger flares inside me. I have a decision to make about my future, and I have to make these decisions now, apparently.

I'm halfway to my office, ready to close the door and shut the world out when I sense a presence walking up to me. I peer up and am met with the familiar grin.

"According to Lucy, you had an appointment this morning." He smiles large, and normally, it would make butterflies take flight in my stomach, but today I'm empty.

"That's right, I did," I respond, my voice tense, my answer tight.

"Is . . ." He pauses, the Adam's apple in his throat bobbing. "Is everything okay?"

"Yes."

"Want to talk about it?" he asks as if we are pals, and I would want to talk to him about my reproductive issues.

"Now why would I want to do that?" I clip.

"I just figured—"

I hold my hand up, and he stops talking.

"You figured what, I'd want to talk about my female problems?"

There, I said it. Nothing scares a man more than talking about lady problems. I watch as his face becomes flustered.

"Ah. Got it. Period problems."

I narrow my eyes.

"Or are you pregnant? Please tell me you're not." He laughs, trying to lighten the mood. It doesn't. It only makes me hurt more.

"I'm not."

All the emotions swirling through me start to work against my psyche because before I know it, my eyes are filled up with tears "Everything is fine, thanks," I mumble, picking up my pace to get away from him.

"Let's grab dinner?" he asks.

I keep up my pace, firing my response over my shoulder. "I can't."

"You can't?"

I stop at his question and turn to face him completely.

"That's what I said," I respond, glaring at him.

"Why?"

"I'm not done yet."

"I'm actually not done yet either, but we both need a break."

I tilt my head at his comment and furrow my brow.

"What?" he asks.

"I'm just shocked by how hard you've been working," I admit. As much as I want to find fault in him, I'm finding it harder and harder each day because he really is trying.

"Are you thinking maybe you were wrong about me?"

"Heavens no." My answer comes out too quickly, and it makes him chuckle.

"Oh . . ." he leads, his lip turning up. He's enjoying this way too much.

"I mean, maybe I wasn't one hundred percent right about you, but most of what I thought was right."

"Such as?"

"Such as . . . you really aren't ready to grow up," I retort.

"I'm here, aren't I? Working hard?"

"Yes, for now. But have you really changed?" I narrow my gaze in question.

"Yes."

"You don't even know what I'm talking about."

"I'm trying, Tink. What else can I say?"

"This whole thing. Pretending . . . that proves you haven't changed. You haven't actually grown up."

We stare at each other for a beat. A silent war waging over what I said. His jaw is stiff, his lips thin.

"So what? You want me to walk away?" he grits so harshly my lower lip trembles. "It's my legacy." He lowers his gaze to the floor, and I watch as his shoulders rise and fall with his intake of oxygen. "How can you expect me to walk away?" When he lifts his stare back up, his green eyes pierce the distance between us, imploring me to understand.

"I don't. I just don't see why you have to do it this way. Why it has to be like this." At my words, his expression stills, the anger fading into a somber look.

"Is it really that awful to spend time with me?" It's unnerving how he looks at me. He looks at me like my words will cut him, and I don't know what to say. I feel tongue-tied and confused.

"No. It's just . . ."

"It's just what?"

"The lie. This, we are deceiving someone you love. Don't you feel bad about that? I feel like a fraud. Lying to my coworkers, to your family, to mine . . ."

His left hand lifts and scrubs at his temples. "I don't feel good about it either, but doesn't the end sometimes outweigh the reason?"

"I'm not too sure. What if you lose a part of yourself along the way?"

"Then you get lost, I guess. Is that really that bad, Tink?" he asks.

"Guess not, Peter. You go get lost in Neverland. I just don't know if I can join you there."

"I can't do this without you . . ."

"I know."

We're both silent for a minute. The room becomes suffocating with the unspoken words. The ramifications of my words hovering over us.

He knows how I feel, but at the same time, I understand how he does. We are at an impasse. The road has already been laid out, and to renege on the deal, well, the consequences would be devastating.

The truth is, as much of a condescending prick that he can be, what I have realized is he's not a bad guy. In fact, he's kind of a good one. He hides behind the asshole persona, but he's been nothing but good to the staff. I'm not sure why his level of assholism was aimed at me, but as soon as I agreed to his crazy plan, he moved out of my office. Sure, he still teases me and sometimes annoys me. Of course he's cocky, but when he's not . . .

When he's just there, working and being himself, he's not that bad.

*And when he kisses you?*

I shove that thought away. No thoughts on kissing him.

I step outside the warehouse. It's dark outside as winter is still upon us. Now it gets dark earlier and earlier. The air is cold; the chill making my body shiver, but the good news is the city isn't as busy now that the work hours are over. It's cleared up, and since most of the foot traffic around here is restaurants and clubs, it won't get busy again until after eight p.m.

I walk a few blocks. I'm not sure where I'm heading, but I just need to breathe. I might not have grown up in the city, but now that I have lived here for the past ten years, the city acts as a balm to my soul. The traffic, the sounds. Hell, the smell of the street vendors. I need the hustle and bustle to right my endless stream of thoughts in my mind. So much plays in my head. The what-ifs. The things I'm missing. The things I'll never have.

Like Nathaniel.

I'll never have a real relationship with him. It's not that I want to, but I can't fool myself into believing that being a single, independent, successful woman is enough.

In the distance, I realize where my feet have taken me. I've been led to my favorite hole in the wall Chinese restaurant. It's nestled between two larger restaurants, and you have to take the dinky stairs down to it. A million health code violations are probably being broken, but it doesn't matter. Their dumplings make everything better.

I walk the steps until I enter the poorly lit counter. "A dozen dumplings," I say and then I wait, pulling out a wad of bills.

Less than ten minutes later, I push open the door to the office. Once again, Nathaniel is not in the office we cleared out for him. He's sitting at the same table dead center in the middle of the space.

He looks up at me, his eyes wide with surprise. I wonder what he's still doing here. "Peace offering," I say as I lift the bag into the air. "I brought dumplings."

"Chinese dumplings?" he asks while lifting his brow.

"Yep."

"Pork?"

"And fried. Only the best," I tease.

"A lady after my own heart."

I let out a laugh, a chuckle really. But it's fake and nervous. His words hit me in the gut after the walk.

"Sit. Join me."

I take the seat beside him, pulling out the dumplings and chopsticks and the signature sauce.

"These are fantastic," he groans as he places one in his mouth.

"I think so too."

"Thank you for this," he says, but by the tone, I think he's talking about something else completely. I put my chopsticks down and gaze into the depth of his eyes. He looks younger, sad. Unsure.

I move my hand to cover his. "You're welcome."

# chapter eighteen

## NATHANIEL

It's Saturday. Tonight, I'm taking Madeline out on a date. Not a real date, obviously, but one merely for the paparazzi's sake. My redemption. My golden ticket. My way to my much-deserved throne.

Picking up the phone, I hit the button when I reach her contact.

"Tink," I say into the phone.

"Is it Saturday already?" she mumbles through the line, and the way she groans makes me laugh. No matter what she says, I know she secretly doesn't hate me. She'll never admit it, but it's still the truth.

"It seems it follows Friday," I retort back, and to that, she lets out an even larger sigh.

"Fine, what's the plan?"

Rising from my sofa, I walk over to my floor-to-ceiling windows and gaze out at the city. It's dark out, the lights of the city sparkling amidst the vastness of winter sky.

"Shall we say nine? First, we'll go to dinner and then to a popular lounge the paps frequent."

"Whatever you say, boss. Your wish is my command," she

deadpans in the most sarcastic voice I've ever heard out of her luscious lips.

"It will be good fun, Tink. Well, have a laugh, a drink . . ." I trail off, letting her imagination fill in the blank.

"We'll have no laughs. One drink and none of that."

"I'll pick you up." Hanging up the phone, I head into my bathroom and hop into the shower. At nine p.m. on the dot, I find Madeline standing outside her building. I made sure to be punctual knowing full well she'd hate it if I were late. And just as I secretly suspected, I was right, and she is standing here waiting. Apparently even early at that.

Swinging open the door, I stand and retrieve her, but not before sweeping my gaze over her.

She looks stunning tonight. Her hair is blown out, long and sleek, and red lips smile a coy smile at me.

I want to kiss her. Have my way with her. I want her writhing beneath me as I thrust inside her.

Her eyes widen as I continue my perusal, and her cheeks turn a warm shade of pink as if she could hear my thoughts.

"Come on," I rasp out, my voice husky with my need.

She walks up to me, and I place my hand on the small of her back before guiding her into the waiting car.

Through the car ride, I stare out the window, needing to tamp down my lust. Instead, I watch as the cars flash by in a series of colors and shapes.

It helps distract me, and by the time we're at the restaurant, I have reined in my lust.

The restaurant is full when we walk in. I suspected it would be, but it doesn't matter. I never have a problem getting a table.

Together hand in hand, we make it over to the hostess. I look at her name tag and smile.

"Lily, I called earlier . . . reservation under Harrington."

Her lip tips up. "Yes, of course. Such a pleasure to have you here tonight," she croaks seductively as if I'm alone. As if Tink isn't next to me. For some reason, the lack of respect for my date bothers me. I pull Tink in closer to me and place a kiss on her head. *I'm with her.* The hostess's cheeks flush.

"Please follow me." She seats us at an intimate table in the back. It's secluded and romantic with lights twinkling from above for ambiance, perfectly setting the tone for what this dinner is supposed to appear to be.

"Is this typical for you?" Tink asks.

"What?"

"Women throwing themselves at you?" She asks this with a straight face, but by the way her shoulders are held tight, I can tell it upsets her.

"Yes." My one-word answer has her eyes opening wide.

"Fantastic. So is there a long string of exes I'll have to bump into? Jaded mistresses, too. Some warning would be nice," she hisses on a whisper.

"Don't get your knickers in a twist. You knew I was no innocent schoolboy already, so this is hardly worth getting cranky over. But no, there are no jaded mistresses."

"And exes?"

I stop and think of how to respond. I should warn her. There is no way we won't bump into Cecile sooner or later . . . but I don't want to.

"Not really," I finally answer.

"That's not *really* an answer."

"Very well. One."

She leans forward onto the table. She clearly wants to know more, and I'm kicking myself for opening this door.

How much do I tell her, though? I'm given a reprieve when the waitress comes over. It's short-lived, though. Once I order for both of us, Tink is right back to staring, and by the way her fingers tap the table, she's waiting.

"I have one ex. We were serious, until we weren't."

"What happened?" Curiosity drips off her in waves. It would actually be quite funny if she was asking about anyone else. But since it's me, and we are talking about Cecile, I don't find it funny at all.

"What normally happens between a man and a woman . . ."

"She wanted more."

"Spot on."

She shakes her head to herself, and I raise my brow. "Oh Peter." She sighs. "Will you ever grow up?"

I force a smile and give her a terse nod. Something about her question today bothers me, and I'm not sure why. Luckily, I don't have to think about it for long because the waitress is already back at the table filling our glasses of wine.

"Let's get pissed." I raise my glass in the air.

"Pissed?" Madeline asks.

"Drunk. Let's get drunk, Tink."

---

And we do. We drink and drink. And drink some more. It's the most fun I've had in a long time. Ever since Olly went back to London, but maybe even further back. It's the most fun I've had since Grandfather summoned me to his study all those months ago and my life changed.

By the time we get to the club, Madeline's draped around my middle as if we were in love.

The cameras love it.

They snap away. Taking in our bodies touching. Taking in the way I hold her close. And when they scream for me to kiss her, I do. Not just because they ask, but because I want to.

I want to kiss her, spend time with her, and be with her for as long as I can.

The thought scares me, but as I drop her home at the end of the night, I know that I'll be calling her tomorrow because I'm not ready to be alone again.

# chapter nineteen

## MADELINE

S UNLIGHT STREAMS IN FROM THE WINDOWS. IT'S EXTRA bright this morning, unlike the usual gloom we've been experiencing recently. Maybe because it's Sunday. As if the weather has cleared up because today is a day just for me. I work Monday through Friday, but the truth of the matter is I work Saturdays too. Today is the day I relax, read, binge-watch Netflix, and pamper myself.

Lifting my arms over my head, I let out a long-drawn-out yawn. How should I start my morning? My stomach grumbles, answering my question. *Bagels? Delivery from the diner?* The idea of bacon, egg, and cheese on a bagel sounds amazing right about now. The sound of my phone vibrating has me reaching over to the side table and grabbing my it.

Across the screen, I see that I have three new text messages.
Who would text me at . . .
I check the time.
8:03 a.m.?
Seriously?
Who would text me at eight a.m. in the morning?
I'm too hungover for this now.

I expect to see my mother's name, or maybe one of my brothers. Hell, I expect to see one from each. But my mouth drops open when I see they all came from one number. The one number I have saved in my phone as the contact Ass.

Nathaniel.

**Ass: Top of the morning to ya, treacle.**

**Ass: Are you ignoring me?**

**Ass: Tink?**

I groan, the noise echoing through the quiet of my room.

**Me: Treacle?**

**Ass: Yes.**

**Me: What the hell does that mean?**

**Ass: Google it.**

Reluctantly I do. I open my phone's Safari app and type in treacle. Images of a thick, sticky dark syrup show up.

**Me: Molasses? What the hell does that mean?**

**Ass: It means you're sweet . . .**

Jeez with this guy. It's too early for this.

**Me: What do you want?**

**Ass: You still haven't said hello back?**

**Me: And I won't.**

**Ass: Hello.**

I throw my phone across the bed, then pick it back up.

**Me: It's Sunday!**

**Ass: So?**

**Me: Leave me alone.**

**Ass: I'm bored.**

**Me: Sounds like a personal problem.**

**Ass: Entertain me.**

**Me: I saw you last night!**

My hand clenches around the phone as I think of a witty

retort, but instead, I come up blank. So I decide to respond with the universal sign of fuck off. An emoji middle finger.

Jumping out of my bed, I hit the cold of the wood floor with my bare feet. It might look beautiful outside, but make no mistake, it's the dead of winter. The chill in the air is apparent once out of the warm confines of my bed.

Quickly, I grab my robe and pull it tight across my body as I make my way into the bathroom. Once I'm done with my morning routine, I head to the kitchen for some coffee and now stand at the counter holding my mug. The freshly brewed coffee tastes amazing. The smell of the robust beans infiltrates my nose with every sip I take, waking every sense in my body.

A sharp pain reverberates through my body. Great. Just great. It's bad enough when the pain starts at work but is it so much to ask for a pain-free Sunday? Placing my mug down, I walk over to the cabinet and quickly take my pills. I probably shouldn't swallow them with coffee. But desperate times. It shouldn't take long for the pain to subside.

Heading into the living room with my coffee in hand, I place it down on the table, grab my heating pad, and kick my feet up. I'm lying there for a while when I hear the phone ding again. The chime indicates an email has come through. Seeing as my email is from work, I don't answer it right away. I actually just stare at it.

It's Sunday.

I don't work on Sunday.

Who am I trying to kid? I work every day. If Val needed me right now, I'd be there. Maybe it's important.

Maybe it's a buyer.

Not on a Sunday.

Fuck it.

I can't help it. My need to know is killing. You know what they say, curiosity killed the cat.

I swipe open the phone and look down.

God. Damn. It.

It's an email . . .

From him.

**Dear Tink.**

**I have decided to refer you to as Tink again. By your lack of response to my previous text message, I have restored your previous pet name. I also implore you to reconsider meeting me for lunch. I am incredibly bored.**

**All the best,**

**Nathaniel**

Seriously. What the actual fuck. He sent me an email and hell no am I responding. I am not spending my first day off in forever with Nathaniel Harrington. No way. No how. Ain't going to happen.

Before I know it, my eyes are fluttering open. The sound of my phone on the side table waking me.

"What?"

"Still no hello?"

"Jeez. Nathaniel. Do you ever stop? And before you tell me you're bored, I'm going to tell you again . . . that's not my problem," I huff.

"I have no one to bother. And now I'm hungry. Do you want to eat?"

I roll my eyes even though he can't see me. "I'm taking a nap."

"First, you were sleeping, and now you're napping. Are you okay?"

"I'm fine, Nathaniel. And as much as I appreciate the offer."

I try to make my voice sound sugary sweet. Honey and all. "I can't. I have an appointment soon. So I'll see you tomorrow."

"Tink—"

"Bye, Nathaniel." I hang up.

All the talk of food has me starved. When I look at the clock, I see I still have a few hours until my standing nail appointment. Pushing up from the couch, I place my heating pad on the table and stand. I'm already feeling a bit better from my nap.

I pad into the kitchen and grab a bagel from the counter and cream cheese from the fridge. Once it's out of the toaster, I recline back in the chair and lift it to my mouth. The first bite is the best bite. It's just a bit salty, and the cheese feels smooth against my tongue. As I swallow, a large sigh of contentment escapes my mouth as if my stomach is thanking me for giving it just what it wanted. I sit eating in silence, and the quiet makes me wonder what Nathaniel is doing.

I don't get it.

Why do I care?

I'm not sure, but what I do know is that I do. It actually makes me feel a little bad for him. Not a lot but a little. I know what it feels like to be lonely. But my heart froze a long time ago, so now I crave the solitude.

A quiet day alone beats everything. Just being able to get up from this table and take a long shower, take my time getting dressed, and enjoy my afternoon is such an amazing feeling that, no matter how bad I feel, I still don't accept his offer.

I spend the rest the day in the same manner, and I'm actually surprised Nathaniel gave up pestering me.

I wonder what he's doing?

Stop.

Just stop.

Don't think about him.

I only have twenty minutes to get to my pedicure appointment. I have given up a lot in my life for my job, but my weekly manicure and my monthly pedicure are two of life's luxuries I continue to indulge in.

When I finally push through the door, I head over to my regular seat. It's quiet today. Normally, a middle-aged woman sits beside me. She has a standing appointment too, but she's not here. Today the chair is empty.

Tanya, my manicurist, fills the tub of water and starts scrubbing my feet. The water feels so amazing that I close my eyes and groan.

"Wow, Tink. If those are the sounds you make every week, I might need to make a standing appointment."

The sound of his voice has my lids opening and turning to him.

There he is. In my place, in the seat beside me, feet in the bowl next to me, getting a goddamn pedicure.

"You have got to be fucking kidding me," I groan. He followed me here. "How?"

His lips tip up, and a large devilish grin plays against his face. He inclines his head in challenge, and then it hits me like a ton of bricks. My calendar. He still has access to my calendar and my schedule. "Do you have any boundaries?"

"Not particularly."

"Not acceptable. You can't keep looking at my calendar," I hiss. My foot jerks in the bowl and causes water to splash out against the floor. "Sorry," I say to the woman kneeling before me, and then I turn back to Nathaniel. "You have to promise to stop."

"Fine. I will." He turns away from me. "I'll take that scrub," he says to the woman doing his pedicure and then looks back at me. "Are you having the sugar scrub? The lady on the phone said they are wonderful."

I stare at him, dumbfounded.

He leans back in his chair and relaxes. He's dressed in his normal laid-back attire. Ripped jeans, that are a bluish-gray shade. A white thermal and his sleeves are pushed up. His forearms are visible and even though he's relaxed his veins are present.

Lord.

Why does he have to be so good-looking?

I only imagine beneath the shirt he's ripped. Even with it on, I can see that he's long and lean. He has the body of a swimmer, and I wonder if he does that often.

I shake my head violently, trying to push aside the image of him wet. Water dripping down his chest, down past his abs until it reaches the V above his swim shorts.

"This water is too hot," I murmur to myself. Because the water has to be the reason I'm flushed, not the erotic images dancing behind my eyes.

He opens his eyes and catches me staring, his lip tipping up into the damn smirk again. "Hot?"

"No."

"Your face says otherwise as do you . . ."

"I meant . . ."

"Yes . . ." His smile broadens.

"Never mind."

"Would you like to get a massage?" a lady asks us both, and I welcome the distraction. Jump on the opportunity, actually.

"No."

"Yes," he says at the same time. "You should have it, too. You seem stressed." He moves his hand in the air and points at me. "She'll have one too."

"I won't," I say to the lady and then turn back to Nathaniel. "And the only reason I'm stressed is because you are ruining my one day," I deadpan.

"Don't be like that. Can't you just relax and enjoy my company? We're going to be spending a lot of time together. This will give us a chance to get to know each other."

"I know everything I need to know."

"Enlighten me, darling."

I open and shut my mouth a few times. He's right. What do I know? Not very much of anything. "You're right."

His eyes widen, and I can see I've shocked him. "How did that feel?"

"How did what feel?"

"Admitting I was right."

I lift my head and cover my face. "You are—"

"I know. I know. Intolerable."

"And here I was going to say a little boy."

"What color would you like on your toes? The usual?" Tanya laughs, knowing full well I'm not going to deviate from the norm.

"What's the usual?"

"Red."

His eyes sparkle. "Interesting. But I think you should do something fun. Paint them green."

"No."

"Live outside your perfect box. Stop being uptight."

"I'm not uptight." Lie. I'm the most uptight person I know. Unless you are my family. Even with as close as I am to Val, I still keep parts of me at arm's length.

"Prove it."

"Fine, pick it . . ." I mutter, knowing full well no matter what he picks, I'll be coming back tomorrow to change it.

"She'll do rainbow."

"What?" I holler.

He lifts a pointed eyebrow. I sigh.

"Fine. There, I'm spontaneous."

When it's over, I have a different color on each toe. It's insane, but the most insane part is I'm laughing. And not just giggling but a full-fledged belly laugh. I don't remember the last time I've laughed this hard.

"I look ridiculous."

"You look cute." He winks. "So where to now?" he asks as he opens the door so we can exit. I pull my coat closer to my body, preparing for the cold.

"We are not going anywhere," I say as I step outside, and my nose instantly scrunches from the chill that hits my face. "You have ruined my relaxing Sunday."

"Does that mean you aren't going to dinner with me?"

I halt my steps, stop, turn around, and then stare at him.

"No. I'm not going to dinner with you. Believe it or not, I do have a life. Albeit small. I have plans." This man is unbelievable.

"But I'm hungry," he whines, pouting his lower lip. *Seriously*?

"Your sad, pouty face will not work on me, Peter." That just makes his lips pout more. He looks adorable. He is not fighting fair.

"I have no one here . . ." He pauses for emphasis. His big green eyes boring into me. "My friends are away . . ." Sigh. "My grandfather is away . . ." Another dramatic pause. "I have no one."

Air escapes my lungs in a long-drawn-out groan. He wins. He always does. I might be ice but even that melts me.

"Fine." I clench my teeth, knowing I'm full of shit. I'm trying to pretend I'm pissed, but I'm not. "You can come with me to my parents' for dinner."

"Great." He smiles. "I'll drive."

Hours later, we're at my parents', and everyone is having fun. Even my parents are laughing at Nathaniel's jokes. He's so laid-back here. It's a whole different side to him. They welcome him into the fold with open arms as if he really were my boyfriend. When the truth is we're barely even friends. But it is easy. I tilt my head, taking him in. He's telling the worst British jokes I have ever heard. I'm not even sure how they are funny, but I think that's the funny part.

"Did you hear about the guy who broke both his left arm and left leg?"

No one says anything as they wait for the punch line.

"He's all *right* now." He laughs, and it elicits a round of chuckles from my dad.

Jeez, that was bad.

"Another one," my mom says cheerfully. Her large smile makes my heart pitter-patter in my chest. It feels natural to have him here, and I like the feeling. Maybe he isn't so bad.

"What do you call a deer with no eyes?" he asks my mom this time.

She shakes her head.

"No eye-deer. What do you call a deer with no eyes and no legs?"

Nothing. Crickets. So his lip tips up into a silly grin.

"Still no eye-deer?" At that, my mom loses it, and hearing her laugh makes me laugh too.

"He's fabulous," I hear from behind me, and I turn to find Eve standing there. "Why have you been keeping him a secret?" Eve asks, tilting her head.

"I haven't been hiding him. It's just new and all." She nods, and then her lip tips up. "He's really hot too."

I look at him. This whole time while I've been laughing, I stopped looking at how hot he was. I was enjoying his personality too much to notice, but now that Eve has called attention to it, I'm gawking. I'm watching as his lips move. His full lips that I know are soft and delectable. I watch as his Adam's apple bobs up and down and remember what he tastes like . . .

"You guys will have beautiful kids."

My back goes ramrod straight at that comment. A poison seeping into me at the thought.

"It's not like that. It's casual." I shrug, trying not to let her words get to me, but they do. I can feel it sweep through my body, into my heart, through my soul.

"Yeah, so were we"—she rubs her stomach—"but look at us now."

"You're different."

"Never say never." But it doesn't matter what she says, or how she says it, it doesn't change the truth, and the truth is there's no future. There's not even a present. This is all a facade. A wicked charade. If they only knew the truth, I wonder what they would say.

My tongue feels heavy with my unspoken words. With nothing more to say, I smile and walk to Nathaniel, who's still entertaining my parents. "I'm ready to go," I whisper.

He leans down to my ear. "Are you okay?"

"Yes. But can we go?"

He nods.

Forty-five minutes later, we are back in the city. The drive was tense, and neither of us spoke. When he pulls up to the side of the road in front of my building, he turns the engine off and faces me.

"A penny for your thoughts."

"I'm just tired," I lie. But the truth is, I can't tell him the truth. That he was too perfect tonight, and I hate it. Seeing my family with him made me hope and dream of a future I won't have.

"Did I do something to upset you? I thought we had a great day," he asks.

"I'm just tired."

He nods and steps out of his car. I'm a bit shocked that he's following me. I didn't expect him to be so chivalrous. "Thank you for today," I whisper. He surprises me when he steps up close and leans down, kissing my cheek. His lips linger for a moment, making me feel warm. I'm still standing there basking in the heat when he pulls away, and with one final smile, he turns to walk away.

Once he's gone, I lift my hand. I can still feel his lips on me. Like he branded me.

I'm sure he did.

# chapter twenty

## NATHANIEL

I'M RUNNING LATE. NOT UNUSUAL, BUT THESE DAYS, I HAVE been turning over a new leaf. I've tossed and turned the last few nights, the sexual tension coursing through my veins keeping me up. Now today, I feel exhausted, and my vision is blurry from the lack of sleep I've been getting.

A block away from the showroom, I stop at the coffeehouse. It's her favorite. I know this because she is a huge pain in the ass over her coffee. The thought makes me laugh. The idea of showing up makes my smile broaden on my face. She is so obnoxious with coffee that I can't wait to show up with it.

No foam, soy mocha latte.

I order quickly and then step off to the side after I pay. Now five minutes later, I'm walking into the door and heading into her office.

"Yes?" she asks, not even looking up from her desk.

"I brought you coffee," I say, lifting it up for her to see.

That gets her gaze to lift. "You don't know how I drink my coffee," she responds, not impressed.

"I know more than you know." I present the steaming cup on her desk. "Try it. I dare you."

"If I drink this, will I die?"

"What good would you be to me if you were dead?" I say with my signature smirk. The one I know drives her insane. The one I can't fucking stop flashing ever since I'd noticed that.

"True story. You need me too much." She lifts one eyebrow as she takes the coffee in her hand. "Smells good."

"Would I lead you astray?"

"Yes."

I nod. "Right. Right. I probably would."

She just holds it to her nose, inhaling. Even from where I'm standing, I can smell her coffee. Robust with a fragrant smell of espresso wafts in the air. "Just drink the damn coffee, Tink."

"God, you drive me crazy."

"I could really drive you crazy if you let me." I smirk.

"You're impossible."

"You've mentioned that already."

"Fine, you're a little boy in a man's body."

"But what a body, huh? Plus, you mentioned that, too."

I cock my head and look at her. Really look at her. Her skin is pale. Dark circles rim her eyes. As tired as she looks, she's still beautiful. Gorgeous really. From where I'm standing, I can see her stifle a yawn as if she hasn't been sleeping. Before I know what I'm doing, I'm stalking in her direction and taking her hand in mine to help her up from her chair.

"What are we doing?"

"We're playing hooky."

"Hooky from what?"

"You've been working too hard."

"Not really . . . this is normal."

"It's not just this, all the nights with me, pretending. I can see it in your eyes. You look exhausted."

"Wow, did you just tell me I look like shit?"

Bollocks, it didn't even dawn on me that it could be construed like that. "Of course not. You could never look like shit. You're beautiful."

Her cheeks turn a warm blush. "Thank you."

"I just think you need some time off, and you've been with me, being photographed. I wanted to . . ."

"I can't play hooky."

"Sure, you can. You're too uptight."

"I am not uptight . . ."

I narrow my eyes at her. "Oh no?" I raise a brow.

"No," she says.

"If that's so, then why don't you tell me what color your toes are?"

"What the hell does that have to do with me being uptight?" She looks down at her feet, thinking I don't see the slight movement of her head. But I do. I know I have her.

"Because I know you went back to the nail salon and changed the color."

"I did not." She shakes her head, but she's not fooling anyone. Madeline Montgomery is too controlled and serious to have not changed the color back to her "normal" color.

"A day of playing hooky says you don't have rainbow toes," I challenge.

"I do," she insists. I plant my feet firmly, and drop to the ground in front of her, about to remove her shoes.

"What color are your toes, Tink?" I ask again.

"Playing hooky sounds great. What did you have in mind?" she says, trying to change the topic.

"Tink . . ."

"Red. Red. Are you happy?"

I start to laugh. "Yes, I am. Now for playing hooky, fancy a trip uptown?"

She lets out a sigh. "Fine. Where to?"

"It's a surprise."

That makes her eyes widen. "I don't like surprises."

"I promise it's a good one."

"Fine." She nods. Together we walk to the entry closet. I pull out her coat and then take mine.

"Thank you," she whispers as she pulls her gloves on and slides her hat on. She looks adorable. Like a child about to play in the snow. Her small stature reminds me of the fairy I so aptly named her after.

"Let's go."

When we step outside, the familiar Mercedes is parked outside.

"Do you ever drive?" She laughs.

"Not if I don't have to. Actually, that's a lie. I love to ride my motorbike, hate to drive cars. You Americans drive on the wrong side of the road."

"So does that mean you only drive in England?"

"If I can get away with it, yes."

She shakes her head in mock shock, and I chuckle.

This time my driver, Roger, is out of the car and waiting to open the back door for us. She scoots in, and I slide in beside her.

"Where to, sir?" Roger asks once he's in the driver seat.

"Rockefeller Center."

"Rockefeller? Really?" Her eyes are wide when she speaks, and she looks like a little child who just entered a candy store.

"You looked like you could use a day of ice skating."

"Do you ice skate?" she asks.

"I do."

She cocks her head, studying me, then nods as she takes the information in.

Through the afternoon traffic, it takes us over thirty minutes to get there. I'm shocked that we're here as we walk to the ice rink and I rent us skates.

"I should probably tell you," she starts, "I don't know how to ice skate."

"Really?"

"Like, at all." She confirms.

"Don't all Americans know how to ice skate?"

"Don't all British people know how to drink?"

"Damn right, we do." I chuckle.

"I think you mean Canadians, anyway."

"Oh, not the same thing?"

She pretends to hurl her bag at me, and I laugh harder at that.

"How do you know how to skate? I thought it rarely snows in England."

"It doesn't snow often, but remember, I might have gone to boarding school there, but I usually spent my winter holiday in New York."

"Right. Right. Your gut-wrenching sad story of a childhood full of magical places and luxurious trips."

"Yes, nothing is lovelier than New York for Christmas, or at least that's what my grandfather said."

"I never knew my grandparents, but yours seems lovely. Your grandfather has always been nice."

"He's a solid bloke."

She nods. "You're lucky to have him."

"Even if I'm an utter arse half the time?" I wink.

"Yes, even when you're an arse," she jokes. The sound of her laughter dances over the chill in the air, warming a place inside me I didn't even realize was cold.

"Come on."

"I'm not sure . . ."

"I got you, Tink. I won't let you fall."

Together, we wobble on even ground to the rink, and I step on first, holding her hands in mine to help her onto the ice. She falters, but with my arms now tightly wrapped around her, I don't let her fall. Just as I told her, I have her. She lets out a puff of air, her shoulders uncoiling.

She pushes off with one foot and then tries to pretend she's not scared. It's cute. But I can see past her false bravado. I can see the tightness of her jaw and the lights that crinkle beside her blue eyes.

"I got you," I coo again. "Push off with your left foot. Here . . . wait." I release her hands, letting her stand there like a little lost doe, then turn to face her, looking deep into her eyes. "Like this. Push off."

"Are you going to skate backward?"

"Indeed."

"Show-off."

"Always."

I start to skate backward, and like that baby doe taking her first step, she's wobbly, adorable, and most of all, enchanting.

In all aspects of her life, she's in control. But right now, she relinquishes her control and gives me all her trust, and I have never felt anything so empowering in my life.

Being this woman's rock is invigorating.

Blindly, she skates. Her movements are off balance, but there is no longer stress. She knows I have her, and I won't let her go.

And I don't.

As we move farther into the ice rink, I never let her go. She's bundled tightly in her coat, her little nose bright pink, but thirty minutes later, she's shivering, so we head back to the benches.

"I'll be right back," I say and step away as she pulls off her skates.

After making my way to a vendor to buy hot chocolate and then heading back, she smiles. A real genuine smile, one I wasn't expecting but am happy I got.

"Thank you for today," she says as she puts her mouth to the cup. She sips slowly, the little bit of skin exposed by her throat bobbing as she swallows.

"This is delicious and perfect."

I want to say like you, but I don't. I hold it back, not wanting to confuse what we are doing right now. As wonderful as she is, this can't be more. I've been hurt once, and I'm not willing to be hurt again.

She takes another sip, and I smile. "Let's head back to the car."

"Time to leave Neverland," she responds, her voice low and full of an emotion I can't place. It's almost as if she sounds sad, somber.

"Not yet." I smile, and at my words, her eyes widen. Her lip turns up, and her shoulders relax. She didn't want today to end either.

"Lead the way."

# chapter twenty-one

## NATHANIEL

I HATE THAT I HAVE TO GO TO THIS EVENT. IT'S A BIRTHDAY, and when your best mate has a birthday, you go. The biggest problem is, Madeline isn't with me.

It's not that I need her. We have taken enough pictures to appease the paparazzi, to appease my grandfather and hopefully the board, but I've gotten used to having her around at these functions.

It's almost as if she keeps me in check.

Almost.

I reach for my coat and head out the door. My driver is off duty since it's Friday night, and technically, this isn't a work function. That and, the truth is, he's on my grandfather's payroll. I don't need the questions.

Questions never lead to anything good.

I walk to the end of the street. Little flakes of snow drift down, landing on my nose. I love the first day after it snows.

Pristine.

Clean.

And most of all, enchanting.

Images of Tink float through my head. Her skating. Her

cheeks rosy from the cold.

I lift my hand, and a cab pulls up.

I fire off the address of the ultra-posh club where Olly is having his party. The city flashes by in a series of bright lights and yellow cabs. I love the city, but I miss London. Pretty soon, the whole team will be flying down for the meetings I set up. The idea of showing my London to Madeline has my lips spreading into a smile.

When we reach Soho House, I pay the cab and then provide my membership information to gain entrance. I might give Olly shit for being such a pretentious arse and having his party here, but I'm a member too.

Frequenting private clubs is how we grew up.

When I walk into the private room, Olly, who apparently is never leaving America, greets me with a hug and a pat on the back.

"Glad to see you're alive."

"Not everyone gets to live the life of leisure," I jest.

"I do work," he deadpans.

"Work on what, shagging every American on your visit?"

"It's hard work." He shrugs.

"And someone has to do it."

"It's my royal duty," he jests.

"You're not the crown prince."

"I'm in line for the throne . . ." He laughs even though there is truth to his words.

"Thirty-one people have to die to see you get that crown."

"Thirty-three," he corrects, and I lift a brow. "My cousin had twins."

"Congratulations." I lift my eyebrow. "Or should I say my condolences?"

"Congratulations. You know I hate that shit."

"I do."

"Let's grab you a libation."

"After you." He flags over a server and orders us two shots of tequila. I appreciate it's not a scotch or whisky. I need something stronger tonight.

"When in America . . ." He lifts his glass.

"Yes, when," a soft voice coos from beside me.

I turn around and see her in the flesh. Cecile. It's like I came to America, and everyone followed. She slides over seductively and thrusts her breasts out as she leans toward me. "So good to see you, Nate. Olly told me you'd be here."

"Funny, he never mentioned *you* would." I shoot him daggers, and he stifles a laugh.

She lifts her hand and playfully touches my arm. "Oh, don't be like that." She drags her nails down my skin. "Aren't you happy to see me?" The feeling of her hand on my skin makes my back tighten. I haven't felt her touch in a long time, and it takes me off guard.

I lift her hand and remove it, and she scrunches her nose, a gesture I used to think was cute, but now I'm too perplexed by what is happening to even understand.

"Don't you miss me?" she asks, confusion evident in her voice.

It's like I'm in the twilight zone right now. I have no idea what's happening. Did I take a time machine? This isn't the same girl I saw at the event a few weeks back. This is not my happily married ex.

"Where is your husband?"

She shrugs.

"Trouble in paradise?"

"You could say that. I found him in bed with Monica . . ."

Her best friend.

"Funny how sleeping with someone's best friend is in bad taste." It might have been in bad taste to say that in public, but she *did* shag my friend and then marry him.

She cowers at my rebuttal. "I guess I deserve that."

"You guess?"

"Okay, I do, but I was wrong."

I stare at her as if she has two heads. Is this really happening?

"We were good together—"

"Save it."

I walk away, leaving her mouth hanging agape at the bar. I find Olly and then walk over to him. "I'm leaving."

"I should have warned you."

"Yes, you should have."

I turn without another word and leave.

I'm outside, the cold blasting my face. I don't know what to do. Where to go. My hands find my mobile before I can think twice.

**Me: Where are you?**

**Tink: At my apartment.**

I imagine her at her flat. Is she alone? Did I interrupt? The thought makes my blood boil, and I continue down a path I'm not sure where it will lead.

**Me: I need you.**

**Tink: ?**

**Me: We need a picture op**

**Tink: But you said I had the weekend off.**

**Me: I did, but I changed my mind.**

I see her type.

. . .

183

And then erase.

Then type . . .

I wonder what my fiery little Tink is going to say.

Then finally, it pops up.

**Tink: When and where.**

**Me: Lux Lounge**

**Tink: Fine.**

A smile spreads across my face. This is exactly what I need. I'm not sure what it is about her, but when she's around, everything seems a little better. And I got what I want.

The perfect little distraction.

I'm at the bar waiting when I feel her presence. I don't actually feel it as much as I smell it.

Lilacs.

They float through the space, tickling my nose. One would think that at a lounge at ten p.m. on a Friday night, I wouldn't be able to smell her, but those people have not met Tink. She's intoxicating.

I turn to look at her. Or look down at her. My six-foot-two frame dwarfs her five-foot-two petite body. Even with the heels she's wearing, she's still almost a foot shorter than me. I look down and chuckle to myself. She must be wearing at least four inches, but she still looks small enough that I can put her in my pocket.

She's exactly what I needed right now. Something about Tink calms me, which is funny, seeing as our relationship started with a sparring match. But that's changed now. She's become more than that to me. I'm not sure when it happened, but somewhere along the line, I have started to consider her an alliance and now a friend.

Without a second thought, I crash my mouth to hers. A

moan escapes her, but then she relaxes into the kiss and allows me to take over, to push harder, to plunder her mouth with mine. As the kiss continues, Madeline sweeps her tongue in my mouth. Our tongues begin a battle for possession. It's desperate. It's filled with so many conflicting emotions. Want. Desire. And most of all, hate. As if she wants this but doesn't at the same time. Finally, she pushes off me, and I grin down at her.

"What was that for?"

"What?"

"The kiss. Was someone watching?"

I furrow my brow. Shocked and dazed. "Yes," I mutter, allowing the lie to slip off my tongue.

No one was watching.

I just needed her.

I needed her more than I needed air to breathe.

# chapter twenty-two

## NATHANIEL

TONIGHT IS THE NIGHT. THE HARRINGTON FUNDRAISER. The whole board will be here. Photographers will be here. My grandfather will be here. Everyone who is anyone will be here.

Her chestnut brown hair is swept up, showcasing her long and elegant neck. Tonight, she's taller. Not the usual pixie I have grown accustomed to. Tonight, I imagine the heels she wears beneath the hem of the long gown are high. I stifle a groan; she's beautiful, gorgeous, and completely stunning tonight.

That's the thing about Tink. I shouldn't want her, but I do. I can't help it. At first, I thought she was a pest, but the more I get to know her, the more and more I like about her. This whole situation isn't easy, and she has handled herself with nothing but grace at every turn.

I let my gaze trail over her. She's always been pretty, but today, she's otherworldly. I know this is fake and that each kiss is well orchestrated—well, other than the one last week—but the desire to be more drifts over me.

Shocking me.

I never thought I would want that. But the idea holds some

merit right now.

*No.*

I can't allow myself to get swept up by her beauty or my desire for her. This is an arrangement and nothing more. I don't want to settle down, and I have no desire to let myself fall for someone right now. There is too much on my plate as it is.

She looks up at me, a timid smile ghosting her face. It's her eyes, though, and the way they look at me. It knocks me in the chest, making my heart thump rapidly.

I don't understand the feeling, but when she looks at me like that, I feel as though I can't breathe. She looks at me as if I'm more than I am. As though she sees me, and I'm her savior. Which is ridiculous because I can barely save myself.

"You look lovely," I say, my voice husky. When her cheeks turn a warm shade of red, I know she hears the desire in my tone, and that's okay. The color suits her, and when we step inside the room, it will bode well for us to have this attraction. As hard as it is to calm, it will be good for us for everyone to see how much I want her. Desire her. Need her. I shake my head at myself.

I don't need anyone.

"Thank you, so do you," she whispers.

I'm taken aback by her. This woman beside me is unlike the self-assured woman from the office. She seems more timid now, unsure. It's strange how much I have gotten to know her at work, yet I have never seen this side of her. I don't necessarily understand it, but I want to calm her nerves.

Stepping up to her, I place a kiss on her soft lips. She exhales a breath.

"What was that for?" The blush on her skin spreads down her jaw, now painting the hollow of her neck.

Down.

Down

Down.

All the way to the swell of her breast, making my own body come alive as I peer down and take her in.

I let my lip tip up. "I kissed you because I wanted to." Then without letting her say anything, I take her hand and tug her to the door. She follows, more like trails slowly. When I glance back, I can't help but chuckle. She looks dazed. Confused. To be honest, she also looks turned on as all fuck.

My eyebrow lifts, and I wonder if I stopped right now and kissed her again, if maybe, just maybe she'd let me have my way with her right here in the hallway.

Unfortunately, I can't see if my assumptions are correct. The event is about to start, and we are already late.

I slow my pace and allow her to catch up, still hand in hand, until she's finally beside me. I release her hand and secure my arm around her waist.

"Ready?" I ask.

"As ready as I'll ever be," she groans.

I'm prepared. And I have prepared Madeline. Well, as much as you can prepare anyone before you throw them into the lion's den without a weapon. But that's where she's wrong. That's where everyone is wrong. Madeline doesn't need a weapon because she is one. *She's mine.*

Arm in arm, we enter the ballroom to The Lancaster Hotel. When we step inside, I see Madeline's eyes go wide. She was here a few weeks ago, but this room has been transformed.

The plush trees and vines decorating the space remind me of the Garden of Eden, and if this is Eden, then Madeline is Eve because as I watch her eyes widen in wonder, I realize she is the temptation to man. I gulp down the desire brimming at the surface. Temper it and pull her closer.

"It's beautiful."

"It is," I respond. Not bothering to look away from her, I make it clear by my perusal what is beautiful in my eyes. I watch her swallow at my words.

"Let's go find my grandfather," I say. Walking us farther into the room, I spot him in the corner. He has a few members of the board around him. No one Madeline has met yet. These men were not at the meeting; they flew in for this event, though.

When we step up to them, my grandfather smiles while the two middle-aged gentlemen ogle my girl. Fury rises within me; no one can look at her but me.

*But why?*

*She isn't really yours. She's not your girl.*

They don't know that, though, and I tell myself that's why I'm mad. I tell myself it's not that I want her to be mine; it's that I don't like them disrespecting me.

"Tobias, Richard," I say as I extend my hand in greeting. One by one, I shake their hands before I step back and turn toward Madeline. "This is my girlfriend, Madeline." Tobias steps up first, taking her hand and lifting it to his mouth. My back stiffens, and I hate the response I'm having to his touching her. When he moves away and Richard does the same, kissing her hand, I stake my claim right then and there. Placing my hand on her waist again, I trail my fingers down the curve of her hip and pull her closer, so close that our bodies merge into one. My grandfather is last to approach her; he looks at her warmly.

"It's so nice to have you here," he says, but he makes no move to take her hand or pull her away from me. Instead, he looks at where my hand is wrapped around her and smiles. He actually smiles. A genuine smile of approval of my possession of her. "You look lovely as always, my dear."

"Thank you, sir."

"Please call me Nathaniel."

"Okay, Nathaniel," she says to him, a sweet and innocent smile lining her face. She looks like a little girl right now. Young, innocent, and sweet. Like a pixie. I move my head closer to her ear and whisper, "Would you like to dance?"

She shivers as my words fan over her skin. "Yes."

"Excuse me, gentlemen, but it seems this enchanting woman would like to dance with me." Without waiting for their response, I pull her toward the crowded dance floor. Together, we slowly sway our bodies, allowing the orchestra to transport us away from the crowd and into our own world. Splaying my hand across her back, I pull her so close that the swell of her breasts touch my chest.

"How was I?" she whispers.

"Perfect."

"Those men . . ." She starts but trails off.

"They are arseholes," I grit. If I despised them before, I really hate them now after the way they leered at what's mine.

*Mine.*

My voice plays in my ear. A need to claim her drifts over me, and before I know what I'm doing, I'm sealing my mouth over hers again. I have no idea what's come over me, but it's like I need to brand my body to hers to tell all the men in the room that she's not available. Even though technically she is.

I feel crazed.

*Like Adam.*

She is my own personal Eve right now, and truth be told, I don't even hate it.

"You keep kissing me," she states, "but everyone already knows that I'm yours."

"I'm just trying to remind them," I huff out, pushing down the feeling . . . *she makes me completely irrational.*

"You're doing a good job. Your cousin is glaring at me from across the room." She tilts her head in the direction to where he must be standing.

"Let him glare." I pull her tighter to me. There is no space between us now.

"Aren't you nervous about how he will react to us?"

"No," I say flatly. *I'm too busy wanting you to care.* I don't say that, though, because it makes no sense. Needing a distraction from my thoughts about Tink, I pull her closer and whisper in her ear. "See that lady to your left?"

"Which one?" she whispers back as her head turns slightly to peer around.

"The one with the yellow ball gown."

"The one that looks like a banana?" She laughs, and I love the sound.

"Yes, that one."

"She's having an affair with her stepson." I can feel her inhale of breath.

"No way."

"Indeed." I chuckle as I look down at her. Her big blue eyes are wide, and a large smile showcases her white teeth. It's such a broad smile, it's like the sun is shining on me, blinding me. *I need to make her smile more.*

"What else do you have?" This time, her gaze is mischievous. So I give her what she wants, and as we dance, I fill her in on all the drama, gossip, and dirty deeds of the elite crowd surrounding us. When the song is over, I walk us back to grab a drink.

Madeline excuses herself to go to the ladies' room, and I stand by the bar, waiting my turn.

"Wow, she's stunning," I hear from beside me. Turning toward the voice, I see two men openly gawking at Tink. I don't like it. I want to pull her toward me, fling my arm around her, and tell them she's mine. But that would attract the wrong type of attention. I need to react above reproach, not like a caveman. So I temper down my feelings and lift my glass to my mouth. With each gulp, my anger fades but my need for her to return peaks.

"Nathaniel," I hear from beside me.

"Cecile." Not wanting a confrontation, I head toward the hallway where the bathrooms are. When I hear heels clicking, I know Cecile has followed me. "What do you want?" I ask her, stopping my pace and leaning against the wall.

"She's adorable," she says, and I know she is talking about Tink. Her own five-foot-ten stature makes Madeline seem like a tiny pixie beside her. Where Madeline is small and petite, Cecile is her polar opposite with long sun-kissed hair, large pouty lips, tall stature, and rail thin.

"Yes, she's rather special to me." My words are curt, and I hope the meaning filters into her. I'm here with Madeline.

"She's lucky to have you," she says, placing her hand on my arm.

I glare down at where her skin touches mine. "What are you doing, Cecile?" I raise an eyebrow.

"I'm sorry," she says as she lifts it. "I just . . ."

"You just what? Is the ink even dry on your divorce?"

She swallows and bites her upper lip. "I was wrong."

"Wrong about what?" I can't believe I'm even humoring

her by asking that question. I don't give a bloody care in the world what she's wrong about. But for some reason, I allow social graces to take over and ask the question I don't care to hear the answer to.

"Wrong about everything. You." She gestures between us. "Me. I thought—"

"What did you think?"

"I thought you would never settle down. I thought you would always be a boy, but I was wrong about you. Seeing you here. Seeing you with her. I realize I was wrong."

Her words make me falter, and I don't notice that she's upon me, so close that now I feel her hands on my chest. "What are you doing?" I grit, staring down at where she's touching me. Hating her hands on me. The warmth that should spread doesn't. It doesn't feel like it does when Tink touches me.

"I want another chance." She steps in until her chest almost touches mine. She rises to her toes and hovers so close, too close. I need to push her away, but muscle memory has me standing there frozen in place, remembering a time before. Her hands trail down my chest, and it wakes me from my stupor.

"Stop." I grab her hands, stopping her movements.

"Nathaniel," I hear, and my back goes ramrod straight. Turning toward the new voice, I see Madeline staring at us. Her mouth is hanging open, her eyes wide with a mixture of emotions.

Anger.

Betrayal.

Sadness.

But why?

"Leave," I hiss, pushing Cecile back. She stumbles on her heel but rights herself quickly before whispering, "Sorry," and scampering off.

Madeline stares at me for a beat. Her cheeks sucked in. I try to read what's playing behind her big blue eyes, tilting my head to get a better view, but she blinks it away too fast. It's no longer there.

"Friend of yours?" She lifts an eyebrow.

"No."

"Didn't seem that way."

"You're right." I sigh. "That was my ex. Cecile."

She nods as if this exchange means nothing, and for some reason, I want her to argue. I want her to fight. I want her to show she feels something. But she doesn't. Instead, she takes a step to leave.

"Since your grandfather saw us, I'm going to punch my card. I'm leaving . . ."

"Stop." My voice is forceful, but she doesn't stop, her heels clicking on the floor as she gains speed.

"Go away," she mutters.

"Let me explain," I implore. I'm not sure why I'm chasing her because it shouldn't matter what she thinks.

But it does. It matters so much more than I want to admit.

"No need. We're fine. I'll see you tomorrow." She's halfway down the hall, but I'm gaining on her.

"I said stop." This time she listens, halting her steps and turning back to face me.

We are at a standstill. I don't speak, and neither does she. We're both waiting for the other to say something.

"If you have her, why the charade?" Madeline finally says, straightening her back. I watch as the curtain falls over her emotions and features, and she presents me with the front, the charade that gave her the nickname "Ice Queen" at work.

"I don't want her." I shrug like what she just witnessed was no big deal. Because it's not, and I can't afford for her to think it is. Nothing has been further from the truth. There is no way I would want Cecile.

Not with Madeline in my arms.

"Didn't seem that way to me," she retorts, and the defiance in her voice makes me want to show her just how wrong she is. So I do. I step in close to her until her back hits the wall.

"You think I want her?" I press myself against her, and as I move closer, my cock hardens against her. "Don't you feel this? This wasn't there before. Do you feel how much I want you?" I pull back and look into her blue eyes. A myriad of emotions plays back. There's fire. There's ice. Two opposing forces wage war against each other. "You drive me mad," I grit out.

"I drive you mad?" she hisses. "You were the one with someone touching you. Not me."

I take her hand and lead her down the hall, deeper into the hotel. I'm not sure where I'm taking her until the familiar door of the conference room comes into view. I pull her in. She steps back, and back, and back until her legs hit the table with a thud.

"All I can think about is you." I move until my legs press against hers. "All I can dream about is you." I take my hands and lift the hem of her dress until it pools at her hips. My fingers press against her upper thigh, digging into her skin. Her breathing comes out in short bursts of air, her eyes completely dazed at what is happening. "I imagine how it would feel to be inside you." I lean in. She leans back until her weight balances on her elbows. "Do you imagine it?" I move forward, placing my face in the crook of her neck, my lips against the shell of her ear. "Do you wonder what my cock would feel like?" I whisper.

"Yes."

That's all the invitation I need.

I swipe my tongue out and taste her skin. It starts a trail down her neck, across her jaw, and up until my mouth fuses with hers. She opens on a sigh, and I take full advantage of the situation, pressing my tongue into her mouth.

"Spread your legs," I command. She does as instructed, making me smile. I smile a wicked smile as I crouch down, and she shivers some more.

I lean forward, inhaling her essence, and then with a swipe of my tongue, I taste it. I taste her need. I taste her desire. It's intoxicating. *The sweetest elixir.* I can't get enough. My tongue runs a trail. Up and down. Tasting every inch of her. With each swipe of my tongue, she moans out in pleasure. Music to my ears. She's begging for more. I don't answer her mewls right away. No, I draw it out, needing her to fall apart before I fuck her. I lap at her once, twice, and on the third swipe of my tongue, she's convulsing. But that doesn't stop my ministrations; I devour her as she comes down from her high.

"Fuck me," she pants on a whisper.

"Are you sure?" I say while I grab a condom from my trousers.

"Yes," she groans, so I push back from where I'm perched and start to unzip my pants. With fast work, I roll it over my dick and spread her until she's open for me.

I place myself at her entrance, and then with one quick thrust, I'm inside. She gasps at the sudden invasion, her walls tightening around my length. Once fully sheathed inside her, I pause, allowing her to accommodate me, but instead, she lifts her hips.

"Oh, God. P-please," she begs, so I give her what she wants. But at the pace I want. The need to torture her is all I can think about as I slowly drag my cock out and let it hover at the entrance before sliding back in painfully slow. When I pull out again and try to continue the slow, leisurely pace with her spread before me on the table of a conference room in The Lancaster, she is having no part of it. Instead, Madeline lifts her hips, pulling me deeper inside her.

*It feels sublime.*

With that, I pump harder. Faster. Eager to give her everything she wants.

*Needing to.*

Picking her hips up with my hands, I have her angled just the way I want. My dick throbs as she squeezes it, milking it. I shudder at the sensation as she swivels underneath me, showing me how desperate she is to find release. I love it.

I love the sounds she makes, so I pull out again and wait for her groan of displeasure. When she answers me with a long, primal moan, I then let myself slip back inside her.

In. Out. In. Out.

Her hips push back as I thrust myself inside her. As her breathing becomes frantic, I place my finger on where I know she needs it and massage her in time with my cock. I'm so close, but I need her to fall over the edge first. I press harder and firmer against her with one hand as my left hand moves to her breast, palming it and tweaking the nipple.

"More," she begs.

"You want me to fuck you harder?" I swivel my hips and she answers my question with a desperate groan.

I pick up my pace and she mewls with satisfaction. *Message read loud and clear.* My thrusts become harder, deeper. Now moving in sync, our hips meet thrust for thrust. It's not long before I feel my balls tighten, and my vision goes spotty from the impending orgasm. I can't hold it much longer. I increase my speed until I feel her flutter around me and only then do I release everything I've got into her.

# chapter twenty-three

## MADELINE

THE WORLD STARTS TO COME BACK INTO FOCUS THROUGH the haze of my orgasm. Suddenly, I'm back in the present, and as that comes crashing down around me, so does the nature of what just happened. I'm in a conference room, on a boardroom table, in The Lancaster. My dress is bunched at my hips, and Lord knows where my panties are. My lids flutter shut again, but the cold bite of the table under me is a constant reminder that even when I close my eyes and wish it were different, I'm still on the table and he . . . Nathaniel Harrington is still inside me.

"Tink," he says softly. "Open your eyes."

I do, and what I see is an emotion I can't place. As soothing as his words are trying to be, it's his eyes that take me aback. If possible, they are softer than the tone of his voice, like soft green moss after a storm. Dewy from the heat, vibrant and alive. It's funny when you think about it, the color perfectly depicts this moment. Isn't that what this was, a storm? It battered down hard, broke down my resistance, but now that it's passed, and the skies have cleared and are back to normal, I can't help but think what the hell did we just do?

So I say exactly that.

"What the hell did we just do?"

"Tink . . ." he says again, and I shake my head back and forth, hoping, praying that I will wake up from whatever this is. A dream? A nightmare? Both at the same time? I push at his chest, and he places his hands on the table and lifts off me and out of me. Instantly, I miss the feeling of him inside me. I feel vacant and needy, and I hate it. I narrow my gaze as I push my own body up to sitting and glare at him.

"No," I say as he buttons his pants after discarding the condom and tucking himself back in. "Don't '*Tink*' me. What the hell did we just do?"

"Something we should have done a long time ago, Tink," he says as he leans down and stands back up, holding my discarded underwear in his hand. He looks down at the little scrap of lace and smirks.

"Don't smirk," I grit out through my clenched jaw.

He tries to keep a straight face as I stand, grab my underwear from his hand, and try as graceful as possible to put them back on, all while still wearing my heels. When I start to topple over, I'm met with a big laugh and an arm reaching around me so I don't crash to the floor.

I'm completely and utterly mortified right now, and he won't stop laughing.

"Don't. Just don't." My hands lift to cover my eyes as if I'm trying to remove the memory of what just happened from my head.

That stops him, so I remove my hands and look up. His features straighten as he takes his fingers and lifts my chin. "Relax, Tink. It's really not a big deal."

*It's really not a big deal*, he says.

*Ass.*

It's a huge deal.

I never have sex. Haven't had sex in over a year.

*This isn't me.*

I want to scream these things at him. I want to hit him in the chest and tell him to stop smirking at me. That, believe it or not, I never allow myself to get lost in the moment, and I never allow myself to have sex, let alone have sex in public.

But I will not do that. Nor will I say any of that. Because I can't let him see this side of me. I lost control, something I never like to do, so I won't let him see me fall. Instead, I take a deep breath, square my shoulders, and look up at him. "I'm going to go to the bathroom and clean up. Then we can go back in."

His eyes widen at my fast change of attitude. I've shocked him.

Good.

I've shocked myself for my careless behavior, but now, I'm back in control. Without another word, I walk away from him, out the door, and back down the hallway that started this mess. I see from the corner of my eye the place where he was with her. A strange feeling of jealousy and possession start to spread through my body, but I squash it down like a bug.

I will not be that person.

From behind me, I hear footsteps and know he's followed me.

"I'll be back," I say over my shoulder as I walk toward the bathroom and push the door open. First, I head into the stall, and when I'm done, I wash my hands and stand in front of the mirror. My cheeks are rosy, and although my hair is still pulled back, small wisps have fallen. I try my best to calm them, but there isn't much hope. I look freshly fucked.

Nothing I can do about it now. If anything, maybe this will work to our advantage. If I put on a good show in front of the board, maybe I'll buy myself some freedom in the upcoming week. Maybe there will be no need for more "appearances." With one more glance at myself and a fresh coat of lipstick, I step out and take his hand. He looks down at where our fingers are locked. Eyes wide.

"All part of the act," I say, and I swear he lets out a breath.

As if I would read more into it. As if I would want more.

*You would,* a small voice says inside me. But once again, I move to kill that thought. There is no place for that type of thinking here. The sex was a one-off, and I refuse to allow myself to think about it one more time.

"Lead the way," I say, my voice leveled again as if I have no cares in the world. When he doesn't move, I lead the way back into the lion's den, but this time, I'm playing the part even more, a part I'm playing for myself as well. A part of not only a girl in a relationship but to him the part of a girl who doesn't care.

---

I have tried my hardest to act normal after the "conference room" incident, but I don't think I'm doing a very good job. To be honest, I'm probably doing a piss-poor job.

Day one, I avoided him like the plague.

Day two, he walked into the room, and I walked out . . . again avoiding him like the plague.

Day three wasn't much different from day one and two.

Okay, if I'm being completely honest, avoidance has actually been my go-to plan since the fundraiser. I didn't even stay around long enough to find out how much was raised, and I haven't asked. That would require speaking to Nathaniel, and I'm not sure I can after . . .

Now that I have lost control, I'm trying my hardest not to let that happen again. I have a feeling that if I was ever alone with him again, we'd have a repeat performance. Why? Because every damn time I see him, my heart races, and the need to have him touch me consumes me. I hate the feeling of losing control.

There are some things in life you can't control. I'm well versed in these things, so when it comes to things under my control, I do not relinquish it. Ever. Except that one time.

Shit.

Just thinking about that one time has me standing from my desk and pulling at my sweater to get some air.

"Hot?" I hear from behind me. There is no need to turn around to know who has entered my office and caught me fanning myself.

It's him.

The man whose face has been playing on repeat in a very naughty, very detailed movie in my mind.

"It's a bit hot in here," I say with a shrug.

"Is it?" His eyebrow rises. "Funny, Valentina has her winter coat on in the common room. Apparently, the heat is broken." He smiles. *He fucking smiles.* Not only did he catch me with my eyes closed, fanning myself, but he also just caught me in a lie.

A very obvious lie, apparently.

"Well, it just might be my office then . . . it's obviously hot in here."

"Hmm, strange. It doesn't feel hot. Actually, it feels quite . . . frigid."

The way he says the word frigid has my stomach dropping.

Is he trying to imply I'm frigid? No. He wouldn't do that. Would he?

"From what I can tell, it's more often cold in here than not." He crosses his arms in front of his chest, blocking my door, not allowing me to walk away.

I glare at him. Then at the door.

"Plotting your escape, Tink?" he muses with a chuckle.

"Maybe," I say, grinding my teeth together. In order to leave, I'd have to go through him. I'd be too close. So close that his delicious smell will penetrate me and make me weak. Cinnamon. Coffee. A faint hint of the leather jacket he wears even when it snows.

You would never think he was the heir to a billion-dollar fortune. Even now, in his white thermal and ripped jeans, he doesn't come across as anyone's heir. The only reason I know it's true, know he has been born and bred for this, is the way he fills out a three-piece suit or a tuxedo when the moment calls for it.

Today, here, it obviously doesn't.

"What seems to be the problem?" he asks, pulling me out of my inner rambles. Something I have done far too often since the first time he kissed me.

Chewing on the inside of my cheek, I wonder how I'll answer. I can't tell him that being this close to him sets me spinning. That he sucks all the air from the room, and I'm stuck without oxygen. Being near him is too much for me. It makes me think of leaning into him, raising my arms up, and touching the stubble on his jaw.

It makes me weak.

I don't do weak.

"There's too much on your mind. Won't you talk to me?" he asks, and I snap out of my stupor, startled to see that he's caged me. He's left the space within the doorjamb, and he's now standing directly in front of me. I look around, wondering if anyone sees how close we are.

"No one is here," he says. His voice, deep and rich, drips like chocolate over a succulent strawberry.

He bends, leaning down until his head is level with mine.

He's only a breath away.

"Do you want me to kiss you?" Each word from his mouth tickles my parted lips.

"No," I whisper, but my voice betrays me yet again.

"Is that so?" His lips are almost on mine. If I closed my eyes, I would think they were already upon me.

"Yes," I answer louder. So loud that it's as if I'm trying desperately to believe my own words.

*God.*

He's close. Too damn close.

I allow my eyes to close. If they close, I can pretend. Pretend I'm not here. Pretend I'm not losing control.

"Good. Because I won't," he states.

My eyes spring open, and he's no longer standing in front of me. He's stepped aside, allowing a clear path to the exit.

I let out the air in my lungs, wringing it out as if I'd been holding it this whole time. Maybe I was.

And I don't like it.

---

This is how it goes for the rest of the week. He teases; I avoid. It's ridiculous, and to be honest, I'm sick of it. It takes every bit of composure by Friday for me not to beg him to fuck me again already.

There is only so much a girl can take. Small touches at the

coffee machine. Public kisses in front of the staff. I'm a panting beast by Friday with a need for release. So, unlike most weeks when Lucy asks if I want to go to happy hour, I'm quick to say yes.

As soon as the words fall from my mouth, I see him smirk. Nathaniel is loving the fact I'm so stressed out. He knows I'm ignoring him; he also knows that his every quip is weakening my resolve.

"Let's go." He takes my hand in his and walks to the closet. He helps me slip into my winter coat and then loops his arm through mine. It's snowing out, so I hold on tightly as we walk down the block over the sleek city streets to get to the bar.

"Be careful," I hear him say a second too late as my foot slides forward on a piece of black ice. As I feel myself lurching forward, his arm tightens and the other wraps me toward him. Air from my lungs billows out in a cloud of cool air as my pulse picks up from the near fall.

"I got you," he whispers, and I look up at him. He's leaning down and hovering above me. He holds me so tight that my movements are limited. "Where do you think you're going?" he coos as I try to push away.

"I can walk."

"Can you?" he teases, and I roll my eyes.

"I have been managing to walk by myself for thirty-some years. I think I can handle a little snow."

"It's obvious that you can handle a little ice . . ." His words are leading, and I'm not sure what he's saying. Is he still making fun of me and my title of Ice Queen? Or is he giving me shit for almost falling? Doesn't matter. I refuse to let him rile me up today. He helps me straighten back up, and I drop my hands from him as I carefully maneuver my way through the street, pedestrians, and cars to get to our location.

Once we are inside, I don't even bother to see if he's entered before I head to the bar.

"Champagne?" he asks from beside me.

I turn my head to the left and shake it. "Tequila."

"Oh, it's one of those days." He smirks. "Stressed about something . . . or *someone*?" His green eyes gleam at me with mischief. He knows what he's doing to me, and to make matters worse, he moves his body closer, lifts one hand in the air to get the bartender's attention, all while placing the other hand around my hip until our bodies are flush.

"What are you doing?"

"Keeping up pretense." He shrugs.

"No one is here yet," I remark, looking around the room. "We are the only people from the office here, and please do not pretend there're paparazzi in the bar."

"You caught me."

I widen my eyes at his admission.

"I like to touch you."

I shake my head. "Well, you shouldn't."

"Why not? We're both adults. Why can't I touch you?"

"Because I don't want you to."

"Why, because you liked it too much? Did you like me fucking you, Tink?"

"Can you please stop?" I say as my face heats at his words. Because the truth is I did.

"What's the problem?"

"What's the problem? Really, you have to ask that? There are so many problems."

"Such as?" He cocks his head.

"What? You want me to list all the problems with us?"

207

"There's no us, Tink." And as much as I don't want his words to hurt or mean anything to me, I can't help the feeling of my chest tightening.

"I know that, what I meant is—"

"No. There isn't us; this is just sex. Just fucking. I don't see what the problem is."

"W-we work together," I respond harshly. It's the lamest excuse I can come up with, but what else can I say. I'm trying to pick my brain for another reason we can't when the bartender finally comes over.

"Two shots of Don Julio 1942, extra chilled. Actually, make it four," Nathaniel orders.

I turn my head to him. "Four?"

"I see where your brain is going, and I think you need to lighten up."

The bartender walks away, and I use the movement and Nathaniel's distraction to move his hand from my waist and cross my arms in front of my chest.

"And where is my brain going?" There is so much ice in my voice, I'm surprised the bar hasn't frozen over.

"You are reading way too much into this. We fucked. And if I had my way, we would do it again."

My mouth opens and then shuts, not even sure what to say to that. If he had his way, we should fuck again.

*No. Just no.*

"Why not?" he asks, answering my unspoken question. "Why shouldn't we? I liked shagging you, and by the way you came around my cock, it's obvious you liked shagging me too."

"Because . . ." My brain is mush, not knowing what to say in response. The bartender comes back, and I grab the glass without waiting for him and take the first shot. Then I take the second. I do it in rapid succession, so I don't notice the burn with the first, but when the second one slides down my throat, I feel the burn. A burn so intense, it melts all the ice inside me.

He's right.

I hate that he's right, but he is.

I did enjoy him. I enjoyed—no I loved how he played my body. It was unlike anything I have ever felt. Why shouldn't I allow this to happen again? It is just fucking as he so poignantly said.

The truth is, I might not have this chance again. My options as I get older are becoming more limited. I might never get married. I might never find someone who will love me and all my faults, all my broken pieces, so shouldn't I get the enjoyment while I can? It might be fleeting, but isn't having something right now, even if just for a moment, worth it? When it's over, at least then I will always have the memories.

"Okay," I whisper more to myself than to him.

"Okay?" he responds, lifting his eyebrow in question.

"Yes." I raise the glass that's in front of me and take the shot.

One word. One simple word and everything is about to change. That should scare me, and it does, but it also makes me feel something entirely different.

Excited.

# chapter twenty-four

## NATHANIEL

NOW THAT WE HAVE ALL THIS BULLSHIT SETTLED, I NEED to be inside her.

I take her hand and pull her with me.

"Where are we going?" she asks, but I ignore her question. We start our way to the loo. She doesn't know that yet, and I'm sure she will object, but I won't give her a choice. I just pray there's no queue.

"Why are we at the bathroom?" she asks, confused as I push the door open. She hovers behind, so I reach across and grab her by the waist and push her through it. Before she even realizes what's happening, I lock the door and turn toward her. Stalk toward her more like it. Her knees buckle. When I'm only a breath away, I slam my mouth to hers, not giving her time to object. Our lips mold together. Hers are soft, full, warm, and everything I need right now. I could get lost in her if I let myself.

But I won't.

I kiss her harder, making sure not to confuse this with something more. The kiss is desperate and filled with so many conflicting emotions: want, desire, but mostly just confusion. She wants this but hates herself for taking it. We're so close now that I can feel her heart pattering fiercely against my chest. It drives me crazy, making me want to consume her completely. This kiss isn't enough. I need more. So much more.

Pulling away, she looks at me with wide eyes and heavy breaths. Her chest rises and falls as she waits.

"Turn around." When she doesn't, I say it again, this time more authoritative. "Turn around and place your hands on the sink." She doesn't move fast enough, so I turn her around myself. With a tap to her lower back, she bends forward, giving me a view of her arse. "I said place your hands on the sink. Do you have problems following orders, Tink?"

"Here?" she mutters under her breath, her confusion evident.

"Yes, here. I need to be inside you. Now," I state, and her body begins to tremble at my words. "Is that what you want? Do you want my cock inside you? Do you want me to fuck you here in this bathroom?" I run my hands up and down her back, and she lets out a moan. "Are you wet right now? I bet if I reach my hand . . ." I place my hand on her upper thigh, and she quivers against my touch. She might not say anything, but I know when I lower her pants and place my fingers inside her knickers, she'll be wet.

Needing to know, I push her leggings until they bunch at her ankles.

"I wish we weren't in a bathroom. I wish I had more time. All I can think of is how you taste . . ." My fingers pull her thong to the side, then dip inside her needy body. Her walls clench around me.

"Jesus," she moans as I continue to work my finger in and out, curling a finger to hit her sweet spot inside. When she starts to quake, I pull my hand and place it in my mouth. "Just as I remembered, you taste amazing."

"Please," she begs, and it makes my lips tip into a smile to hear the desperation in her voice. "Please."

"Tell me what you want."

"Fuck me."

I pull the lace down to meet the leggings at her ankle and then reach in my back pocket. The sound of my zipper echoes through the bathroom, and she trembles with anticipation. Normally, I would toy with her and make her wait, but our time is limited in the bathroom, and I just need to be inside her already. Moving my body forward, I align myself with her core and start to tease her entrance.

I circle my cock, dipping just the tip inside to coat myself with her essence. When I feel her squirm back and hear her groans, I slam inside, seating myself deep in her core. Her walls contract instantly. She's so tight I swear I'm already close to coming. Holding myself still so she can accommodate my size, I can feel a sweat break out along my brow. When her body relaxes, I slowly pull out . . . she starts to quiver again, trying to fill the emptiness, so on a chuckle, I slam back in. I keep up the slow, punishing pace until she begs me to go faster. I do.

I fuck her harder, this time snaking my hand around and stroking her where I know she's desperate for me to touch. I feel her tighten around me. That's all I need because knowing she's coming sets me off. With one last thrust of my hips, I spill inside her.

I stay pressed against her for a minute, trying to get my breathing to calm. "Fuck," I murmur, and it's her turn to chuckle. I follow suit.

"Fuck is right," she squeaks out.

A knock on the door has us both going rigid.

"Shit," I hiss in her ear so only she can hear.

"Hold on a second," I say to the door. She goes tense as I pull myself out of her and dispose of the condom. I kneel and help her get dressed. "I'm going to sneak out now. Then you pull yourself together and go out there." She looks dazed. "Understand, Tink?" She nods. Without a second thought, I unlock the door.

"What were you doing in there? That's the ladies' room," a middle-aged redhead hisses as I stroll out, closing it behind me.

"What's a bloke to do when he has to use the loo?" I wink while laying my accent on real thick, knowing full well that American women are suckers for a British accent, and I'm happy to oblige. Her face turns a bright shade of red, and she giggles. Mission accomplished. Hopefully, by the time Madeline exits, the lady will be too distracted to badger her. I go straight to the bar and order us another round. This is going to be a long night, I can feel it, because what we just did wasn't enough to quench the thirst I have for Madeline.

Not at all.

By the time the two shots of tequila are placed in front of me, she steps up. "Hey," she says timidly. We might have just fucked, but she still doesn't know how to act. Her face is still flushed, and she looks gorgeous with her post-orgasmic haze lingering on her skin.

"Here, have a drink. I think you need it."

"That obvious?" she asks, and I nod. She takes the shot and grimaces when it goes down. I take my shot and barely feel the burn. There is still too much energy coursing through me.

"Now what?"

"We fuck." I wink.

"We just did that," she deadpans.

213

"No. I mean . . . regularly. At all hours of the day. And, if I may suggest, in various places."

She looks at me like I'm crazy, so I lift my hand to stop her from asking questions. "Here is the thing. We are going to be spending a lot of time together, be it at work or with my family or with the board, so we might as well enjoy ourselves. I don't want a relationship, and one of the reasons I picked you for this, other than the fact you are gorgeous, is because I thought you didn't want one either."

"I don't," she says, a bit too quickly, but I shake it off.

"See, that's why this is perfect. Neither one of us wants anything more. This way not only do we both get what we want from this arrangement, but we are also both satisfied."

She doesn't speak for a few seconds, but I know she is thinking about my words as her teeth nibble at her lower lip. Her gaze is at her feet as if she's weighing out all her options, then she raises her head and locks her eyes with mine.

"Okay," she says before allowing herself to smile. "I agree."

I let out the breath of oxygen I didn't even know I was holding as a realization hits me in the gut. I wanted this more than I had let on, and I don't like it. Not one bit. But as much as I know this, I can't find it in me to care or back away. Instead, I pretend I don't want more. I shut down all the pieces inside me that say otherwise, grab her to me, and seal our new arrangement with a kiss.

# chapter twenty-five

## NATHANIEL

S INCE THE BAR, THINGS HAVE CHANGED.

There is an energy around us now. It courses through the air like a storm brewing. High winds, thunder crackling, lightning. If I thought the tension was high in the office before I bent her over the sink and fucked her, I was wrong.

Now the tension is almost unbearable.

We all sit around the table in the common room. Valentina's swatches and the samples of clothing are missing because they're all packed up for our meetings and pitches. "When do we leave?" Valentina asks. She might design the clothing, but when it comes to the business side, that's Tink's job.

Madeline opens a folder in front of her. "Six weeks, four locations. The cities are as follows . . . New York followed by London, so we will throw our party right before. Also in Milan, we'll do the same MO. By then, the hype will be up. If we play this right, people will be begging for an invitation to the final kickoff in Paris, which falls at the beginning of April." She looks through more papers between looking back at me and nodding. "After discussing, planning, and making phone calls, we have pop-up shows in most of the cities, not official, but we will have a show in Paris."

"The final night we're there?" Valentina asks, her eyes wide. "We are throwing a cocktail party on our last night?"

"Yep, one last hurrah, and hopefully, it will set the world on fire." I smile. There was something I was able to do for them, and well, for myself. I called in a shit-ton of favors, but it was well worth it just to see the look on her face. I had told Madeline about the possibility weeks ago, but now it's official. In only a few weeks' time, we will show the whole world Valentina Fisher's designs.

When I first started here, it was merely for show, kind of like Madeline's and my arrangement, but now things have changed, and I'm enjoying my decision.

"We have so much to do," Val says, furrowing her brow.

Madeline reaches across the table, grabs her hand, and squeezes. Instantly, Valentina relaxes. Tink has that effect on the world. It's like just her presence is pixie dust. She sprinkles it on you, and you relax.

Fuck.

I sound like a sap.

What's wrong with me?

Working too long with Lucy and Valentina, that's what. These women are so hormonal all the time, it's a wonder I don't have a pussy yet. I swear I know more about their time of the month than any man should. Same with Madeline. I have only been here for a few months, but I have learned to stay the fuck away from her. She pops more pills than a drug addict and sequesters herself to her home office.

It's actually kind of strange . . .

A sound from the other side of the room has me turning my head. Valentina has a sketchbook out, and she's apparently showing the ladies the design she has for the final number.

I stand, and all eyes turn to me. "This is my time to go," I say, gesturing to the sketchpad.

"Oh, come on, you know you want to give input on the fabric."

The truth is, I probably should stay. Textiles are in my blood, and now that Harrington will be sourcing the materials for this line, I should be here, but I don't want to pick colors. "I'm good." I turn my head toward Madeline. "Lunch later?"

She nods and then turns back to the girls, going over the details of which pieces and which models we will be hiring for the pop-up shows in Europe.

I make my way into my office, the office I rarely use because it lacks the "Tink" effect. I groan. Did I really just think that? I am starting to sound like a woman. I pick up my mobile, dialing the only person who will knock some sense into me.

"Hello," Oliver says in my ear.

"Hey," I respond.

"And it's me who gets to say to what do I owe the honor?"

"I'll be in London soon. Fancy a cocktail when I'm in town?"

"Of course. Will you be bringing the American?"

"The American has a name, Olly," I say a tad too aggressively.

"Down, boy."

I blow out some air and sigh. "No, I won't be bringing Madeline to drinks."

"Then to Blacks it is."

"Brilliant." Having some time with my best mate is exactly what I need.

As I place my mobile back on the desk, my door opens and a very lovely, very fuckable Madeline walks in.

"How was the rest of the meeting?" I ask her.

"Good."

"Come here."

She moves closer until her thighs touch my bent knee. I trail my hands up her tights-covered legs.

"It's a shame you have these on," I say as I snap the material.

"And why is that?" she responds in a coy voice.

My fingers trail circles on her covered skin. When I reach the place I want, I put a little more pressure until her mouth opens on a gasp.

"Because I'm hungry and want lunch." I watch as my words flutter inside her. I watch as her eyes glaze over, and I watch as she moves against my finger when I increase the pressure.

"Stop," she whispers.

"Do you really want me to?"

"No." The word comes out so low I'm not sure I heard it, but I did.

I pull my hand away, and this time, the sound that comes out of her mouth is a groan, not a sigh. "You said stop." I wink and then stand, leaning down and placing a kiss on her lips. "Come on, let's get lunch." This time, there is no innuendo.

She lets out a long-drawn-out sigh. "Fine. But I'll remember this," she whines.

"Good. I'm waiting for it."

# chapter twenty-six

## MADELINE

STILL SITTING AT MY DESK, MY PHONE RINGS.

Jace.

"Hi," I answer cheerfully, always happy to hear from my older brother.

"What are you doing?"

I let out a long groan. "No hello?"

"Hello, sis."

"Sis? Now I know you need something. What's up?" I move back from my computer and recline in my chair, wondering where this is going.

"Are you busy?" he asks, and I laugh.

"Hmm. Let me think about that. It's five on a Thursday night, and I'm the CEO of a fashion brand. Nope, not busy."

"Stop being a smart-ass."

"Here's how it works, Jace. I'm going to teach you a thing called manners." I laugh. "You need something from me. So . . . you're supposed to be nice."

"Hello, Madeline. I've missed you. How have you been? You look lovely in that dress, by the way," he says in a more chipper voice. "Better?"

"Better. For the record, though, I'm wearing a skirt. So now what can I do for you?"

"Are you free tonight?"

"Technically no. But for the father of my favorite niece and nephew, I'm free."

"Well, that's exactly why I'm calling. I need you to come over and watch the kids." I can hear the plea in his voice, and I know I can't say no.

"Okay," I say without having to think twice about it. I love those kids. "Is everything okay?"

"Yes, of course. But Sydney and I haven't been alone since the wedding, and well, she's stressed with work and the kids. I want to do something nice for her."

A smile spreads across my face. "I'll be there in thirty."

"You're the best."

"I know."

"Always so modest, Mad."

"Bye, Jace."

Thirty minutes later, I'm walking past the doorman into the elevator and then down the hall.

Sydney throws her arms around me once she opens the door. "Thank you so much, sis," she says, still holding on to me.

"Needed a night out?"

"Yes."

"I don't have kids, so I don't get it." I smile weakly. The words feel sour on my tongue.

"We just need to convince your man to marry you," Sydney says, misreading the look on my face.

"Who needs to get married?" Jace steps up behind her and places his hands around her middle. "Thank you again for this. Being alone with my wife . . ." His lips part, and he looks so damn happy I can't help but feel jealous.

The sound of pitter-patter on the floor gets closer and then arms envelop me. "Aunt Maddy!"

"Avery. Logan. Lord, you guys are getting tall."

"We saw you last week," Avery deadpans with her usual sarcastic bite.

*I love that girl.*

"Leave, Mom and Dad," Avery says.

My eyes widen. Mom. She called Sydney mom. Tears well up in my eyes.

"We're going. We're going." Jace chuckles.

As soon as the door closes, Logan has my hand, and he's pulling me toward the living room. Once I'm there, a full giggle erupts. "Board game night, I see?"

"It's on, Aunt Maddy. Revenge. I'm taking you down tonight."

There must be six board games set up along the floor. It appears back-to-back games are in order.

"Where do we start?"

"Clue, of course. You might have won last time, but I'm coming for you."

"Fine, but no cheating," I say to both kids.

"We don't cheat," they answer in unison.

"Sure, you don't."

It takes five minutes before Avery is casually walking behind me, trying to get a look at my sheet. "I know what you're doing."

"What?" She raises her brow and feigns ignorance. My breath leaves my chest when she does. She looks so much like her mother. Her real mother. The way her brow lifts and her eyes sparkle, it's like looking at a picture of Claire. My heart tightens. She's a mini Claire right now. Claire would have loved to see this.

I keep looking at her, wondering what it must be like to have your own child. To have a mini you. *Mini version of yourself.* The entire attitude, all the sass, the Montgomery blue eyes. I want that.

I shake my head violently.

*No, you don't.*

*You want a career.*

*You want to succeed.*

*No, you want a little girl to smirk at you. You want the smile. You want the giggles.*

I push back the thought.

Not right now.

Right now, I'm going to hang with my family. I spend the next two hours doing just that. That is, until they are in bed, and my brother and Sydney are home, and I find myself standing on the corner of the street not wanting to go home.

**Me: What are you doing?**

**Nathaniel: Missing me, Tink?**

After we slept together, I decided it was only fitting to change his name in my phone. I can't be sleeping with an *Ass*.

**Me: Yes.**

**Nathaniel: Wow. I didn't expect that.**

**Nathaniel: Your place**

**Me: No**

**Nathaniel: Where then?**

I start to type, but I can't think of anyplace.

**Nathaniel: Meet me at the office.**

**Me: The office?**

**Nathaniel: I want to shag you on the tidy, uncluttered desk you are so fond of.**

My mouth hangs open . . .

**Nathaniel: Spoiler alert: we'll be making a mess.**

Yes. Please.

---

It's crazy how fast the past few weeks have gone by.

Everything is ready.

At least on my end, it is. Today is the big night, our official launch into the world of high luxury fashion. We're about to kick off our version of fashion week, a six weeklong tour of all the biggest cities, pop-up shows, cocktail parties, and presentations.

Things have been changing at Valentina Fisher, and we need this night to be successful. This will be the first show since I have been brought on as CEO. It will make or break us, and that thought hangs heavy in the air. Not only will this prove to the fashion world we are a company they should take notice of, but it will also prove my worth. We need this to be a success.

So now as I take my seat along the runway, I silently pray I've done enough.

An old converted bank built in the 1800s with gilded ornate ceilings and marble columns makes the perfect setting for the show. The red lights illuminating each column give the space an intimate quality. As large as the room is, it feels like the perfect place to seduce and carry on an illicit affair with all the private nooks and alcoves. We chose this location for that reason. Valentina Fisher designs are seductive and sexy, but classy all merged into one. They are made to make the wearer feel sensual yet like she can conquer the world.

Which is how I should feel right now, wearing my one-of-a-kind dress, custom-made to fit my petite stature. Most of Valentina's dresses are cut for women quite a bit taller than me, but when I came aboard, Valentina designed a line solely for women of different shapes and sizes with the intention that all women should feel amazing in their own skin.

I'm a fraud.

I may look the part, but in truth, I'm a hypocrite pretending to be in control of my life and my body.

Shaking my head back and forth, I don't think about that right now. Instead, I focus on the task at hand, the show. As the lights dim and the music filters through the air, it begins. The first model steps out. Her chestnut brown hair bounces around her in full curls, and her striking smoky eyes and red lips give her a classic Hollywood look as she flounces down the runway, swaying perfectly to the beat. I pull my gaze away from her to take in the crowd and make sure she is capturing the audience. The need to gauge their interest is all-encompassing.

Do they love it? Hate it? It's hard to tell right now. I'm normally pretty good at reading people, but tonight, this means too much to me. This is the culmination of months of planning for us, and I can't see past the thud in my heart. Willing myself to move past the anxiety that has captured my stomach, I continue to allow my gaze to sweep across the audience. Taking in every person who is there. From the head fashion editor at *Posh* to the social media influencer sitting next to her. Next, my eyes land on a man leaning forward in a suit looking off into the distance, bored. Then my breathing stops.

I see him, Nathaniel, and he's making his way over to me, to the open seat I've saved for him beside me.

He looks handsome tonight.

Devastatingly handsome, actually.

My face warms as I think of the feeling of him inside me.

With all the force I can muster, I turn my head. I can't day-dream about fucking him when I need to pay attention. From beside me, I feel the warmth of his body as he sits down, and then he takes my hand in his, and trails slow patterns on my skin. They're warm, and as they touch me, I can't help but imagine them spreading my legs apart and having his way with me right here, right now.

*So much for not thinking about him.*

It's been too long since he's touched me. Not since the night he had his way with me on top of my desk. It feels like forever. I'm desperate for him again, and I hate myself for the desire that courses through me.

Needing a distraction from the way my heart pounds against my rib cage when he touches me, I do a final sweep of the room, and then I look back at the runway and follow as each model walks down the center of the bank. The crowd eats it up, applauding over and over again, and for the first time in weeks, my corded muscles uncoil.

I think we did it.

The show goes on without a hitch.

We receive standing ovations. And for the first time since we set up today, I let out the breath I've been holding.

The show ends, and the models begin changing into the next round of outfits. Outfits we've chosen for them to wear and be photographed in tonight. Waitresses dressed in Valentina Fisher original pieces come out holding trays filled with flutes of champagne.

Everyone takes a glass, and chatter starts to fill the air. There are two parties being held tonight. One downstairs, where models will showcase the pieces, and the one upstairs, which is a private, more exclusive party and invite only for friends, family, and important business associates. Stepping into the lounge that sits above the main room, I find the white couches and dim lights evoke a seductive feeling. The models are still wearing the line, and the party is the who's who of fashion. We have celebrities and social media influencers wearing our clothes tonight. It cost us a pretty penny, but as I see the editor of *Posh* magazine staring at the Instagram influencer with over three million followers, wearing our crop leather jacket over the mini, I know it was worth it.

Tonight is important for us, but what's more important is tomorrow. Will orders roll in?

I hope so.

As a cocktail waitress passes, I grab a glass of champagne off her tray. Taking a long sip, I let my eyes scan the room. In the far corner, I see Preston, Eve, and then Jace and Sydney. When they spot me, I give a wave, lifting a finger to tell them I'll be over in a second. But first, I need to find Valentina. Peering around the space, I find her and make my way over.

"Great show," I congratulate her, leaning in to give her a hug.

She embraces me back. "Thank you for everything. I would've never been able to do this without you."

"Oh, stop. Of course, you could. I'm happy you didn't, but you would have been just fine." I wink.

"Do you think they liked it?"

"Liked it? Obviously, they liked it."

"Thank God." She beams and then looks over my shoulder and waves at someone. "I have to talk to the buyer from Lux."

"Good luck. I'll make my rounds after I talk to my family."

With a final smile, I make my way over to my siblings. "Hi, guys!" They all turn toward me, brimming with excitement. "Thank you for coming."

"This was amazing." Eve smiles.

"It really was. I'm dying to get my hands on a ton of the stuff." Sydney laughs.

"Well, I might be able to help with that." I wink.

"It's really amazing," Preston says. "We are very proud of you."

"Thank you. It's not me, but thank you. Valentina is the talented one."

"Don't sell yourself short. Valentina might have designed the clothes, but getting this far . . ." Jace gestures around the room. "This is a team effort. We all know how hard you work. All these years of endless hours and traveling the world. It paid off, Mad."

Hearing my brother's praise makes a smile spread across my face.

I have always looked up to Preston and Jace. Always valued their opinion. Jace a little more so because he isn't as forthcoming with the compliments. For Jace to compliment is a big deal, so you know he means it. Not that Preston doesn't, but he tends to look at the best in people. Unlike Jace, who always looks for the worst.

I didn't realize how much his praise meant to me, but it's what I need right now. Exactly what I need.

---

The week of our New York launch came and went, and since the major success of our pop-up show, we've concentrated on securing all the details to make our travels abroad more beneficial. Our first stop is London, and we leave in three short days. Although we aren't doing a show there, per se, Nathaniel has been a huge help to us. Not only has he secured the most important meeting, but he also secured a space for a cocktail party so we can have models milling around wearing our line. Since he's from London and lived there most of his life, he knows everyone. The fashion directors of every posh magazine have been invited to our event, and better yet, they all accepted. All the top department stores will be there too, and the next day, we have meetings scheduled with all the buyers.

We hope that, by the end of our trip, we will have secured placement in every place that matters.

I'm lying in my bed. It's early. I have been working hard and not feeling well. I take Advil, followed by another prescription pain pill my doctor has given me. I feel like shit, absolute shit, but I'm thankful that I feel crappy now and not when we are abroad. Typically, the worst passes after a few days, so by the time we go to London, I should be able to function again.

My phone rings, and I see it's my mom. "Hey, Mom."

"Hey, sweetie," she chirps. Her chipper voice always makes me smile no matter how crappy I feel. "What are you doing?"

"Just lying down."

"Not feeling well?" she asks.

"Nope. It never ends," I groan.

Through the earpiece, I hear her sigh. "I'm so sorry. What did the doctor say?"

"Same old shit, different day. New pain meds, but it's only a temporary thing. I just don't know how much longer I can take this pain, you know?"

"I do, sweetie. Well, you have a lot to think about, but whatever you do, you have your father's and my support."

I breathe out as my eyes fill with tears. Pain is a part of my life. Surgery is one of the only options, that and pain management, but the pills make it almost impossible to work, and although I've been lucky as of late to be able to work from home, but that option isn't always feasible. But surgery is a big deal, bigger than I want to think about, so instead, I don't. I take my meds and pretend I can go on like this forever, knowing full well I can't.

My mother proceeds to tell me all the gossip of every member of my family before she hangs up.

The phone rings again. "Hello."

"Tink," I hear through the line.

"Peter," I respond. My voice is dry. I'm in no mood to deal with him now.

"Peter? Bad day?"

"You can say that . . ." I move in my bed to get more comfortable and place the phone on speaker. "Is there something you needed?"

"No."

"Then why are you calling?" It comes out much harsher than I anticipated, but I don't feel well, and I just want to go to sleep.

"I was concerned about you," he says, and I can hear that he's not lying. He is.

"No need to be concerned," I answer.

"You can't tell me what to be concerned about. If I want to worry about you, I will."

"I'm surprised you care."

"Why do you say that?" he asks.

"Well, why should you care? We aren't anything—"

"That's not true," he says, cutting me off. Even though he

can't see me, I furrow my brow, not understanding what he's saying.

"We're just fucking. And seeing as we haven't in a while, we aren't even doing that."

"We might just be fucking, and yes, Tink, maybe we haven't shagged in a while, but that doesn't mean we won't again. Yes, I do want you. Yes, I love being inside you and no, we aren't more. We aren't in a relationship, but you're not just a warm body to me."

"Then what am I?"

"You are a woman I respect. A woman I like to spend time with, and if you will let me, a woman I will fuck again." He chuckles.

"Jeez, thanks," I deadpan.

"Listen, I like you. And I don't like many people."

"That certainly makes me feel better," I quip.

"That's what I like about you. You give as well as you take. I like spending time with you. We're friends."

His words take me aback.

*Friends.*

I never expected a man like Nathaniel to want me as a friend. I actually can't see him being friends with anyone. Not because he's not charming because he is. And not because he's not fun. He's that too.

But I can't see him as being friends with anyone because from what I have seen over the past few months, no matter where he is, who he's with, and even more so how much he drinks, he never lets his guard down. He never lets anyone in. Even his grandfather, he keeps at arm's length. Maybe he is afraid to form attachments because he's afraid to lose anyone else.

He did have a girlfriend once.

The thought makes my stomach sour, and I'm not sure why. I wonder about her. What he was like with her? Is she the reason he's like this? Maybe she broke his heart. For some reason, I don't like thinking about that.

"Tink?"

"Yeah."

"Are you still there?" he asks, and I realize I had grown quiet, lost in my thoughts, and forgot I was on the phone with him.

Maybe I can be friends with him? Even if it's just sex, I can be friends with him. I don't want anything more. I have nothing to give, but I guess I could use a friend.

With my brain resettled, I move farther into my bed and yawn.

"You're tired."

"I am . . . but, Nathaniel."

"Yeah?"

"Thanks for calling. Thanks for checking up on me. I appreciate it."

"You are welcome. Call me if you need anything."

"I will."

Once he hangs up, I settle, closing my eyes with a smile playing on my face.

Maybe this isn't so bad.

# chapter twenty-seven

## NATHANIEL

THE FLIGHT TOUCHES DOWN A LITTLE PAST NINE A.M. FROM beside me on the plane, I see Madeline rub the sleep from her eyes. She's only just woken up while I barely slept. It's not that I don't sleep when flying back and forth between England and America. It's just that I have too much on my mind these days.

I'm back in London, which means I'm back on Edward's turf. My grandfather is often in America, but Edward lives here full time. The idea of having to see him makes the muscles in my back go rigid. Lifting my hand, I try to loosen the tension.

"What's wrong?" Madeline asks, her eyes moving to where my fingers are trying to work out a knot that has formed beneath the skin.

"Nothing," I mutter.

"It's obviously not nothing. I can see how tense you are."

"London."

Her brows stitch together in confusion. "London?"

"Yep."

"Is everything okay?"

"Yes and no. I'm looking forward to the trip. I love London, obviously, but—"

"But?"

"My cousin lives in London."

"So?"

"He'll want to check up on me. He'll make it his mission to prove how incapable I am."

"So let him try. You are working your ass off, Nathaniel. Anyone can see that. And as for us. You don't have to worry about us."

She's right, I don't. Ever since we decided to fuck, I no longer have to worry about people not believing our story. It's obvious to everyone. We might not be in a serious relationship, but the chemistry and the connection are there. Not having to worry about Edward finding out anything different takes a huge boulder off my back.

As soon as the plane stops, I stand and reach out my hand to help Madeline stand. She gives me a heart-stopping smile, and without any resistance, she lets me help her. Normally, Madeline isn't like this. Normally, no one can help her, but she's warmed to me, warmed to my touch, and I like it.

Together, we walk out of the jet, down the stairs, and onto the tarmac. The rest of the staff follows. A few feet away is a fleet of cars ready to whisk us to London. Everyone is staying at the Mandarin in Knightsbridge. Madeline, however, doesn't know yet, but she's staying at my flat. I turn to the group.

"Everyone, those cars will take you to the Mandarin, where I booked rooms. Tink, you're in that car with me."

"What?" she asks as she squeezes my arm.

"You're with me."

"As in?" She pulls my arm, and I turn to face her. As I lean in, my lips hover over hers when I speak.

"They expect you to stay with me."

I pull back and watch as the news settles down on her. She's my "girlfriend." People will expect me to spend time with her and sleep with her. She nods but still looks unsure.

"See you lot tonight," I say to Val and the group as I wrap my hand around Madeline and lead her to my car and driver. The luggage has already been loaded into the boot, so when I sit inside, I take Madeline's hand and squeeze.

"It will be fun," I say to her. I let my lips split into a reassuring smile, but the truth is, even I'm confused by what I just did. Sure, we're supposed to be seen together, and sure, we've fucked, but sleeping together, in a bed, in my flat, in my space? Well, that is a whole other level of intimacy I'm not sure I can do.

This is a bad idea, but since I already announced she was staying with me, I have to follow through. I'll just have to be upfront with her about what this is.

Two people putting on a front and enjoying ourselves at the same time.

Nothing more.

Nothing less.

It will be fine, I tell myself, but even I'm not buying this shit.

The city comes into view, and before long, we are weaving our way through traffic until eventually we pull in front of the flat I keep in Notting Hill. Madeline has been watching the whole trip, smiling at every turn. She seems lighter on this trip than she is in New York. It's as though she left her baggage behind and is here on holiday.

She's obviously not. There is work to be done, but she doesn't look like it's bothering her.

"Have you ever been to London?" I ask as the driver gets

out of the car to open the door for her.

"No," she replies.

"I didn't think so."

"I'm excited that we don't have a meeting for a few days."

"It was smart to add a few extra days before so everyone can get over the jet lag."

"Just because I'm going to be jet-lagged doesn't mean I'm going to stay in bed all day. I want to see the city." She turns to me and lifts a brow in challenge.

"Are you sure? Staying in bed all day has its merits."

She drills me with her eyes.

"Okay, okay, Tink. I'll show you London. But first . . ." I smirk. "First, I'll show you the bedroom . . . if, after that, you choose to leave, and I can't convince you to stay in, I'll take you on a tour of London. Sound good?"

Her face turns a lovely shade of pink at my words. "Yes," she squeaks.

"Good." The door opens. "Hurry up so I can start your British tour." I laugh. She giggles back and lets me escort her in.

The moment we step into the space I move to kiss her, but she pulls away as her mouth goes wide at the flat. The space is immense, and although I know Madeline is from money, by the way her eyes go wide, she is shocked by the extent of my wealth.

"Wow, this is where you live?"

"When I'm in London." I shrug.

"Is your apartment in New York like this?"

I laugh. "Yes, Tink, it is." I take her hand. "Come on, I'll give you the tour."

I have my way with her all morning. After, we had to shower. I had to refrain from touching her, though, as I was sure a wicked cycle would begin, and we would never stop.

Now she's in my bathroom getting ready, and I'm sitting on the sofa, waiting. It's so domestic. Having her in my space, in my shower, in my bathroom putting on makeup. It's been a while since I've done this. Years really. I haven't had a woman sleep over here since Cecile.

With all the women over the years, I've either gone to their place or fucked them at a hotel. Always leaving before they could ask to cuddle. To be honest, I wasn't sure how I would feel about it, but with Tink, it doesn't seem like a burden. I know she knows what this is, so I don't mind her being in my space.

Tink is too motivated, too driven to give up what she's worked so hard for, even for a man like me. She is too independent, and where she is in her career doesn't bode well for a family, so I have nothing to fear where she's concerned. She's actually the perfect woman in that sense. She's fantastic in the sack and independent enough that she won't be clingy.

When she steps out, I take her in. I'm not sure how it's possible, but even in her jeans, jumper, and trainers, she looks gorgeous. As beautiful as she does in a dress. She's a natural beauty who doesn't need makeup to be stunning.

"You ready?" I ask.

"I am."

"Good, let's go. Plenty to see."

"Where to first?" She's watching me, waiting.

"Well, since you've never been here, I assume you want to do all the touristy things." I roll my eyes.

"Don't make fun of me. Of course I do."

"Wouldn't dream of it."

"I saw you roll your eyes." She places her hands on her hips, and I chuckle.

"I didn't roll my eyes. I just had something in them," I say nonchalantly.

"Likely story. So where to first?"

"Well, since you are the tourist, how do you Americans say it 'It's your rodeo.'"

"Oh Lord. Are we doing this? Should I start making fun of you now?"

"Have at it." I walk over, place my hand on her jaw, and tilt her face up, pressing my lips on hers. "But be forewarned, there will be a punishment." I lick the seam of her lips, and she lets out a moan. "Are you sure you want to leave?" I whisper against her.

She places her hands on my chest and pushes off me. Turning her back, she fires over her shoulder, "Chip, chip cheerio."

"We don't actually say that, you know?" I deadpan.

She just giggles as she walks out of the room to the front door.

Twenty minutes later, we are standing outside Buckingham Palace. "I can't believe this is the first place you wanted to see," I groan.

"What? Every girl wants to see the palace." She shrugs.

"Please tell me you aren't another American dreaming of meeting a prince, getting married, having royal babies, and living happily ever after?"

Her eyes darken, and I have no idea what I've said. "I am not that girl. Nor do I want anything you just said." With that, she turns her back to me and starts walking closer.

The moment is tense as we watch the changing of the guards. She stands so still and stiff, I'm not even sure what to do. But whatever I said is a sore topic for her. After the show finishes, I take her hand. She is stiff under my touch.

"I didn't mean to insult you by that," I say, and I'm shocked by how much I care what she's thinking. I haven't cared about anyone's feelings for a long time. The feeling is strange, but I find that I do care. I wasn't lying when I told her I wanted to be friends with her. I might not have it in me to be more, but I do want her friendship, and seeing her angry or sad is not something I care for at all.

"I know."

"Then what are you on about?"

"I'm just sick and tired of everyone assuming that's all women want. That's all I can want. I don't need a man to ride up on a horse and rescue me. I can handle my own damn life myself." She grits so harshly that her teeth are bared.

"I know you can." I lean forward and place a kiss on her head. "That's what I like so much about you, Tink. You don't need anyone. You're strong and independent. You can handle anything life throws at you. I respect that."

With that comment, she instantly relaxes. "I wish I could go in," she says dreamily, still staring at the ornate gold gates.

"You can."

"I know, but I mean really see it. Plus, it's not open to the public now," she says.

"Maybe not, but I have ways," I respond. She turns her face toward me, and I smirk. "We might not be able to see it this time, Tink. But I can get you in . . . I know people." I wink.

"Of course you do." She laughs.

I make a mental note that I love it when she laughs, and I should make her laugh more. After that, though, I catalog that I need to ask Oliver about getting Madeline in to see the palace.

"Where to next?" she asks, pulling me out of my thoughts.

"What else is on your list?"

"Westminster, Parliament, Big Ben." She continues to rattle off a list so long I'm shocked.

"Aren't you tired at all?" I ask.

"Nope. I want to see it all."

And so we do.

# chapter twenty-eight

## MADELINE

TODAY HAS BEEN AMAZING. AND SURPRISINGLY, BEING WITH Nathaniel has been amazing too.

I think back to the first day when I walked into my office and there he was. Cocky, arrogant, and his damn feet on my desk, but now looking at him, watching with delight as he pretends to be a tourist with me, I can't help but smile.

Right now, we are on a double-decker bus. *Yes, that is correct.* The great Nathaniel Harrington is sitting on the top level of a shiny red tourist trap all because it makes me happy. We are bundled close together, his arm around me to keep warm. I point like the tourist I am.

"Look, kids, there's Big Ben." I laugh, pointing into the direction of the landmark.

"Parliament," he responds to my movie line quip, pulling me closer into his ribs. I can feel him laughing against me, and it makes my lips spread across my face until my cheeks burn.

I can't remember the last time I've had this much fun or the last time I've felt this free. It's like when I'm with him, I'm flying above the ground. Off to Neverland where there are no responsibilities. No worries. For the first time in I don't know how long, I have fun. And it's amazing.

Not a care in the world.

I'm just living.

I know it will be short-lived, and that I only have a few more days of this before we need to work, but for now, I'll enjoy myself.

We ride the bus for about thirty more minutes before we end up back where we started at Notting Hill. I'm not ready to go back to his apartment. Not that I mind what we will do when we are alone. No. I'll enjoy that immensely, but until then, I want to feel the cold air on my face. I want to enjoy a taste of normalcy without deadlines, without pressure.

Hand in hand we get off the bus. "Home?" he asks.

"I'd like to walk around a bit more if you don't mind."

He pulls me close and places his lips on the shell of my ear. "Sure I can't persuade you to go back to my flat?"

I shake my head, and he nips at my skin. "Nope," I mumble, my eyes fluttering shut at the feel of his tongue trailing on my skin.

"Let's have a stroll." He stops his assault and moves away. I feel the lack of his warmth instantly.

"Which way?" I ask, and he takes a step back, grabs my arm, places it in his, and walks us in the opposite direction. We stroll for a while, admiring the scenery. The buildings, the gates, and snow-covered grass.

"I imagine this is beautiful in the summer," I say dreamily.

"It is. You'll have to come back one day and see."

His words hang in the air. Oppressing. There won't be a summer trip. I know this; he knows this. He will show the board through Valentina Fisher's success in the next month that he is ready to take the helm, and then shortly after he has won their bid of confidence, we will part ways. It's inevitable. We might not have spoken of our shelf life, but it will happen and probably sooner rather than later. The thought weighs heavy on me, making my lungs fill with tension.

"Come on, this way." His words pull me out of my thoughts, and I am thankful for it. I don't need to dwell on the future. The future is unforeseen, and right now, here in London with Nathaniel, I want to live in the present and enjoy every minute of it.

"Where are we going?"

"It's a surprise."

"I hate surprises."

He laughs at my answer because it's true. I hate the unknown.

"I promise you, you will love this one."

My interest is piqued with that, so I follow him down a cobbled stone street past whimsical stores and beautiful buildings. We finally stop in front of a quaint little bookshop. He pulls me in with him. The smell of new books and old books fills my nose.

"What are we doing here?" I ask.

"Thought you could use a book."

"I hardly have time to read . . ."

"You're right, you don't. When we get back, I won't allow you."

"Oh, you won't?"

"Nope."

"Do you have other things in mind?" I say, lifting a brow at him. He smirks.

That damn smirk. The one that makes my knees go weak and my cheeks warm. The smirk that makes me constantly throw caution to the wind. That makes me step toward the fire, reach out my finger, and get burned.

"I do. And if you're a good girl, I'll tell you."

"You wouldn't dare." He steps up, pressing his body to me, and leans down. His hand moves to my hips. My breath lodges in my throat as I wait for him to say wicked things to me.

But instead he steps away, and I swear I almost fall from the lack of his presence. "You're right. I won't. You'll just have to wonder." Then he grabs my hand and pulls me toward the back of the store.

Once we get to the far wall, he starts to search. Rummage. He's on his knees looking for something, and it's actually quite cute.

"What are you doing?"

"One moment," he responds. "Found it."

He stands, holding a royal blue book up in his hand.

"What do you have there?"

"It's a surprise."

I cock my head at him. "I told you I don't like surprises."

"This one you will like."

"Promise?"

"Scout's honor."

Without showing me the book, we walk to the register where the elderly man rings up the purchase and places it in a bag. It's not until we walk the many blocks back and I've pondered what he bought, that I finally find out. Standing in his living room, he reaches in and pulls out the book. The moment I see the cover, I can't help but stifle a laugh. It bursts through my mouth as I shake my head.

"You really shouldn't have."

"It's a reprint. One day, I'll locate the original," he says with confidence, and I know without a measure of a doubt he will.

"It's perfect."

"Anything for you, Tink."

I look down at the book he handed me and run my fingers over the title as if it's Braille. A warm feeling spreads through my heart that I can't temper.

*Peter and Wendy: Peter Pan, the Boy Who Wouldn't Grow Up.*

"You're speechless. Never thought I'd be able to accomplish that goal," he says, and I want to respond—I do—but he really has rendered me speechless. The gesture and thought. I understand the nickname started from a bad place, but like him, it's evolved. I no longer get angry when I hear it. Now I smile because it reminds me of how much I hated him and how far we've come. Not just as lovers, but also as friends.

Without words, I walk up to him, wrap my arms around his neck, and rise onto my tiptoes. I'm so much shorter than him that I feel him bend his knees so our mouths meet.

First, it's slow. My lips on his, his parting mine. Then our tongues start a slow dance. Circling, teasing, saying all the words I can't say. No one but my family has ever done something that thoughtful for me before. I push down that thought, though, because that thought will make emotions I don't want to have boil to the surface, so instead, I lose myself in the kiss. Let myself become swept away in it.

It deepens.

He pulls me tighter toward him, wrapping his arms around me, and then with one swift move, he lifts me. I wrap my legs around him and, still kissing, he walks us to his bedroom. I'm placed down.

He looks down at me with hungry eyes. They drink me in;

they devour me. They tell me of all the wicked things he wants to do to me, and right now, I need all of them.

He moves in and pulls off my pants. My panties go with them. He smirks. "Take off your shirt," he says, and I do, and then remove my bra until I'm sitting at the edge of the bed, naked and ready.

I watch with hooded lids as he quickly removes his clothes. He's long and hard and ready for me.

He moves quickly to the dresser and pulls out a condom. I hear the familiar rip, and then he's stretching it over his impressive length. I move back up the bed until my head hits the pillow, and he crawls up my body, parting my legs and settling in the juncture.

I wait for him to press in, but instead, he frames my face with his hands and gives me another earth-shattering kiss.

"Please," I find myself moaning. Because as much as I love kissing him, I need him inside me. He removes one hand from my face and then slowly guides himself to where I need him most.

Still kissing, he plunges in.

The feeling is too much. As if he belongs there inside me. I'm overwhelmed with emotions and want to hide, want to close my eyes, but he isn't having it. He kisses me again but then pulls our mouths apart.

"I want to see you. I want to watch you," he groans, and he does.

He thrusts over and over again, but his gaze never leaves mine. It feels so intimate my heart wants to burst. This is more than I wanted, more than I expected, more than I can handle, but I can't find it in me to break away. Because as much as I know I need to, as much as I know I can't and shouldn't get lost in the green of his eyes, I can't turn away.

Instead, I push forward toward the storm, not heeding any warning from the screaming in my brain, and while our eyes are locked and he rocks into me in the perfect rhythm, I fall. I fall into an abyss so deep, I don't know how I'll ever pull out from it.

A moment, a second, a minute must pass. Nathaniel's weight is on me, and he's buried his face in the crook of my neck, spent, as drained as I am from what just happened.

I'm not sure what that was, but now as the haze has lifted, as the storm has passed, I need to breathe. "I'm going to shower," I finally let out.

"Okay, we are supposed to go to the bar at the Mandarin?"

I think about this, and right now, after this, I'm too un-nerved to be nice, fake smile, and act for everyone. Not that it's really acting with him anymore, but in public, I still need to be "on," and I don't want that.

"Do you think we can cancel? The jet lag is finally getting to me."

"Of course," he says as he places one kiss on my forehead and then stands. He walks out of the room, and I admire him from where I am perched on the bed. Once he's gone, I head into the shower, turn the water on, and step under the hot stream. My muscles loosen. My heartbeat calms. My brain rights itself.

*Just because the sex is amazing doesn't mean you will fall for him*, I tell myself. I say the words over and over again as I wash my hair, and as the final suds fill the drain, I think I've finally convinced myself of this fact too.

Stepping out of the shower, I grab a towel and the robe. Nathaniel must have hung one up for me while I was show-ering. I'm happy he didn't join me because I needed to right myself and get my emotions back in check.

And I did.

Now, I'm no longer floating out to sea without a life raft like I was when he made love to me. Now after my shower, I washed those thoughts away, and I'm ready to take this on again.

Now I'm ready to face him without losing my heart to him.

# chapter twenty-nine

## NATHANIEL

GIVE HER TIME. AS MUCH AS I WANTED TO GO INTO THE shower, I didn't. She needed a moment, and truth be told, so did I.

What the fuck was that?

I don't stare into someone's eyes as I make love to them. Because as much as I want to say I bedded her, I didn't. I made fucking love to her. What the hell is going on with me? Maybe this was a bad idea. Having her stay with me, showing her London. I'm all fucked up and confused now. Buying her that book.

*Jesus.*

It's like we're actually in a relationship. I could feel her freaking out after, so I got up and pretended I was busy. But really, I fired off a text saying we weren't coming, and now I'm sitting on the sofa in sweats and no T-shirt, drinking a glass of scotch.

*Now, what do I do?*

*Nothing.*

*Because you don't want more, and she sure as shit doesn't want more.*

Never has a woman pushed me away so fast after sex. It's actually laughable. A part of me is relieved, a very large part, but the other part, the part that's a little confused by the feeling that has rooted in my belly and her dismissal, is being drowned by booze.

I finish the glass. She'll be out soon, and I hope we are back to normal because as much as I don't want a long-term thing with her, or anyone for that matter, I like what we are doing and don't want it to end.

After a few more sips, she walks out, eyes me on the sofa, and gestures to the glass. "Got one for me?" she asks, surprising me. But I'm not sure why it does. Tink is not like any girl I have ever met, so I shouldn't be surprised by her candid attitude and her dismissal of everything, playing it off like it's no big deal.

Which it isn't.

Again giving her points in my book.

I stand, grab another tumbler glass, and pour hers. Her petite fingers take the glass and place it to her mouth. She takes a small swig and grimaces.

"How do you drink this?"

"How do you not?" I retort.

"So now what?"

"Order takeaway?" I suggest. "What are you in the mood for?"

"I could go for some noodles or something."

"Sounds good." I stand and go to grab a menu from the place that sells noodles up the road. "I'll place an order, and you can get dressed while I go get it, and then we can have dinner. Anything in particular?"

"Surprise me." She smiles, and I laugh.

"I thought you didn't like surprises?"

"You're proving me wrong."

Grabbing my mobile, I dial the number and order a few of my favorite dishes, and then I leave.

Twenty minutes later, bag in hand, I see that Madeline has made herself at home in my flat. She's lying on the settee in her pajamas, reclining back. The telly is on, but I'm not sure if she's watching it or asleep. She must hear the door because she moves, yawns, and then looks up at me.

"You're back," she murmurs in a sleep-laced voice.

"I'm back . . ."

"Good. I missed you." She stands and takes one of the bags from my hands. "Smells delicious. Let's eat."

After I show her to the kitchen, we set up the noodles buffet style, each of us taking a set of chopsticks and plates, and then sit down.

"What would you like to drink?" I ask.

"Wine?"

"I have some here." I hand her two glasses. "I'll go get a bottle." I bring back a bottle of Screaming Eagle, and she laughs.

"Is it weird that we're drinking a cab from Napa with noodles in London? Shouldn't we be drinking a sake or something?"

"Nothing is weird as long as you like it. Normally, I would drink scotch."

"So let's do that," she says, taking me by surprise.

"Really?"

"When in Rome, or I mean London." She laughs, and the sound makes me smile. I walk up to the table, remove the wine glasses, and replace them with two tumblers of scotch.

"Cheers," I say, lifting my glass.

"Cheers. What are we cheering to?"

"Us," I say. "To friendship."

"To friendship," she says. "And fucking," she adds, and this time, I'm the one taken aback.

"You're a little minx, you know that?"

"You bring out the worst in me."

"Or the best," I retort.

"I guess it depends on who you ask." She shrugs. She lifts her glass and takes a sip. Her nose scrunches as she swallows.

"It's an acquired taste."

"You don't say."

Soon, we are both using chopsticks and eating. We don't talk much for the first few bites, but eventually, we slow down, so to stop the silence, I place my chopsticks down and lean into the table.

"As strange as this is to say, I really don't know much about you."

She places her own down and cocks her head.

"What do you want to know?" she asks.

"Everything."

That makes her let out an uncomfortable chuckle. "There isn't that much to tell. Plus, where is the mystery and surprise if I tell you everything?"

"I see I really converted you on the surprises front. Now you're full of them."

"Only with this one. For you, it's a different story." She winks.

"Is that so?"

"It is."

"Fine," I huff. "Just tell me a few things... Tell me about your family. Or how you got into fashion. Just tell me something."

She lets out a long-drawn-out and overly dramatic sigh. "I went to school at FIT. From there, I landed an internship working for a fashion brand. Over the years, I have moved up the ranks in different companies. I started working at the bottom until, eventually, I became the merchandising director for a luxury brand of clothes. Then when Valentina approached me about her branching off to start her own clothing line with me at the helm, I jumped at the opportunity."

I realize when she's done talking that as fascinating as her career is, it's not what I want to know. "And your family?"

"What about them? You met them."

This is like pulling teeth, which is odd since she's normally so talkative. "Anything else you want to tell me about your 'family,'" I air quote, obviously teasing her. She rolls her eyes.

"Fine. You know they are married. And you know both their wives are pregnant." With that, she picks up her chopsticks and takes another bite.

"Anything else?" I press. "Were you close growing up?"

"Kind of. They're older, so I was always the kid sister if you know what I mean."

I shake my head. "I don't. Only child." She worries her lip, and I smile. "It's okay." It grows silent, and I think of something to say. I'm not sure why I ask my next question. I shouldn't care; I shouldn't ask her stuff that could be leading, but I can't help it. For some reason, I want to know the answer.

"Do you want kids?"

"No."

Things get quiet after that. I'm not sure what answer I expected, but her one-word answer wasn't it. Sure, she had mentioned to me that her career was important and that she didn't have time for a relationship or kids, but the idea that she didn't want children, even maybe someday, takes me off guard for some reason.

At some point, maybe not now, and most certainly not in the next ten years, but eventually, I would do my duty and have an heir to pass down the legacy to.

*This is why you picked her.* An incessant voice plays in my head. *You picked her because she was perfect. She would never want more from you. Never want to be with you, not really. Would never want a relationship, a family.*

So why does it feel like I've been stabbed in the chest with the reality of her words?

It makes no sense.

This is just casual. A quick fuck. A way to pass the time. Her answer is exactly the answer I wanted. She's exactly what I want right now.

No fuss.

Simple.

Easy.

Temporary.

So why do I feel bothered about it?

# chapter thirty

## MADELINE

S O DINNER IS TENSER THAN I WANTED IT TO BE, BUT I LET IT
go. I have no choice. I offer to clean, using that as an
excuse to get some space from the topic that has made me such
unpleasant company. It's not his fault. He doesn't know that the
subject of children is a sore one for me. Truth be told, he didn't
deserve my one-word answer or my attitude. By the time the
last dish is put in the dishwasher, I find Nathaniel sitting in the
living room with his scotch in hand.

"Hi," I mumble from across the space.

He turns his head away from the television and looks toward me. He smiles, and it instantly makes my shoulders uncoil.

"Can I join you?" I ask like a timid little mouse, which is
so not like me, but at this moment, I can't help it. I'm here, in
his place, but I'm unsure of where we stand now. I feel out of
control, and I don't like it.

He motions for me to come over and then pats the couch
when I step up to him. I take the spot next to him, and he lifts
his free arm for me to snuggle against him.

Once beside him, I notice he has something in his hand. A
picture.

"What are you looking at?" I ask, and he holds it up for me to take.

It's a picture, a very old picture. The color has yellowed over time, and the sides are beginning to crinkle. Two men stand next to each other, but it is obvious it's father and son. Right off the bat, I know who the older man is; it's Nathaniel's grandfather. The younger man must be his son. He looks in his early twenties. His hair is long and unruly, and his eyes are a vivid green. Even with age, the green hasn't faded. It's striking. Just like the man sitting beside me. I continue to stare at the picture. My heart thuds a little heavier in my chest when I see that a toddler is on his lap. If I had to take a guess, I'd say the boy is around two in this picture. The little boy in this picture hasn't changed much over the years, he's aged, but his eyes are still the same. Green like the color of moss after a storm.

Turning my head to Nathaniel, I give him a tight smile. One I hope conveys that I know looking at this picture must be hard for him. The pain is evident in his eyes, his irises large and glassy.

"He looks so much like you," I whisper, and he nods. "Like your grandfather. You have your father's eyes."

His lip tips up, and he reaches over and takes back the picture. He studies it for a minute as if he's memorizing it. "Family trait," he answers before turning back to me. He inclines his head down. "Maybe one day . . ."

"Maybe one day?" I ask, but as I wait for him to answer, my stomach tightens.

He lifts his chin and then meets my gaze. "Maybe one day . . . my child will have his eyes too."

The words hang heavy in the air, or at least they do in my heart. Instead of speaking, I settle in, allowing the warmth of his body to give me the peace I need over my inner turmoil. As he holds me, his words replay.

Before I know it, my lids grow heavy, the words "maybe one day" replaying in my mind as I fall asleep

I wake sometime later to being lifted in his arms and cradled close to his chest. The intoxicating scent of cinnamon and Nathaniel filters in through my nose. I want to inhale him; he smells that good. But I'm too tired to do anything. He walks us to the room and places me on his bed.

A few minutes later, I feel him settle in beside me. I can't remember the last time I've slept in a bed with a man. Years probably. Not since my last long relationship, and that was almost four years ago when I was younger and more naïve. When I thought love and a family were possible. The reality was ripped away from me, though. A painful memory that will live inside me, guarding my heart to future heartbreak.

I wonder if I'll be able to sleep with him, or if he will be okay with me in his bed. He answers my question by pulling me closer to him, his arms wrapping around me and bringing me to lean into his chest. With a soft kiss on my head, he whispers, "Sleep."

And I do.

---

Early morning sunlight streams in through the windows. I stretch out my arms and let out a yawn, but then I try to stifle it when I remember where I am and who I'm with.

Blinking the sleep away, I turn to my left, expecting to see him there, but the side of the bed is empty. I touch the sheets, and I realize they are cold.

I continue to lie there, wondering if he actually slept in the bed with me all night. Wondering if maybe he couldn't. But somewhere deep inside me, I know he did. I've never slept more peaceful as I did last night. I remember how he held me, comforted me, quieted my brain, and I know without a measure of a doubt that my well-rested state today is because of him.

With one more stretch of my arms, I kick back the blanket and move to stand. My bare feet touch the cold wood floors. I find a robe at the foot of the bed, and I can't help the butterflies that swarm. This man has thought of everything.

Once the robe is on, I head to the bathroom for my morning routine, and then I head to the kitchen, and that's where I find him.

He turns to face me. I swear drool collects in my mouth at the sight of him. He has gray sweats on, hanging low on his hips, and no shirt. His hair is damp like he's showered or worked out, and his torso glistens, making each ripple on his chest look tighter and more delectable than before. He definitely just worked out.

"I was just making coffee," he says.

"Did you work out?"

"I did." He walks over to the machine and pours me a cup. He adds the perfect amount of sugar and cream. "It's not as fancy as your normal." He smirks.

"I'll make do."

"I promise to take you to a Starbucks today so you can get your fix."

I roll my eyes at his comment. "I'm not that high maintenance."

"You're right. You're not." Then he hands me the coffee, but not before placing a kiss on my lips. "Delectable," he says against my lips.

"Me or the coffee?"

"The coffee, of course."

At his words, I swat at him playfully with my free hand.

"You'll be punished for that."

"Promises. Promises," I say with mock annoyance, then head to the table and take a seat. "So what's on the agenda? More sightseeing?"

"If you'd like."

"What about what you'd like to do?" He lifts a brow, and I shake my head. "Head out of the gutter."

He thinks for a minute and then smiles. "I have just the thing."

"Do tell?"

"No. It's a surprise . . ." He laughs while shaking his head and then standing up.

"Where are you going?" I ask.

"To shower."

"Aren't you going to ask me to join?" I bite my lip. This isn't like me. I'm not this girl. I've never had a sexual appetite like this, but Nathaniel brings out another side of me, a side that is unquenchable. That coupled with pain pills and wine, and I'm actually able to enjoy sex . . . for now. I don't know how long this Madeline will last, so I welcome it.

"I'm playing hard to get."

I place my mug down, stand, and put my hands on my hips in protest.

He stares at me for a moment, assessing me, and I think he's actually going to keep the charade going that he doesn't want me. Instead, he surprises me yet again when he leans down, throws me over his shoulder, and swats me lightly on the rear.

"Come on, you're dirty. It's time to clean you."

Once we're out of the shower and dried off, both of us stand in the bathroom. I'm in a bathrobe, and he has a towel tied around his waist, his perfectly shaped V staring back at me.

"What's the plan today?" I ask, trying hard not to let the saliva pooling in my mouth drool. How can I want him again when I just had him?

"I changed my mind. No plans today," he responds. Pulling the towel from around him, he stands naked before me.

Shit.

Now I really want another round.

I walk over to the counter and pop my pills. His ass is to me now as he scrubs his torso with the towel.

"I figured you were jet lagged and needed a day off to recoup."

I stare at his naked body and lick my lips. "And by recoup, you mean . . . ?"

"Shag all day."

I nod, still willing myself to keep my cool and not jump his bones. The truth is, I need to wait for my pain pills to kick in. I'm not used to having this much sex, and the more sex I have, the more pain I have. Back in New York, we only had sex a handful of times, so I was able to drink a bit and loosen up my body, and I always took pain medication beforehand so I could enjoy it. But here, it's been so often, I'm not sure how my body will respond, and I'm a bit worried.

I'm lost in my thoughts when I see a towel being thrown at me. I catch it even though I'm surprised and stare at a naked Nathaniel.

"Do you mind putting that on the side?"

"On the side?" I ask, completely perplexed by what he's saying. "On the side of what?"

He lets out a throaty chuckle. "On the side," he repeats as if I should know what the hell he's talking about.

"What the heck are you talking about?" Still naked, he walks over to me, takes the towel, and sets it on the counter that's beside me.

"On the side." He winks.

"Seriously?" I scratch my head. "What is that, a Briticism?"

"It is. I'm just taking the piss." He grins like the cat who ate the canary.

I glare at him with mock annoyance, which only makes him throw back his head and laugh.

"Stop being an ass."

"The proper way of saying it is arse."

I drop his towel on the floor and shake my head, all while stifling my own giggle. "Get dressed."

---

Staying home yesterday was just what I needed because I woke full of energy today. I'm not sure what Nathaniel has planned, but I'm excited to find out.

As soon as we enter the park, in the distance, the palace stands like a dream. A light dusting of snow must have fallen overnight because the Kensington Garden has a majestic feel to it. Everything is white and pristine. I wrap my scarf tighter around my neck and look up at Nathaniel.

"This is beautiful."

"It is," he says while staring at me, never pulling his gaze away.

I cock my head at him. "Kensington Palace." I give him a stern look and then point in the direction. "Look at it."

"Lovely." He grins.

"Look at the damn palace."

"I have everything I want to see right here," he says offhandedly.

With a shake of the head, I push past him and start walking through the snow-clad gardens as if I know where I am going.

"All right," Nathaniel finally says as he picks up his pace to meet my step. "Follow me."

"Is this the first of my surprises?" I ask.

"What makes you think I have multiple ones?"

I stop walking, turn to him, and give him an "are you being serious" look.

He laughs. "Fine, I might have one or two up my sleeve."

"See, I knew it. Only you would plan surprises for a girl who doesn't like surprises."

"You love it, Tink." He takes my hand in his like he does so often these days, and I welcome the warmth of his fingers. Although I have a scarf on, I don't have gloves. It's not snowing now, but it certainly is cold. Gloves would have been smart. Luckily for me, I have him to warm me up.

"This way."

We continue to walk, each step transporting us farther into the winter wonderland that surrounds us. It's like a dream. Or a fairy tale. A perfect fairy tale where anything can happen and everything is possible.

Standing in front of me is a statue. But it's not just any statue. A light dusting of snow covers the bronze, but that doesn't hide the shape of a little boy standing on what seems to be a mountain. In his hand is an instrument he's playing with his mouth, like a flute or a pipe.

"Is that . . . ?" My words trail off as I look at this beautiful piece of history.

"Why, Tink, it is." He pulls me closer to look at the statue of Peter Pan in front of us.

"It's amazing."

"I thought you might like it." His voice is soft and low, and I realize this means as much to him as it does to me.

"Like it? I love it. It's amazing." I step even closer, as close as I can get. It's close enough I can almost touch it, but I don't dare.

"How did it get here?"

"The author, JM Barrie, had it commissioned in secret, and then one night as if by magic, it appeared in the same spot as Peter lands his bird-nest boat in the story, *The Little White Bird*."

"Wow," I mutter. It's really the only word I can say.

Together we stand there, his arm now wrapped around me. Neither of us speaking, just staring at Peter. He reminds me of Nathaniel at this moment, whisking me away on an adventure. As I stare, I wonder if it could really be that easy. Can one just never grow up? Not have real problems.

No, unfortunately not.

Even Peter had to grow up someday.

Liquid starts to form in my eyes. It's freezing, so he won't notice. He'll just think I'm cold. As if my body understands what my heart needs, I shiver.

He tucks me deeper into his chest. Rubbing his hands up and down on my back to warm me up. "Fancy a cup of tea?" he says, finally breaking the silence.

"I would love one."

"Brilliant. Follow me."

# chapter thirty-one

## NATHANIEL

W E SIT ACROSS FROM ONE ANOTHER AT A SMALL TABLE along the window with a perfect view of the gardens. She was right when she said it was fantastic. It's truly lovely.

Like her.

She's caught in a daydream, staring out the window in the direction of Peter. I knew she'd like it. My little Tink. But I didn't realize how affected she would be seeing it. She doesn't think I know, but I saw the tears. I let her pretend she was cold, but I know better.

I'm not sure what that was about.

Was it me?

Is this too much for her? Is she starting to have feelings for me?

I narrow my gaze and shake my head. No. That's not it. It's more. Something else is going on with her.

I want to know what.

I need to know what.

But I'll never ask. I can't. That would be crossing a whole other line, and as much as I like spending time with Madeline, I can't make this real. I refuse.

I lost my heart once, and it was stomped on. Finding the person you thought was the love of your life in bed with another man is one thing, but when it's your best mate, that's a whole other level of betrayal.

I really thought Cecile was the one for me. Her family had a long-standing relationship with mine. We grew up together, but the truth is, I drove her away. She was ready for more, and as much as I loved her, I wasn't.

I'm not ready to settle down, and I'm not sure I'll ever be. Eventually, the time will come when I'll need to secure an heir. I know it seems like a prehistoric tradition, an heir. But when your family lost everything, a legacy is all you have, and my grandfather built that legacy. With the loss of my parents, it rests on me to secure our future, and I can't fail that.

"What are you thinking about?" Madeline's voice pulls me from my thoughts, and I have to grin to myself. She was lost and now I am.

"My parents."

I'm shocked I admit that. But when I do, her face softens, and she leans forward in her chair. "Would you like to tell me about them?"

Lifting my drink, I take a sip, wetting my throat. It's dry for some reason, probably from my thoughts. "I was just thinking about . . ." I don't want to say about me having a child one day. But at the same time, I don't want to lie. "My legacy," I finally say.

She furrows her brow, not understanding.

"When my parents died, it fell upon me to carry it out since I'm an only child."

"That must be a lot of pressure." She sighs.

"It is. My grandfather is everything to me. But honoring his wishes, after all he's done, it's worth it."

"He's a lucky man to have you."

"No, I'm the lucky one."

"No," she argues. "You don't see it, but you're a good man."

"And you see this?" I laugh. "Just a few months ago, you wanted to hire a hit man to take me out."

"I would've never gone that far . . ."

Perhaps not, but only because an assassin would be bloody expensive.

"A mere accident then?"

"Well, obviously." She smirks, and I answer her with a chuckle. "No, seriously. I was wrong, and I see that now. When the time comes, you'll do it."

"I'm not so sure I'll be able to."

"You will. We all have to grow up one day." She looks over at the garden, and I know she's referencing Peter Pan. If she only knew how wrong she is. I might never grow up.

---

When we arrive at the next location an hour later, trekking the blocks in the cold was worth it. Her nose is pink now and tucked behind her scarf, but she's a trooper, never showing how cold she is.

"It's March . . . shouldn't London be warm right now?"

"Apparently, our weather is as unpredictable as yours." I laugh as I pull her closer to warm her up.

When we turn the corner, and she sees her next surprise, her smile extends across her face. It's so broad it reminds me of the first rays of sunlight at dawn. You want to bask in its heat, its warmth, and feel its rays awaken every nerve in your body. That's what Madeline does. She awakens something that lies dormant in me.

I should mind, but I don't. Instead, I bask in it.

"Ready to skate?"

"As ready as I'll ever be."

"I'll make sure you don't fall. I won't let you fall."

She stares at me, and I can't read the look in her blue eyes, but then she whispers, "I know."

Children's laughter filters through the air as we skate hand in hand.

"You're better today," I assess.

"Well, I couldn't be any worse."

"No. You couldn't."

"You're an ass."

"It's arse. We're in London now."

After a few more laps, I can see she's shaking, so I lead her back to the exit. We retrieve our boots and quickly set on our way back to my flat. When we are only a few blocks away, my mobile rings. I groan.

"What's wrong?"

"It's my cousin," I mumble.

"Are you going to answer it?"

"No."

She gives me a hard stare.

"Very well," I say to her and then answer. "Hello."

"Nathaniel . . ."

"What can I do for you, Eddie?" Contempt drips out of my mouth.

"We heard you were in town."

"You heard right. How can I be of help?"

"How, indeed. Imagine my surprise when you never called, dear cousin. Well, no worries, we found out."

"Good for you, Sherlock. Is there a point to this call?"

"There is a baby shower being thrown in Gretchen's honor tomorrow, and we would like you to come."

"I'm not alone."

"We would like both of you to come."

I look away at Madeline. "A party," I whisper.

She shrugs.

"We'll be there."

I hang up, and I can feel her still looking at me.

"Where are we going?" she asks.

"It's just a party," I say. Still walking, we are no longer holding hands, and she trails me. I don't mean to be this way, but my cousin sets it off in me. We don't speak for the remainder of the block.

When we enter my flat, I hold the door open for her, but once she's inside, I focus on other things, not wanting to speak for fear that I will take my anger out on her.

"What's going on?" she asks, putting her hand on my shoulder.

I turn around and face her. "We have to go to the baby shower tomorrow."

Her eyes go wide, and her face blanches. "Why do we have to go?" she finally asks.

"Don't ask daft questions. Of course, we have to go. You know this."

Her jaw tightens. "Well, why do I have to go?" she grits out. As her words filter through my mood, I realize I've upset her with my snide comment.

Reaching out my hand, I pull her toward me into a hug. "I'm sorry for what I said."

"I don't want to go," she whispers.

"I know. I don't want to go either."

She moves away from me and crosses her arms in front of

her chest. "No. I'm not going," she assesses, and she sounds like a petulant child. I've never seen her like this. Sure, Tink can be difficult, but this is different. She's cold, distant, and nothing like the woman I have grown to care about. If anything, she's actually acting like a spoiled brat. My head inclines, and I look at her head-on. She looks at me back, her posture straight and her jaw clenched.

"I know you hate him," I say, moving closer.

She shakes her head. "It's not that."

"What are you on about? Make me understand."

"I can't," she whispers, and I step back into her.

Wrapping my arm around her shoulder, I start to rub her back. "Please." I pull back and tilt her chin up, making her meet my gaze. "I need you with me."

"Why?" she mumbles, biting her lip. This isn't the strong woman I know, and it breaks something in me to know I did this to her. But regardless, I still need her with me but not for the reason she must think, and as much as I know I should say what I'm about to say, she has to know.

"I need you with me, Tink," I say again, imploring her to read between my words.

"Why?" she asks again, this time a tad more forceful.

"Because I can't do it without you," I admit on a sigh.

She stares at me for a second, digesting my words. Her shoulders rise and fall with her breath, and then finally, when I'm not sure what she will say, she gets on her tiptoes, places a kiss on my lips, and mutters, "Okay."

Instantly, her words relax me. I might hate that I have to go, but having Madeline with me is what I need and not just for our charade.

No, it's so much more than that.

# chapter thirty-two

## MADELINE

THIS IS ONE HUNDRED PERCENT THE LAST PLACE I WANT TO be. I would rather be standing at the gates of Hell right now, buzzing the goddamn intercom until someone escorted me in. At least there, I might get a tan. I shiver as we approach the building. Or at least be warm, for that matter.

I told him I shouldn't come, and I meant it. I don't want to be here right now.

*Not at all.*

But then he said those words to me, so here I am. Standing beside my fake boyfriend, but now my real friend, entering a place worse than Hell.

As we stand outside the large estate waiting for the door to open, I'm taken aback by the sheer size of the place. Nathaniel must see it because he groans. "Edward is doing quite well for himself."

"Yeah, you can say that again. If he's doing this well, why the need to take more?"

"That's how some people are. Nothing is ever good enough for them. All they want is to take, take, and take."

"Are you like that?" I ask.

"Hardly."

"But you want this." I motion to the building standing tall in front of us.

"No, I don't want this." He lifts his hand in gesture. "What I want is what is mine. Nothing less, nothing more. I want my legacy and all that entails. I want what was meant to be my father's." His voice drops low on the last word, and a feeling of sadness engulfs me.

"You'll get it," I say with a sincerity I didn't think was possible for me. It's not that I'm not sincere, but I'm also not warm and fuzzy. Ice Queen and all. But here I am holding his hand and comforting him, and even though this isn't natural for me, it feels natural with him.

I'm mid-thought, about to micromanage the statement my brain just said, when the door flings open. A butler. I shouldn't be shocked. But I am. I know the level of money is leaps and bounds above what I am used to, and I'm used to a lot, so that says something. But for some reason, even though we rode the corporate jet to get here, and even though I know Nathaniel has more money than God, I have a hard time reconciling him with this.

He might be arrogant, but he's not ostentatious.

He might have money, but he doesn't flaunt it.

Even now, while I'm wearing a knee-length black fit and flare dress with black tights and knee-high boots, he still looks more casual than I do in his dark-wash fitted jeans, button-down, and blazer.

His hair looks like a good case of bed head, which, since we did have sex just before we left, makes sense. But while I freshened up from the midmorning romp, he didn't, and to me, it's obvious.

That's not to say he doesn't look sexy. Oh Lord, does he ever, but even I know a post-orgasmic bed head isn't appropriate for a baby shower.

Baby shower.

The idea of it makes my heart lurch in my chest.

"The party is being held in the parlor."

As we step in through the large foyer, I follow Nathaniel into what must be the parlor. The room is set up for tea service, and it appears we are here for high tea rather than a party. Across the room is Nathaniel's cousin Edward and his very pregnant wife.

I hate that I have to be here.

I can't shake the feeling weaving its way through every molecule of my body. I hate how I respond to this stimulus. Seeing her, seeing her round belly and her hand resting on it, seeing the couple before me. I don't know them, and I don't know if they are, in fact, in love, but from where I'm perched, it appears so. He puts on a front of utter devotion to her right now, and it makes me feel weak watching. I know what this feeling is oh too well, and as it slides into my blood, its venom spreads.

Jealousy.

An uncontrollable jealousy is poisoning me. As it spreads, it strips me of all feeling of happiness and leaves me bitter and empty inside. It hammers home just how fake all this is.

Nathaniel's hand on my back. *Fake.*

The kiss on the street. *Fake.*

Everything in my life is *fake*.

The only thing that is real right now is a painful reality. Everyone around me is moving on, having kids, and getting married, but I'm in the same place.

The feeling rises to a point I can't control it, so I turn,

looking down, and whisper, "I'm going to find the bathroom."

"Let me show you. The loo is this way." He takes my hand. I try to fight it because right now, I don't want to be touched, but he won't have it.

He pulls me down a corridor. I know this isn't the bathroom for the public, this is a bathroom for a family member, tucked away and secluded. When we reach it, he turns the knob and pushes me inside.

I can feel his eyes. They bore into me even though I'm looking at the ground.

"Look at me."

"No."

"Goddammit, Tink. Look at me."

I oblige.

When he sees a tear, he wipes it. "What's going on with you?" he asks, but the way he says it is with concern.

"I just don't feel well," I say, but he's not buying it.

"Is this too much?" he asks softly. "Is being with me here too much?"

"Yes," I admit on a sigh. He lets out his own breath.

"Are you falling for me?" he asks, and I lift my head and meet his gaze. He's reading this moment all wrong, and I'm not sure how to respond to that. He sees a girl who wants more, but he has that more wrong, and I'm not even sure what to say.

"That's not it."

Now he looks confused. His forehead furrows and fine lines form on the normally perfect skin.

"What is it then?"

"It's okay." I force a smile. "I'm okay, I-I just . . ."

"You just what? You can talk to me." He lifts my hands and places them on his lips, an intimate gesture that threatens to destroy what little composure I have left. I rack my brain for an answer, anything feasible other than the truth.

"I just miss my family." I make my voice sound meek as if this is my weakness and I'm admitting it to him. I make myself sound small. It's not my truth, no, this is a lie, but he never needs to know my truth.

His eyes widen, and then he does the one thing I don't expect. He laughs.

I look at him confused.

"I don't even really know your family, and I miss them too when surrounded by these vultures."

His joke works. It makes my lip rise into a smile of its own accord. We stand there laughing for a bit, then he cocks his head.

"Ready to face the vultures?" He winks, and I nod.

As ready as I'll ever be.


When we stumble back into his apartment sometime later, I'm beat. My body aches, and to be honest, I'm emotionally drained. I step past him and make my way into the bathroom. Walking over to the sink, I open my pill container and pop a few of my pills. It won't make me feel perfect, but it will make me feel good enough. The truth is, I need a bath and to relax. I stretch my arms and then start to knead my corded muscles.

"You okay?"

"Yeah, just tense, I guess." *Nothing a glass of wine and a few pills wouldn't fix.*

"What did you take?" he asks, catching me off guard.

"Nothing, just my prescription."

"For?"

"Nosy much?" I chide, but I don't want him asking these

questions. It feels personal, and right now, I don't want personal. When he continues to stare at me, I sigh. "Pain pills. And before you say anything, for my stomach. And yes, my doctor gave them to me."

"What's wrong with your stomach?" He looks concerned, and I feel bad for worrying him, but this is personal, and I hate talking about me.

"I appreciate that you're concerned, but this is kind of a private thing. I don't like to discuss—"

"Just tell me you are okay."

I let out a forced laugh. "Of course, I'm okay." I look at him, and he looks visibly unsettled as he frowns at me. "It's not life-threatening or anything. It's just embarrassing." I smile.

"Ohhhh," he says, and I'm not sure if he does know, but I just nod anyway. Easier that way. "Can I do anything?"

"Would you mind if I take a bath?"

"Of course not. You should. Today is our last day before we have to go back to work, planning the event next week, so you should relax. How about I run the water, and you grab a glass of wine for yourself? Can you drink on your pills?"

"Yeah, it's fine," I lie because I really shouldn't, but right now, I don't care.

I need the relief.

I pad into the kitchen, grab a bottle of wine from the fridge and a glass, and then pour. The combo of the pills and the wine will take it all away. I don't drink on my pills often, but sometimes, I need the extra help to get through the pain. The combination I'm sure is not something my doctor will approve of, but I'm here with Nathaniel, and I don't want to ruin the moments I have with him. I don't want it to hurt when he touches me. So instead, I'll numb my body and hope it works.

When I return, there are foamy bubbles floating to the surface.

Placing the glass down, I strip down and step into the water. I'm not sure where Nathaniel went, but I welcome the solitude. Slipping into the water, I stifle a moan. It feels so good. Once settled, I take a sip and then lean back and relax.

I'm halfway through the glass and most certainly buzzed when I hear him approach. I look up at him.

"Hi," I whisper, my eyes half closed in relaxation. A euphoric feeling spreads through my limbs and rests in my belly.

"You look comfy."

"I am."

He tilts his head and stares. "Room for one more in there?" He smirks. I move forward, allowing space behind me, and peer over my shoulder.

"It seems there is." I smile.

"Brilliant."

I watch with hooded lids as he strips down bare. Then he steps in behind me, nestling me in the juncture between his legs. It's a very intimate position, but I love it. Right now, this is exactly what I need.

He touches my shoulder, massaging the tight muscles. I moan at the touch. My sounds of enthusiasm just grow as he touches me until he's groaning himself.

"Tink, if you don't stop making those noises, I'm going to have to fuck you in here."

"So fuck me," I say.

"We don't have protection."

"No worries there. All clean, and no pregnancy," I say.

"I'm clean too."

That's enough for me. Maybe I shouldn't trust him after his

previous exploits, but I do. It's a crazy feeling, but I do trust him.

I turn my body and then straddle his hips.

His erection settles between my thighs. We are nose to nose, his lips open, mine as well. Each breath I exhale, he inhales as I push down and take him inside me. Once he's fully sheathed, I start to rise and fall on his length, riding him slowly, leisurely, as though we have all the time in the world. Each movement intensified by our locked eyes and our shared breath.

It feels too good.

Deep.

Meaningful.

If I allowed myself to believe I would think this is more, but I don't. I just decide to live in the moment. And enjoy. With one last rise, I fall over the edge and shatter into a million pieces, coming apart around him.

"I'm going to come," he groans. And then he does. He follows me over the edge into bliss, coming apart inside me.

---

"We are so fucked," I hear Valentina shout as Nathaniel and I walk into the large suite in the Mandarin where the team is working today. I have no idea what is going on, but whatever it is doesn't sound good. Especially since Val always keeps her cool. I'm usually the one who gets angry, not her, and by the sounds coming from the room, she's pissed.

When we walk into the living room, I'm taken aback by what I find. All the fabrics are on the floor. Clothes are everywhere.

And Val is on the floor, back against the wall, her hands buried in her hair.

"What the hell, Val?"

"Oh, thank God!" she exclaims.

"What's going on?"

"I need you."

I narrow my eyes at her and her position on the floor. "Yes, that's obvious, but why?"

"It fell through," she cries out.

"What fell through?"

"The venue. It's gone."

Nathaniel chooses that moment to step out from my back. "What are you going on about? There is no way—"

"It's true. I just got the call," she groans loudly, cutting him off.

"Val, I'm going to need you to calm down and tell me exactly what happened," I say. I perch myself directly in front of her, and she needs to crane her neck to look up at me. I can see the tears in her eyes.

Shit.

This is bad.

"I got a call from the event space. Apparently, there was a mistake . . . They can't accommodate us."

I hear Nathaniel behind me.

"I need to speak to George." A long-drawn-out sigh. "Now." His voice is loud and assertive, and it makes a chill run down my spine. I have seen many sides of him, but never one this angry. "What do you mean you overbooked?" He goes quiet. "That's horseshit."

Quiet. "No. I don't want to hear any excuses." More quiet. "I will have your job for this."

He hangs up. "Fuck!"

"What happened?"

"Apparently, there was a mistake . . ." He goes silent again.

"What are we going to do?" I walk over to him and place

277

my hand on his arm. He looks pissed and stressed, and I understand why. Everyone from the London office is invited, including the entire board.

"Do you trust me?" he asks.

I look at him, his eyes imploring me to answer. I run my fingers across his skin, down his forearm, and over his clenched knuckles. "Of course."

"Then please trust me to handle this."

I lift on my tiptoes and kiss him on the lips. "I trust you, but what can I do to help?"

"I'm going to make a few phone calls, and when I'm done, I'm going to need that beautiful brain of yours to come up with a plan."

"I can do that."

"I know you can, Tink. If anyone can, it's you."

"I'll just sprinkle pixie dust." I wink.

For the first time since walking in, he smiles and looks calmer. I watch as he walks into the bedroom. I hold up my hand to Val. "Let's clean this place up."

"Okay." She gets up, and together, we start to clean. By the time the room looks again like a hotel room and not like a bomb exploded, Nathaniel walks in.

"What have you got for us?"

"A location." He smirks. "And I think it's going to be great."

"Talk to me."

"My friend owns a gallery."

"An art gallery?" Val asks.

"What other type of gallery is there?" he mocks, rolling his eyes. I swat him.

"Just tell us. Jeez. It's not like we have to plan an event in four days."

"Okay, okay. My old friend from university owns an art gallery."

"And by old friend, you mean . . . ?"

"Yes, I slept with her. Really, is this important now, Tink?"

Feeling chastised, I groan, "No."

"She offered us the gallery for the night."

"Is it in our budget?" I ask, always being practical.

"Let me worry about the budget. You worry about the plans."

"I can do that. Val, is this okay with you?"

"Yeah." She turns to Nathaniel. "Thank you. You really saved us."

His face turns a bit flushed, and I want to laugh. She's made him uncomfortable. I never thought I'd see that. It's cute. He's cute.

I stare at him for a minute, thinking about just how wrong I was.

He really is amazing.

"Stop staring, Tink . . ." He laughs, and I lick my lips.

"God, guys. We have work to do," Val teases.

"We do."

All three of us sit down at the long wood table in the dining area of the suite. Each with a job. Each working on our own task. Six thousand miles away and we're all back in an office together.

And I love it.

# chapter thirty-three

## NATHANIEL

DAYS HAVE PASSED, AND ALTHOUGH MADELINE IS STILL staying with me, I have barely seen her. We both work all day, side by side like a team, but it's work, nonetheless. No more day trips around London, laughing and smiling. At night, we fall into bed. Some nights we have sex. Some we don't. It's like we are an old married couple except we're not.

The thought should scare me, but it doesn't. What actually scares me more is that it doesn't scare me at all.

What does that even mean?

This will run its course soon and then what? Why does it have to end?

It does.

It has to.

There is no bloody way I'll leave myself open to anything more, so when the time comes—and it will come—we will part ways.

For some reason, the thought makes me feel angry.

Not wanting to know what the anger means, I throw myself back into what I'm working on. Tonight is the cocktail pop show. The ladies are getting ready, and I'm dressed. With time to kill, I call Oliver, and we decide to meet at Blacks.

Looking at my watch, it's time, so I shut down my laptop and head out the door. A short ride later, I'm walking into the private club.

I find him in his usual spot with a newspaper or maybe a magazine in front of him. He's staring at the cover, but I'm not sure what it's about. What has me wondering is when he takes it in his one hand, crumples it, and throws it in the trash.

"Olly," I say as I approach.

He looks up, completely taken off guard by my approach. "Nathaniel." He stands and gives me a one-arm hug, patting my back. "It's been too long."

"Bollocks, I just saw you."

"Yeah, mate, except you bailed."

"Only because Cecile was there."

He shakes his head. "Would that be so awful? If I remember correctly, she was a good shag."

I shake my head. "She was, but she was also a big cock-up on my part."

"Don't be so hard on yourself. You couldn't possibly know she was fucking all of England." He winks.

"Not all of it."

"Just your best mate."

"Sod off."

He reaches over and takes the bottle of scotch and pours me a glass.

"Ready for me, I see?" I ask.

"Always."

We both lift our glasses and take a swig. "You coming tonight?"

"Maybe," he responds.

I look down at him over my glass. "What's going on with that?" I say, pointing at the crumpled-up magazine.

"Just a thorn in my side."

I lift my brow at his nondescript answer. "Anyone I know?" I ask.

"Just an American."

"Interesting . . ." I ponder who it is as he lifts his drink and takes the rest in one gulp. "Very interesting."

"Enough about me. What about the American you're with? Are there wedding bells in the future?"

"Jesus, we aren't women." I laugh.

"True, true, not sure what came over me. Okay, well, is she a good shag at least?"

"I can't take you anywhere."

"Apparently not." He shrugs.

We don't talk about shagging or Americans. The topic is officially off-limits. After one more drink, I leave Blacks to head to the event space.

The party is being held at a posh little art gallery. Each model has a piece of the collection, and Valentina's sketches are displayed on the white walls. I find the team standing together laughing. Madeline's back is to me, her short neon pink cocktail dress showing off too much leg for my taste. Not that she doesn't look gorgeous, but she'll enthrall every man in this place.

A feeling of possession sweeps over me. I reach my arms around her waist and pull her toward me. She lets out a little giggle as I place my lips on her exposed neck and kiss a trail up. Oohs and aahs are heard around us. After one last peck, I pull away and turn my gaze toward Val.

"You ready?" I ask her.

"Yeah, I think I am."

"It's going to be brilliant."

"Thank you for everything," she says to me.

"My pleasure."

Still holding her, the doors open, and I finally have to pull away, but I secure her hand in mine.

"You know, at some point, you'll have to let me go."

"Never." I laugh, but something with that word resonates.

When the crowd starts to filter in, and the music is flowing through the air, Madeline is in her element.

I did finally let her go, and like Tink, she's flittering around the space. I watch her for a while.

"You have it bad," Oliver says from beside me.

"You decided to show up?"

"Beautiful women, how could I say no?"

"Well, don't let me stop you. Go catch yourself a model."

"Catch? No. Distract me for the night? Yes."

Just as if conjured by our talk, a beautiful, leggy blonde strolls by, and just like that, as fast as he came, now he's gone. I can't help but laugh.

"Too bad your original venue fell through. What a shame."

I turn toward the new voice to see my cousin beside me. Obviously, he did something. "It was you?" I ask, but I don't need his confirmation. The smug look on his face is confirmation enough. I grit my teeth and move in toward him.

"Enjoy it while you can, cousin. But this . . . this doesn't prove anything. While you are fucking the help, I'm securing your grandfather and the board another billion. And as for the new location, it's cheap just like your American . . ."

I step up to him and grab his shirt. "Don't you ever speak of her again."

"But isn't she? You are her boss, she's the help, and she's—"

283

I tighten my grip, and his face turns darker. A crowd starts to form, and then I feel a hand on me.

"Let him go."

I don't.

"You have to let him go," she whispers. "You are causing a scene."

That snaps me out of my haze. Lucky for me, the only bodies around me are Oliver, Val, Eric, and Madeline.

"Leave."

And he does. Smart move.

Olly has blocked the view, so no one but us knows about the scene, and I'm thankful for it. Now that he is gone, the tension settles in. But in typical Oliver form, he reaches his hand out to Madeline.

"You must be the girl who has my mate so tied up."

"I don't know about tied up, but I'm certainly the girl." She winks before she places a kiss on my lips and strides away. When she's too far to hear, Olly's face grows serious.

"What the fuck was that? The board is here, mate."

"It's one thing to go after me, but to go after Madeline . . . I just couldn't let him."

"And why is that?" His eyes glint of something.

"She doesn't deserve it, man. She's amazing. She's the hardest worker I know. She's smart, funny . . ."

"And beautiful . . . Hmm, is this more than you're letting on?"

"Don't be daft. You know I don't do relationships."

"Why not?" He shrugs. "So your ex was a shrew. That doesn't mean there's no chance."

"I don't want a relationship, and neither does she."

"Maybe neither of you knows what you want, but if you

care about her and have fun with her, why not see where it can go?"

I shrug him off before stepping away, needing distance.

But Olly's words have already hit their mark, playing on a loop over and over again in my brain. Why can't it be more? Who says it can't? Not everything is black and white. Our relationship can be shades of gray.

We can make our own rules.

———————————

Before I know it, weeks have passed and we are done with Milan and in a car driving from the airport to Paris. I look over at Madeline, who is staring out the window, lost in thought. She looks peaceful resting her head on her hand, and I wonder if she is actually sleeping.

"I can't believe we are here," she says, her voice soft and in awe as Paris comes into view.

"It's quite lovely, right?"

"It is," she agrees. The car continues to roll on, and soon, we are navigating the busy streets.

"I wish we had more time here."

"After all the shows, we should be free. Have you considered taking a vacation?"

She laughs at my suggestion as if the idea is preposterous. "I can't take a vacation."

"Why not? You never take off. What are you saving your days for?"

"Maybe I'll need them one day." She shrugs but turns her head out the window to face away from me.

I wonder if she's thinking of taking time off after this is over and doesn't want to tell me. That way, we can part ways without her having to see me. The thought makes my mouth dry. In only a few more weeks left, this charade is going to end.

We never set a time limit, but it's always been assumed that after the Paris show, I'd have the power to sway the board. With all the success that Valentina Fisher is having right now, it only seems fitting that they would agree. Not only in the past few months since I acquired the brand have we signed deals for the largest and most exclusive retailers to carry our brand, but every celebrity is wearing us. We have been covered in every magazine, and now we will be featured with our own show in Paris.

It's pretty incredible what we've accomplished, but my place here is coming to an end. Sure, I'll still own it, but it will become just another profitable endeavor like most of the Harrington investments.

Hopefully, after this, I will take my proper spot in Harrington. The thought should make me excited, but I'll miss Tink. I'll miss seeing her every day. And the joy she brings me. Not just the sex, but the friendship. Because that's what I realize; she's become a close friend of mine. Maybe after this is over, we can still talk.

Lord, I have become a bloody woman.

I'm luckily pulled from my thoughts by the car coming to a stop. We're here at the hotel. Everyone gets out of the cars and heads straight to the lobby. I had my team pre-check us in. We have so much to do; there isn't time for much else but working.

It doesn't take us long to make it up to the room. Of course I'm sharing my room with Madeline. I have been basically living with her for well over a month now. In London, in Milan, and now in Paris.

I find her staring out the window, lost in thought. I walk up to her and bracket my arms around her waist. "What are you thinking about?" I say as I place a kiss on top of her head.

"It's almost over," she whispers, and I wonder what she's referring to. Is she like me, dreading the inevitable?

"What?"

"All of it," she says on a sigh.

I turn her around until my eyes meet hers. "The show?"

"Yes, that but also . . ."

"Us?" I ask.

She nods.

"It doesn't have to be," I say, and the words shock me. I don't even know where they came from, but they did.

Her eyes widen. "What are you saying?"

"It doesn't have to be over, Tink. We can . . ."

"Date?" she asks, perplexed.

"I mean we already are, aren't we? We can make this real."

She stays quiet for a moment, thinking about my words. Then she swallows, and I dread what she's about to say. "What I want hasn't changed," she says. And I know she's talking about not wanting to get married, not wanting children.

"I know and I'm not saying I want that either. I don't. What I'm saying is for right now, we don't have to end. We can see what happens, where this leads . . ."

"I won't change my mind," she insists. For some reason, her words anger me, but I'm not sure why. I have always said the same thing, so why does it bother me so much?

Do I want more?

I decide not to dwell on that. I'm not ready for this to end, so instead of scaring her off with any more talk of the future, I bite down every rebuttal and argument that sits on my tongue.

"I know."

"And you're okay with that?"

"I am."

She thinks a bit longer, her face scrunching in thought. "Okay."

"Okay?"

"Yes."

I lift her jaw and trail my fingers over her lips. "Well, good." With that settled, I move forward and kiss her, parting her lips and devouring her. She entwines her arms around my neck and kisses me with abandon.

Pulling away, I turn her toward the city. The lights twinkle in the distance, the Eiffel Tower staring back at us as I place her hands on the window for support and then move to lower her pants and expose her arse to me. I push her forward so she bends at the waist. With her in position, I work to free my cock before thrusting into her waiting heat.

She feels amazing. She is amazing.

So right there, in front of the bright lights, in front of the city of love, I tell Madeline without any words how much more I want from her, how much I need her, and how I'm not ready to let her go.

---

Nerves are high. Everyone is excited. This is a turning point. Everyone who is anyone in fashion is in attendance. It's a who's who of the rich and famous.

The energy in the room is electric, and I drink it in. I'm going to miss this. After the event, I won't be flying back to New York with the team. I'll put them on one of my planes, and I'll be proceeding to my grandfather's estate in the country. I meant to ask Madeline to come with me, but I'll do it after the show. What we will do from there, I'm not sure. But right now,

I'm not going to dwell on that. We have a show to throw.

Unlike the last runway show I attended back in New York, I'm not sitting front and center. This time I'm backstage. This event isn't like the one in New York although the location is just as interesting. This time we went classic, not cutting edge.

"You ready?" I say as I pass Val.

"So ready." She laughs while pumping her hand in the air like a cheerleader. I can't help but laugh.

The models are lined up. All are beautiful and impeccable, but not one catches my gaze right now. There is only one woman I want to find. One woman I want to seek out. From across the room, I see her. She's stunning. I swear every day I know her she becomes more and more beautiful.

With quick strides, I make my way over to her. "Beautiful," I say, sweeping my gaze over her. "You are the most beautiful woman I have ever seen."

"Hardly. Have you looked over there? I bet every modeling agency in the world would beg to differ with you."

"Those women don't matter. Only you do."

A small smile plays on her lips as her face warms. Then she sweeps her gaze over me. "You don't look so bad yourself."

"Thanks. Happy to oblige."

"I'm sure you are." She laughs.

"You ready for this?"

She nods. "I am. I think it's going to be amazing."

"You've worked so hard. It will be."

Her eyes soften, and she takes my hand in hers. "You've worked hard too. None of this would have been possible without you and all your help."

"I didn't do that much."

She steps on her tiptoes and places a kiss on my mouth.

"You did. You should be proud. I'm sure your grandfather is. I'm sure the board is."

"Guess we'll find out soon."

"Is he here?"

"Who?" I ask.

"Your grandfather."

"No." I let out a sigh and she lifts her brow in question.

"He said he was ill."

"Is he okay?" Her voice cracks with concern.

"He said he was, but I'll see him at his house, and I'll make sure. Speaking of my grandfather . . . I wanted to know if you would come with me."

"To your grandfather's?"

"Yes, Tink. To my grandfather's."

"You want me to go with you to visit your grandfather with you? Won't that be weird?"

"Not really. The estate is large. You'll hardly know he's there. It's like being at a hotel with all the luxury and staff members."

"I-I'm not sure if I can . . ."

I move closer and tip her head up. "Please consider it."

"Okay. I will."

"Now let's go watch this show."

# chapter thirty-four

## MADELINE

I F I THOUGHT THE OTHER PROPERTIES WERE AMAZING, I WAS wrong. This house, estate, castle more like it, is a whole other meaning of wealth.

My mouth must be hanging open because I hear a chuckle beside me. "You should probably close your mouth, or a fly will fly in."

I turn my head and shoot daggers at him. "Shut it. Will you?"

"Never," he retorts.

I do as he says, though, I shut my mouth as we walk inside and make our way through the large foyer and down a long, wide hallway. Before I know it, we are in a parlor, but not the same type of parlor as Edward's. Nathaniel's cousin's home was big, but this home . . .

This is where I imagine a duke would have lived in the Regency period. I imagine this is where the wallflower would have tea. I smile to myself as the mental story takes root in my mind.

"Please have a seat. Your grandfather will be right down," a man in a suit says.

"Thank you, Rupert."

Nathaniel takes my hand and leads me to a very formal couch. Together we sit until the door opens and his grandfather walks in. This is only the third time I've seen him, maybe fourth, but I can tell he looks tired and run-down. His skin appears waxy. Dark circles surround his eyes.

"Grandfather, we didn't expect to see you." Nathaniel stands. "You remember Madeline."

"Of course I do, son." Hearing him call Nathaniel son makes me smile. I know how much Nathaniel values him, and it warms my heart to see them together. He slowly makes his way to us and takes my hand in his, placing a kiss on the top of my hand. "My grandson seems to think I'm senile. But what he doesn't know is I would never forget a beautiful woman." He winks.

And I giggle. "I like your grandfather," I say over my shoulder to Nathaniel.

"I'm happy to have you both here. I hope you enjoy your stay. Make my house your house, dear," he says. "I'll try to stay out of your hair."

"We wouldn't dream of not spending time with you," I answer back.

"I like her," he says as he turns to Nathaniel. "Don't let her get away."

It gets quiet after that comment, and we all sit down. Soon, a lady I haven't seen before comes in with a tray of tea. We make small talk, and before long, his grandfather excuses himself to rest. Once he's gone, I look over to see Nathaniel deep in thought with his brow furrowed.

"Everything okay?"

"I don't like seeing him sick."

"He did seem like he's still run-down."

"It's not that. I can't put my finger on it. He just seems more off than a cold. I need to talk to him about it. I hope everything is okay with him."

"I'm sure he's on the mend," I say, tilting my head and staring into his eyes. The green of his irises isn't its normal vibrant color today. No, today they look tired and far away as if something weighs on him, and it breaks my heart.

"I hope so . . ." he says.

I take his hand in mine and squeeze once. "How about you show me the house . . . castle you grew up in?"

His shoulders visibly relax with my comment.

"It's not a castle." He chuckles.

I roll my eyes. "The only thing you're missing is a moat."

He looks down while stifling a laugh.

"What?"

"We used to have one."

"What? You can't be serious."

"I am. But it's not what you think . . ."

"How can it be anything other than what I'm thinking? Was there or was there not water surrounding your *castle*?"

"There was."

"Unreal. So what happened?"

"There was water when he bought the estate. It was half empty, and it was disgusting. A casualty of neglect and WWII. Half of it was gone, so he filled it."

"Wow." I shake my head in awe. "So tell me more . . . Where do you keep the dragons?"

"In the dungeon, obviously."

My mouth drops. "Don't tell me you have a dungeon too?"

He shrugs. "Okay, I won't."

"You do?"

He looks off with a grin.

"Oh my God, you do. This place is really amazing. Show me everything."

His wicked smile spreads wider. "Don't worry, Tink." He steps in, trailing his hands on my arms. "I'll show you everything."

"Dirty boy."

"Only for you."

*Only for you too*, I want to respond, but I don't. I can't.

We spend the next few days enjoying each other's company. Being here with Nathaniel and his grandfather is the most relaxed I have ever been. We wake each morning and have breakfast with his grandfather in the morning room, then we throw on warm clothes and Nathaniel shows me the property. We trudge through the grounds damp with spring rain, and he shows me everything. From the tree he used to play in as a child to the pond where he skated. I feel so close to him, and no matter how much I know this isn't forever, I will never regret this time I've spent here.

Today I stretch my arms above my head as the early morning light streams in through the large windows that overlook the gardens down below. I wonder what we'll be doing today. Will it be another walk? Or maybe today Nathaniel will take me into town. Turning my body, I move to snuggle into him. He's still asleep, which I find strange because normally these past few days when I wake so does he.

A loud groan escapes his mouth as if on cue to my inner rambling. It actually sounds like an animal is being tortured. I pull back, sit up, and look down at him. He looks flushed in his face. I lift my hand and touch his head. He's warm.

"I'm dying," he croaks out.

"What's wrong? What do you feel?" I ask, concerned. I'm no stranger to feeling awful.

"Everything hurts."

I place my lips to his forehead this time, the same way my mom always did when I was a child. He feels less warm this way. I stand from the bed and pad over to the chair. "I'm going to see if anyone has a thermometer."

"Thank you." His voice is low and hoarse.

Once I have the robe wrapped around me, I walk down the hall. I'm not sure who to ask, but when I find a member of the staff cleaning the stairwell, I figure that's as good a place to start as any.

"Excuse me?"

"How can I help you, miss?" the young lady I've never seen before asks.

"I was wondering if you happened to know where I can find a thermometer?"

"Is everything okay?"

I lift my hand to calm her. "Yes, Nathaniel is not feeling so well. I just want to make sure he doesn't have a fever."

She nods. "Of course. Is there anything else I can bring you?"

"Would it be a bother to also have some ibuprofen, and maybe soup brought up to the room?"

"Yes. I'll make sure you have everything."

"Thank you so much . . ."

"Charlotte."

"Thank you so much, Charlotte."

She scurries off, and I head back to our room. Within five

minutes, a knock on the door delivers all the provisions I ordered. Placing everything down on the table, I make my way over to Nathaniel, to see if he, in fact, has a fever.

"What is it? How high?"

I look down at the strip I placed on his head, and surprisingly, it reads no fever. "Normal," I say. "I'm sure it's just a cold."

At that, he sneezes. "It's not a cold. I'm bloody dying." Turning my head from him, I have to stifle back a grin. Seeing as Nathaniel has no temperature and no other symptoms other than a sneeze, it's pretty obvious what his infliction is . . .

*The man flu.*

This is going to be a long few days.

Hours later, Nathaniel is even more convinced he will die. "I'm telling you, Tink. You need to take me to the hospital."

"You are not dying. You have the man flu." I laugh, not holding back anymore.

"I need water. My mouth is parched."

I let out a long breath. When will this end?

The man flu lasted for two days. *Two very long days.*

Finally, on day three, he's back on the mend. We spent the days with him curled in bed, and me reading to him. Today, I'm reading *Peter and Wendy*. He's better today, but in typical fashion, it's raining outside, so we decide to hole up in our room for one more day, just in case. His color is back, his body no longer aching, and by the way he looks at me when he thinks I'm not looking, he's better.

Halfway through the story, I hear his voice.

"Thanks for taking care of me," he says.

His words have me putting the book down and staring at him. This time with him showed me so much about Nathaniel. There are so many layers, so many pieces of the puzzle, but with each story he tells, with each touch, I know without a measure of a doubt that I am in love with Nathaniel Harrington. But I also know as each day passes that the end is coming soon. He says he wants to try, but we both know that's not possible. How can it be? One, he will start at Harrington Textiles in London. It's where he needs to be, and I need to be in New York. Long distance is hard enough, but we have so many other obstacles against us, and if I think about the fact I allowed myself to fall in love with him, I will fall to the floor and cry, but I won't do that. Instead, I will treat each day here with him as a gift, and I will enjoy every second of it. Every last minute. I will take the minutes, those seconds, and each memory and place them in a little spot in my heart to remember them forever.

As if he heard my brain running rapidly, Nathaniel brings it up a few hours later. Instantly, my back goes ramrod straight. He's stroking my naked back, his fingers trailing up my skin. He touches me all over as if he's memorizing my body. As if he is taking every divot and making a map.

"I love your body. It's perfect."

"I'm not perfect. I have scars."

He turns me over and places his finger over the small line on my abdomen. One of my many tiny incisions. Small white lines, so small you can barely see them.

"What's this from?"

"Laparoscopic surgery."

"For what?"

"Stomach issues," I respond. Not wanting to talk about it, I lift his hands and place them higher on my stomach. Right below my breast. He must understand because he stops, but now he just stares at me, not saying anything.

"I want to talk to you."

297

"Okay," I whisper, not knowing what he wants to talk about, but my stomach hurts and my chest feels heavy with uncertainty.

He crawls up my body. His weight is on his arms, but he hovers over me. "I know I said I wasn't ready to end this . . ."

*Thud.*

*Thud.*

My heart rate picks up, pounding in my chest.

"I didn't make it clear what that meant for me."

"What does it mean?" I whisper.

"I want to really try."

"But—"

"Listen. I know you have your reservations too, but why can't we see where this goes? We don't have to make any promises, but I'm not ready to walk away. I'm not ready to let you go to New York."

"What are you saying?" I ask, peering into his green eyes.

"I'm going to speak to my grandfather."

"But you need to be here."

He leans down and places a kiss on my lips and then lifts up again before he speaks.

"I can work from New York," he responds. His voice is soft and sincere, and I know if I ask this of him, he will.

"You want to come to New York . . . for me?"

"You make it sound like you never considered that as a possibility."

I nibble at my lower lip, staring at the ceiling. "I didn't."

"Well, it is. And I'm going to talk to him."

I don't know what to say. My breathing is all over the place. On the one hand, it's everything and more, but on the other hand, just because we are trying doesn't mean he'll want to be with me for the long term. Or forever. *You could just say okay and cross the bridge when we come to it. Not think about the future.*

As if reading my mind, he says just that. "Can't we just live for the present? Worry about the future later?"

Can I do that? I'm already in so deep. Can I put aside all my issues? Can I just enjoy him? *You love him. When he leaves, and he will, you will be devastated.*

"Just say yes. Don't think past yes. Just say yes." He leans forward, placing a kiss on my lips. "Say yes." He kisses me again, this time more forcefully. "Say yes." His tongue licks at my seam. I moan into his mouth, but he doesn't give me more, he just hovers. "Say yes, give me a chance."

"Yes."

His lips seal over mine. His tongue thrusts into my mouth, swirling against mine. I feel him grow hard between my thighs, and I open my legs for him. He doesn't break our kisses as he thrusts into me. It takes my breath away. The fullness, the kiss. The possession.

With each swipe of his tongue, he tells me how much he wants me, needs me, owns me. And I can't pull away. I can't think. I give all of myself to him. Moaning into his mouth, clawing at his back, I give him all my heart. I give him every part of me I have held back. I answer his thrust with my own, lifting my hips to take him deeper and remove any distance between us.

At this moment. No matter what obstacles we have, we are one, and together as one, we reach our high. We fall over the edge together.

A perfect match. In perfect symphony.

It's everything.

# chapter thirty-five

## NATHANIEL

W^AKING UP NEXT TO TINK IS SOMETHING I CAN GET USED to. No, allow me to amend—that I am going to get used to. This morning, before my eyes are even open, I'm rolling on top of her, spreading her legs, and thrusting inside. I hear the gasp as I enter, and my lids open. Lifting on to my elbows, I look into her eyes. They are tightly knit, and a deep line separates her brows.

"Open your eyes," I whisper, but she doesn't. She keeps them closed, so I halt my movements.

"I'm okay." She cringes.

"Please, Tink." I lift my hand and stroke her temple with the pads of my fingers "Open them." I need her to. That gasp wasn't one of pleasure.

Slowly, her lids flutter open. The blue of her irises is hazy, and her eyes are filled with tears, diluting the color. "Are you okay?"

She inhales, and I stifle a groan at the movement. I'm so deep inside her I feel everything. I feel every breath, but as much as I want to move, I need to make sure she's okay.

"It was just—" She lifts, and her nose scrunches as another

tear falls. Moving my hand, I swipe it away and place a soft kiss on her nose. "Just sudden. I guess I'm sore from this week."

"Do you need me to stop?" I ask, concern evident in my voice.

"No, I'm fine," she answers too fast.

That and the word she used—fine—means she's not. Fine is the worst word a woman can say.

I know what I need to do. I need to stop regardless of her words. I move to push off her, but her arm brackets around me, halting my movements.

"No," she implores. "Don't stop."

I gaze down at her, at my strong girl, and I can see and feel her strength in her words. She's giving me her heart, her body, and I want to take it all. I move slowly inside her. I kiss her mouth, and as I lose myself in her body, I realize in her I'm found.

The pace is steady, and I feel her loosening up to me, her body welcoming me in. I still see the small twinges of pain, but I continue thrusting slowly until I feel her tightening. With a gasp that I hope is pleasure, she comes undone. I allow myself then and only then to chase my own bliss.

It takes only a few more seconds, but it happens it's as my world turns on its axis.

Falling down upon her, I inhale her neck as our hearts beat together. Seconds or minutes pass, and she squirms and cringes again. I know I must be hurting her, so I lift, removing myself from the confines of her body. What I'm met with takes the air out of my lungs.

Blood.

Everywhere.

It coats my skin, it's splattered across her thighs, but it's the linens that make me gasp. Against the stark white, it's grizzly, reminding me of a scene from a murder movie.

"Bloody hell, Tink."

She looks down. Her eyes widen in shock, and then her lip starts to quiver. Tears fill her eyes again.

"I-I," she stutters. "My period . . ."

"It's okay." I place my hand under her jaw. She won't look at me as tears streak down her face. Her jaw is clattering from her sobs.

"Look at me." She does. "There's nothing to cry about." I run my finger up her jaw. "These things happen."

More sobs leave her mouth. Her face red and flushed from what I can only imagine is embarrassment. I can't even comprehend how she must feel right now. I'm uncomfortable, and it didn't even happen to me. I don't show her how I feel, though, because that will only make it worse. She needs me to be strong and show her it's okay. That everything will be okay.

"Here"—I stand—"I'll run the water, and once it's hot . . . we can wash together."

I walk to the en suite and turn the shower on, placing my hand under it to make sure it's warm enough.

When I walk back in, she's trying to strip the bed.

"Leave it."

"I can't. People will see," she whispers while she lifts her hands to cover her face.

"I don't care what people see."

"I do . . ." Lowering her hands, she continues to move, pulling the bloody sheet back.

"Stop."

That makes her, finally.

"I'll do it."

"I can't let you—"

I lift my hand. "You took care of me. Now let me take care of you. No saying no. March yourself to the shower, and I'll strip the bed. Once it's done, I'll join you."

She worries her lip before finally nodding. I hand her the towel in my hand, and then as soon as she's out of eyesight, I start to strip the bed. When I'm finished, I find her in the shower still crying. I understand she's embarrassed, but this reaction seems pretty severe. I cough to announce my presence, and she moves to straighten herself.

When I step in, I let the warmth of the water wash away everything. Together we lather and rinse until no remnants of what happened remain.

The only thing lingering are the shadows in Tink's eyes.

# chapter thirty-six

## MADELINE

L AST NIGHT WAS HARD. THE TRUTH OF MY LIES WEIGHS heavy on my tongue; they're so heavy I don't even know what to do. After the incident with the blood, Nathaniel held me, took care of me, and if it was possible, I fell even more in love with him than before. However, last night proves that sometimes love isn't enough, and I'm not sure what to do about this situation.

Today, he is off doing an errand, and I welcome the solitude to help me formulate a plan. Right now, I'm sitting in a large wingback chair in the library, thinking of my options when a noise startles me. Looking up, I find I am no longer alone in the room. His grandfather has joined me.

I place my book down. He looks at me with so much warmth, my heart expands. "I'm sorry for interrupting you, dear."

"Oh, you aren't interrupting. I'm just waiting for Nathaniel to come back."

"He should be back soon, but I'm happy he's away right now. I get the opportunity to talk to you." He smirks.

I smile in return. "What did you want to talk to me about?"

"Nathaniel."

That makes me sit up. "What about him?"

"My dear lad." He laughs, and I wonder where he's going with this. "You know I raised him?"

"Yes."

He nods. "When he told me about you, I knew he was lying."

My pulse picks up. "You did?"

"Of course, my dear. I raised him. I know everything about him."

"So you let him lie . . . ?"

"I had my reasons."

"Which were?" I ask, my head cocked. I'm not sure where this is going, but I'm getting uncomfortable. He must sense it because he takes the seat next to me and takes my hand in his.

"I saw how he looked at you at that very first meeting. My grandson has always been a lost boy . . ." His choice of words is so penitent to our story, I'm taken aback. "I saw you and what you brought out in him, and I knew you were perfect. You would be the woman who would make him grow up."

"But I didn't."

"You did. I see it. I can see the man he's become because of you. And what I see even more is how you complement each other."

"We aren't—"

He holds his hand up. "I know it didn't start off real, Madeline, but it is now. He loves you."

"He doesn't."

"He does. And I'm happy. That's all an old man like me wants. Nothing means more to me than family. I'm sure you know how the Harrington family lost everything. Everything but our name. Since then, all the men in my family have been Nathaniel. Our legacy. After we lost my son . . ." he croaks, holding back tears. "Nathaniel is our future. His children are our future. My whole life I worked for this, to build up our name. *For them.* They will carry on my name. Our name. All the Harrington men will be Nathaniel. My legacy. Our legacy. The idea that you will help bring me that legacy brings me more joy than you will ever know."

His words make me feel cold. Like an arctic breeze filters through me. All the lies I tell myself rush over me. I can't be ignorant to the truth. Not anymore. Not after yesterday. Not after the blood.

*This will never work.*

Nathaniel and I will never work.

I can't give him children. I want to. I have never wanted to give someone anything as much as I want to give him this . . .

But I can't.

Every single surgery. Every single appointment. Every single pain ricochets in my mind as each memory clouds me. Hovers over me.

*The blood.*

A stark reminder of my shortcomings and what the future will hold for me.

As this dear old man, the man who means every single thing to the man I love, looks at me, I see this is about more than just Nathaniel and me. I can't give them their legacy.

Ever.

That right, that blessing has been taken from me.

My uterus . . .

My body.

My ability to be the woman he needs is broken. I will never

have a child of my own.

I can feel the beat of my heart. It feels harder, heavy, broken. The reality of this situation comes crashing down on me. I need to end it. That will be my gift to this man. This will be the end of it. There is no question I will never love anyone the way I love him, but I can't. Regardless of what I want, or how heartbroken I will be, I can't be selfish.

Not anymore.

Needing the space to cry on my own, I smile. I force my lips to spread. "Nathaniel is lucky to have you." I stand.

"You're leaving?" he asks.

I beg myself not to cry. Not to let the tears that are begging to fall come. "I have to make a phone call," I say and walk up to him and place a kiss on his cheek. "Thank you for everything."

"My pleasure, my dear."

When I'm back in my room, I let the tears fall. They come in a torrent. Each tear is like a drop of blood. My blood. And I bleed.

The tears finally stop, and I stand. Wipe. And set off to pack.

I know he will be home soon. I need to be packed and call a car before he arrives, but the time comes before I know it, and he walks into our room. He stops. He seems to know something is wrong. He certainly knows when he sees the suitcase.

"What are you doing?" He steps farther into the room, his arms crossing in front of his chest.

"I got a call . . . I have to go back."

"What call?" he asks, his voice strained with concern.

"It's nothing for you to worry about," I say. I know he won't drop it, but I'm too weak, too exposed to say it, so I lie. What's one more at this point?

"Okay." He nods. "I'll pack . . ."

"No," I breathe out before I can stop myself.

"What do you mean no?"

I shake my head. I'm falling. I can feel the murky tears filling my eyes. "You can't come."

"Why the fuck not?" His voice rises in anger.

"I have been thinking . . ." *Why is this so hard? Because you love him. But you love him enough to know you can never be the right person for him.* "I can't do this anymore."

"What?" he hisses.

"Nathaniel . . ."

"No. Don't Nathaniel me."

"I have been thinking . . ."

"You have been thinking? I leave you alone for one afternoon, and this is what I come back to? It was just the other day when you said you would try. What the fuck happened?"

"I was thinking—"

"So you keep saying. Care to share your thoughts?" he grits.

"I spoke to your grandfather and—"

"What did he say?"

"He said how happy he was for us. He said . . ." I try to stifle the sob that is threatening to expel. "He said how important legacy was. How one day we would have children."

"So?"

"Nathaniel, I told you this. We spoke about this. I don't want children. We have been fooling ourselves to think this could be more. I don't want kids. I never will. The truth is, you should go back to your ex. She's willing to give you everything you want. Kids aren't in the picture for me. That's not the life I intend on having for myself. And it never will be."

"Don't give me this shit about intentions. That's bullshit, and you know it. What are you so scared of? Why don't you want children?"

"I have issues," I say and leave it at that, turning my back to him.

"What the fuck does that even mean?"

"You wouldn't understand."

"Try me."

"No."

"Tell me," he shouts.

Hatred. Fear. Sadness, not for him but for myself, and before I can take it back, I scream. I scream so loud, everyone in this place must hear. But it doesn't matter because it doesn't change anything. Nothing will.

"What?"

"I. Can't. Have. Children."

"No. You won't have children," he yells. As if he knows me, as if I would ever be that selfish.

I snap.

"I can't have children. I'm broken . . ."

"Nothing broken can't be fixed—"

"Listen to me. I *do* want children, but I can't have them."

Understanding falls over his features. "I-I'm sure—"

"I'm not able to ever have children." The words fly out of my mouth, and they hit the mark. He finally understands. I will never have his children. "I'm not able to," I whisper. "That's already been taken from me."

He doesn't say anything.

The tension courses, and suddenly, I feel more broken than I have ever felt. I knew this would happen. I'm not worth fighting for. I'm too broken for him. I'm too broken for anyone.

Without another word from either of us, I walk toward the door.

He doesn't speak.

He doesn't stop me.

I walk down the stairs. He doesn't follow.

I open the front door. The car I called is parked in front, waiting. He still doesn't come. He doesn't plead. He doesn't beg.

He lets me go because I am broken and he can't fix me.

*Goodbye, Nathaniel.*

# chapter thirty-seven

## NATHANIEL

S HE LEFT.

I can't move. I'm stuck, standing in the same place, staring at the same place where she just stood.

She left.

As if I'm a statue, I can't will myself to follow her. Her words rush over me.

She *can't* have children.

How had I never seen it? But now, like the wool has finally lifted from my eyes, I see it. All the signs were there—every last sign—and I was too fucking blind to see them. The pain when she talked about family. The sadness that always lingered in her eyes when she spoke of not wanting kids. It's not that she didn't want them. No, it was the fact she couldn't have them.

And now I'm standing here like a bloody idiot, instead of going after her, because I don't know what to say.

She's right. As angry as I was, as soon as she said those words, I knew she was right. I owed it to my grandfather, to my father, to have children. Maybe not now and maybe not in five years, but eventually. I would eventually get married, and I would continue the legacy.

It doesn't stop me from hating this. For feeling like a part of me has been broken with her news. I never allowed myself to think that far with Tink, but now that I know she can't be that woman for me, it feels like I'm mourning the death of the children I have never even had.

I'm not sure how long I stand here. I hear the front door slam, so I know she's gone, but I couldn't bring myself to stop her. I'm too confused. Finally, as my legs start to fatigue from standing, I shake myself out of my haze.

I look down at my watch.

Fuck.

She's probably at the airport already. I think about heading to the airport myself, but what's the point? She made her thoughts clear.

*Fight for her.*

I can't.

Without another thought, I walk over to the closet and throw my stuff into my suitcase. I head down the stairs. My grandfather sees me and walks up to me.

"You're leaving?"

"I am. I have some business."

"And Madeline? I thought I heard her go."

"Yes, she had to go back to the States."

"Is everything okay?"

I open my mouth to say something, but what?

"What's going on?" he asks earnestly, and I think about what to say. Less is more in this situation.

"We broke up."

His mouth falls open and then closes. "Is it because of me?"

I know that it has everything to do with what he said, but nothing at the same time. This issue would have come to pass no matter what. Maybe not today, but this was inevitable. We had a shelf life, and unfortunately, we expired long before we even knew it.

"She's a very independent woman. She . . ." I pause.

"Was it because of what I said about family?"

"Yes," I admit on a sigh.

"I'm sorry, son." He moves to me and places his hand on my arm. "It's better this way," he says, and his words feel like an attack on Madeline. I want to tell him he's wrong, but he's not. Maybe if I were someone else, it wouldn't matter, but as I stare at my grandfather, I know what this means. "You did the right thing. You know the importance of family, of being a Harrington. Today, you were man enough to realize that sometimes we have to make sacrifices. I am proud of you. I will do everything in my power to ensure you are at the helm of Harrington."

His words should make me feel better, but they don't.

With one last smile, I head for the door. Only one place to go now. London. By the time I arrive, it's night. I dial her number. Voicemail.

I head to bed.

———————•———————

The rest of the week is the same.

I call.

She sends me to voicemail.

I call the showroom. She's unavailable.

Now I'm beside Olly at a run-down old pub. What it lacks for décor, it makes up for in character. I've had more scotch than I care to discuss.

"Want to talk about it?"

"No."

"So you just want to sit here and get pissed?"

I lift my glass in the air. "That sounds like a bloody brilliant idea." I swallow a big gulp.

"Spill."

"We aren't women, Olly. We don't gossip like silly lilies."

"Yes, that is indeed true, but sometimes you have to. So what is it? She dumped you?"

"Something like that."

"So you are going to drown yourself in booze?"

"That's the plan."

"Indeed. I can see that, but at what cost? You finally are where you want to be. Is some girl worth it?"

"She's not some girl."

"Well, then why aren't you going after her?"

"You don't understand . . ."

"Why don't you enlighten me?" he asks, and I let out a breath.

"We want different things in life."

"Let me ask you a question. When you see your future, do you see her in it?"

"Yes."

"So what are you doing, mate? Go after her." He looks at me with a quirked brow.

"I can't."

"Here's what I know. If she's the one, don't let her leave without a fight."

"What do you know about this?"

"More than you know . . ."

I study him. I'm not sure what he's talking about, but right now isn't the time to ask. Right now, I need to decide what to do with Madeline. I don't want it to end the way it did. Even if we can't make this work, I need to talk to her.

With one more sip, I slam my glass down and stand.

"Where are you going?"

"To New York."

"Brilliant." He laughs. "Let's go," he says, standing too. I shake my head, and he shrugs. "Well, if the plane is going, I might as well hitch a ride."

# chapter thirty-eight

## MADELINE

I'M SITTING IN THE DOCTOR'S OFFICE. A PLACE I HAVE SPENT far too much of my time in, but unfortunately, after what happened in England, I'm back, and this time I know I'm running out of options.

"The doctor will be with you shortly," the nurse says, leaving me alone and naked except for the little plastic gown. I feel exposed and alone. My fingers drum on the exposed skin on my thigh, and my jaw rattles. If someone saw me, they would think it's from the cold, but the chills that run up my spine are for what the doctor will say. What he will say about my bleeding.

This has been a long time coming . . .

When I was ten, I started my period. It was also then that the first discussion of birth control came in to play. Most would think that's too young to start discussing methods of contraception, but for me, it was never about safe sex, and even though I didn't start the pill when I was ten, that's when it was first brought up.

My period was too heavy.

The cramps . . . *crippling.*

Every month, the pain was debilitating, causing me to miss

school. Causing me to miss life. I don't ever remember not being in pain during my period. By the time I was thirty, my doctor had inserted the Mirena IUD. The idea being if I had no period I wouldn't be in pain.

Time went on. Everything was looking good. Then one day I was at work. I'll never forget that day. My internship.

Something felt wrong in my body. It was as if I was floating above it, but then came the pain. The pain I hadn't had in so long I almost forget what it felt like. I almost believed I was normal. I can't remember how I got to the hospital, but I remember the shot of morphine. I remember the CT scan. I remember what they found.

The blood.

The ovarian cysts.

I remember an emergency surgery to see what was wrong.

*The first of many.*

The first of the tiny incisions that litter my skin, telling a story of pain and isolation.

Some time later, I'd learn my fate.

Endometriosis.

My ovary had twisted, the left one to be exact. The symptoms were sudden, and I was too late. I lost that ovary to torsion.

It was then that I learned the actual definition of a disease that I had never heard of before. A disease where cells that normally line the inside of the uterus grow outside the uterus.

The diagnosis made sense looking back, the pain of the past years floating in my head. All the pain I had during periods and during sex, it all made sense.

After I went home, the pain didn't go away. I just learned to mask it better.

Take more pills.

Drink more.

Until I was numb.

I have learned to deal with it the best that I can. I work from home when I'm too sick, and I avoid men just in case I have a flare-up. In the past two years, I have had five surgeries. I've had more overnight stays at the hospital than I can count. After the last procedure, I had a reprieve. I was handling my pain, and my symptoms were controllable. Things got better, or so I thought . . ..

"Hello, Madeline," Dr. Martin says as he walks into the room.

"Hi, Doctor."

"It's been a while . . ." He looks over my chart, probably checking the date of my last visit.

"It has."

"I was hoping you wouldn't be back until your next checkup." He sighs, and I know he doesn't want this for me. We've been through a lot together over the years, and at the last appointment, we spoke of options in the future, including fertility preservation treatments. He had told me at my last appointment that freezing eggs before my condition damages my right ovary would offer a real chance of future pregnancy. I thought I had more time to decide, but the grim expression on his face tells me my time has run out.

"Me too."

"Tell me what's going on?"

"I bled."

"Okay."

"Not during my period this time. This time . . . during sex." Tears sprinkle down my cheeks. "And the pain . . ."

He bites his lip in thought, and my heart pounds in my

chest. "We spoke about this at your last checkup. The possibility of freezing your eggs before the uterus—"

"I know."

I knew what he was saying. It's time. Over the past few years, this has been an ongoing discussion.

Chances are, I might need to consider having a hysterectomy in the future. It's meant to be the last option. My doctor has always been reluctant to consider it, my age a defining factor, so we have done every procedure and exhausted all other resources.

The blood.

When I saw the blood, I knew that this new development might have tipped the scales, which is why I told Nathaniel what I did. Which is why he isn't here.

"We are going to run a few tests."

I nod. "I figured."

"We won't make a decision until we know for sure." He tries to sound reassuring, but it only makes me sob harder. I know.

I know I only have one choice.

———————•———————

Three days have passed since my doctor's appointment. Everything he said is weighing heavily on me. It's been hard to work, but at the same time, I welcome the distraction. So here I am now, still at the office well after five p.m. because I have nowhere to go. Sure, I could go home, but at least here I can silence the voice in my head with spreadsheets and PowerPoints.

"You've been avoiding me." The rich baritone of the voice makes my heart hammer rapidly.

I hear his heavy steps as they approach, but I don't need to turn around to know who it is. I have dreamed of him every day. Missed him even more. But he was right. I had been avoiding him. I couldn't face him, still can't. I wasn't ready, and although I'm still not, he's giving me no choice. I turn slowly, and instantly my gaze finds him. I feel as though a hot metal rod has been shoved in my chest.

So this is what it feels like to be heartbroken?

This is what all the stories told about star-crossed lovers never meant to be. Because what I realize as I stare at him is how painful it is to love him because this fairy tale will never be. I try to mask my emotions. I bite back the sob lodged in my throat and will the moisture in my eyes not to fall.

"I have."

"Please talk to me."

I shake my head and then start to walk away, heading straight for the door. When I hear his footsteps behind me, I pick up my pace. I just hope I can make it out the doors before I lose it. Before I fall apart.

"Tink."

"No. I can't."

"Turn around."

His voice is hypnotic, and I find myself doing as he says. I stare down at the floor. The unshed tears in my eyes make the floor seem blurry.

"Look at me."

Tentatively, I do. Our eyes lock. He must see my tears because his own eyes become glassy. His lip trembles. A tear falls from my eyes.

"I love you."

What he says catches me completely off guard. He has never said that before. I knew I loved him too, but it didn't matter. It didn't change anything. My love for him wouldn't give him what he so desperately needs, and as much as I want to be selfish and not care, that's the thing about love . . . I do.

The realization floods me. I love him enough to put him first. To put his needs first.

"Did you hear me? I love you. I want to be with you. I want to try." His voice is angry. Desperate.

It makes no difference. The end is still inevitable.

"For how long?" I respond. "For how long this time?"

"I-I," he stumbles over his words, something I've never seen. This strong, arrogant man is showing me his weakness, and it severs me completely.

"You don't know?" I say in a soft voice because herein lies the problem.

"I don't need to know. All I need to know is that I do."

"Until what? Is your love enough, am I enough? What about your legacy?"

"I . . . we don't need to think about what happens in the future. Let's think about now."

"That's the thing. I can't. I need to think of my future, and I have no future. You might not see it now, or maybe tomorrow, but you will. I can't give you what you want. I will never be able to give you what you want."

"I don't care."

"You might not care today, but one day you will. And you will resent me. It will start off small, but one day you will leave. It's time for me to leave Neverland," I say sadly.

"So that's it?"

"Yes."

"I gave my heart to you, and I never—"

"I know you did," I cut him off. "But I never asked for it. I told you from the start . . . I'm sorry, Nathaniel."

I hate my words, and I hate myself for saying them to him, but my future is already written. Maybe I lied. Maybe I hadn't had the hysterectomy, but I had already made up my mind. The pain would just get worse. How many surgeries could I have? How many pills could I take?

How long before he would grow bored of it?

"It was never my intention to fall in love with you." He looks down at the floor, then back up at me. There is so much pain it breaks me in two.

"I'm sorry."

"I can't just let you go."

"You have to," I whisper.

Neither of us speaks, and then he reaches out. I step away. I can't let him touch me. If he does, I'll be lost.

"You know . . . you know that place between sleep and—"

"Stop," I whisper. I can't hear his words right now. They will crush me. But I know what they are, nonetheless. I have read *Peter Pan* too many times not to know what he is going to say.

He's going to tell me he loves me again.

He's going to tell me he'll wait. I won't let him, though.

I can't.

"Don't wait for me. It's over."

# chapter thirty-nine

## MADELINE

'M NOT MY USUAL SELF. I KNOW IT, AND THE KIDS KNOW IT. Fuck, anyone who sees me would know.

I feel bad. Truly, I do. But no matter how much I tell myself I need to smile and pretend, I can't. Instead, I stare at the kids. I look at them while they eat popcorn and laugh. I imagine what it would be like to have my own kids, and I feel like my heart is breaking all over again.

I about lost it when I saw Sydney's pregnant bump when I arrived tonight. Tears still fill my eyes at the thought even hours later. I want what they have.

*You can still have this.*

But then the doctor's words about viability and frozen eggs play out.

*Adoption is an option.*

Looking at Avery, I see so much of her mom. Sometimes she's so much like her it's as though Claire is still here.

I want *that*.

A part of me has always dreamed of a mini-me.

*Someone with my eyes.*

*Someone who will be my little twin.*

323

I never voiced my dreams, but it doesn't change the fact that I want it all the same.

*Get a new dream.*

Pulling myself from my thoughts, I watch the TV. Both the kids are asleep when the door to the apartment opens. Sydney walks in with Jace behind her.

"Hi." She yawns. "I'm so tired." She rubs her belly as she speaks. A stab in my heart, that's what it feels like to watch the small gesture. "I'm going to go to bed. Thanks, Mad."

"My pleasure." I force the words, stuffing the vomit back down my throat.

Jace lifts Avery and motions for me to wait. I do. Now both kids and Sydney are asleep in their rooms. I wait on the couch for Jace to come in, and when he does, he sits next to me.

"Thanks for staying."

"What's going on?" I ask.

He takes my hand in his. "Madeline, I'm here for you. I wanted you to know that."

"What did Sydney tell you?" My voice prickles.

"Not that much. She told me you broke up with Nathaniel."

Tears form in my eyes.

"What happened?"

"I can't," I whisper, not wanting to sob.

"Maddy."

I turn my face to him. Tears streak down my cheeks. He pulls me toward him until I'm in his arms.

"You can talk to me. You can tell me."

"I'm sick."

"How sick?" The concern in his voice is evident, and it makes me cry harder.

"I have endometriosis."

His head shakes. "I don't know what that means."

"In a nutshell, my uterine lining is outside the uterus."

"What do you mean?"

As I explain it to him, I try to keep my voice steady. I try to sound clinical, but the more I tell him, the more the truth hits me. The more I break apart. I tell him about all my surgeries, all my pain, and when I'm done, his own eyes are glassy.

"But why would you need to break up with him? That's what I'm not understanding."

"I can't have children." I sob.

"So . . . ?"

He doesn't get it. No one gets it. His eyes penetrate me, judging, waiting . . . and I can't take it. "Are you kidding me right now?" I hiss. "It's too much, and nobody understands. I did it for him."

His hands fly up to stop me. "No. You're misunderstanding me. Yes, you might not be able to carry a baby, but you don't know that you can't have a baby. There are options. You can have a surrogate."

A desperate laugh bubbles up. "The chance of my eggs being viable . . ." I trail off, breaking apart just thinking of the little girl who might never have my eyes or the little boy who won't resemble my brothers.

"You can always adopt."

"It's not the same."

"It's not? Tell that to Sydney. Tell that to my kids who love her like a second mother. Syd might not have birthed them, but they're her kids."

"I know, but—"

"You have options."

"Not with him."

"Why the hell not?"

"He needs his legacy," I whisper. "He lost his parents. Having a biological child is important to him. I wouldn't take that chance away from him."

*I wouldn't take away the chance of having a little boy with his father's eyes.*

"It could happen." Jace's words come out too low, and I know he doesn't believe it either.

"I can't take the risk."

"You're worth the risk." Jace pushes back and looks me in the eye, imploring me to believe him.

I don't.

"Thank you, but I'm not." Fresh tears fall down my cheeks.

"If he can't see your worth, he's not worthy."

He's wrong. He is worthy of me. He's the best man I know. He is enough for me.

I'm just not enough for him.

---

The following day after my doctor's appointment, I find myself in my apartment. My mom, Eve, and Sydney are over. They knew I wasn't okay, so they stopped by unannounced.

"What's going on with you, Maddy?" Sydney asks.

"It's official. I have to have a hysterectomy," I say as a tear drips down my face.

"What do you mean?"

"I just had a doctor's appointment. I have fibroids in my uterus and—" My voice shakes as an unsuppressed sob lodges in my throat. "The doctor he told me that my uterus has attached to my intestines. H-he told me that my uterus would never be able to carry a pregnancy to term."

"Oh my God." My mom's hand flies to her mouth, and I can see a tear drip down her nose.

We all sit in silence after my admission. The only sound is the sniffling from my mother. Sydney finally breaks the silence.

"Why didn't you tell us?" she whispers. "We could have come with you. You didn't have to go alone . . ." Her voice cracks, and my eyes well up again in the pain she has, in the pain I have.

"For this exact reason. I didn't want you treating me like glass. I want to be normal. I didn't want you to see me for what I was . . ."

"And what's that?" Eve steps forward and places her hand on my shoulder.

"Less," I whisper back. My broken uterus. My inability to have children. Less.

"You think you're less?"

"No. Yes. I don't know," I mumble. "Society tells us—" I start to say, but Sydney cuts me off.

"Fuck society. Birthing a child doesn't make you any more of a mother than if another did. Look at me. Look at Logan and Avery." She implores with her eyes for me to think of my brother's children from his previous marriage. "I love them like my own. I don't love them any less just because they didn't come from my womb."

"I know."

"Do you?"

"Sometimes . . . sometimes I'm so strong. So put together. And other times . . ."

I shake my head, not wanting the wall to break. I always knew this was a possibility since the first procedure for my endometriosis, to the second, and then to the third. With each year I've suffered in silence, I knew in my heart it was leading to this. But somehow, somewhere I thought if I didn't say anything, if no one knew, it would change the reality.

It didn't.

I let my tears fall, and Sydney pulls me into her arms.

"Let it go. Cry. Scream. Take the pain and let it go."

So I do.

I scream.

I shout.

I curse.

When I'm done, my voice is sore and my eyes are swollen. But a burden has been lifted. I can't have a baby, but that doesn't make me less. That doesn't define me.

Birthing a baby won't define me. Sydney is right.

———————•———————

The time is finally here. I'm in the hospital with my mother, waiting . . .

"I'm scared."

"You'll be okay, darling."

"How do you know? What if I regret this decision?" I whisper.

"There was no decision to be made. Your uterus would have never been able to carry a baby. Your quality of life would only deteriorate more. You made a brave choice. This is your body, and you choose to live."

She picks up my hand and kisses it. "I'll be here, baby, when you wake up. I'll be here."

"Promise?"

"Of course."

My stomach knots up as the nurse walks in.

"It's time."

I'm transported into another room, this one more sterile, colder. That's how I feel. Frigid. Empty. The scary thing is, I'm about to be emptier. I'm about to lose everything. I'm trying to be strong, but it's so hard. My mouth feels dry. Fasting robbed me of the saliva I should have, but instead, I'm barren. I stare at the ceiling, the walls, anything to keep me from thinking about what's about to happen, what I'm about to lose. But it's useless. Nothing will make this pain go away. Before long, a woman dressed in scrubs walks in, and she introduces herself as the anesthesiologist. When she tells me to count down, I do. Staring at the light above that flickers in my eyes, I count.

100

99

98

97 . . .

My eyes blink open, groggy. They flutter closed.

"I'm here, sweetheart."

I try to say mom, but the anesthesia must still be lingering because the words are hard to come out.

My hand is engulfed in hers. "I'm here, baby girl."

It's over.

I know it is. And although I can't feel the pain, I feel it in my heart.

My dreams of being a mother are gone.

I know my mom will argue that I had my eggs frozen, but the doctor said if my uterus was hostile, the chances of a viable egg being harvested were slim, and the chances were even more slim that those eggs would ever take root and grow.

"Baby, can you open your eyes again?"

With all my strength, I do.

"So good, I'm so proud of you. Do you think you can talk?"

"Mom," I croak.

"Thank God," she cries, and tears start to stream down her face. "You probably think I'm being ridiculous but—"

I know what she's saying. Anytime someone goes under anesthesia, there is always the chance that they never wake. I can only imagine that's a mom's greatest fear. Losing their child.

A choked sob escapes.

Losing a child.

I lost mine.

I lost my chance.

And for what?

Why?

I can barely breathe. I sob. My mom just holds me. "Let it out. Just let it out," she coos.

"What am I going to do now?"

"You're going to live. You're going to love. You're going to be fine, baby girl, because you are the strongest woman I know."

"Will anyone ever love me?"

"You will find someone who will love you."

"My faults, too?" I whisper.

"Look at me." I meet her stare. She looks at me fiercely. Like a lioness who will do anything to protect her cub. "Baby, one day you will meet a man who will see every single fault of yours as a beauty mark. Different, and unique, but yours all the same—and therefore, beautiful."

"Thank you, Mom."

"I love you."

The day goes by in a series of family visitors and naps.

When I open my eyes, I'm met with a familiar pair of green eyes. "Tink."

"What are you doing here?"

"I thought you could use a friend," Nathaniel says.

"How did you find out?"

"Val."

"Do you hate me?" I whisper.

"I don't hate you. I could never." He looks away for a minute, gathering his thoughts maybe. "Why didn't you tell me? I could have been there for you."

"I couldn't. I needed to make a decision. One for me. For my body. For my quality of life. I couldn't take you into consideration. That might sound selfish, but—"

"It's not."

"I am sorry I lied. I didn't feel like I had a choice. This is why I didn't want to let you in. I always knew this would need to happen. The question was when. How much could I take? How many surgeries? By the time I met you, I'd had a few procedures already. I just . . . I just want to be able to live again. You saw me. I hide it well, but even you saw the pills I took. The pain I was in."

"I just wish I had known." He places his hands over his face.

"It was wrong of me not to tell you, but I never thought . . . You always insisted . . . "

"I did. So what now?"

"You coming here, Nathaniel . . . although it means the world to me, it doesn't change anything. The problem is still there, and nothing will change it."

"So I can't change your mind?"

"No. I can't have your children. I can't give you the legacy. I can't give you the little boy with your father's eyes. I can't be who you need, and no matter how much you live in the clouds and believe it doesn't matter, we don't live in Neverland. And you're not Peter and I'm not Tink. Time to come down and be what you are meant to be"—tears fill my eyes—"without me."

He stands, leans forward, and places his lips on my head. "You were never Tink." He walks to the door.

"Nathaniel," I say, and he stops, his back still to me, so I ask, "What do you mean?"

"You were always Wendy."

# chapter forty

## NATHANIEL

THERE WAS REALLY NOTHING TO SAY AFTER OUR LAST conversation, so I did what I had to do. I drove myself straight to the airport, got right back on our plane, and went back to London.

Now I sit in my flat. It feels different. Empty. In every corner, I see her. I remember the way she laughed while we ate in the kitchen. I remember her curled up on my sofa. I walk into my bedroom. I see her in my bed. I remember how her hair fanned across the white sheets while she slept.

Everywhere.

She is everywhere.

I need a drink. And I keep drinking until I wake up in my bed with a raging headache the next day.

The early morning light gleams blinding. It penetrates my lids and burns my retinas, so I cover my eyes to keep it out. But eventually, I need to get up. I need to go into Harrington today.

If not, then what was all this for?

After a shower that luckily sobers me up, I'm out the door and heading into work.

It takes me about forty-five minutes to make it into the

office. The building looms like an imposing force in the middle of London. It's all floor-to-ceiling windows. Surprisingly, it's sunny today for spring. Still. This morning, I was sure it was a fluke, but now as the light bounces off the glass, it brings my headache back to the forefront. It's strange what a beautiful day it is. I don't want it. I don't want the beauty. Not when I don't want to be happy. Unfortunately for me, I can't dwell in my own misery. Edward would eat that shit up. So instead, I square my shoulders and walk in like I own the place.

"Look what we have here," I hear when I step into the main room on the tenth floor.

I turn to the side to see Edward standing in the doorframe of his office. "What are you doing here?"

"Taking what's mine." I smirk.

"One success doesn't mean anything. You know it. I know it."

"That's what you think."

"You didn't fool anyone with your act of stability. The board knows if you ever had power here, you would sink us. I'm just biding my time. Your grandfather will be gone one day, and I will rise."

"What did you say?"

"You heard me. Are you going to do anything about it?" He looks me up and down, then crosses his arms in front of his chest. "Please do. It will only prove me right."

My hands close into fists. I grit my teeth. As much as I want to fight him, I can't. Maybe before I would have, but now after Madeline . . .

I know I can't.

"Interesting," he says, narrowing his eyes. "Maybe you have changed. Not that it matters. The outcome is still going to be the same."

"If that's all, Eddie . . ." I start to walk away.

"How's the pretty piece, by the way? Oh, that's right, I heard that's over. So sorry to hear that it ended."

"No, you aren't," I mutter through gritted teeth.

"Nope, you got me. I'm not . . . but you know what I do care about? What she's going to feel like wrapped around my cock."

I step forward until I grab him by the neck. He flashes me a sadistic smile, and that's when I realize that was all a show, and I'm the number one performer. From the corner of my eye, I can see all eyes on me.

Fuck.

So much for a good first day.

---

The weeks pass.

I put my time in, but the truth is, I'm in a goddamn haze. Every day I walk through the door, I allow my mask to fall. I'm the perfect grandson and the perfect employer, but it's hollow. It's not that I miss working for Valentina Fisher. I do enjoy working here, that's not the problem at all. The problem is her.

I miss her.

The banter is missing from my day. I don't know how she's been. After her surgery, I checked in a few times, but she stopped answering, so I stopped calling. Now I have no excuse to speak to her anymore. There is no reason for me to sit and dwell, so tonight although I didn't want to, I'm going to a fundraiser.

I have to.

I'm dressed already and drinking a glass of scotch when my mobile rings. The number looks familiar, but it doesn't register on my phone.

"Hello," I say.

"Hi, Nathaniel." It's Cecile. "I was wondering if you can do me a favor."

"No."

She laughs nervously, and the sound is so pathetic and so incredibly unmoving to me that I can't help but indulge her. A predator doesn't play with dead prey.

"What type of favor?" I press the base of my palm into my eye socket.

"I was wondering if you could pick me up on the way to the event tonight."

"You're going?"

"Of course I'm going, silly. I always go."

It really was a terrible question. She does always go. I have no desire to pick her up, but at the same time, I'm getting tired of being an arsehole, or—as Maddy calls it—an asshole. "Sure."

"Thank you so much."

An hour later, Cecile and I appear at the V&A museum. The museum is open tonight for a large fundraiser, my family being one of the largest donors. When I step out of the car, I turn to help her out. She takes my hand and stands. I move to let go, but she holds on tight. "Do you mind? My heels and the wet pavement are not a good combo."

"Very well."

She wraps her arm within mine. Together arm in arm, we make our exit from the car. Flicks of light flash in my face as the paparazzi swarm. We push past them and enter the event.

For the rest of the night, Cecile remains glued to me. She holds my arm, and she doesn't let go. She smiles coyly all night.

It's not so bad.

She helps me enjoy myself, and at one point, I find myself

dancing with her. Her body close to mine as we sway to the music playing. "This feels good," she says to me.

"Mmm," I agree because, in truth, it does. It feels like old times. Like I'm young, and the world is ahead of me.

"This. We work. I'm sorry I ever doubted you. That I ever let you go. Do you think . . . ?" she says, pulling me out of my thoughts, and suddenly, all that we went through comes crashing back down on me. "Do you think you could give us a try?"

I think of all the bad times, but I also think of all the good times. All the laughs. All the fights. I see her in my bed.

And then I see *her*.

Not Cecile. I see Madeline. I smell Madeline.

I hope and wish I could feel more for her because that would be easier, but as I hold Cecile close, I feel nothing. All I see is the past. I don't see the future. I'm still in love with a woman I can't have.

I doubt I'll ever stop loving Madeline.

Nothing will change. Now to think of what I'm going to do about that.

As if reading my mind, Cecile moves in closer, so close I can smell her perfume. It's tart, like sour fruit, and I can't believe I used to find the scent alluring. Now I find it to turn my stomach. *Only one woman's scent makes your mouth water now.*

"We should try again," she whispers.

When those words leave her mouth, I realize how this must appear. How everyone around us must see this. How she must see this. Without responding, I pull her into another room. She's quick to pounce once alone, stepping into me and placing her hands on my chest.

"I loved you. You don't understand. I loved you," I hiss, removing her hands from me. "I would have grown up for you, but you never gave me a chance. I would have been the best man for you. I was going to propose. Three weeks from the day I found you in his bed, I was going to propose." I lift my hands and scrub at my brain, scrub out the vision that has molded me into the man I am today. "I have been so mad at you for so long, but now I'm not. I forgive you."

"You forgive me?"

"I do. Because had you never broken my heart, I would've never met Madeline. Madeline makes me a better person than I ever could have been for you."

She looks cross at my words, staring off into space, and then she steps back and looks at me, the haze lifting from her eyes.

"I never knew how you felt. I-I thought . . . It was my fault. I know that now, but what I also know is if that's true about how you feel for Madeline, I don't know what you're doing here. If you love this girl like you say you do . . ." She pauses and lifts her brow in speculation. "It doesn't appear you do, Nate. Because if you really did, why are you here?" she asks, challenging me. "You're in the wrong country, aren't you?" My eyes widen at her words.

"You know what? You're right."

"What?" she answers, confused by my response.

"I *am* in the wrong country," I clarify, and now she looks shocked. "Bye, Cecile."

And with that, I go.

---

It takes me a full week to get my shit together to speak with my grandfather. I'm not sure what I'm going to say to him, but there has to be something I can say to get his blessing. I love Madeline, and I'm not even sure if she will take me back, but I have to try again.

I used to think that legacy was everything, but that was before I had nothing. A life without Madeline is not a life I want to live. This stop is only a courtesy. No matter what, I'm going for her. Last week was an eye-opener for me. I know I will never want anyone else. I know she can't have my children, but we have other options. I never spoke to her about them. And if there are no options, it's no matter to me. I realize now I can be happy with just her. As long as I have her.

Not giving myself any time to change my mind, I call my grandfather. He sounds tired, but he lets me know he's back in New York.

Good.

Kill two birds with one stone.

First, I'll talk to him about Madeline, and then I will get my girl.

Six hours later, I'm back in the city. The last time I was here, my heart was crushed. I confessed my love, and she shot me down. My love wasn't enough. But now as time has passed and I've gotten some distance, I see it for what it is. She was trying to protect me. She gave away her happiness for me, to do right by me. She did the most selfless gesture. She sacrificed her own future with me to give me the future she thought I wanted, but what she didn't get, and that's partially my fault for being too slow to understand, was that I just wanted her.

When I pull up to one of my many childhood homes, I go straight to my grandfather's study and then the parlor. Finally, I find him and my heart stops. Everything around me stops.

There on the floor is my grandfather.

I rush over to him. "Grandfather." I put my hand on him and shake him. I can't breathe as I touch him, shake him. All the oxygen in my lungs seizes within me, and it feels as though I'm suffocating.

This can't be happening. It can't. I feel moisture drip from my eyes, and the room feels too cold.

"Wake up. You need to wake up." I place my hand on his skin, feeling for a pulse. It's faint, but it's there. I grab my mobile from my pocket and dial.

"Nine-one-one, what's your emergency?"

My arm shakes as I try to wake him again, but still nothing. "My grandfather is unconscious."

Words leave my mouth, but I barely know what I'm saying. I hold him until the EMT comes, my heart thumping, my breathing shallow.

He has to be okay.

What would I do without him? I need to talk to him, to tell him how much he means to me. He's all I have. I can't lose him. Without him, I'll have no one.

If I lose him, I'll have lost everyone.

The trip to the hospital is a blur with a wave of lights and words I don't understand. He's wheeled into the emergency room, and they whisk him away. I'm not sure what to do. So I sit and wait and pray that he doesn't leave this earth.

Not yet.

"I can't believe he has stage four-cancer," I say to myself more so than to his longtime doctor and friend. When my grandfather woke for a moment, he told me. It felt like a knife was stabbed in my heart at the news. Now that he's asleep, the pain has not subsided, it's just spread through my body, encasing me in grief.

"I'm surprised you didn't know. He promised me he would tell you."

"He didn't."

I turn to my grandfather. I don't know what to do or say. I feel like the rug has been ripped out from under me. I had no idea. But then I think. I think over the past six months, and the question is how had I not known? But the answer hits me in the face. First, I was too self-absorbed, and then I was falling in love, all while my grandfather was dying. He knew and never told me. I want to be mad at him, but how could I possibly be mad?

My eyes well up, and a tear falls from my eye. I swipe it.

He starts to stir, and I know he's waking. When he opens his eyes, he tries to smile, but his movements are slow, and more tears fall from my eyes.

"Nathaniel," he croaks out.

"I'm here. I'm here." I take his hand in mine. "I'm not leaving."

"You know?" he whispers, and my breath lodges in my throat. *He doesn't remember telling me.*

"I do."

"I'm sorry," he whispers. His voice is so weak I can barely make out the words.

"I know. I wish you had told me."

He lifts his hand to his mouth. "Water?"

I reach across the table next to me and give him a glass the nurse left. I bring it to his mouth, and he lifts it and takes a small sip.

"I couldn't. You've lost everyone . . ."

"So you thought it was better to leave me without telling me?"

"I thought I'd have more time. I thought you would've found someone."

"Is this what it was all about? The board. The rush. The need for me to succeed and find someone. Was this why?"

"Yes. I don't have much time. I needed to make sure you were ready. I won't be here much—"

"Don't say that."

"No, listen to me. I won't. I know how long I have, and by the look on your face, you know too. I needed you to prove you could handle Harrington. Not for me, I always knew you could, but I needed you to show them. It's not going to be an easy road. I have done everything I could to secure your future, but once I'm gone . . ."

"Please, don't. I don't care about any of that."

"You have to. For me. For your father. Harrington is our legacy. When we lost everything, I made it my life's goal never to have a child of mine go through what I went through. You might not be my son, Nathaniel, but I raised you as though you were. This is yours, and I needed this. I know after all you've grown that you will succeed. I know that you will take over, and the future generations of Harringtons will be safe. You will do me proud."

His talk of legacy makes me feel ill. He's dying, and that's all he wants, but I don't know if I can fulfill that wish because, without Madeline, I'm nothing. What he's asking for is for me to give up the woman I love.

And I don't think I can.

# chapter forty-one

## MADELINE

"OH MY GOD, MADS." I TURN TO SEE VAL MOVING TOWARD me, carrying a newspaper in her hand. "Have you seen the news? Nath—"

She starts to say, but I can't hear it, so I raise my hand. I can't hear her tell me he's featured. I can't look at another picture of him and Cecile. The one from the V&A nearly crushed me. I can't see him moving on. I know I ended it. I know it was my choice, but it doesn't hurt less. I still love him, and I always will. I know that now. Even though I chose to do the right thing, it doesn't mean it hurts any less. This feeling. This hollow feeling in my chest will always be there. I know I'm broken. I know I'm missing a part of me, but that doesn't even hurt as much as the part of me Nathaniel took with him. I'll never be able to have a child, and that is devastating, but not having both is too much for me to handle.

"I can't, Val. Please don't show me," I say, defeated. "I can't see a picture of him moving on," I whisper.

"No. That's not it."

I stop and turn my body around so I'm facing her again. "What do you mean?"

"Here. See for yourself."

She thrusts a newspaper at me. I don't see anything at first, but on the front page, there is a small article.

***London business tycoon Nathaniel Harrington rushed to the hospital. The family is with him, but there is no comment on why he was admitted. Nathaniel Harrington is the owner and CEO of Harrington Textiles.***

The newspaper drops from my hand.

"Shh. It's okay." I must not realize I'm shaking because Val is holding my hands and soothing me.

"I have to go," I mumble. "Where is he?"

"Here, let me see." She reaches to the ground and picks up the paper I dropped, scanning the remainder of the article. "It says here that he's been admitted to Sinai Grace."

I know that hospital well since my brother worked there. Before Val says anything else, I'm out the door, in a cab, and heading toward the hospital.

I walk straight up to the front desk. "What room is Nathaniel Harrington in?"

She starts to type in the computer before telling me he's in room 609.

"Thank you," I say as I start toward the elevators. Pushing the call button, I wait. I need to be there. I don't care what's happening between us. The only person Nathaniel has is his grandfather. I'm halfway down the hall to his room when a sinking feeling falls upon me. What if she's there?

*It doesn't matter. You are there for him as a friend. You are his friend. No matter what happened, you will be his friend.*

I see the room, and my hand touches the knob. I will be devastated, that much I'm sure. *Don't think about it. Be strong.* I need to be strong. I can do this.

344

Pushing the door open, I step through. What I see makes my heart lurch in my chest. In the chair directly in front of the door is Nathaniel. He's leaning in an awkward position in the hospital chair, his eyes closed. Sleeping.

I step farther into the room and sweep my gaze away from him and around the room. The rest of the chairs are empty. As I continue my perusal, my eyes finally land on his grandfather. His eyes flutter open, and his lip splits into a small smile. "A beautiful woman. Am I dreaming?"

"Nope. I'm really here." I laugh, but I don't want to laugh. I want to cry because it's obvious he is very unwell.

"Come sit and keep an old man company. He's useless." He laughs. I do as he asks, and I take the chair next to his bed, opposite Nathaniel's.

"I would love to spend time with you," I say as I place my hand over his. "You were always my favorite."

"When he wakes up, I'm going to tell him you said that."

"You should." I wink.

"I bet you're wondering why I'm here," he says, and I nod. "Cancer. Stage four. It's the end of the road for me," he croaks through a cough.

"I'm so sorry."

"It's okay. It's been a good journey, and I'm ready. I'll see my girl again. You would have liked her. She was an American too."

"I know. Nathaniel told me."

"Nathaniel . . ." He trails off as he watches him. "I'm very proud of him, and I have you to thank for that."

"You never need to thank me. Helping him . . . working with him . . ." I stutter, but my voice cracks, and I know tears have filled my eyes.

"Nathaniel didn't tell me much."

I swipe a lone tear that fell from my eyes.

"You love him?"

"I do."

"Enough to let him go?"

"I do."

He nods. He's very quiet for a minute, and I think he's fallen asleep, but instead, he squeezes my hand.

I'm thankful he doesn't ask more.

# chapter forty-two

## NATHANIEL

JERK AWAKE. MY BODY IS STIFF, AND I HAVE NO CLUE WHERE the hell I am. Then it all comes rushing back. New York. Grandfather. Cancer . . .

I'm at Sinai Grace.

And by the crick in my neck, I've fallen asleep on the chair. My eyes feel like they are glued shut. As I lift my hand to rub the sleep out of them, a familiar voice rings through the air.

Like the sound of an angel, it filters in.

"I do," she says. There is so much sadness in her voice, and it pains me. I don't want to open my eyes. I don't want to see the pain in them. Because I know it's there, and I know it will kill me.

But as much as I don't want to, I need to. I need to see her face. Because she came.

She came.

Despite all I've done to her.

Despite everything.

Despite every bit of pain, she came for me. I know without a measure of doubt she came to bring me her strength, and I love her even more for that.

I open my eyes. Her gaze is downcast, so she doesn't see me. But even with the angle of her face, I can tell she's crying.

"You're up," my grandfather says, and she lifts her head. Our eyes meet across the distance of the bed. I want to reach for her. I want to comfort her.

"Hi," she whispers.

"Hi," I respond.

"Hello, son." My grandfather's voice cuts through my haze. I know I need to look at him, but I can't bring myself to look away from her. Not when she's here, and I have so much to say to her.

We continue to stare at each other, neither of us speaking, until she finally gets up. "I have to get back to the office, but I'll be back. I can bring you fresh food," she says to me. I smile.

"That would be great."

She leans forward and kisses my grandfather's cheek. "I'll see you soon."

I stand to walk her out, and she gives me a tight smile. "I'll be right back. Will you be okay?" I ask, and my grandfather nods. We walk to the door and out into the hall. She turns back and pauses. I can see all the emotions playing out in her eyes.

"Goodbye."

And then she's gone again, and again, I haven't stopped her.

Once she's gone and out of view, I walk back into the room and sit back down. "Grandfather, I know you want your legacy—"

He holds up his hand, and a sick feeling weaves its way through me. I don't speak. I wait for him to say something I don't want to hear.

"I was wrong," he says in a low, weak voice. So low I'm sure I was hearing him wrong.

"What?"

"Son, will you forgive me?"

"For what, Grandfather?"

"I told you that legacy was all that matters, but I was wrong. I was so very wrong. Family isn't about the blood that runs through your veins, it's about the love you have. And you love that girl?"

"I do, very much."

"And she loves you." It's a statement, not a question.

"She never . . ." I trail off.

"She does." His words are final, resolute. "Your happiness is more important than a name, Nathaniel. Does she make you happy?"

"Yes."

"And you make her happy?"

"I try," I admit, and a chuckle escapes at the thought of it.

"Then that's all that matters. Now, go get your girl."

"Can I leave you?" I ask, not wanting to leave him in his state.

"Yes, I'll be fine. I love you, and I'm proud of the man you have become."

I head to the door and look back. "I hope to one day be as great a man as you are," I say.

"You already are."

I stare at him for a moment. A moment that seems to stretch, and for some reason, I memorize it.

As if it's the last.

———————————•———————————

She's not even out of the hospital when I find her.

"Madeline. Madeline," I shout, and she stops.

"What are you doing here? Shouldn't you be with your grandfather? Is he okay—"

"Stop speaking."

"What—"

"I said stop speaking because these past few times, you got the time to talk, but now it's my turn. And I have things to say."

"Okay."

"You don't get to tell me what's right for me. I let you walk away, and for that, I was wrong. I never should have let you leave."

"I-I—"

I lift my hand. "No. I'm not done."

She bites her lip.

I almost want to laugh, but I won't. I have too much to get off my chest. "I'm sorry."

She looks confused at my words.

"I'm sorry for everything. For how it all started. I'm sorry for how I treated you. I'm sorry for making you think you couldn't confide in me, and most of all, I'm sorry for making you think you weren't enough. You are enough. You have always been enough. I don't need anything as long as I have you. I will never resent you. Our love will be enough for me."

"What about your grandfather? Your legacy?"

"Fuck the legacy. Without you to live my life with, that's bollocks anyways."

"But your grandfather?"

"Understands. Gave me his blessing."

A sob escapes her mouth, tears falling freely down her face.

I step closer. "The one thing I am not sorry for is whatever brought you to me. I want you so much. I don't even know where to start."

"What do you want?"

"I want to watch you laugh. I want to be who you smile at. I want to love you. I know I've made mistakes. I've made a lot of mistakes. But the biggest mistake I ever made was letting you walk out that door."

"That's where you're wrong. Nothing you would have said at the time would have made me stay. I needed to learn for myself."

"And did you?" I ask.

"Yes."

I stare at her for a minute, looking at the woman who made me want to be a better person, who made me want to grow up and be the man she needs. I smile.

"What? Why do you have that look in your eye?" she asks.

"Because I love you, Tink . . ."

"I thought I wasn't Tink anymore?" She looks at me confused.

"You'll always be Tink," I declare, and now she looks at me even more confused. "But yes, you're also Wendy, and I'm finally ready to leave Neverland."

"What does that mean?"

"I want to grow old with you. I'm ready. And I hope you'll have me."

Tears cloud her eyes, and her jaw trembles.

"I will." Her voice breaks with an unsuppressed sob. I pull her into my embrace and hold her tight.

Minutes stretch in that embrace until I feel the vibration of my mobile. I don't need to check to know who's calling. But when I see the number of the hospital appear on the screen I know.

*He's gone.*

# chapter forty-three

## NATHANIEL

STAND AT THE PEW, MY HANDS SHAKING SO HARD I CAN'T control them. Madeline stands up and walks beside me. Taking my hand in hers, she squeezes gently, giving me her strength.

I feel the energy. I feel how it fills every molecule in my body. I feel how it lifts me up out of the murky abyss and pulls me out of the depths.

"I love you," she whispers. It's not audible, but it doesn't need to be. I feel her love, I see her love, and she gives me exactly what I need right now.

Still holding her hand, I pull the paper out. The one we wrote yesterday, together. I crumple it up.

"I wrote a whole speech. How he grew up, and how he fought tooth and nail to build his legacy. But instead, I'm not going to tell you who Nathaniel Harrington was. I'm going to tell you who my grandfather was. He was a great man. He was the best of men. Not because of the money he made but because of the man he was. My grandfather came to America with no money. There he met a beautiful American. She was the love of his life, and he was hers. Together, they built an empire. He never left her out, always saying she was the bones of the business. They had one child, my father. I didn't know my father well, but my grandfather told me stories, and through the stories he told me, I felt I did. When my parents died, my grandparents took me in. They raised me to be the man I am today. I didn't know he had cancer. He didn't tell me. I'm not sure why he didn't. But knowing him, I can only assume he didn't want to be a burden." I take a deep breath.

"My grandfather gave me everything. He gave me strength, character, love, and understanding. I never understood it, or maybe I took it for granted, but on the last day of his life, he gave me peace. Not the other way around. Because that was the man he was." I wipe a fallen tear and look toward the casket where he lies.

"Thank you, Grandfather. You will be missed, remembered, and honored for the rest of my life."

When I step away, Madeline pulls me into a hug.

Tears run down her face.

And together we hold each other, giving each other strength.

———————•———————

You can hear a pin drop. That's how silent it is sitting around the boardroom. Someone needs to speak, but no one is.

I move to open my mouth when the sound of a file being flung on the table echoes through the room. I lift my gaze only to be met with the smug as fuck look on Edward's face. The will was read, and my grandfather's shares were handed over to me, so what then was this meeting about?

"I assume you all want to know why I've asked you here."

"You can say that," I growl.

"Well, everything you need is right there in that file."

The file is passed around. Sounds from each board member can be heard as the folder moves across the table.

"What is this all about?" I ask just as the file makes its way to me.

Opening it, my heart starts hammering in my chest at what glares back at me. It's the contract. And not just any contract. It's the contract with Madeline. Every ridiculous thing I made her sign.

It all seems so silly and trivial now looking at it, a way to drive her crazy at the time while protecting my interests.

Funny how in the end none of it mattered.

I fell in love, and none of it matters.

As I stare down at the sheets that started a course of events that changed my life, I know that this little piece of paper could put the final nail in my coffin.

This could destroy everything.

"So what," I say, trying to sound unfazed, when, in fact, my stomach is twisting inside. "So I wrote a contract with my girlfriend."

"According to this document, she's not really yours."

"It's a silly document. A little spot of fun we had. I can promise you this has little effect on my ability to run Harrington. These past few weeks I've been at the helm, and I've done a mighty fine job."

"That's not the point, Nathaniel," he hisses.

"So then what is the point? My grandfather started this company . . . he wanted me to take over, and I've proved I can. If that's not the bloody point, then what is?"

"You're a liar."

"I hardly think—"

"No, you don't, do you . . . isn't that what got you into this mess? I, for one, don't want to put the future of this company in the hands of a man who doesn't think. I put forth a vote."

"This is preposterous."

"Is it, though? You might single-handedly own the largest share of Harrington Textiles, but your grandfather made sure not one single person owned the majority. If the board decides to remove you . . ." He trails off, letting his words hit their mark. And they do, right in my chest, like a sharp knife twisting.

"This is a serious matter," Tobias says. "We will have to vote on it."

"Certainly," the smug bastard says.

"This is ridiculous. You can't just vote on my future."

Tobias cocks his head. Yes, he can.

"Not without giving me time to counter."

"Why should we? So you can come up with another lie?"

I glare at Edward, but then I hear the sound of a hand hitting the table.

"Enough," Richard says. "We will give you one week. In a week's time, we will vote."

"Only a week?"

"You're lucky we are even giving you that."

---

Once back in my flat, I pour myself a drink. Madeline is beside me, her hand resting on my knee as she strokes me, gently trying to calm me.

"This is bloody bullshit," I hiss into my glass.

"I know."

"What the fuck am I going to do?"

She takes my hand in hers and lifts it to her mouth, placing a kiss on my clenched knuckles. "I'm not sure. We'll figure it out."

We stay like this through two glasses of scotch before I'm grabbing my mobile off the table.

"Hello," Olly answers.

"Let's go out." The words slip out of my mouth, and in response, I feel Tink (the nickname has stuck) squeeze my hand. I turn my attention back on her, and she's shaking her head in disapproval. "You shouldn't go out," she mouths.

"I need to drown my sorrows," I mutter regardless of the looks I'm receiving from beside me.

"You know me. I'm always up for a good time," Olly says.

"He's not going out—"

Madeline finally hollers loud enough for Olly to hear, which causes him to chuckle.

"A problem with the Mrs.?"

"No."

"Then what? I haven't heard you like this since you two broke up. And now you have her back and you want to go out. What's going on with you?"

"A lot."

"Why don't you start from the beginning," he says, and I sigh, putting my now empty glass down and reclining back. This is going to take a while.

Thirty minutes later, I have purged the past few months of my life to him, starting from the summons to my grandfather, to the contract, to the board. The only thing I left out was Madeline's private story because that's her story, not mine. When I'm done, the line goes silent.

"I'm going to give you a number," he says, and I have no idea what he's talking about.

"It's for an American I know. She might be able to help you.

If anyone can find something to help you out of this mess with your cousin, it's her and her brothers."

"Um. Okay."

"Oh, and one more thing . . ."

"Yes?"

"Whatever you do . . . don't tell her you got the number from me," he mutters.

***

It takes less than one week to get what I need, but now I find myself striding into Edward's office, back straight, head held high. When I push open the door, his eyes go wide in shock. He didn't expect me for two more days. But I don't need the two days because he's not forcing me out. Not with what I have in my hand.

"You can't just barge into my office," he hollers, and I flash him a grin.

"Of course I can."

"The board will hear about—"

I hold my hand up, silencing him. "I don't think so." I smile. "See this"—I raise my hand—"I have my own folder. Would you like to know what's in my folder . . . ?" He doesn't say anything, and I know he's scared. Because inside he knows what he's done, and he's realizing by the cocky look on my face, I know too. "I have the proof to get you out. I have the proof of the funds you took. Of where you got the money to buy the monstrosity you call a home. I have it all here."

His eyes are wide, and a bead of sweat trickles down his face. It makes me grin wider. He might have proof that I lied, but I have proof that he stole from Harrington Textiles.

"What are you going to do with that?" He stands and

marches forward until he's in my face. "I don't think you're going to do anything. And you want to know why?"

"Indeed. Please enlighten me," I say smugly.

"Because your legacy will be tarnished," he hisses. He knows what I have, but what he doesn't know is what I have learned about legacy. Of course, I don't want Edward to drag my company or me through the mud, but I know the truth . . . No matter what he does, we'll get through it. But just in case he doesn't heed my warning, I open the file and slowly start reading through the documents I have attained through Oliver's connection.

Edward stares at me, his nostrils flaring as he waits for me to speak.

"Hmm, now this looks a bit dodgy . . . It seems that I have in my possession evidence of an account you set up under your wife's name and your daughter's."

"So?" he bites out. "That doesn't prove anything."

"No, it's not the accounts that are so dodgy . . . it's the time of the deposits and withdrawals. It seems they correspond with missing funds from Harrington."

"You have no proof."

I lift the printed email and shove it into his hands. He stumbles back at the force. "But don't I?" I smirk.

His eyes go wide as he reads the printed copy of the emails he's now holding in his trembling hand. All the damning emails that I have had pulled from his server. Encrypted emails he thought no one would ever see.

He rips them up and throws the shreds of paper on the floor.

"You don't really think I haven't made copies, do you . . . I wonder what the board will think of years of embezzlement of company funds."

For the first time since I marched in here, his face goes white. The proof is everywhere and now he's seen it.

"What do you want?" he asks, his voice cracking in fear.

"I want you out. The way I see it, I can really fuck you with this, but my grandfather loved his brother . . .and he wouldn't want you in jail . . ."

# epilogue

## NATHANIEL

IT'S BEEN FIVE YEARS SINCE MY GRANDFATHER PASSED. FIVE years met with triumphs, tribulations, tragedy, heartbreak, some more heartbreak, and miracles.

Madeline and I got married in a very small ceremony. Only her family and a few of our closest friends were invited. That was one of our miracles.

Today is another.

*Today we meet him.*

Today we meet our baby.

Over the years since our wedding, we have tried unsuccessfully to use the eggs Madeline froze. It turns out, due to the endometriosis, her biggest fear came true, and they weren't viable. It was hard for Madeline to get past it. I knew how badly she wanted to give that to me.

For me, I just needed her.

Finally, after many unsuccessful attempts, we decided to adopt. This isn't the first adoption. The last one fell through, and we were devastated. But together, we knew that when the time came, we would be blessed with our baby. The baby that was meant for us.

Today is that day.

Now we wait. All the papers have been drawn up and signed. Legally, he is our baby. Together we walk through the halls of the hospital hand in hand until we get to the nursery.

The nurse smiles. She knows us. The whole hospital does. They all smile, knowing how important this moment is for us. Madeline holds me close, her body shaking with unsuppressed sobs. My own tears form in my eyes as a little bundle is brought out to us.

"Would you like to meet your son?"

"Can I hold him?" Madeline asks as she sits in the rocking chair.

"Of course, Mom," the nurse says, and at that, the sob she's been holding is released.

Tears roll down my own cheek as I watch the nurse place my son in my wife's arms.

"It's really happening."

"It is."

"We have a baby," she tearfully says.

She holds him for another minute before I sit and take him into my own arms. When I hold my son in my arms, I instantly fall in love. Today is the anniversary of the day my grandfather passed away, the only person in my world, but now, five years later, it feels fitting that my family is growing. I touch his soft nose and think back to five years ago and when my grandfather told me, "*Family isn't about the blood that runs through your veins, it's about the love you have.*" He was right.

"Hi, Nathaniel," I whisper to my son, my namesake, my father's namesake, and my grandfather's.

*Our legacy is his now.*

# acknowledgments

I want to thank my entire family. I love you all so much.

Thank you to my husband and my kids for always loving me. You guys are my heart!

Thank you to my Mom, Dad, Liz and Ralph for always believing in me, encouraging me and loving me!

Thank you to my in-laws for being so cool and supportive!

Thank you to all of my brothers and sisters!

Thank you to everyone that helped with in-ten-tion.
Lawrence Editing
Jenny Sims
Becca Mysoor
Indie After Hours
Livia Jamerlan
My Brother's Editor
Marla Esposito
Champagne Formats
Sophie Broughton
Lori Jackson
Hang Le

Thank you to Specular Photography and Olly Hines for the most perfect image of Nathaniel EVER!

Thank you to Shane East, Andi Arndt and Lyric for bringing in•ten•tion to life on audio.

Thank you to Ena from Enticing.

Thank you to my AMAZING ARC TEAM! You guys rock!

Thank you to my beta/test team. Leigh, Melissa, Callie, Christine, Jessica, Kelly, Mia and Becca. Thank you for your wonderful and extremely helpful feedback.

Thank you Parker S. Huntington.

Thank you to K. Towne Jr for allowing me to use your poem as the epigraph of in-ten-tion. (For more work follow @k.towne.jr on Instagram

I want to thank ALL my friends for putting up with me while I wrote this book. Thank you!

To all of my author friends who listen to me complain and let me ask for advice, thank you!

To the ladies in the Ava Harrison Support Group, I couldn't have done this without your support!

Please consider joining my Facebook reader group Ava Harrison Support Group

Thanks to all the bloggers! Thanks for your excitement and love of books!

Last but certainly not least. . .
Thank you to the readers!
Thank you so much for taking this journey with me.

# by Ava Harrison

*Imperfect Truth*

*Through Her Eyes*

*trans·fer·ence*

*Illicit*

*Clandestine*

*Sordid*

*Explicit*

*ab·so·lu·tion*

—

# about the author

Ava Harrison is a *USA Today* and Amazon bestselling author. When she's not journaling her life, you can find her window shopping, cooking dinner for her family, or curled up on her couch reading a book.

**Connect with Ava**

Newsletter Sign Up: bit.ly/2fnQQ1n

Book + Main:
bookandmainbites.com/avaharrison

Facebook Author Page:
www.facebook.com/avaharrisonauthor

Facebook Reader Group: bit.ly/2e67NYi

Goodreads Author Page
www.goodreads.com/author/show/13857011.Ava_Harrison

Instagram:
www.instagram.com/avaharrisonauthor

BookBub:
www.bookbub.com/authors/ava-harrison

Amazon Author Page
amzn.to/2fnVJHFF

Made in the USA
Lexington, KY
14 March 2019